ANGELS CREST

ALSO BY LESLIE SCHWARTZ

Jumping the Green

ANGELS CREST

A Novel

Leslie Schwartz

DOUBLEDAY

New York   London   Toronto

Sydney   Auckland

PUBLISHED BY DOUBLEDAY
a division of Random House, Inc.

DOUBLEDAY and the portrayal of an anchor with a dolphin are
registered trademarks of Random House, Inc.

Book design by Caroline Cunningham
Title page photo courtesy of Barbara and Andrew Barthelmes

Library of Congress Cataloging-in-Publication Data
Schwartz, Leslie, 1962–
Angels Crest : a novel / by Leslie Schwartz.—1st ed.
p. cm.
1. Missing children—Fiction. 2. Fathers and sons—Fiction.
3. Custody of children—Fiction. 4. Wilderness areas—Fiction.
5. California—Fiction. 6. Blizzards—Fiction. I. Title

PS3569.C5666A82 2004
813'.54—dc22
2003064635

ISBN 0-385-51185-X

Forever
Greg

ACKNOWLEDGMENTS

———————◆———————

I owe an infinite debt of gratitude to the following people: For their vision, counsel, and faith, Henry Dunow and Deb Futter; for their kindness and professionalism, Rolph Blythe and Anne Merrow. For reading the novel in all its incarnations: The Grrrs, Krista Eulberg, Amy Scripps, and Georgene Smith; also Kayla Allen, Diane Arieff, Judith Dancoff, Hope Edelman, Denise Hamilton, Kerry Madden-Lundsford, and Diana Wagman. I must also thank Kisha Xiomara Palmer, who kept me laughing. To the people who mean the most to me in the world, Greg, Shashi, and Ezra, I've no doubt you'll settle my hash. And finally, my Muse, thank You for Your boundless grace.

We shall find peace. We shall hear the angels. We shall see the sky sparkling with diamonds.

—ANTON CHEKHOV, *UNCLE VANYA*

ANGELS
CREST

ETHAN

◆

Ethan woke slowly. The metal scent of a storm in the air. His heart quickened at the marvel of his life. *Me*, he thought, and the word came and went like a flash of light.

He got out of bed and put on his jeans. On a pallet on the floor, Nate lay sleeping. Ethan stood for a moment and gazed at him. Since the day his son was born, Ethan had always thought of Nate as his North Star. Now, he bent down and pushed the hair back from Nate's forehead.

"C'mon, buddy, time to go."

Nate stirred. Ethan didn't bother to change him out of his footie pajamas; he simply put a parka over him and picked him up. He knew, if need be, there was a pair of shoes in the truck.

"Balloon, Daddy," Nate said, still half asleep.

Ethan bent down and picked up the now-deflated balloon from Nate's third-birthday party the day before. Nate grabbed it and held on to it while Ethan shimmied into his coat, balancing Nate first in one arm, then the other. He was getting so big, almost too heavy to hold anymore.

Dawn was at least an hour away. It was cold, but Ethan could feel the subtle warmth of the coming snowstorm. He knew by the fragrant scent in the air that the storm was close. It was early for snow—just the first of December—but Ethan could feel how it threatened, how monstrous it would be. He imagined the way the clouds had journeyed almost four hundred miles from the coast along the jet stream, packing more and more power on their way here, to this place, on this day of his life.

He bundled his son into the car seat and started the truck, turning the heat on. As he pulled out of the driveway and drove down the dirt road to the main highway, Nate said, "Brother Powell says I need to go to church."

He said "Brother" like "bruver." And the r was missing from "church." It killed Ethan, the way Nate talked, the things he came up with. Once, he called a daddy longlegs a long-legged daddy, and Ethan had to pick him up and hold him and kiss him after that.

Still, no matter how charmed, Ethan had to make an effort now to keep the asshole out of his voice. He'd never liked Brother Powell, but he tried to make his tone smooth, without too much sentiment.

"We're going to church now, buddy."

"We're going to the woods, Dad."

"Well, a church doesn't have to have four walls and a door to be a church."

Ethan heard the edge in his voice. He wanted to go on, but Nate had already lost interest, and by the time they had driven a mile out of town toward the mountains, he had fallen back to sleep. Ethan drove up the winding, narrow roads, higher and higher. Darkness was giving way to a weak, gloomy light. He thought of Nate at the Christian preschool. He had no choice but to send him there. He would not lose the full custody he'd just won because he didn't like the church school mandated by the settlement. He didn't like church schools and things that were organized, like religion and politics. But Ethan chose his battles well. The woods could knock the Jesus out of anyone, if you went there enough. So that's what Ethan would do. Indoctrinate his son with the divinity of the forest.

Ethan wished the storm had waited another two days. Or that hunting season really opened this morning. He knew, from years of hunting, that deer stuffed themselves with zeal before a storm. Though they were swift and intelligent animals, they were also lazy. Ethan had learned that they did not like to expend too much energy searching for food. That meant on a day like this, they'd be everywhere, eating along the game trails, gathering nervously in the valleys, seeking shelter against the cliff faces. Easy targets.

Eventually, he made his way to the fire road that ended at the old Angels Crest trailhead. He loved this spot. He felt the anticipation inside him, like a tight wire holding him together. He wished he could hunt today, but he was not the sort to stoop to poaching.

He let the engine idle and watched the forest. Very few people knew of this place. Very few people would undertake it. It was the hard way up to Angels Crest, and Ethan knew that most hunters were too lazy and liked to drink too much to find the footing a place like this required. It was a beautiful spot, with woven carpets of arctic willow spreading out among the towering stands of pine and fir. In the distance, the tip of Angels Crest glowered above the clouds. He had never been up there in a storm. But he could well imagine the fury.

Almost immediately, he spotted a mature buck over the rise. He looked back at his son. This was what he had come here for, as he did almost every day, to show Nate the beauty of the woods, the wildlife, the sanctity of this place. But Nate was fast asleep. Ethan felt a twinge of regret, but he didn't want to wake his boy. He turned back toward the woods, and two more buck appeared over the ridge. He thought he would go have a quick look, track them for a minute. He promised himself he'd keep the truck in sight and not venture too far.

He turned off the engine, pocketed the keys, and looked back at his son. Fast asleep. He looked out beyond him. The lure of the woods was like a drug to Ethan. He felt the sway and pull of the forest as if it touched him, tugged on his coat sleeve.

He quietly shut the door and headed into the forest. He left the gun in the truck. It was an ancient dual-sighted .30-30 Savage he'd bought in Los Angeles at an army-surplus store years before and then restored and maintained. He knew there were better guns out there. But over the years, Ethan had grown used to the old Savage. He knew its rhythms and feel. It was a gun that rarely failed him.

The buck had gone upwind, into a narrow crag. Ethan walked a few feet and then stopped to look back at the truck. He could still see it, still see the outline of the car seat and Nate, his head forward in sleep. He told himself he'd go a little farther and only for another minute. He wasn't a gambling man, especially when it came to Nate. But those buck were beauties. Mature trophy buck. They'd provide food for the rest of the winter and an enviable rack for the garage wall.

He walked a ways longer and then, pausing, stopping, gambling, he followed the deer trail into a steep ravine, where the vanished glaciers had left behind silver-white rock surfaces, so polished and smooth that one day last spring, Ethan had watched as Nate licked the side of one. He remembered he hadn't stopped his son, only wished that he had thought to do it himself.

The deer themselves were out of sight, but Ethan, who had trained himself to spot such things, knew that they would keep traveling in the same direction, into the wind. They would not venture into the open ground. They would stay under the cover of trees and close to canyon walls, hidden among the kalmia and cassiope.

Once more, Ethan looked back. The truck was no longer visible, but he knew it was not far. He told himself that just this once, he'd keep walking. Luck was with him. Hadn't he just won custody, *full* custody, of his son? Hadn't most things gone his way in life? He figured that just this once, he could let his guard down. He'd walk just a few more feet along this old, now-abandoned trailhead, savor the solitude, forget just for a brief moment all of his responsibility and pretend. *I am free.* Then he'd get back to the truck— Nate would probably still be asleep—and head into town to open the hardware store. Maybe on the way home, Nate would wake up and Ethan would tell him how beautiful the woods were, how fine and strong the deer. He would promise to take him out again later, because Ethan knew Nate would be disappointed to have missed this morning sojourn.

The air felt tense. It would probably snow within the hour. He walked on, lured, as if to a woman, by the balm of his solitude. He thought aimlessly about his failed marriage, the custody battle he'd just won, but the cost at which it had come. He thought about how pitiful it was that lately all his sexual pleasure had come from the labor of his hands, burrowing into the bed. A mattress, he thought, was a poor substitute for a woman. He thought about the hardware store. Taxes were due on the building; money was short. Why had he bought the place? He knew at the time that he could barely afford it.

He walked on a few more feet, and there before him the buck stood majestically, partially hidden by a hedge of alpine goldenrod and the dry brown Indian summer grasses. The animals were so beautiful, so regal. He felt strangely joyous and relieved.

But then, as if coming to his senses after a long, slow dream, he looked at his watch and felt a shock. Fifteen minutes had passed. He couldn't believe it. How had he traveled this far for this long? What the hell had he been thinking? He felt a quickening and a tightening inside. Fifteen minutes at that pace meant he'd walked at least a mile into the woods. And then he thought of all the things he'd failed to think of before. He'd left the truck unlocked. Nate knew how to wiggle out of the car seat. He hadn't dressed him very warmly, hadn't even bothered to put on his shoes. Ethan knew in that surreal, certain way you do sometimes that he'd made a terrible mistake by letting the truck disappear from his view. Later, he would not be able to explain the certainty of his intuition, how clearly he knew he had gambled and lost.

He rushed quickly through the woods, not wanting to run because he was afraid to give in to the fear. He lost the scents of the woods, the earth smells, the smell of iron in the brewing storm. The world around him passed by in a blur. There were no longer distinct trees with buck rub or bear claw. Instead, there was a flurry of trees. Cartoon trees in a cartoon forest. He thought of Nate. His most beautiful son, his North Star. Nate, whom he'd finally, finally won for himself.

By the time he reached the clearing where he'd parked the car, the snow had started to fall, and Ethan saw, as he knew he would, that the door to the truck was open. His heart went to his throat. His head burst into pain, sharp and blinding. He felt himself splitting apart, everything about him tearing wide open.

"Nate," he yelled. "Nate."

There was no answer. Ethan raced to the truck. Nate was gone. He'd taken the deflated balloon and vanished into the woods.

GLICK

—————◆—————

Glick stirred. Darkness. He wanted to sleep some more, but Cindy was lying there in bed beside him. He thought about last night, their awkward sexual fumblings in the dark, the way they'd finally abandoned sex altogether, he with a sense of relief. He thought about how drunk she'd been, how useless and stupid their encounter.

Glick sat up and peered out the window, pulling the curtain back. Fresh snow, as white and downy as goose feathers. Deer tracks everywhere. Instinct made him turn his head toward the closet. The shotgun was there, leaning against the wall. The thought crossed his mind that he might never hunt deer again. He wasn't sure why.

The cats were curled up on the dresser. When they heard him moving, they lifted their heads. One of them let out a small cry; the other began to lick itself.

"C'mon, Cindy," he said. Ethan's ex-wife was still asleep next to him. Dead drunk asleep. Probably would have a hard time remembering. He recalled the other time, two years ago now, that he'd actually fucked her. He remembered how Ethan had walked in and seen the two of them together in bed. Now, as back then, he felt a sickness in his throat. He'd have plenty of time later to give himself grief for last night. To go back in time and regret that other night, too.

"You got to go, Cindy," Glick said.

She made a noise and pushed his hand away. She was only twenty-five, but she looked ten years older. The liquor had toughened up her features. There was a deep sorrow in her face. Glick knew the sorrow had as much to do with the drinking as it had with the harshness of her life. He didn't drink much himself, but he knew what it was like getting into something deep and not finding your way out.

"Cindy, girl. Get up."

She opened her eyes. She really looked like hell. He knew she'd just lost custody of Nate. The battle had been fought on Main Street. Everyone taking sides. Such ugliness. The boy so small and sweet with his green eyes and blond hair. How could two people mess up so badly? His role in it was not lost on him. Maybe if he hadn't fucked her while they were still married . . .

"Cindy. Jesus Christ. You know. You have got to get up."

"I cannot move this head of mine," she said. "And it's so goddamned cold." Her words were gummy.

As she lay beneath the covers, he leaned over her and found the bottle of whiskey on the floor beside the bed. He knew her. He knew she'd been drunk for years, would stay drunk for longer. He felt his insides tighten.

"C'mon now. This will get you going."

He poured some whiskey into an empty cup by the bed and helped her sit up. Her hair astonished him. Aside from the bleached-out ends and the pink streak she'd dyed down one side, he had never quite seen hair that tangled. Idly, he thought it over, wondering if she'd get a brush through it.

The dog moved. Glick could hear the cry in his yawn. The dog had no name. Just Dog. Glick got up and pulled on his jeans. Cindy said, "Where you going?"

"Let the dog out."

The dog, a ninety-pound black Lab, all muscle and sweet as a pea, stood up. Glick had found him as a puppy by the side of the road, scrounging for food in an overturned Dumpster. Even as small as he was, the dog had bitten him hard when Glick nabbed him, but Glick had felt some kind of empathy for him, and in some way, it was this act of defiance, this bite, that had won him over. He'd trained the dog diligently and turned him into a good tracker, a reliable hunting partner. He never bit Glick again. And he never seemed to want any more than Glick could give him.

The dog ran outside, and Glick stood there in the doorway, the storm waiting off in the distance, about to unleash. Winter had come too early and would last too long. Glick had a way of feeling these things in his bones. For the last ten years, ever since he moved to this town, he had never been wrong about the weather.

The morning was still blue-gray. He looked down and found some coins half-buried in the dirt. He bent down to pick them up and put them into the pocket of his jeans. Seventy-five cents. She must have dropped them when she tripped over the steps last night. Good for a cup of coffee later.

He whistled for the dog, and when he didn't come, Glick went back inside and shut the door. Cindy, by now, had made her way to the bathroom. He could hear the water running and the pipes groaning. She made little noises. He heard her say "Shit." She blew her nose and said "Shit" again. When she came out, she was still naked except for her socks. Her hair had been brushed, and Glick was struck more by that than by her nakedness and the boldness of her body's loose flesh and form.

She was, beneath it all, a really pretty woman. But so tired and worn. He knew she'd lived with her alcoholic grandmother all her life, had barely known her folks, had buried the old lady and moved in with Ethan after high school. He knew her marriage to Ethan had been rocky and passionate from the start, that the divorce had nearly killed them both. He wished again he had not agreed to let her follow him home last night. What had he been thinking?

"You should put some clothes on," he said. There was impatience in his voice. There were times he could not stand being in his own skin.

She nodded and went back to the bathroom. She was smoking a cigarette. Glick did not much care for cigarettes.

"You sure live a plain life," she said from behind the bathroom wall.

He didn't reply.

"How come you don't even have a showerhead on that shower? And no shower curtain."

"No need for it," he said.

"It's just a hose shooting hot water out."

"So what? It does the job," he said.

It all seemed so wrong. Glick was fifteen years older than she was. Sleeping with her the first time had killed his best friendship, and still he had done it again last night, or tried to at least.

"Is this towel clean?"

"You have to go, Cindy. Now hurry up and get dressed."

She emerged from the bathroom dressed in her jeans and the brown sweater from the night before. Everything about her looked better wrapped up in clothes. Her nakedness had been shocking in retrospect. It angered him now that she would have stood there so daringly without her clothes on. It seemed to him as if she had meant to mock him with her shabby wear-and-tear body. As if to say, You men did this to me.

She was wearing a red baseball hat, her hair piled into it. She drank what was left in the cup of whiskey that he'd poured for her earlier. In her other hand was the bottle.

"Mind if I take this?" she said. She held up the bottle. There were still two or three shots left.

He nodded. "Go on, then."

"We didn't do nothing last night, did we?"

Glick shook his head. He could not look at Cindy in the eyes. He wanted to go to Angie's Diner and have some breakfast. He wanted to be anywhere but here, in this cabin at the end of Cage Road. Cindy walked to the door. She raised her lips to him. Though he wouldn't have otherwise, he bent over and kissed her, feeling the pity and humiliation in it.

"We don't much care for each other, do we?" she said.

"Now, Cindy . . ."

"It's okay," she said. "Now be your usual self and don't give nothin' away." Then she walked outside and looked toward the ground, as if she was searching for something. Glick closed the door behind her and felt the coins in his pocket.

❖ ❖ ❖

Glick started the truck. It rumbled halfheartedly to life. He had the money. Why didn't he just buy a new one?

Dog was somewhere in the forest. Glick had left some food by the dog bed in the old barn. He'd be back later to take the dog up the mountain and track some deer before the start of season in two days.

He drove into town. He felt Cindy's seventy-five cents roll out of his pocket, but he left the coins where they fell on the plastic bench seat. The morning light began to pierce the clouds with a creamy blue glimmer. It would snow within the hour. The town was still asleep. He passed the bar and saw Cindy's truck parked there. He kept on until he got to Angie's. He grabbed his thermos from the backseat and went inside.

Angie was inside talking to her sister Rocksan and Rocksan's girlfriend, Jane. They seemed animated. Too excited for this early in the morning. Glick sat at his usual booth and Angie came over with a menu. When he saw her, something in him relaxed. It felt right being near a woman so close to his own age, someone like Angie, who was always so serene, so calm. When he looked at her, he thought, as he always did, that she was beautiful. Her lean, strong body appealed to him, the high cheekbones, the blond hair, which she now wore in a loose ponytail, so that wisps of it fell by her face. But most of all, he loved the color of her eyes, so deeply green, so quiet and tender.

"Did you hear the news?"

Glick looked up. Nothing ever happened in Angels Crest, but when it did, people always said the same thing. *Did you hear the news?*

He shook his head no. Angie poured him a cup of coffee. At the counter, Rocksan and Jane seemed to be arguing. Glick could not fathom the two of those ladies in bed together, Rocksan so big and manly, Jane so thin and ladylike.

"What news?" he asked.

"Nate's gone missing in the woods."

"What?"

"About an hour or so ago. The rangers are out there now. They've called in a helicopter."

"I don't understand," Glick said. He felt his heart pounding in his chest. He'd been there when Nate was born. He'd fucked Ethan's wife while they were still married. He'd just tried fucking her again last night.

"The ranger said he'd had a report of some poachers up at the old Angels

Crest trailhead. But when he got there, he found Ethan hysterical. Something about tracking a deer. That he'd left Nate in the truck. He said he was gone fifteen minutes. But when he got back, Nate was gone."

"Well, he couldn'ta got too far," Glick said. But already he was thinking that you didn't have to go too far to meet bad luck in woods like that, especially if you were three years old. Already he was thinking of the things he would pack: the flare, a flashlight, a stove to melt snow, in case he needed water once he found the boy. Already he was in those woods, looking for his ex–best friend's son. In his head, he had already found the boy, alive and well, his and Ethan's friendship mended in the celebration.

"Shit, Ang. It's gonna snow."

She nodded, then looked in the direction of the window. Glick looked, too. Already the snow was beginning to fall. He saw the blind preacher from the Calvary Church walk by the window and head next door to the town records office.

"You gonna head up there?" she asked.

"Yeah," Glick said, standing up. "Fill my thermos, would ya?

"Sure thing," Angie said. "I'm telling everyone. I'm sure they'll find him."

❧   ❧   ❧

When Glick got home, he called the dog, who came running out of the barn. He went over to the truck and opened the door.

"Get in, boy," he said.

He kept the engine running while he went inside to grab a few things: his hunting knife, some rope, a few old rolls, a round of salami, a couple of old cakes that Angie had given him along with the thermos of coffee, and some dog food, which he sealed up in a Baggie. He also threw in a flashlight and an extra couple pair of silks, a hat and some glove liners. It was snowing. He'd need some extra clothes if he got wet, or to give to Nate, who would be cold and scared and likely wet himself. He found the flare and a box of all-weather matches and put them in his pack. He filled his dad's old army canteen up with water. He also threw in a small camping stove and an old pot. To melt the snow, just in case.

Quickly, he popped the hood, checked the antifreeze and the wiper fluid, then shut the hood again. The engine idled rough, and Glick hoped, like he hoped every time he had to drive it, that he'd make the pass.

As he drove up the winding mountain road, he remembered all those years he and Ethan had gone up there together on the first day of hunting season. How they always drank too much the night before and how the cold, brisk air of early December always killed the hangover.

He pictured Nate again. His tiny self running blindly through the woods. The snow was falling harder now. If they didn't find the boy soon, things could go bad. And Glick knew all about things spiraling out of control. Prison had taught him that.

ROCKSAN

Rocksan had taken the last bite of her breakfast and pushed her plate away. Nate was missing. She felt torn. She wanted to join the search, but she was late exchanging the queens. With the snow starting to fall, she worried about the hives. Without new queens, all could be lost. And she still had to check the combs, clean the feeders, and supply the winter food. She wondered how she could do both, keep the hives alive and search in the woods for Nate.

"What should we do?" Rocksan asked.

Jane put some money down on the counter and started putting on her coat. "You go home and exchange the queens. I'll go up to the mountain," Jane said.

"I'll meet you up there in a few hours."

Jane nodded. "Nate'll be found by then."

Just before they left the diner, a crowd of people, a few of them strangers, showed up. Then a rumor swept through the place: The boy had been found unhurt. But it quickly proved to be false. Reporters began to arrive from the next town over.

Angie walked over to them to say good-bye. Rocksan loved her sister in a plain and simple way. It was the most uncomplicated love she'd ever experienced.

"You guys heading up to help with the search?" Angie asked. She put a pen behind her ear.

"I'm going to work on the hives first. Jane said she'd go."

"Look at those reporters. How did they find out so fast?"

Rocksan looked at the reporters who'd gathered in the diner. There were a bunch of people she didn't recognize. City people. She felt something strange and gripping. The anxiety of disturbance. "It's a sexy story, Ang. A huge snowstorm on the way. A small town filled with us dumb hicks. A boy lost in the woods. They should probably get it over with and just crucify Ethan now."

Angie pursed her lips. She looked worried. "I wish I could go," she said. She looked at the crowd. Rocksan saw the glimpse of sorrow in her sister's eyes. The regret had lodged itself there when her daughter left town with a married man, leaving the baby behind. "But I got Rosie. And this place is filling up fast."

"It's best you stay," Rocksan said. She caught a glimpse of Angie's granddaughter asleep on one of the booth seats. "Rosie will be awake soon. And you can fill a need here."

Angie nodded. "You're right," she said. She turned to Jane. "Good luck. He can't survive out there very long in this weather."

Rocksan and Jane went to the truck. Even though six years had passed since she'd moved here, it still struck Rocksan as entirely ridiculous that she was in a truck at all. In a truck, driving through snow like this. She'd been a city girl all her life, had earned a secretly coveted reputation as a badass San Francisco lesbian who'd spearheaded the ouster of more than a few conservative politicians. She'd made a pile of money gambling on real estate. A speculator. The new face of the modern Wild West. She had held court in their Hayes Valley digs. But then she woke up one day and literally saw how a lifetime of ball-busting feminism and city life, with all its stubborn bureaucratic claptrap, had worn her thin. Now, she was here, near her sister, in this small town with her girlfriend of twenty years, driving home to tend to her beehives. If anyone had told her this was where she'd be in her forties, she probably would have kicked their ass.

"What do you suppose Ethan was thinking, leaving his kid in the truck like that?"

"I don't think he was thinking at all," Jane said.

Rocksan saw the worried look on Jane's face. It had been there for a couple of weeks now. She knew Jane. Jane, with her crying jags and delicacy. She was afraid to ask after it, to prompt Jane's fragility. Instead, she reached over and held Jane's hand. It was cool to the touch, a tight hand, filled with anxiety and need and love. Rocksan had been holding this hand for so long. It seemed such a long time to know one hand. To know all the tiny lines and grooves and blemishes. To watch the bees gather in its palm. To feel it touch her in the darkness or to tend to her when she needed tending. It was a hand Rocksan knew could withdraw in melancholy, and lately more often than Rocksan cared for. It occurred to Rocksan that the last few weeks, Jane's tendency toward seemingly inexplicable sorrow was high, like the color in Jane's cheeks.

Rocksan rolled the window down. She felt hot, pink. The goddamned change taking over. Jane made an exaggerated show of being cold.

"You know, it's really cold out there," Jane said. She sounded so snotty.

"What the hell is wrong with you today, Jane? You're acting like it's a full moon."

"Well, isn't it?"

"No," said Rocksan. "You got something up your ass, though."

Jane folded her arms tightly across her chest. She looked like she was about to cry. Rocksan felt her heart beating, the steady thrumming of her veins pounding in her temples. What the hell was wrong with Jane?

"You wanna talk about somethin'?" Rocksan said. She hated how her own clumsy attempts at gentleness made her sound so country. But being around all these mountain people had tenderized her accent. Jane was always telling her to quit sounding like a goddamned cowboy and put her g's back in her words.

"I guess I should tell you," Jane said.

This made Rocksan's pulse rocket. Jane had been to the city for a doctor's appointment a month ago. Was this some delayed bad news?

"Your health okay?" Rocksan asked quietly.

"Yeah," Jane said. "It's nothing like that."

"Then what the hell?"

Jane began to cry. She shook her head vehemently. Her hair hung down over her eyes. Pink splotches everywhere, covering her neck and cheeks.

"Now, Beanpole, you're startin' to scare me."

Jane sobbed loudly. Jane was the crier. Rocksan reminded herself of this: Jane is the one who cries.

"I got a call from George," she said.

Rocksan felt her insides tumble and lurch. George. The son. The big festering lie that had plagued their relationship for five years, until Jane finally fessed up to giving birth, then abandoning her infant son. George, the revealed secret that continued to haunt their lives like an old attic ghost that had no intention of leaving.

"George? Your son?"

Jane nodded. Tears were streaming down her face.

"Isn't that odd?" Rocksan said. "How many times has he ever called? Three? Four?"

"Thirteen," Jane said.

"Well, let's have it. What'd he want?" Rocksan wondered if George knew she was rich. She hated the crass thought, but she couldn't help herself. When she got rich, people had come running out of the woodwork with their hands out.

"He's in some kind of trouble," Jane said, gulping air, trying to silence the sobs. "He didn't say what. Only that he needed a place to stay."

"You say that like he's in the next town over, Jane."

"He might be," Jane said. "He said he left Ohio a few days ago. He's coming here."

Rocksan gripped the steering wheel. Her knuckles were actually turning white. She hated entanglements. She hated that when you put your life with someone else's life, you took on their crap forever. She hated that the son—George—was the source of all of Jane's fears and sorrows.

"Goddamn, Jane, you know how I hate teenagers."

"He's twenty."

"That's even worse."

"I couldn't abandon him again," Jane said.

"Why the hell not? It oughta be easier now. At least now he can feed himself."

Rocksan couldn't believe this had come out of her mouth. Just like that. Tumbled out like tiny snakes.

"You can be such a bitch sometimes, Rocksan," Jane said.

Rocksan had no reply. Jane was right. She felt sorry instantly. She remembered the way she had felt when Jane had told her about George the first time, fifteen years before. How she had almost left Jane over it because it had brought up too much for her. She remembered how they had patched it together after that, both agreeing that they'd never talk about it. But like all resentments, that had proven impossible, and over the years, it was all Rocksan could do to keep it at bay, to love Jane in spite of the fact that she had done to her own son exactly what Rocksan's father had done to her.

Rocksan looked at Jane now. She loved Jane with all her heart. She loved Jane with a passion that sometimes scared her. She loved Jane because Jane was kind and good. She even thought that maybe in George's arrival, Jane would finally find some way to free her guilt, and Rocksan wanted that. She did.

But the other pain it brought for Rocksan was always there, always lurking, like a boil that kept rising to the surface. Jane looked heartbroken, and Rocksan felt her deeply buried tenderness trying to get out, the delicate tendrils of an apology yearning for light. But she had screwed it up now, so that her pride, her embarrassment and fear, kept it stuffed down there, accompanied by all the other phantoms of her heart.

JANE

———————◆———————

Her husband's ultimatum had been fairly straightforward: "You seek out the Lord and repent, or you leave, you goddamned whore dyke." He promised he'd tell the world what he'd caught her doing outside that bar in Cincinnati if she didn't renounce her ways. Her filthy, naked self in another woman's arms. "You could have at least fucked a man," he'd said. "You whore." He was that way. He wore Jesus on the surface of his skin and the testosterone everywhere else.

What was the better choice? Stay in that small, crappy, cow-smelling town and let her son eventually find out, too? Or leave. Leave and be free. No more hiding her love for women beneath her summer shifts and aprons, her bingo with the girls and Sunday church bake sales.

Eventually, she came to believe that leaving would set her free, because though she prayed with all her might, the Lord did not deliver. Prayer only opened her eyes to who she really was: a nineteen-year-old closet lesbian in a small town that welcomed you with a huge billboard featuring a picture of Jesus nailed to the cross and the words JESUS SAVES EVEN YOU. All her knowledge of freedom and bondage seemed somehow wrapped up in the competition between that billboard and the urges of her flesh.

She saw her husband's threats as worse than leaving, because she knew she would never change. She would never be anything other than what she was. Her heart, which was nineteen years old, and even younger than that in so many ways, told her it was the best thing for her son because it would spare him knowing about the freak he had for a mom.

Still, it took almost an entire bottle of schnapps to say good-bye in the dark night to the boy she'd loved since he was a zygote, since before that. Since he was an idea in her head. His pure skin, his small heart, beating as fast as a bird's, his little man's face and balled-up fists. She loved him with everything she had and it took that bottle and maybe a half of one more to convince herself that leaving was the best thing for everyone. And because she hated her husband, she also stole from the cookie jar the money he had been saving—for a *lawn mower*, for Christ's sake—and she took the only decent photo of her baby, taken just a week before his fifth month, and she left.

She left and left and left, until she got to San Francisco, which was where she stopped, because that was where she was when she found out her bastard husband had told the world about her anyway, and also, she'd met Rocksan in a bar, slept with her, and, a few days later, moved right in.

Now as the snow barreled down, white and thick and lovely, Jane felt everything converging. Nate, who she sometimes pretended was her own left-behind boy when she babysat him, was lost in the woods. And George, whom she dreamed about constantly, never as the man he was, but always as the five-month-old she'd abandoned, was heading her way. You make your bed, she told herself, you lie in it. It was about as original as she could muster.

"I'm gonna walk," Rocksan said. She'd stopped the truck at the end of the driveway. She had to get out, she said. She couldn't goddamn breathe. Jane could feel Rocksan's furies pushing her from the truck as if they were wicked little sprites with wings. "You go help find that boy. I want to be alone."

Jane watched Rocksan step out of the truck, leaving the keys in the ignition, and march up the driveway toward their house. It was a quarter of a mile away, hidden behind trees and a thick tangle of manzanita. The blackberries and dogwood had receded into the hillsides, bare and brown, succumbing to the start of winter. Jane got out, too, because she'd need some good boots and some water and her hat and gloves. It was cold, and the snow seemed to be falling harder. She thought of Nate. How little and alive and spirited he was. She wanted to get up there to help. She also wanted to linger here, to resolve this fight or fight some more.

She walked quickly down the driveway behind Rocksan. The property had once been in such disrepair, they'd needed a machete to hack their way through it. The place had been on the market for years. No one would buy it because it was said to be haunted, and besides, there was no water, no septic. She thought of the way she and Rocksan had painstakingly brought the land back to its fullest glory, fixed up the ramshackle house so that its history and beauty shone proudly, how they'd rebuilt the old barn and restored the old furniture left behind. She saw the place as their crowning achievement, the gift they gave themselves for all they had had to sacrifice as two women in love with each other.

She watched Rocksan ahead of her and could feel the anger sparking off her. Rocksan could power a small village with that anger, Jane thought. Her hips were wide and her gait lumbering. Sometimes, Jane thought Rocksan resembled an old Chevy. Ample and sleek and bullish. Beautiful, but a little heavy on the muscle.

"Rocksan, wait up." She hated that she ran after Rocksan. She hated that she always felt so beholden to Rocksan. It was her fault. She'd come to Rocksan a bird with a broken wing. Rocksan had seemed so mythological to Jane. Manly and cocksure, but beautiful with her dark, soft skin and the supple flesh of her body, so rare and pure. Someone who could rescue her. Someone who had.

"Jane," Rocksan said. "I don't feel like talking, okay?"

"Why are you so mad?" It was a stupid question, Jane knew. But she didn't know what else to say.

"Well, let's just say, for starters, that you coulda asked me. You coulda said, 'Hey, Rocksan, what do you think about my son coming for a visit?' "

"I was afraid."

"Goddamn it, Jane. How is this any better?"

Jane shrugged. "It's not."

"Look," Rocksan said. "I just want my life to be simple. That's why we left San Francisco. I just want things to be simple. What do I know about a teenager?"

"He's twenty."

"Twenty. Ten. Five. Who cares? He's someone from your other life."

"Why is that so hard for you?"

Rocksan stopped moving for a moment. Everything about her seemed to get smaller, quieter. Jane thought she could hear Rocksan's heart beating. The snow fell, but all else was still.

"I can't say," Rocksan said. "Except that you were once with a man. You chose a man. You made a baby with him. Why did it take you five years to tell me?"

Jane felt herself caving in. The world was a big open circle growing smaller and smaller. She was a spot on the head of a pin.

"But I did tell you, Rocks. I did."

Rocksan nodded and looked off in the distance. "Yes, you did. But you also left a *baby* behind," she said. Her voice was barely above a whisper. The words seemed to fall delicately to the ground like the snowflakes. Jane heard in them the regret. She heard Rocksan's diminished voice, the way she struggled so. Even when it started out with Jane feeling wronged and attacked, she always saw that it was really Rocksan who was afraid.

"Please don't judge me, Rocksan. Please don't do this anymore."

"I don't mean to. I try to get over it every time, Jane. I know that I can love you in spite of it. I do love you in spite of it. But every time George comes up, I can't help but be reminded that he represents a side of you that has always scared me. You know my own father did the same. It's just one of those fucked-up ironies. I'm sorry."

Jane was determined not to cry. She read those stories in the paper of all those young girls having babies in the bathroom at the prom. The way they threw them in the trash and went back to dance. It sickened her for sure. But at the same time, she was probably the only person on the earth who understood how they could do such a thing, and it made her feel bleak and unacceptable. Someone whose choices had always forced her to live secretly on the outskirts of the world. It wasn't the lesbian anymore that made her feel like a freak.

"I told you why I did it."

Rocksan nodded. "And I can see it. I can sometimes understand. But I can't lie to you, Jane. Just the mention of the boy's name and I'm off and running. You understand. I go places I don't wanna go."

Jane nodded her head. She couldn't turn her back on George again. She saw his coming as her second chance. But at what risk? Rocksan might leave her. She might jump off the fence she'd been sitting on for twenty years and finally decide that for all her good qualities, Jane was too flawed a woman to keep on loving. Jane turned and walked away toward the house. She would gather her boots and her hat and her gloves and join the rest of them in search of Nate because it was the only thing she could imagine doing.

ANGIE

Right after Glick left, Angie wanted him to come back. She couldn't explain this feeling. It had been with her since the day he showed up in town ten years ago. He would leave the diner; she would feel wistful and alone. She would think, Come back and talk to me.

She thought of him spending all that time in prison for a crime he hadn't committed. She knew it was foolishly romantic of her, but she thought the right woman—herself perhaps—could set him back to a time before prison turned him so remote. No matter how pathetic it made her feel to harbor these desires, she could not seem to stop.

And now she wished she was with Glick and everyone else who was out helping search for Nate. All the things she longed for seemed to be outside the door, away from this diner and her life, which sometimes felt so small, so inconsequential. But her sister was right. She could serve a better purpose by keeping the diner open, especially for that moment when the word would spread about Nate's rescue. People would go to one of two places, the diner or the bar. She'd need to be here for the people who didn't celebrate by getting drunk.

But still the hours swept by. It seemed the longer there was no word, the quicker time went. It would not stay light forever. And a convincing snowstorm was blanketing the town. Angie could just imagine how fiercely it was snowing at the higher elevations.

Rosie had been awake for a while, and though she was playing quietly with her stuffed penguin, whose wings were worn thin from all that frantic clutching, Angie knew her granddaughter would soon lose patience. She thought she'd take her home for an hour or so and take a break herself from the news as it blared from the small television on the counter. By now, most of the local stations were carrying the news of Nate's disappearance and people were already taking the moral high ground one way or the other about his father.

She went to the back of the kitchen, where Rosie had her toys and a small cot. She knelt down and kissed her granddaughter on the forehead.

"Wanna go soon?" she asked.

Rosie nodded. She was deeply involved in the baffling task of how best to shove her penguin's plump round body through the small opening of a milk jug. Her cheeks were red, almost feverishly so, but that's how she looked sometimes, as if she knew deep down that things were not as they should be, that her life was without things that other children had.

Angie went back out to the dining room. The place was fairly packed, and someone else, someone she had never seen before, walked in and sat at one of the booths by the window. He was a large man with gray hair, older, perhaps in his middle sixties. He was clutching a dog-eared clothbound book and he seemed lost, but in the shocked way of someone who'd just narrowly avoided death.

It was rare to see strangers at the diner. Sometimes in the summer, campers stopped in, and occasionally someone's relative would drop by to say hello to Angie. But with the quick spread of news about Nate's disappearance, it was only a matter of hours before people began to show up, arriving from the city, underdressed and overeager, dangerously so. Angie, who'd lived in these parts since her first marriage, twenty-five years ago, did not trust city people. They always said something stupid about how adorable the little town was, how fresh the muffins at the diner tasted, how old-fashioned everything was, and do you really have a library and a school? Angie felt like she was on display, a monkey in the zoo. It was the condescension that irked her. As if she and the people who lived here were imaginary people, quaint distractions from the real people who led real lives in the real world.

By the time she walked up to the stranger, she had convinced herself he was just another journalist. She made a point of greeting him without too much warmth.

"Coffee?"

"Please," he said.

He smiled at her with kindness. She was taken aback. He was so pleasant-looking. And when she studied him, she realized that though his gait and style made him seem older, there was also a youthful quality to his face. Only his mouth, behind the gray beard, revealed a spot of tension, an unhappiness.

"You ready to order?"

He looked at the menu. Then he smiled again, this time sheepishly. "I have a terrible time making up my mind."

"I'll give you a minute and come back with your coffee."

"I appreciate that," he said, returning a worried gaze to the menu.

Just then, a crowd of high school boys barged in. Angie knew that her part-time waitress would be there in moments, but she seated the boys herself. They all ordered sodas, except for one, who said he wanted a hot chocolate. Angie gave them menus just as Hilda, her part-timer, walked in and tied an apron around her ample waist. As Angie walked away from the table, she heard the boys talking about Ethan, the search, finding the kid. They seemed in a hurry. They were cutting school and they wanted to get to the trailhead to help.

She put her order pad in the back pocket of her jeans, grabbed the coffeepot, and returned to the stranger. She poured him a cup of coffee and pulled out her order pad.

"Did you decide?"

"I'll have a sandwich. Tuna. No fries."

"Okay. I can bring you a cup of fruit instead."

He nodded. He appeared nervous and preoccupied.

"Anything to drink besides coffee?" she asked.

"No thanks," he said.

"Okay." She put the order pad in her pocket and turned to go.

"Excuse me," he said.

There was a long silence. She said, "Yes?"

"Well, I was wondering if you could help me. I heard on the radio that there was a missing boy. I thought, since I'm here, I would go help with the search."

Angie looked at him for a moment. She knew it was rude.

"Are you a journalist?"

"Heavens no," he said. "Like I said, I just wanted to help out."

Angie studied him. He seemed sincere.

"It's a rough road up there. Hard to find. You got a good car?"

He pointed meekly out the window. A black Mercedes.

"It'll get dirty," Angie said.

She could tell she was making him uncomfortable, and she felt bad about that. What difference would it have made had he been a journalist? That's a living. People had to make a living. And if he wasn't a journalist, if he was telling the truth, then all her scorn was being wasted.

"See those boys at that table over there?"

He reached for his specs and put them on. He followed her gaze and nodded.

"They're heading up there, too. I can arrange it so you can follow them. They'll make sure you get there."

He took off his glasses. "That's very nice of you."

"No problem," she said.

"It's a terrible business, isn't it? I have three sons. They're all grown now. But you never forget how small and vulnerable they once were. I hate to imagine what that poor father is going through. Or the boy. I ache when I think of that boy lost in the woods."

The man briefly touched his heart, which made Angie feel sad. She pictured, for a moment, her granddaughter lost in the woods. The landscape of such a thought was barren and silent. It was a place deep inside her, without words.

Just then, several more people walked in. A couple of rangers and what seemed like more reporters. She had never been this busy before. She looked at the man's worn and tattered book. Hebrew letters on the cover, a Star of David.

"I'll let those boys know you need to follow them up there. Be careful. Those shoes you got on won't keep the cold and the wet out for very long, and believe me, those woods can swallow a person whole."

He looked at her briefly. Then he disappeared behind something in his eyes, a memory perhaps.

◆　◆　◆

Angie packed Rosie's toys and coloring books and crayons into the bag and piled it all in the truck, then buckled her granddaughter into the car seat and drove home. She lived in town—a five-minute drive from the diner—in a small, neat house with a white fence surrounding a lawn and Rosie's swing set. Four years ago, when her daughter, Rachel, dumped Rosie off with twenty dollars and a bag of diapers, Glick came by and hung a tire in one of the trees for her. Rosie wasn't able to use it for a long time. But Angie remembered how he hadn't asked her a single question. The empathy was in the act alone. Now as the snow fell into the balding trees, the swing seemed stark and abandoned.

The summer blooms had all faded and the hand-size leaves from the sycamore trees littered the lawn. She would have to rake them up, another thing to do. It seemed that her life was a series of things to do, a long list she just kept checking off and filling up again. There was a time, after her second marriage ended, that she dreamed of taking a vacation. In her mind, there was always the same beach, the same palm trees, the same hammock, something her memory had cribbed from an ad in a magazine somewhere.

But even that eventually faded out after her daughter had sneaked into the house one black autumn night and dumped off the baby. "Dear Mom, maybe you'll do better with her than you did with me." That was all it said on the note. After that, there was no room in Angie's head for vacation dreams anymore.

Angie parked the car and helped Rosie out. Rosie clutched her stuffed penguin and ran into the house. When Angie caught up with her, Rosie was feeding the fish, taking just a pinch out of the food container, the way Angie had showed her, and sprinkling it in.

"Grammie, how come Nate ran into the woods?"

Angie shook her head. "He went to look for his daddy."

"When are they gonna find him?"

"Soon, baby."

Angie was always surprised at how raw and vulnerable children were. She didn't remember it that way with her own daughter. She watched Rosie watching the tank. Spellbound, a captive of the movement, the bubbles, the underwater weirdness. She had told herself that she *would* do better with this one. Not a day went by that she didn't feel some regret for the way she'd raised her own daughter. She blamed herself for her daughter leaving like that, pregnant, skulking off with another woman's husband. The woman ended up stuck with three kids, a mortgage, and the hardware store. It was a relief when Ethan bought the hardware store and the woman and her kids finally left town. She looked at Rosie, the product of that union. She wished that Rosie would never have to know the truth.

"Tonight, I have to go back to the diner," Angie said.

Rosie turned around and looked at her. She walked over and sat beside Angie on the tiny bed. She put her hand on Angie's thigh and rubbed her jeans. She seemed overly serious and contemplative for a four-year-old. She smelled of the diner and of something else, something sweet, like bread or pudding.

Rosie said, "I don't want to go."

"You'll stay with Aunt Rocksan and Jane. I'll pick you up in the morning."

Rosie looked into Angie's eyes, but Angie knew she was really thinking over this latest development. Angie knew how much Rosie loved Rocksan and Jane. They lived in the old place at the edge of town—a big wooden house with lots of land and places to explore. And it carried the thrill of being haunted by the spirit of the old man whose entire family had lived and died there, who'd let it run its course and fall into disrepair. Rocksan had a giant heart, despite her temper, and a large squishy body that Rosie liked to sink into. Rosie had asked Angie once if Rocksan was a man.

Now she looked at Angie and said, "Rocksan told me that after the summer, the lady bees kill all the man bees."

"Well, that doesn't seem nice."

"Rocksan said it's because they're lazy and they aren't needed anymore, so all the lady bees kill them."

"She should know."

"Real ladies don't do that."

"You're absolutely right."

"Was my mom a lady?"

Angie stood up abruptly. She had waited for this. Now it was here. She thought of her daughter at thirteen, sneaking off into the night to be with boys, to smoke dope and have sex. She thought of her first husband's death. The stupidity of her second marriage, this one to a fat, dumb, no-good trucker. She thought of herself watching her daughter's back disappearing through the front door. They were all gone now. There was just her and this house and this child. That was the only story anymore.

She put her hand out for Rosie. Rosie got off the bed. Angie hoped that if she changed the subject, she could avoid this conversation, this now, this moment. She made a mental note to talk to Rocksan about those damned bees. She'd had it up to her ears in drones and queens and virgin bees, and even though they were just a bunch of flying bugs with stingers, the hives held no less mystery for her granddaughter than her own mother and father's absence.

"Honey," Angie said. "Let's go look at the Sears catalog, pick out some winter woolies for your hands and feet."

Rosie seemed agreeable. She was not usually so easily distracted from her questions. But Angie knew how smart Rosie was. She had that radar that kids have. The good sense not to pull the one rock that kept the avalanche from releasing. Not just yet.

CINDY

After Glick, Cindy had meant to go home. But she couldn't muster it. Everything inside her boxy apartment was brown: brown carpet, brown wallpaper, brown furniture. Shit-colored. It twisted her heart up just driving into the complex and reading that sign—SKYVIEW MANORS—on the side of the building. There was no reprieve there, no hiding from her loneliness and the rage prowling around inside her.

She knew Trevor would be at the bar, just waking up, cleaning the mess from the night before so he could open by ten o'clock for the morning drunks. So she decided to give herself just a little more fortification against the day.

Trevor let her in and poured her a drink. She took off her red baseball cap and set it on the bar, along with five dollars she found in her wallet. Trevor left the money there, as he always did, and lit a cigarette.

"Cindy, I got some real bad news for you," Trevor said.

She felt her heart skip a beat. The first thought that came to her head was Nate. Nothing specific, just Nate, the world of Nate and all its possibility for hope and tragedy. But then she thought maybe Trevor was just pissed off that she'd left with Glick last night. He was the jealous type, and even though she told him time and again there was no future for them, he couldn't listen.

"What is it, Trev?"

"Baby," he said. "Your boy is missing."

Cindy instinctively went for her drink. She downed it.

"What do you mean, 'missing'?"

"Ethan took Nate up to the old Angels Crest trailhead to scout some deer. He left Nate in the car, and when he got back, Nate was gone."

"What the hell do you mean, 'gone'?" By now, she was standing up. Her veins were sparking, little flashes of electricity coursing through her, igniting her.

"He's missing. People are heading up there to search right now."

"I'm going," she said.

"Hold on a sec," Trevor said. "I'll go with you."

She didn't wait for Trevor. She ran out to her beat-up old piece-of-crap Toyota, the whiskey still burning in her throat, and started the engine. Trevor jumped into the passenger side just as she was taking off.

"It's gonna snow," Trevor said. "You'll need something warmer than that."

She felt his eyes on her. She heard the slut slur camouflaged in his words. She understood that he was seeing her again in the same clothes she'd been wearing last night when she'd left with Glick.

"You're right," she said. "A coat. And some better boots. We gotta hurry, though."

All of a sudden, she was so cold, so afraid. She saw the trajectory of her life careening slowly out of control to this here, this now. Her parents leaving her with her drunken grandmother before she was three, the near marriage to Trevor, till Ethan showed up. Those first good years with Ethan and the way she lived off that happiness with greed and waning hope. And Nate being born, falling into her life as if from a dream. Now here she was, divorced, the loser in a custody battle so brutal it had aged her by half a life, already drunk at eight o'clock in the morning, heading out to find her boy, who was inexplicably lost in the woods.

"How long has he been missing?" she asked. She didn't want to hear the answer. She never made excuses for being a drunk, but she knew that, depending on the answer, she might just sit this one out in a blackout. The truth was, she had always had an ominous fear that something terrible would happen to Nate. She didn't know why it would creep into her head. When she broke it down in her more lucid moments, she thought it probably had more to do with her own fate, the way she was running her life into the ground. Still, the only thing that ever made her pray was her son, and it was always the same prayer, the words rushing together like a train wreck: Dear God I know I'm a drunk you don't have to forgive me or let me into heaven but please keep Nate safe forever.

"He's been gone a couple hours now," Trevor said. He lit two cigarettes and handed her one. She was speeding down Main Street, heading for her shit brown apartment. Her son was missing. *DeargodIknowImadrunkyoudonthavetoforgiveme . . .*

"Damn," she said. She reached over and opened the glove compartment. Inside was the bottle of whiskey she'd taken from Glick's. She opened it and took a long sip. She thought about Glick and the way he hadn't wanted to kiss her good-bye this morning, the way it went through her and humiliated her. She thought about Ethan finding her and Glick in bed that time, the way she'd planned it, her trump card, and the way it backfired on her. Then she pictured her boy, lost in the woods, and somehow everything seemed to follow everything else, one perfect downward plunge into this moment. She was amazed by the order you could find in chaos. She thought maybe if she had done one thing differently, maybe even years ago, this wouldn't be happening now. But the problem was how to settle on the one thing. How to know when you took that wrong turn to begin with.

"Are you sure he *left* Nate in the truck? Ethan is always so careful. This just doesn't sound like him at all."

Trevor nodded. "I told you he's selfish. I told you that you shouldn'ta married him. That was a stupid move on his part, a damned stupid move, leaving a three-year-old in that shitty truck of his. He ain't smart, I can tell you that much. I mean, even I wouldn't have left a three-year-old in a car."

She looked at Trevor. He just went on and on. She wished he'd shut up. She pulled into her carport, spot twelve, and raced up the stairs, leaving Trevor behind in the car. She grabbed a backpack and started throwing things in it. There was, first of all, a bottle of whiskey under the kitchen sink. And some gloves and a hat. She put on some wicking socks and her sturdiest boots. She stopped long enough to open a beer and drink some of it down. She took two or three huge gulps and then she saw it, lying there on the countertop, that paper plate with the macaroni pieces glued around its rim. Nate had made it for her.

It made her think about the preschool he'd just started going to at the Calvary Church. It seemed a good-enough place for him, except for the pastor, Brother Powell, who was always stopping her and holding on to her hand and telling her that God did not love a sinner. She remembered, so that it made her skin crawl, how one time he'd taken her hand and said she ought to come by for some spiritual counseling. She hadn't been able to shake the feeling that he was after more than a little soul-searching with the good Lord.

Just yesterday, Nate had glued down this pile of macaroni on this paper plate. Glue globs and all, it was a work of art. Nate had been so proud. She'd promised him she would hang it up. He was doing things he'd never done before, and every day it was like a light going on over his head. She picked up the plate and thought of all the things about him—his skin, his hair, his smell—while keeping the rest of it—the woods, his fear, was he wearing a coat?—out of her mind. She thought again of Ethan, the only man she had ever loved, and how he had failed her by not doing the one thing she wanted him to do, which was for him to love her forever. She wondered again what she could have done to prevent this morning, this day. She saw herself as the one to blame, because maybe if she had done one thing differently—for instance, if she hadn't slept with Glick two years ago—maybe Nate wouldn't be lost in the woods today.

Trevor walked into the apartment. He saw her holding on to the plate with one hand, the beer with the other. "Nate will turn up."

She nodded.

He kissed her. She nodded again. She wished more than anything he hadn't done that. It made her think of Glick and the way he'd sympathy-kissed her this morning. On any other day, she would have stewed about that for hours—all the humiliation and the pity that had been wrapped up in that kiss. But now, she just forgot about it and walked to the car and gave Trevor the keys. While he pulled out in his irritating, careful way, she sat hunkered down in the seat, wishing so many things—that Ethan still loved her, that Nate was safe, that she wasn't such a drunk. It just went on and on. She took a sip of whiskey and watched silently as the snow began to fall.

GLICK

The truck groaned over the summit and slid on the ice. The silver light of the snow was dimmed and muted by the forest. As Glick drove higher, the trees began to crowd closer together, like people waiting for something to happen. Or like prisoners in the pen, gathered round a betting table or a bloody fight.

He maneuvered the truck off the road and onto the fire trail. The earth was hard and slippery beneath the wheels. From time to time, he looked back in the mirror at the dog, who was panting and yelping gleefully, oblivious.

The storm had darkened the mountain. The headlights illuminated the narrow road, and the broad overhang of trees and brambles made a wide canopy over the truck. The air up here was denser, wetter, the snow fell harder, and condensation swirled into willowy shapes among the branches.

Finally, Glick came upon the clearing. He turned the headlights off because they had landed directly on Ethan, who was standing by his truck with a cigarette in his hand. It reminded Glick of the spotlight in the prison yard. The way lights were used to flush out criminals hiding in places, thinking they could escape.

He killed the engine. It was bitter cold outside and snowing hard. He rubbed his hands together. The dog whined in the back, and before Glick greeted Ethan, he let the dog loose. Glick heard him disappear into the woods. He didn't have to whistle. The dog would be back.

"Hey, Glick," Ethan said. He looked away before their eyes met.

"Any word?"

Ethan shook his head and Glick got a good look at him. He had spent too much time behind bars not to know, just by looking at a man in the eyes, the degree of his guilt. He caught Ethan's gaze for a moment and he knew the extent of Ethan's crime. Foolhardiness. Carelessness. Maybe selfishness. But that was all.

Ethan, who had been leaning at an angle against the truck, now pushed himself away from it using his back. He hit on his cigarette. Glick noticed how Ethan's hands shook, but he could not be sure if it was nerves or the cold. Glick felt something keen and sharp in his gut, though he didn't have the name for it.

"I just got back," Ethan said. "Been out there for hours. The rangers are out there. Sheriff. A few people from town are starting to show up. I needed to get out of those woods for a minute. But now that I'm here, I feel like I should head back."

Glick had a hard time looking at Ethan. He peered into Ethan's truck. A cooler in the back. His gun against the window.

"I packed up a lot of shit," Glick said. "I could last for hours out there."

Ethan nodded, and Glick was about to say good-bye and head into the woods, when Ethan let out a sob. He jerked forward and awkwardly embraced Glick. He was a big man, bigger than Glick, and Glick could feel the heaviness of Ethan's muscles, the weariness of his bones as he briefly accepted the embrace and worked to keep himself from falling back into the side of his truck.

Ethan then moved back just as suddenly, released Glick, and wiped his nose with the arm of his shirt. The act was filled with shame and regret, a sense of loss. Their history was left behind in the space of Ethan's withdrawal, and Glick remembered when Ethan had caught him with his wife. The words Ethan had said then. "I oughta kill you." He saw this embrace for what it was, the erasure of the past, the confirmation that whatever had gone bad between them was now departed, overtaken by something of far greater import and with far graver consequences.

"I'll find him," Glick said.

"Of all the people, man, I hope it's you."

Glick nodded. He felt a calm welling-up of sadness. In his heart, he

knew the boy was in very bad trouble, possibly even dead. Anything could
have happened. He could have fallen off a cliff face, landed in one of the
creeks, twisted his ankle.

"You know Dog here's a good tracker," said Glick as his dog came running up, tail wagging, his tongue lolling out and the steam of his breath filling the air.

Ethan bent over and stroked the dog.

"I remember when that bastard bit you." Ethan laughed miserably. "Talk
about biting the hand that feeds you."

Glick wished suddenly to be out of the range of Ethan's misery. It was so
strong as to be physical, and he was feeling the weight of it in his own body.
But he didn't want to run out too early. This moment, his showing up and
bringing the dog to track, worked like an apology, and he felt their grievances
vanish in the wake of Ethan's tragedy.

"Guess I'll head in. I can look for fresh tracks before anyone else steps in
them, and maybe the dog can catch a pure scent." It occurred to Glick that
he'd used these words before when hunting deer with Ethan. It made him
feel sullied. He hoped Ethan hadn't noticed.

"I searched these woods all morning. Rangers, too. They got a helicopter coming. A couple of hunters came by with horses. It's like he disappeared
into thin air."

"Nothing just disappears," Glick said. But he knew these woods. He
knew a person could get lost within a matter of minutes. You didn't even
have to wander far, and you'd stay hidden by the trees, or the light would re-
fract off granite and transform you into the shape of a shadow. The sounds
of the creeks or the winds could easily drown the call of searchers, or the
cold could force you into unseen corners for shelter, leaving you concealed
from view.

Ethan smiled sadly. Glick saw that Ethan knew, too. He took a drag of
his cigarette with trembling hands. He said, "Nate was wearing footie pajamas, white, with blue moons on them."

Glick nodded, turned, and went into the woods.

◆　◆　◆

The outline of the woods was obscured by the soft, weak light of the morning. If Glick hadn't walked these mountains for ten years, if he hadn't had the memory of incarceration, he would have felt exposed and vulnerable. But in the woods, he found a certain reassurance. He and Ethan had taught each other about the woods. One step at a time, they had learned the language of the seasons, how to track deer, to watch for bear scat when hunting alone, to smell the scent of a storm on its way. And Glick remembered how quickly he had taken to it. In the woods, it was as if prison did not exist, had never existed. The solitude, the scent of the earth, the privacy; in the woods, he could exult in his freedom.

Glick looked up. The trees were quietly crowded and drew together around him kindly, with consolation and comfort. The smell of the storm seemed somehow stronger within the warren of the pines and their branches. Glick could feel the dry crackle in the air even as the snow blanketed the earth. The dog ran off. Glick could hear him tramping through the brush.

His first thoughts as he walked into the gathering darkness of the woods were of his six years behind bars. He only allowed himself to think of it when he was alone. There was a reassuring edge to the rage. When they'd set him free, he'd waited for an apology. The money from the settlement, which, if he was careful, would last him his lifetime, wasn't enough. He wanted the words. He wanted to see another person's remorse. He didn't know who should have granted it. The overzealous prosecutors, whose handling of the evidence had been shoddy and illegal. The woman who had picked him out of the lineup, who'd failed, *failed*, to see that he was not the one. The gang bangers inside who'd beaten him relentlessly because he was white, had no posse, refused to join any group, and lingered alone in the yard, reading tattered paperbacks. It seemed the entire world owed him an apology, and he'd drunk himself into a stupor waiting for it to come. Then one day, he simply realized there would be no acknowledgment for the stolen years of his life. He'd picked up the bottle he'd been nursing, poured it down the drain, and left Los Angeles.

Now he could only faintly remember the humiliating abuses. It was as if a curtain had come down over that part of his life. Nothing much remained

of it but the calm reassurance of his rage and the memories, opaque, iridescent, like dreams.

He heard something rustle beyond him, a squirrel or a mouse scurrying
for cover. Above him, the mournful knocking of a woodpecker, vainly at-
tempting to siphon out a few last insects before the onslaught of winter,
echoed among the trees. The snowfall had obscured any tracks. But it was
also beautiful, and the murmur in the woods quieted down, as if to make
room for his thoughts.

He walked on. He pictured Angie, her blond hair tied up in a bun. He
remembered how one day he had walked into the empty diner and had seen
her taking her hair out of the bun and brushing it so that it fell down her
back. She had brushed it idly, as if she were unaware that she was doing so,
and the way she'd stood, with her feet apart, her back slightly arched, and her
head tilted just so to one side, had stirred him. He had stood there motionless, watching, and when she'd sensed him, she'd turned around quickly,
caught his eye, and blushed. He remembered it now as invoking desire,
though in honesty he had felt something deeper and less articulated than
that.

For a moment as he walked, he let his thoughts drift into an image of the
two of them embracing, perhaps outside her house, near the tire swing he
had hung from the tree for her granddaughter. But he wouldn't let his
thoughts go further than that. There would have been something disre-
spectful in it, and behind it was something he dared not hope for, or desire.

Soon the light began to shift and the shadows grew heavier. Glick
checked his watch. He had been walking for nearly three hours. There had
been no sign of Ethan's son. The dog seemed to be growing restless and
tired. And the snow, which had been falling intermittently all day, now
turned. It swirled around him, darkening his tracks and narrowing his field
of vision.

He thought then of Cindy, and to get her out of his mind, he opened his
backpack, ate some of the sausage and one of the cakes from Angie's. He put
on his hat and gloves and checked the flashlight out of a growing sense of
nervousness. He checked that the matches were still intact, that the flare and
the stove were within easy reach. But none of these tasks could take his

mind from the memory of the crude way he had kissed Cindy by the bathroom at the bar and, later, tried to fuck her on his bed, even while she went in and out of her drunken stupor. He remembered the way the cats on the dresser had stirred and opened their eyes as the bedsprings screeched, how their eyes had caught the light from the moon outside and glowed almost translucently in the darkened room.

He knew he could no sooner avoid rehashing the night with Cindy than he could forget the six years of his life in prison for a crime he didn't commit. It was all somehow one and the same, the same dark road, the same wrong choices, the same glum hangover from the same bad dream. It was what he had been trying to run away from but what he could never seem to escape. This dark journey. This shame. Since his release, he'd hungered after the things that made him feel the worst. And when he gave in to the desires, it was almost with relief.

He remembered the way Cindy had rolled over after they had aborted their attempts at sex. He saw how barely conscious she was and he was aware that she would remember little of it. And even though they hadn't consummated the act, he felt like he had committed the crime for which he had been wrongly accused. It seemed to him that all his sexual needs were met and released in this way. The string of one-night stands after he'd been freed, the faces of the women he had fucked but barely knew, now rose before him, apparition-like, and left him with sadness and regret. He was not the man he'd thought he would become.

Disgusted with himself, aware of his failures and the fact that for a long time now he had forgotten his purpose in the woods, he decided to turn back. But just as he made the decision, the dog suddenly lifted his head into the wind and stood erect, catching a scent. Just as quickly, the dog took off into the woods, and Glick followed, his heart racing. But though they ran for a long time, nothing came of it. And when Glick turned around, he realized he was utterly and completely lost. He thought back to the things he had packed and realized he'd forgotten his compass.

"Damn you, Dog," he said.

The dog, who had always been sensitive to the varying tones of praise and admonishment in Glick's voice, cowed slightly.

"We're lost, you mongrel."

The dog looked away, a dumb look on his face.

Night was nearing fast. Glick's sense of direction had all but vanished and so, too, apparently, had his dog's. He searched for the tip of Angels Crest for bearing, but in vain. The clouds were low. The world had disappeared. He could not determine which direction he faced. When he stumbled up a hill, he lost his footing and fell several feet into an icy ravine. The dog slid down with him and the two of them—it occurred to Glick that there was something comical and vaudevillian in it—got hopelessly tangled.

"Shit," Glick said. He pushed the dog off of him and gave into the miserable fact that he had allowed the bitterness and disgrace of his thoughts to trick him into getting lost. It had never happened before. He was struck by the sudden memory of his first day in prison, on his hands and knees, the crushing and humiliating gang bang, the hoots and calls of the inmates, those who participated, those who watched. The blood. And then the degrading tears.

The tears, of all things, had been the final blow. Streaming down his face, his silent cries had somehow ruined him. Had changed him, but from what into what was never clear. It had simply *changed* him, and though he would never suffer that same fate again—why, he was never sure—he'd left prison six years later with an untamable anger.

Now, as darkness fell and the snow barreled down with a temper, Glick let out a brief cry, almost a sob, at the same time aware of how the panic had set in without warning. He looked at the dog. The dog appeared sheepish and guilty.

Beaten, Glick sat in the ravine, cross-legged, whipped by his memories, his vain and stupid longings, and the parade of his immediate failures, first with Cindy and now with Ethan. In the end, not only had he not found Nate, he realized, but he had stopped searching hours ago.

He opened his backpack and with a sense of defeat took out a roll and what was left of the salami. He also opened the Baggie of dog food and handed it over. The dog looked at it uncertainly at first, then dived in. As night descended, Glick lit the little stove, melted some snow, and drank, sharing some with the dog.

ETHAN

———◆———

When Glick went off into the forest, Ethan had the sense that something had been taken away from him. He was left with a carved-out feeling, an impression of having been severed, as if from a restraint or a long confinement.

He recalled how they used to hunt together before he'd caught Glick screwing his wife in his own house. He remembered every detail of that moment. But it was only now, with his son missing and the chance that he would not be found alive, if at all, that he understood the truth about how it had made him feel to see Cindy wrapped around his best friend's body.

He had wanted to tell Glick this truth before he'd disappeared into the woods. He'd wanted to come clean. It had never been about Cindy or their marriage. And it hadn't been about his ego. Not so much anyway. What he'd wanted to tell Glick was that when he'd first caught sight of him and Cindy entangled, he'd felt relief. Simple, unadorned reprieve. He had seen the key to his liberation in her infidelity. What angered him was that his best friend had been the one she'd chosen and that his own freedom, or so he had thought then, required that Glick be excised, too. If only it had been someone else, someone who didn't matter, someone whom he could remain bitter toward without also feeling the loss.

And in the end, the years that had passed without speaking to Glick had only equaled a new kind of constraint. Ethan had wanted to speak his forgiveness, to convey the passing of water under the bridge. All the drama with Cindy and Glick seemed suddenly so frivolous and unimportant. He'd wanted to tell Glick all this, but he hadn't found the words. The frustration had bored into him, so that he had sobbed instead. Humiliated, he'd pulled himself together and then, like an idiot, said something about the dog. The chance for it was gone, like everything else, it seemed. Vanished.

When Glick disappeared behind the canopy of trees, Ethan lit another cigarette and opened Glick's truck door. It was still warm inside the cab from the heater, and he sat down behind the wheel and shut the door, smoking. He felt something underneath and found three quarters. Without thinking, he put them in his pocket. Then he reached over and grabbed the thermos that Glick had left behind on the floor of the passenger side. The smell of coffee was strong and he took a gulp, savoring how bitter and hot it was. His mouth was instantly scalded, but he welcomed it. He tasted the metal of blood in his throat.

People were starting to drive up now, more and more as the time passed. Reporters began to converge, talking to one another in tight, excited clusters. One of them walked up and rapped on the window of Glick's truck, but Ethan told him to go away. He knew he had to get back out there, away from this brewing mayhem, toward his son. He looked out at the people he had known most of his life, who were showing up now to help him. It gave him a sense of hope. Of course they'd find Nate. They had to find him. Then tomorrow, he'd go deer hunting, and when he'd killed his limit, he'd go pick Nate up from school, take him back to the hardware store, close up, and go on about the rest of his evening, remembering the fear, grateful that it had just been a close call.

But then he looked at his watch and saw how much time had passed since Nate had taken off. At the same time, he realized that if his son were dead, he would probably never hunt deer again with Glick or by himself. The forgiveness and apology he felt in his heart for Glick would find no recourse in the picking up of old traditions. Though he understood now what had kept him from speaking to his best friend all that time, he knew, too, that after this was over, he and Glick would still find no way to pick up where they had left it so long ago. The fact that Glick had come out to help him shamed Ethan beyond words.

He stepped outside just as several cars in a caravan came around the bend. In the first were Cindy and Trevor. Then a group of kids he'd seen around town pulled up in an old Camaro. There was a small, expensive-looking Mercedes he didn't recognize; the driver was a stranger, an old man not from town. Then came Rocksan's truck, though only Jane stepped out of the cab. After that, several more cars arrived and then the rangers, the sheriff, a couple of paramedics, the media.

Some of the kids in the Camaro, rowdy and spirited as unbroken horses, came up and slapped Ethan on the back or shook his hand.

"It's okay, man," one of them said. "We're gonna find your kid."

There was something bold and hopeful in their enthusiasm that gave Ethan a moment's euphoric optimism. Of course it would all work out for the best. Everything would be fine. Then he saw Jane standing off to the side, wiry and nervous. Ethan thought she might have been crying. She held her arms close to her body and the worry on her face brought him back to his state of anguished waiting, the feeling in his gut that it would never be fine again.

Cindy walked up. There was liquor in her swagger. Her anger and hatred for Ethan were tactile. But he could also see the regret, the unfinished love.

"If he's dead, Ethan . . ." But she didn't finish, and he could see she didn't know what she'd do, that she could not devise a fitting punishment for such an egregious act.

Ethan said nothing. He only nodded. Trevor came up behind her and pulled her away. He and Ethan exchanged glances. When they had walked off, Ethan could smell the tangy liquory vapors they left behind.

Jane walked over and, unclenching her arms, embraced Ethan.

"How ya holding up?"

"Okay," Ethan said. He was a stew of emotions. It was a wonder to him to feel so many things at once. "I can't settle on a feeling," he said.

Jane nodded. "Looks like Glick's here already," she said.

"Yep. He's already gone with Dog and a backpack of supplies. I hope he finds Nate and we can just call this off. These people, this help . . . feels so much like charity. Or pity."

"We love you, Ethan. We love Nate."

Ethan felt something hot behind his eyes. "I can't imagine. I'd hate me. I do hate me."

Jane smiled. It was a tight smile, but still, if you knew her, you could see

the warmth there. "We love you all the more. We'd all want the same for ourselves if it were us."

Ethan tuned out. Her words were landing on dead air. He felt the earth
open up. He felt himself moving away from her. She had always been so
kind to Nate. She'd babysat more than a few times, though Cindy objected
on account of Jane's sexual inclinations. But Ethan liked Jane. He'd just
stopped telling Cindy altogether because he didn't see how being a lesbian
could rub off on a boy anyway. The thing was, Nate and Jane loved each
other. You could see it between them.

Ethan wanted to get back out there and keep looking. He wanted to find
his boy before dark. He eyed his truck in the distance. Through the back
window, he could see his gun propped up on the seat. He watched as Cindy
and Trevor disappeared into the woods.

"I have to go," he said. "Someone brought some coffee and some rolls or
something over there. Help yourself."

Jane looked stricken. Her face had gone white. She raised her arms, and
Ethan thought for a moment she was going to hug him. But then they fell
by her side and he saw her helplessness. He walked away. He glanced at the
old man who was slowly getting out of his Mercedes. Ethan paused and then
decided he was either the law or a journalist, so he kept walking toward the
woods.

He wanted his son back. He wanted to feel his son's body flush against
his own. He wanted to hold his son in his arms. His North Star shimmering brightly in a winter sky. He wanted so many things that he could not
have, and this stubborn thwarting of his will threatened to break him apart.
Once again, he asked himself what had compelled him to chase those buck,
leaving his son, who was a light and fitful sleeper, alone in the truck.

ROCKSAN

———————◆———————

Rocksan could not get the boy out of her mind, the fact that he was lost in the woods and the weather was turning. Neither could she remove the thought that Jane was gone now, too, walking through the very woods that Rocksan knew frightened her. Rocksan saw the day was growing darker and, with it, her spirits.

She thought of Jane's son, whom she had never met, about to show up on their doorstep. She recalled that once a teacher in the next town over had heard about her and her bees. He had wanted her to speak to his senior class, and she'd said she would. She'd felt honored. It seemed like a compliment. And besides, no one had ever asked her about her bees, except Jane. She couldn't wait to talk about them out loud to a captive audience.

But right away, she saw how the students had taken one look at her and written her off. Perv. Lesbian. Freak. For most of the hour, they were rude. They didn't listen. A couple of them seemed to have fallen asleep at their desks, and those who were still awake talked to one another, drowning out her voice. It pissed her off. Near the end of the period, she mentioned the word *sex* and they perked up, the boys on the lookout for some sort of titillating lecture, the girls fussy and flirty, exchanging coy glances with their friends or, more daringly, with the boys.

When she got their attention, she told them that the one drone that managed to mate with the queen, among the thousands vying for the task, paid with his life. Sex, she told them, always had dire consequences. When the male bee entered the female, his sex organs were ripped from him, caught in the queen's open genitals. Rocksan saw the expressions of disgust on the faces of the teens. It goaded her on.

The bee's lust, she told them, was what eventually killed him. With his organ left swaying from the female's vulva, he'd tumble to earth, not quite dead, ripped open from head to stinger. He'd land on the ground, just alive enough to watch the ants and birds make their meal of him.

The boys in the class looked panicky. Was this big lesbian beekeeper going to somehow do the same to them? The girls giggled nervously or glared at her because she was a lesbian and clearly hated men—couldn't you tell by the tales she told? But Rocksan just smiled and thanked the students for their attention. Then she swore off teenagers forever.

Now, if she understood it correctly, one was coming to visit them. A boy. Well, a man really. Jane's abandoned son. The whole thing, at least on the surface, made Rocksan edgy because it threw into question whether Jane could be trusted as a lesbian. Rocksan was dyke through and through—in every blood vessel, every gene, every organ. She had been marked from birth. But Jane, it seemed, had not. That she had loved a man enough to make a baby with him involved convincingly, frighteningly hetero things. It made Rocksan jealous and afraid of what she didn't understand.

These were the things she liked to say, at least, because it was always easier to hurl an insult rather than fess up to the truth. In all honesty, what she could not admit, what brought her too much pain to face, had very little to do with Jane at all. Whenever George came into the picture, Rocksan could barely stomach what she loathed most about her life: not that Jane had abandoned him, not that Jane had fucked a man, but the miserable fact that when Rocksan was six, her bastard of a father had left her and her mother and sister in a badass, crime-infested, poverty-stricken corner of Oakland, California, to fend for themselves. The suddenness of it had sent Rocksan into a lifetime tailspin. One day her father was there and the next day he was gone, leaving her mom to raise her and Angie on nothing but a grocery-store clerk's salary and other people's leftovers.

To blame Jane, to turn the problem into Jane's problem, was selfish and loathsome. But Rocksan knew she was weak, though she harbored this weakness jealously, lest anyone find out who she *really* was. In the end, it was so much easier to pretend that someone else was fucking up her life rather than face her deepest, darkest grief.

Rocksan shook her head. Maybe these thoughts would just fall out of her ears. Why Jane didn't leave her, she would never know. It grew colder outside, and she began to remove last year's feeders, then cleaned them as thoroughly as possible. She filled the jars with bee candy—the concoction of sugar and water that she and Jane had made in vats over the stove two nights before—and hung the jars upside down on the bungholes over the brood combs.

She thought of the boy, Nate, lost in the woods. Of the snow falling harder now, the cold growing crisper, the world so much more menacing because of the things outside of them that could not be controlled. She pictured Nate and his terror. It made her heart falter. Something inside her seemed to crumple up and grow smaller. She felt a broad and plentiful sorrow for all children, for their vulnerabilities, for the way adults always fucked up their lives.

It was getting gloomier, darker. Her spirits were lagging. After she had hung the food jars, she went to the shed and, though she was depressed—the boy, Jane, her past—she pulled the blue, yellow, green, and ultraviolet paint from the shelves. She knew that it was considered "hippie" at best, and, at worst, idiotic, to paint the hives these colors. But Rocksan had seen the difference that second year. The homecoming bees had been so quick to locate and identify the hives. She knew that the colors spoke to their eyes of flowers.

She spent the rest of the afternoon painting the hives under the eaves of the shed, trying to forget all that had passed between her and Jane. The snow fell softly to earth, and the earth seemed to retreat behind it, to hide, to suffer it with patience. She tried to forget her cruelty toward Jane, but it gnawed at her. When she thought of Jane, she thought of her softness, her vulnerability. She hated that she trampled over it so swiftly, so easily.

When dusk arrived, pale, gray, and silent, she put her brushes away and used the remaining light to seal some cracks in the hives and attach mouse screens. She wondered where Jane was but then decided it was too early to worry. Maybe they'd found Nate. Maybe they were celebrating. Before her sister arrived with Rosie, she quickly weighed the hives, made entries into the record cards, and collected the cards from all the colonies. She looked toward the sky and hoped in earnest that the boy had been found.

She went inside the house and put the cards on the counter, placing them by the cookie jar. She reached into the jar and took out some cash for the pizza she would order that night for her grand-niece. She pulled a plastic knife from the drawer and put it near the edge of the counter. As darkness fell, a palpable silence filled the house, and she thought of Jane. In spite of her anger, she felt uneasy, worried. Moments later, she heard her sister's truck turning into the lane.

Angie and Rosie entered the house with a boisterousness that shattered its stillness and brought Rocksan out of her sulk. Rosie ran up to her and jumped. Rocksan caught her, lifted her in the air, and the girl shouted out gleefully, "Aunt Rocksan."

"You gain one more pound, Rosie, and I won't be able to do that anymore."

Rocksan set her down, and immediately Rosie ran to the cupboard and reached for the saltines.

"Rosie, you don't just go into people's cupboards and take out food," Angie said.

"Rocksan isn't people," Rosie said.

Rocksan laughed. "Sometimes that girl speaks my thoughts exactly."

Angie looked at Rocksan and smiled. Rocksan hugged her, taking in her quiet warmth.

"Any word on the boy?" Rocksan asked.

Angie shook her head, her expression grim. "Nothing. This wait . . . I'm just one giant nerve."

"Can you believe it? The timing can't be worse, what with this snow falling."

"I don't want to put the bad thoughts out there, but I'm scared for him. For Ethan."

Rocksan nodded. With the darkness now descendant, the fight with Jane still crisp, still alive and growing, and the boy still lost in the woods, she felt again a sense of despondency.

"Jane and I had a terrible fight," Rocksan said. She turned to Rosie, who was opening the refrigerator. "Use the margarine in the tub, sweetie," she said. "And I put a plastic knife on the counter there to spread it with."

"What about?" Angie asked. She sat at one of the high bar chairs near the counter and dug into a bowl of chocolates.

"Her son is coming, Ang. Goddamn. Her *son*."

"Aunt Rocksan just sweared," Rosie said.

"Sometimes grown-ups lose their tongues," Angie said. Then, turning back to Rocksan, she said, "I don't understand."

"Well, you know she had that son and left him behind. You know the story. . . ."

Angie nodded.

"Now she tells me he's in some kind of trouble and he's coming here."

"Oh boy."

"Doesn't bother talking it over with me. He's gonna be here tonight or tomorrow."

Angie leaned over, resting her elbows on the counter. Rocksan was always amazed at how calm her sister seemed, how unruffled. Angie never lost her temper, never overreacted, always assessed the situation and handled it slowly, thoughtfully, always the right way. Even before her daughter took off, Angie had a stillness about her. Even when Rachel had left the baby, Angie had stayed serene, as if the pain had only softened her, where it might have made others bitter. Rocksan was both jealous and irritated by her sister's serenity. Now, when her sister failed to say anything in support of her outrage, Rocksan said, "Can't you see where I'd be mad? Her not consulting with me. I mean, Christ, it's bad enough she left him to begin with."

"Ummm. Is that a swear word?" Rosie asked.

Angie ignored her granddaughter. "I can see where you'd be upset," she said calmly, earnestly, without condescension.

"I'm steaming mad," Rocksan said, her voice rising. Out of the corner of her eye, she saw Rosie methodically buttering her saltines, trying to appear as if she wasn't listening, the way children do.

"Rocksan, don't waste your energy on this anger. Jane isn't Daddy. She had her reasons, and you, of all people, should understand them. Daddy was just a loser. And you gotta give Jane credit for at least making good for her son now. Besides, she's scared of you, Rocks. You got that temper . . ."

"Oh fuck my temper,"

"Gramma," Rosie wailed. Apparently, she could handle "goddamn" and "Christ," but "fuck" was something else altogether.

"Rocksan, can you *please* watch your mouth," Angie said.

"Sorry," Rocksan said. She saw how worried Rosie was by the way the swearing had escalated. Children were so peculiar. Rocksan liked them, but only as long as she could give them back.

"You know all of this is worse for Jane," Angie said, putting another chocolate in her mouth.

How her sister could eat junk and never gain a pound was beyond Rocksan. It was weird they were even sisters. They looked nothing alike. Their temperaments were completely opposite—Angie like her mother, she like her bastard father.

"God, I hate it when you do that, Angie," Rocksan said. "You're too kind."

"Give me a break, Rocksan. You could learn something by it. And besides, remember how every time some stranger did some asshole thing that made you angry, Mom would say that you had to allow for what you didn't know about them."

"The breast cancer thing."

They laughed. Angie said, "It was always 'Maybe they have breast cancer' or 'Maybe they just learned they have testicular cancer.' "

Rocksan howled. "It was always cancer of a reproductive organ."

"Well, she was Catholic."

"What's reproductive?" Rosie asked.

"I gotta go, Rocks," Angie said. She looked at her watch.

"Great. Do I have to answer the kid?"

Angie smiled. "No." Just make something up till I can talk to her. And listen, don't be too hard on Jane. You love her. You need to love all of her, then, right?"

Rocksan didn't say anything. As Angie walked out the door, Rosie said, "Aunt Rocksan, what's reproductive mean?"

"Come here," Rocksan said.

Rosie walked over. Rocksan looked at her. She said, "Remember last summer how me and Jane had to put new queens in the hives?"

Rosie nodded solemnly.

"We had to do that so we could get more bees. The queen is the one who helps the hive grow. She lays eggs and then more bees are hatched. That act is called reproduction. It's making more bees. And people do that, too."

Rosie absorbed the information with grave seriousness. She said, "Did I come from an egg?"

The inquisitiveness of a child. Why was it so hard to answer these questions? Some cultures made up creation myths, and now she thought she probably knew why.

"Honey," she said, "go eat your crackers."

Rocksan did not tell her niece the other part. That the queen leaves the hive only once, to mate. That she knows neither flowers nor sunshine. She does not experience the companionship of the drones. And worse, she creates the perfect opening for her own death and succession, since any of the eggs she fertilizes can become the queen that will dethrone her. Rocksan did not tell Rosie that for all the queen's sovereignty and privilege, her life is brief, absent of light and love.

❦   ❦   ❦

Cold wind battering the panes of the windows. Snow flurries smashing into the glass like tiny pebbles. When Rocksan turned on the porch light, the snow looked ghostly, a dreamy apparition of white moving light.

Angie had called her to tell her that Jane was at the diner, dallying, talking to some of the others who had come in for pie and a cup of coffee. There was a flask going around, she said, because they didn't want to go to the bar. But no one was getting drunk. Angie had just wanted Rocksan to know so she wouldn't worry. Ever since their dad took off, Angie had always tried to make it so Rocksan's famous temper wouldn't ignite.

Later, after Rocksan had put Rosie to sleep, she drank some tea and read from the *American Bee Journal*. She loved the ads in the back for all the strange accoutrements of beekeeping. But her favorites were the handful of personals from the lovelorn apiarists, especially the women seeking "female companionship and a shared interest in beekeeping."

At 9:30, she got ready for bed and fell asleep immediately. Minutes later, she was startled awake by the sound of the front door closing. She heard the rustle as Jane hung her coat on the rack and then her light footfalls as she mounted the stairs. Rocksan heard her go into Rosie's room. The footsteps stopped. Silence. Rocksan imagined Jane, thin, quiet, peering down at Rosie, lost in the thoughts of her own son, the years she had let go. What grief could be deeper, Rocksan wondered, than to face the loss of what you might have had if only your courage had held out?

She felt a tightening in her chest and wondered why it hurt so much to love. After a moment, Jane began to tiptoe again, and Rocksan could hear her making her way to their bedroom. The door opened and Rocksan, whose eyes were used to the darkness, made out the silhouette of Jane re-moving her clothes, slipping into a flannel nightie, and making her way into the bed. Rocksan could smell the whiskey, and something else. The snow. The cold.

"Hi," she said.

"Hey," Jane said.

They were silent. The clock ticked loudly in the room. Rocksan could al-most feel the weight of Jane's regret and nervousness. For a moment she felt crowded by it, but then she imagined Jane again, looking down at Rosie, re-membering something she had no memory of.

"Did they find him?"

"No. And now Glick is missing."

"What?"

"He started out before most anyone got there. Went alone. Hasn't been seen or heard from since. It's snowing hard. They decided to wait until morning and then go back to find him."

"Oh no. This is awful."

"Ethan's out there sleeping in his truck. He says he won't leave, in case Nate comes outta the woods."

The night bore down on Rocksan. She could not stand this chasm between them, to have it filled with such terrible news.

"Jane," Rocksan said. She found Jane's hand under the blankets. "I'm sorry."

Jane began to cry. She was always the one who cried.

"We can leave it go. We can leave it behind us," Rocksan said. She heard the desperation in her voice. It served to remind her how deep her love was, how much she wanted to love Jane forever.

She felt Jane nodding her head. Jane said, "I'm the one who's sorry."

Rocksan felt relief, a broad liberation from the black mood that had seen her through the day. She couldn't find any more words, though she had a vague desire for everything to go back to the day before. Now there was this new terrain. It was like making a map without coordinates or landmarks.

They turned toward each other. Outside, darkness prevailed. "We'll have to get the back room ready for him," Rocksan said. "And we'll need to stock up on food. You eat like a bird; I can hardly see him wanting all those fussy nuts and fruits you like. He's probably a steak kinda guy. Like me."

Jane laughed. She gripped Rocksan's hand tighter in the dark, and Rocksan felt as though she'd been moored, stilled once more from the private eddy of all her flaws and frailties.

JANE

———◆———

Lying there in bed with Rocksan, Jane thought about how she'd felt that morning at the search sight.

After Ethan had returned to the woods, Jane felt lost. She felt so small with the pines shadowing over her. The forest was an impenetrable place, with all those trees leaning this way and that, the snow, the haphazard way the plants seemed to grow. It looked drunk. A drunken forest.

Jane turned around, thinking she'd just go. She had no one to search with and people were pairing up. She thought of how she had just babysat Nate last weekend while his dad worked late at the hardware store. She remembered how they had put together a puzzle and then later she'd let him have a sip of her grape soda. She remembered the way he'd smacked his lips. The way he'd burped and then fell out laughing.

She started to head back to her truck, feeling confused and over-whelmed. All these people out here for Nate, and Nate just gone, vanished as if into thin air. How strange. How frightening.

As she neared her truck, she saw an old man step unsteadily out of a black Mercedes. She didn't recognize him. She saw Ethan cast a sidelong glance at him, pause for a moment, and then continue on. The man looked out of place. His jacket was too new, too fancy, as if he had bought it to look good skiing someplace like Aspen. His shoes—a pair of lightweight boots—would never hold up against a good snow.

To Jane, he didn't look like he was from the press. He didn't have a pen or a pad of paper. There was no cell phone attached to his belt, no miniature tape recorder with its mini-cassettes. And he lacked the buffoonery and arrogance of the journalists who were showing up, blundering into this small town with its reticence and privacy, like elephants at a glass factory. He took off his glasses and wiped them with a hankie that he pulled from his shirt pocket. The act made him seem afraid and vulnerable.

Jane approached him. "Are you a friend of Ethan or Cindy?"

The man seemed momentarily speechless and self-conscious. Jane knew he wasn't anyone's friend here.

"No," he said. "I heard about the boy being lost. I heard there was a search."

"Where you from?"

He nodded. "Down valley."

That was code, Jane knew, for the city.

"It was nice of you to come."

The man nodded. He seemed both kind and nervous. Haunted by something and trying hard to hide it.

"I don't have a search buddy," Jane said. "You wanna come with me?"

The man seemed surprised. Jane surprised herself by asking. But she had grown suddenly weary of this small mountain town, its people, its gossip, and the oppression of Nate's disappearance. She wanted something different to happen or to be happening. She missed San Francisco, with its predictable pavement, the Muni buses and BART, the high-rises and homeless. All these trees, the hidden scurrying sounds within the woods, it got to her sometimes.

"Why, sure. That would be fine," the man said. He put out his hand. "Jack Rosenthal."

"Jane Childs."

The man's hands were cold. Jane wondered if he had any gloves, but it looked almost like he hadn't planned this trip, hadn't expected to be here. Jane zipped up her parka, put the hood on. The sky looked threatening.

"Let's get started. Spend some time searching before the snow makes it impossible," she said.

They passed by Ethan's truck. He was nowhere to be seen. Jane saw the shotgun propped up on the seat, a thermos on its side on the dashboard. The forest was rich and dense with old-growth trees and berries, delicate fingers of dogwood, now bare and bony for the winter. She knew that if you walked over five miles in from this point, you would find an ancient stand of sequoia. Farther up was the summit of Angels Crest.

Only the locals knew about this old trail anymore, since the Park Service had built the newer, easier trail. She and Rocksan had done the hike once, camping overnight by a stream and lying under the stars. She remembered being afraid. The forest had bellowed all night with the sounds of the wind, the gurgling stream, the nocturnal animals foraging. She'd been convinced they would be eaten by bears, that no one would find them for weeks, and then when they were found, the grisly details of their deaths would end up in one of those books of gruesome deaths. Rocksan was much braver. She'd kept waking Jane from her muddled dreams and whispering, "It's all right, Beanpole."

The thought of Rocksan made her feel regret and worry. She suddenly remembered something that had happened when they'd first met. She had been staying at Rocksan's house every night—a beautiful large Victorian that Rocksan had bought in Hayes Valley and fixed up. The neighborhood wasn't great. They had to share the streets with drug dealers, and there was a lot of crime associated with the projects a few blocks away. But the house was beautiful, with brightly painted turrets and windows everywhere. Inside, with its hardwood floors and creaking closet doors, the house smelled old and comforting, like a library. Rocksan had updated the kitchen, so that even while you felt you were living your life in the 1800s, you could still easily make yourself an espresso.

She remembered how they had been sitting together in the living room on a particularly foggy day. The foghorns were blaring their mournful song and the house was warm and smelled of coffee and the fresh croissants that Rocksan had picked up from a nearby bakery. Jane was wearing one of Rocksan's shirts, which hung on her narrow frame like a billowing muumuu.

The phone rang, and Jane heard Rocksan answer it. Moments later, Rocksan returned, her face white and haunted. Jane asked her what was wrong and Rocksan said that her sister had called to tell her their father had died. Jane remembered feeling a rush of adrenaline. She hardly knew Rocksan. Such despairing news was difficult. How should she react? She stood up and put her arms around Rocksan, but Rocksan pushed her aside rather gruffly, the color returning to her face.

"Just so you know," Rocksan said. "He was a bastard when he was alive. He died a bastard, and as far as I'm concerned, there's no use crying over a dead bastard."

Jane had been stunned. Rocksan had reached for the vodka and poured some into her orange juice, then drank it down. It was like she had turned off a switch. In moments, the phone call and the news that came with it had been wiped away.

She thought of George. Of his birth, how long and arduous it had been. When it was over, she couldn't remember anything except that at one point she had screamed so loudly, a nurse had come in and said, "What's the matter?" Jane remembered how she had shouted back, "I'm in labor, you idiot."

She thought about George arriving sometime soon, probably tomorrow. It made her heart race. She had not seen him in nineteen and a half years. She thought of the night she left him, how much liquor it had taken, how long the sorrow had lasted.

"Do you live here in town?" Jack asked, interrupting her thoughts and causing her to start.

"Yes. We moved from San Francisco about six years ago. My girlfriend wanted to be here, closer to her sister."

If he was shocked that he was in the woods, walking around with a lesbian, on the hunt for a missing boy, he didn't show it. She admired his good manners, the way his surefooted gait and his calm deportment belied his obvious inexperience with the forest.

"What do you do in the city?" she asked.

"I'm a circuit judge," he said. "About to retire."

Jane was surprised. It was odd to be talking so casually to a judge. She had always had a problem with authority. Had always felt shy around policemen and lawyers. She looked at the judge, at his kindly face, and she tried to think of the questions she should ask him. For instance, was there any way to sue that bastard who'd forced her away from her son? But she kept the thoughts to herself. It was too much to give away in the woods when you were looking for someone else's missing child.

"Rocksan and I are both retired."

"So young," he said. "What did you retire from?"

"Well, I didn't really retire from anything. I just worked odd jobs, but Rocksan was in real estate investment."

Jane always felt foolish saying that. What Rocksan did was make loads of money in the commercial real estate boom, buying and selling. She was a gambler. A speculator. She had been lucky. They were rich.

"Now we keep bees. It's really Rocksan's passion. I pretend to share it, but between you and me, I don't have the same level of interest."

"You mean hives? Honeybees?"

"Yep. We make honey. But the thing that Rocksan really loves are the bees themselves. She's always going around saying that God made bees before He made man and that this should give us all pause. She thinks bees are superior to the human race."

"She may be onto something," the judge said, smiling for the first time.

It made Jane smile, too. She remembered that time in the woods, how she and Rocksan had finished their hike, reaching the summit of Angels Crest on a glorious summer morning, and all around, the world shimmered like a kingdom of trees and granite and more splendor than she had even imagined, as if her imagination were too small, too finite to have predicted it. And all her fear had vanished. It was that way with Rocksan sometimes. She could sometimes see Rocksan from far enough away that she inhabited a place outside of Jane's imagination of her.

"Do you have any kids?" she asked the judge.

"Three boys. All grown. One of them works for a bank; another runs a homeless shelter. But the baby—he's in his thirties now—he's got some problems. He doesn't work. Least not last time we spoke."

"I have a son," Jane said. She tried the words out. She wanted to see how they'd feel to say, how it would sound out loud. "He's twenty. He's coming for a visit."

"That's wonderful," the judge said. "Did he grow up with you?"

"Nah. He lived with his father."

"It's strange," the judge said. "So strange that I'm here today. Last night, I went to bed and everything seemed okay. But by the time I woke up this morning . . ."

The judge trailed off. Jane didn't feel right prying. She had learned, from living up here, that you didn't pry into other people's business. You waited until they offered it up and then you didn't say much either way about it.

The forest seemed impertinent, cagey, as if it had snatched the boy and was keeping him for its own. Jane had never liked all the trees, the claustrophobia it gave her. She had always found the woods menacing, and she sometimes wondered why she had agreed to move to the mountains, when it was the broad, dry expanse of the desert she preferred. She had told Rocksan that whenever they hiked, she felt like something was always lurking in the shadows. Rocksan had told her that it was her guilty conscience.

She and the judge followed an animal trail, probably deer, and foraged into the woods much deeper than she would have liked. She tried to remember her purpose, to help Ethan, to find his son. But in the silence, Jane could feel her fears crowding in.

"How did you hear that Nate was missing?" she asked. She wanted to hear her own voice. The stillness in the woods was too loud for her taste.

The judge paused for a long moment. He sighed deeply. Then he said, "I went for a drive and heard the story on the radio. It got to me, I guess you could say."

"I know what you mean," Jane said.

"We are all so . . ." He paused. Jane saw him searching for the word. "So defenseless."

"I know. We forget that about ourselves."

The judge nodded. He zipped his jacket up higher. It was growing colder, more still. Jane knew the snow would start falling harder soon.

"Ethan loves his kid. The two of them do everything together. You'd never see one without seeing the other."

"It was like that with me and my youngest. They say a parent is not supposed to have favorites, but Marty was the light of my life."

Jane stumbled for a moment over a log and the judge was quick to help her. He guided her by the elbow, helped steady her. Jane was moved by the sureness of the gesture, the automatic quality of it. He seemed like such a gentleman, so fatherly.

"What happened with him?" she asked when she had gained her balance.

"Honestly? I don't know. He just never found his footing in the world. He always felt different from other people. He marched to the beat of a different drummer."

Jane wondered if the son was gay, but she was afraid to ask.

"He got involved in drugs," the judge said, as if reading her mind and wanting to set it straight. "We lost him to that world after that."

"I'm sorry," Jane said.

They walked on. Jane began to look in earnest for the boy. She hoped she'd find his footprints or a piece of clothing, something that would give them a clue. The judge, too, seemed suddenly aware that he was there to look for a lost boy. But his navigation of the woods was awkward. He moved self-consciously. Under it all, there was a quality of unease, as if the judge was not convinced he should make too much room for himself in the world.

The snow was falling harder now. Jane thought it beautiful. The beauty of it mitigated the creepiness of the forest, even though she knew it really made it all the more dangerous and inhospitable. At one point as they searched together, walking in a companionable silence, the judge removed his glasses and wiped them on his shirt.

When he put them back on, he looked into the distance and said, "It was like my son had walked into the woods and never came back."

A few hours later, Jane and the judge walked out of the forest and entered the clearing. There were more cars there than when they had started. A couple of rangers wearing brown uniforms and badges stood talking with Ethan. A table was set up, and on top of it sat coffee in a large thermos, some doughnuts and apples, maps. People were milling about. A contingent from the Calvary Church was heading into the woods. A group of boys hung out near their Camaro and smoked while a few more talked to reporters among the trees. When one of the boys near the car saw the judge, he said, "Do you need to follow us out of here? We're takin' off."

Judge Rosenthal seemed momentarily confused. Jane felt a flash of warmth for him, for his awkwardness and for his befuddlement. His discomfort there, during the search, talking with Jane, made him seem familiar and genial. Something about the new parka he wore made her sad. She wanted to give him her phone number. But he nodded at the boys and got into his car, forgetting to say good-bye to her.

When he drove off down the dirt road in the wake of the Camaro's dust, Jane thought he looked solemn and surprised, a man who had never expected to be so alone.

⬧   ⬧   ⬧

Midnight. Rosie was asleep in the room next door. Rocksan breathed rhythmically beside her. Jane envied Rocksan her ability to sleep so easily.

Quietly, she stood up and went to the bathroom. She lit a candle and opened the window, letting the cold air blast inside the warm tiled room. She felt the relief of forgiveness. Rocksan always forgave. She always loved her.

Outside, she could just make out the drifts and flurries of snow. She thought of her son arriving shortly. Of Nate, lost in the woods. She had heard that Ethan was camping out there in his truck, waiting. She pictured him sitting by a fire, smoking in the darkness. She remembered the camping trip she and Rocksan had taken, how the forest cried and whispered at night. How frightened Nate must be. She did not go to the other possibility in her head.

Looking off in the distance, she could see a pair of headlights on the road far below. Silently, they passed by the drive of their house, glittering in and out of the spaces of the trees and bushes. As the car went down the hill toward town, Jane watched the red taillights glisten and disappear. She stood quietly surveying the night. The world was a place filled with stillness and mystery.

CINDY

―――――◆―――――

Once in a while, she and Trevor would run into some of the other searchers. They would want to stop and compare maps or routes that had been searched or those that hadn't. But Cindy and Trevor didn't have a map. She thought of herself as searching blindly, without reason or thought except one, to find her son now.

Trevor talked and talked. It drove her crazy. She thought of Ethan and her gut filled with heat. She wanted so much to hate him. Now she finally had a reason, the best reason, to hate him. He had won full custody of her son and then lost him in the fucking woods. That should have been the deciding factor, the one thing that changed her love for him forever.

But instead, she felt sorry for him. And scared for him. She was so close to it that she kept thinking *she* was the one who had left Nate in the truck. It was something she would have done, not Ethan, with his slow, careful, plodding ways. This should have been her fuckup. But it was his. She knew he would not be able to handle it. She knew that if Nate wasn't found, Ethan would fall completely apart. That was who he was. No one knew that better than Cindy.

She remembered how Ethan had showed up in town when they were freshmen in high school. How quickly she had fallen for him, and the gossipy, high schoolish scandal it had caused when they began sleeping together. She'd had to give Trevor back the promise ring. She'd had to tell Trevor that she loved someone else.

Even back then, her head was a spinning madhouse of voices. She wasn't good enough. She wasn't pretty enough. She wasn't smart enough. But when she met Ethan and he told her she was pretty and beautiful, and not only that but sexy, and could they have a baby together, she was a new person. A different person. A woman. Everyone, even her drunken grandmother, noticed. People she'd known all her life had stopped her on the street and told her she looked different. Beautiful.

Ethan was like magic. He was so quiet, so good. He wanted to do everything right all the time. He said she was raw and beautiful and he wished he was more that way. She should have known then that it couldn't work between them. But for a while, she fell into his silences with a sense of quiet gratitude. She had even stopped drinking for a while. Stopped smoking dope. She had been able to care about him in a way she had never been able to care about Trevor, or anyone.

For once, there was someone more interesting to her than she was to herself. It was easy to listen to him, and though on the surface of things he seemed the stronger of the two, she saw how his silence was a mask for his fragility. He'd told her about his mother's long illness, his father's quiet sorrow. How after she died, he and his dad would sit there watching TV for hours, not talking. He told her that he thought he would just die in that lounger in Los Angeles, until one day his dad had quit his job and sold the house. They were moving to the woods.

He had said that when he'd moved up here and found the woods, he felt like the very trees had somehow sucked up all his misery and kept it for themselves, freeing him from all the old hurts and pains. He told her he'd finally found happiness. And now here she was, he said. A dream. It was all a dream come true.

She'd believed him. For the first time, she didn't hate her parents for dumping her off in this shithole town to live with her alcoholic grandmother. Being loved by Ethan was like looking through a window. But loving Ethan was being the window itself, being the glass and all the light that shone through it.

Now as she and Trevor walked through the trampled forest looking for Nate, calling out his name, she remembered that time when Ethan's gloomy father had found the two of them out back near the shed. How disappointed he'd been to see Ethan with his pants down around his ankles, his butt in the breeze, pumping into her. Ethan had been embarrassed, but Cindy remembered feeling cavalier. She had felt branded, owned. But also powerful. She had taken Ethan away from his depressing life, the memory of his dead mother and the melancholy of his father.

But then she got pregnant. Three years out of high school. A month later, Ethan's dad died of a heart attack. By the time the baby was born, all the stored-up sadness inside Ethan had come to the surface. It pained Cindy to think about it. Because by then, she was drinking again, only with a more powerful and convincing thirst. She couldn't stop, even to nurse Nate, and she saw how he was slow to walk, slow to talk because of the liquor she fed him through her milk. She saw how he would cry in the night, long and bitterly, not the way, it seemed, a baby should cry. Drunk, she would raise her hand to the boy, telling him to shut up, shut up, shut up. Sober, she'd fill with remorse and love him hard and desperately. She saw how much Nate loved Ethan. How much more.

As she walked in the woods, the pain of Nate missing had taken on some kind of physical shape, had latched itself onto her, so that it seemed to penetrate through even the armor of the liquor. It was not just this loss but also the mistakes she had made before and knowing how things might have been different, if only.

"You need to be strong," Trevor said.

"You don't have the slightest idea how bad this feels. You can't know. You've never had a child."

"We've known each other most all of our twenty-five years, girl, and I have never seen you crumble. You gotta stay tough. You hear me?"

Something in his voice. Something sure and familiar. They'd known each other their entire lives. He knew her better than anyone. She felt herself go limp. She reached for the bottle that she'd shoved into the pocket of her parka. She pulled on it and felt the way the whiskey went down. She found an anchor from far away, deep within her, and she nodded her head.

"I hear what you're saying, Trevor. But you talk too fucking much, and you gotta stop calling me 'girl.' "

They heard someone shouting in the distance. He looked straight ahead.

He said, "I may not have a kid, but I love you. I can feel what you feel even when we aren't in the same room. You understand?"

She nodded. It had always been like that with them. She would never love him that way. She heard the shouting again.

"Listen," she said. "Do you hear that?" She started running toward the voices and stumbled into a small group of people gathered around in a circle. A couple of reporters were there, too, the flash from the cameras bursting into the dark sky.

"What? Oh my God, is it Nate? Did you find him?" Cindy shouted. She ran forward, pushed her way through the gathering of people. At their feet was the deflated balloon he'd been carrying. And the string. Nothing else. No Nate. No footprints. Nothing.

❖   ❖   ❖

She walked out of the woods with Trevor. She was exhausted. She knew, in her heart of hearts, her son was probably dead, and though she wouldn't say it out loud, she could feel it, the way she had felt him when she was pregnant. A pull. A tussle inside with her organs.

She emerged from the woods and saw Ethan, and everything, *everything,* she had ever felt for him welled up inside her. She remembered the way he had loved her and then the way he had no longer loved her. She remembered the way their end had been telegraphed in his solitude, the way he kept his distance. She saw how his loneliness made it possible for Nate to be the only thing that mattered in his life.

"I can't believe you did this, Ethan," she said. She saw the hurt in his eyes. She wanted to hate him. She also wanted to grab him, clutch ahold of him, promise him it would be all right. Trevor came up behind her and pulled her away. She went without a fight. The two of them walked back to the truck. They drove back to town in silence. When she dropped him off at the bar, he leaned over and tenderly kissed her on the cheek.

"You'll make it through this thing, Cindy. Okay?"

"Yeah, sure."

"I'll come over after I close the bar."

"Not tonight, Trevor."

She drove off. She felt so much relief to be going home to her shit-colored apartment. She just wanted to sleep this drink off and figure out her next move.

◆ ◆ ◆

Cindy roused herself from bed. It was almost 10:00 P.M. She reached for the bottle and sipped from it before anything could sweep in and hurt her. She stood up and looked out the window. Snow flurries drifted silently down in the glow from the streetlights around the building. Nate was out there somewhere.

She went to the hallway closet and took out her heaviest boots. She put them on. Then she reached for her down jacket and a pair of warm gloves, a hat and scarf. She found her car keys in the kitchen, where she'd left them. She opened the door, sucked in her breath from the cold, and then remembered to get the bottle from her room and the flashlight she kept under the bed.

She drove through town. When she passed Angie's, she saw that the place was still open, unbelievably packed. She drove by slowly and saw people she didn't know and people she did—Jane, Angie, the old blind preacher.

She remembered when Jane and Rocksan moved to town, right after Angie's daughter had gotten herself pregnant and left with another woman's man. She remembered how everyone went around sneaking peeks at them because they'd never seen lesbians in town before. She remembered staring at them herself, sort of shamefully, too, but in the end not seeing anything that different about them. What seemed stranger to her than the two of them sharing the same bed was the thing they had with those bees. She'd seen them once near the perimeter of their property, wearing white suits and big capelike hoods with screens in the front. There were bees everywhere, which gave her the creeps. How could anyone stand having all those bees swarming around them? The sound alone.

She thought of the fight she'd put up when Ethan let Jane take care of her kid. She saw now what a stupid fight it was. What a wasted fight. It was as if she always had to find something to argue with him about, some kind of outside thing to keep wielding over him. It was desperate, she knew. But she needed to stay engaged, and all she had left was the fight.

She drove past Cage Road, where Glick lived, and out of town, snaking up the long, winding road to the spot where her son had last been seen. In the falling snow, she parked her car and then, taking the bottle and the flashlight with her, ventured into the clearing. There she saw Ethan's truck and a small fire burning beside it. But Ethan was nowhere to be seen.

Cindy crept into the woods. The flashlight made eerie shadows among the trees. The forest was silent, sleeping. The snow was very light, very dry, and it squeaked beneath her feet. She walked slowly, not going too far because she was afraid. She remembered the day her son was born, how harrowing it had been to drive the twenty miles to the next town, where the closest hospital was. How unbearable the contractions were, every bump in the road making them worse. She remembered the swiftness with which they came on and the way they grew in size and shape, until she cried out and begged Ethan to drive faster, just drive the fuck faster. Nate was born so quickly, so painfully, and when she'd held him in her arms, she was disappointed because she did not feel the rush of love she'd expected.

He'd cried all day, and she could barely hold him, could barely feed him. She would not admit how much she disliked him. But then that night, he'd finally suckled at her breast and had fallen asleep across her chest, his tiny legs holding him up by her side, so that he was leaning over her body in the shape of an L. He slept that way, and she could hear his breath, so rich and alive. He had seemed then much more a part of her than he had at any time during her pregnancy. And at that moment, she had felt the miraculous and extraordinary fact of him. In that moment, she had felt complete and whole and forgiven in its broadest sense. Pardoned for all her weaknesses and moral lapses, for all her pettiness and little fears. In that moment, she had felt the deepest love, the greatest love.

"Nate," she cried out. "Ethan. Where are you?" She stumbled and grabbed a branch to keep from falling, but her balance was off and she fell to the ground. On the ground, feeling the cold and wet instantly seep through her jeans, she cried out again, "Nate, goddamn it, please come to Mommy. Please. Mommy is here. Mommy loves you. Goddamn it, Nate. Please."

Her cries were met by silence, and then a wind picked up and blew through the trees. She stumbled to her feet, tears streaming down her face. It was so dark, so cold. God, where was he? Where was Ethan? She wanted to pray, to get on her knees there in the snow. But there was so little God inside her, and what had once existed was chased out from the years of drinking and disappointment.

She walked back to her car, wiping the tears from her cheeks. What good were they anyway? They'd just freeze to her skin. She got in her car and, exhausted, drove back down the road. On the outskirts of town, she passed the house where the lesbians lived and saw the faint glow, as if from a candle, in an upstairs room. She thought she saw the shadowy trace of a woman standing there. She turned up the radio, thinking of the woods and how they had swallowed her family whole.

JUDGE JACK ROSENTHAL

———◆———

He used to tell his sons this story. Rabbi Hillel lived during the time of Jesus. He was challenged to explain the entire Torah while standing on one leg. Hillel said, "What is hateful to yourself, do not do to others. That is the whole of the Torah. The rest is commentary. Go and study it."

He often thought of Hillel when he was expected to pass a sentence in court. He had been drawn to the law through the Torah, through the Ten Commandments, through the teachings of Moses. He abstracted meaning from the challenges of secular law through his knowledge of Jewish law, though he would never tell anyone this.

Privately, he made his decisions in court based on his knowledge of Torah. He was drawn to the *people* and their issues. To finding solutions that would embody God's law, even though he had to appear impartial to God's law in his courtroom. These were his secrets. His wife knew them and his sons knew them, even if he himself had never admitted them. They knew he was a jurist and had to maintain that bias away from God in public, even if his every action was driven by his love for God in private.

The fact was, he was a Jew in a provincial city with a Baptist church, a Catholic church, a Pentecostal church, and a Protestant church. His synagogue had a painfully small membership and made up almost the entire Jewish community in town. If not for his assignment to the judiciary here, he would be in a larger city, like Los Angeles or New York. It had always pained him, this aloneness, but he kept it to himself because he knew his wife had felt it, too, and he didn't want to make it harder on her.

But because his faith was second nature to him, he had always been able to withstand the occasional Jew joke, the crank calls from the anti-Semites. Then there was the time someone salted his front lawn in the shape of a swastika, a brown burn on the otherwise-green grass. He'd left it there. He would not make it easy on them. He would not kowtow to the vagaries of hatred. People would walk by, he hoped, and feel ashamed.

The swastika had come just before Adele learned of the cancer. Jack could see the way the image of it right there on their lawn had wounded her. She had begged him to get rid of it. But he would not. He had said, "A man should feel ashamed to do anything which would not be in accordance with the will of God."

She had erupted in anger. "And who are you to decide what that will is?"

When he had continued to refuse, she had stormed off, shouting, "Is it God's will, Jack, or your will, I wonder?"

The cancer had swept through her so quickly, there was barely time to prepare for the inevitable outcome. As she lay dying, Marty, their youngest, the brightest of their children, the one everyone said was too sensitive and the world would break his heart if he wasn't careful, had vanished. He and his drug addiction and his stripper girlfriend had taken off for Hollywood, light-years away from the life Jack had hoped for him.

So when Adele died, it felt as if really both she and Marty had died at the same time. He mourned them both. And he would look at the lawn, at the swastika there, and feel ashamed. For in the end, he knew how unkind he had been, how his unbending desire to teach a lesson to all the bigots in his stupid provincial city had stood in the way of really understanding that God's will was simpler than all that. It was what Hillel had said. He knew that he could not place the responsibility for his own misdeed on the shoulders of God.

But still, even more so after she died, he could not tear it up and lay new sod over the soiled grass. He needed the lesson every day to remind himself of his own wrongheadedness. Then on the day of the funeral, he came home from the graveside and the swastika was gone. He never knew who had rid the lawn of it, and for weeks he could make out the square patch of sod that had been put in its place.

After Adele had died, his life had narrowed in focus. He spent his days on the bench—though he was retiring soon and had scaled his work back. When he'd come home at night, he'd have a sip of scotch and he'd water Adele's plants or, if he had it in him, he'd go back to the task of emptying her closets and drawers.

Then last night, almost exactly six months to the day of Adele's death, everything had changed. He'd been sleeping in the guest room because he could not sleep in the bedroom anymore. His wife, the memories. It was as if she were still in there, watching him.

He was dozing off, thinking how he'd like to sell the house and move somewhere, the desert maybe or Florida, where it was always warm and he could start over, in a new bed, one without Adele's scent, her essence still there. After a while, he'd dozed off, only to wake up with a start an hour later. He'd heard the front door downstairs shut quietly. His heart started racing. Someone was walking slowly, softly up the stairs. A burglar. It crossed his mind that it might be someone he'd sentenced, someone on parole. It was not that far-fetched. His friend Steven, who'd just retired as DA, had been held up at gunpoint by the wife of a murderer he'd sentenced to life in prison. It was not that far-fetched at all.

He sat up. The phone. He'd left the damn phone downstairs. The only other one was in his bedroom, down the hall, by the stairs. His heart was racing. He heard two people whispering. Then they went into his and Adele's bedroom. Someone who knows the house, Jack thought, someone who knows what they are looking for. Marty, he thought.

Jack jumped out of bed. Quietly, he opened the door and looked down the hall. The door to his bedroom was open. He heard their voices, a man and a woman. He felt sure it was Marty, but he also thought it might not be. How, for instance, would Marty know that Jack no longer slept in his old room? In either case, he felt a driving fear. Jesus, he could hear his heartbeat in his head, the thump and roar of his blood. He thought of his blood, and he saw himself on the floor, blood seeping from his head, the intruders running away.

He needed to get to the phone. He had to think. To clear his head. But the pounding blood. He wasn't sure which seemed worse: the prospect of his son sneaking into his house for—what, to rob him?—or a stranger doing it.

Just then, he saw them emerge from the room he once shared with his wife. He blinked a couple of times because it didn't seem possible. But there was Marty with Adele's jewelry box in his hands, and a girl, the stripper, holding on to a pillowcase that seemed filled with books. Jack could not believe it. It was worse, this betrayal, than his wife's death.

"Marty," he said. His voice was barely above a whisper.

Marty turned to look at him. He stopped dead in his tracks.

"What are you doing? Marty?"

"Dad . . . I . . ."

"Are you stealing from me? Your mother isn't cold in the grave and you're stealing her jewelry?"

He was incredulous. Broken. He felt the world yawning open and snatching him inside its putrid depths. He felt as if he were growing smaller and smaller by the second. Soon he would disappear.

"Dad, I . . ."

"Fuck it, Marty. Let's go," the girl said. She grabbed the pillowcase tighter. Jack thought of all the things that might be inside it. He remembered his coin collection. All those rare coins, each one placed in its slot in the thin leather coin books. They were worth a fortune. He realized that his coins were in the pillowcase and that they would probably pawn them for so much less than their value. The possibility of being hurt had not yet left him. In his adrenaline haze, he pictured the girl hitting him over the head with the pillowcase, the heavy coins inside knocking him out.

"Are those my coins?" he asked. He realized he was still hiding partially behind the door. He was in his pajamas. His feet were bare and cold. Everything felt both cold and hot. He was shaking.

"I'm sorry," Marty said.

He and the girl turned and walked swiftly away, heading toward the stairs. Jack watched them disappearing. He heard them take the stairs quickly, this time without masking the sound, and he heard them go out the front door, close the door, and drive off. He remained standing there for a long, long time. It was so hot and so cold. He felt almost like a small child in his pajamas. After a while, he sank to the ground and felt something inside him open up. He began to pray, hoping he could fill it—*God have mercy on me*—but the hole just seemed to grow bigger and wider and emptier.

❧ ❧ ❧

As first light hit, Jack woke up. He'd fallen asleep right there, leaning up against the door, the prayer still on his lips. He was bereft. Everything inside him, emptied out. He wished his life were over, that he had somehow died during the night.

He left his house and got into his car—a black Mercedes that had been his one bow to conceit—with the vague idea of driving up to the mountains and disappearing forever, of leaving all his earthly pain behind. He did not know what these fantasies meant, nor did he dare articulate them in words, but his mind was filled with the strange yet comforting image of the world as a place without him.

He drove on the empty freeways and then, as he neared the foothills, exited and began to take the county roads, a network of well-maintained but increasingly narrower lanes winding their way up the mountain. The plow had been through during the night, but the dip in temperature had frozen the snow in places, causing long patches of ice. Once in a while, the car would swerve and slide and Jack would feel his pulse quicken and a rush of adrenaline pierce his gut.

By the time he hit the marker denoting the eight-thousand-foot elevation, he learned from radio reports that a boy was lost in the woods near a small town called Angels Crest. A search had been mounted. The boy had been missing for several hours.

Jack recalled that he had just passed the turnoff for the town, and, struck by the serendipity of it, he turned around. When he arrived in the town a few minutes later, Jack felt everything within him slow down. He was struck by how small and beautiful the place was. Not beautiful the way you might find in some quaint mountain tourist spot where the buildings were adorned with Christmas lights year-round and every store smelled like incense and soaps. No, it was beautiful for its emptiness and silence. The small houses that lined the main road were well tended, with cars in the driveway, toys on the lawn. Main Street was sprinkled with shops and stores, most of them housed in nineteenth-century buildings. He passed a hardware store, Ethan's Hardware and Sporting Goods, a Laundromat, a dentist's office on the street level of a beautiful old Victorian, a taxidermy shop, a pawnshop, and a bar called Trevor's Echo, which looked like a saloon right out of the Old West.

Something about the town, its earnestness and simplicity, something about a small boy missing in the woods, changed him. It was a shift of subtle proportions. But the now-troubling notions he'd had of disappearing vanished from his thoughts and were replaced by this quiet town, its dawning tragedy and the growing sense that he was meant to be here. He drove on until he found a diner.

Before he went inside the diner, which was called Angie's, he stopped next door at the town records office, thinking someone there might give him some information on the boy, directions to the search site. Sitting inside, on a bench facing a row of pictures, was an old man. It took Jack a moment to realize the man was blind, because he seemed to be looking at the photographs on the wall, but Jack could see his eyes were milky, dead.

"Hello," Jack said.

The old man nodded. He held a flimsy Bible in one hand and his cane in the other.

Jack looked at the pictures taken back in the late 1800s, when the town was evidently first founded. There was one picture that caught his attention. In it were five infants; the date was 1889. On the right, beside it, was another picture of the same five people, only it was taken twenty years later, when they were adults. Four men, one woman. Jack read the title and inscription below the first picture.

A Miracle in the Snow—The Founding of Angels Crest,
or How Five Babies Survived the Worst Winter in History!

These five infants you see here were born that terrible winter in 1889, when the snow was twenty feet deep by January! It only took a few weeks for the cattle to die off. The settlers, their wagons unable to make it through the snow, were trapped! One by one, most of them died from cold, starvation, disease. But miraculously, these five infants survived. Legend has it that the angels, on their way to heaven, stopped at the summit of the highest peak in these parts and watched over the babies until the winter passed. The peak became known as Angels Crest, and that spring, the town officially adopted the same name. You can still find the graves of our town's first settlers in the cemetery on Main!

The old blind man straightened up. "That was my great-great-grandfather," he said. "Third baby from the left."

❧   ❧   ❧

Jack went next door to the diner. He was surprised at the size of the crowd until he realized that most of the people were probably journalists or outsiders like himself who had come to help with the search. The place looked warm and inviting. He stood outside the restaurant for a moment. How odd the world seemed. It was the same place it had always been and yet Jack felt as if he'd just gone through the looking glass. The sheen of a new logic seemed to lie over the last twenty-four hours, so that while the essence and the truth of his life were the same, something felt different. Uncomfortably so. Out of fear and also a mysterious sense of gratitude, he went back to his car, reached into his glove compartment, and grabbed the pocket-size Torah he kept there.

Inside the diner the smell of freshly baked bread made him feel safe, as if someone were taking care of him after a long time of being sick alone. He thought of Adele, the cancer, how quickly it had swept through her. He thought of Marty, stealing from him, the girl holding the pillowcase filled with his coin collection.

A blond-haired waitress was there beside him instantly. Her name tag read ANGIE. She seemed wary, and he was suddenly self-conscious of his overpriced parka, his expensive ski hat, and his Torah, which lay beside his elbow. He was unsure now, under this glare, what had made him bring it inside. He wanted to put it away, but he dared not bring attention to it, to the fact of his awkwardness. She waited patiently, but he couldn't decide what to eat, wasn't even hungry. His gut felt hard, unmoving. He felt his plumbing had reached a stasis and the balance of his life would be devoted to unsticking his gut, his nervous bowels.

When he finally ordered, he mustered the courage to ask for directions. He saw that Angie, the waitress, had seemed to decide something about him, something that made him evidently more favorable in her eyes. When the tightness left her lips and her eyes, her entire face softened and lit up. She seemed extraordinary to him, simple and pious somehow. Still, she made fun of his shoes and his car, which he had to admit was too clean and too expensive-looking amid all those trucks and tattered sedans with their mud-caked wheel rims and bent fenders.

"See those boys at that table over there?" she said.

He reached for his glasses. He felt so old and feeble, the way he groped for them, the way his hands shook slightly as he put them on.

"They're heading up there, too," she said. "I can arrange it so you can follow them. They'll make sure you get there."

And they had. They drove slowly, whether for his benefit or not, he wasn't sure. At one point, they turned off the main highway and drove along a dirt road into the forest. But soon the road became impassable, unplowed and rutted. They stopped and idled for a minute or two, then signaled for him to back up. They came to the main road again, drove on, and then turned off again at another back road, this one plowed. Finally, they came to a stop at the end of the road, where a haphazard array of cars was parked willy-nilly and the trees towered over them, like a ceiling made of pine and snow.

He remembered what the waitress at the diner had said about the woods. How they could swallow a person whole. He saw now, shamefully, shockingly, that he had meant to come up here to the mountains and end it all and that the disappearance of this boy, his terrible predicament, had brought him back to his senses. He understood that once again God had tethered him securely to the edge of the cliff so that he could see, without actually falling, that his life had purpose, even though all else felt lost.

He thought of his own son. He thought dimly that Marty's life, its deterioration, was somehow, deeply, deeply, due to his failures as a father, though he felt blinded to his own faults, unaware of what he had done. He thought of the boy lost in the woods, of his personal terror being too big to comprehend and thus even more terrifying. He closed his eyes and the pain was stilled but not erased. Sometimes he could pray without uttering words.

Later, he found himself walking in the woods with a bright, articulate woman. She was friendly, but her taut, lean body was wired tightly and she had a strange way of blurting things out. He mused for a moment over the odd fact that he was walking in the woods with a lesbian beekeeper, searching for the lost boy of a man he didn't even know. But even stranger to him was that while he and Jane talked, he would suddenly forget his reason for being there. He would be lost in the image of Marty standing there holding Adele's jewelry box, or he would think of Adele, the swastika on the lawn, the patch of sod that mysteriously replaced it after she died. Then it would hit him that they were searching for a child who had been missing more than six hours, who in all likelihood would not make it through the night unless he was found.

He felt foolish telling her about Marty and his problem with drugs. But the forest, with its shadows and the trees with their snow-laden branches, made him feel an intimacy with Jane he might not have felt otherwise. It was a closed, silent place. A sanctuary where, it seemed, all of his uttered secrets would remain once he left.

When it began to snow in earnest, Jack felt the ripening of old hurts and a gripping fear of his aloneness. His wife was gone, his two eldest sons were far away, and Marty had been driven to steal from him—it occurred to him that stealing Adele's jewelry and his coin collection was actually a felony— because of his addiction to drugs. It seemed his life had been swept clean of him, leaving in its wake a long, perhaps bleak future of nothing.

He felt his heart lurch, and to place himself again, he took his glasses off and wiped them on his shirt, feeling the cold against his face and the wet seeping into his shoes. He looked at the quiet congress of trees and the smoky mist that whispered through them. He thought of Marty, how beautiful a boy he once was, how promising his life had seemed.

"It was like my son had walked into the woods and never came back," he said.

◆　◆　◆

On the way home, he realized that he'd never said good-bye to Jane. He felt a twinge of regret. He had liked her. She might have been a good companion for him, someone to have an occasional coffee with or a good meal. He would have liked to meet her lover.

As he left the mountains, the snow turned to rain, and by the time he was on the freeway, it was not much more than a gentle, warmish mist. The day was late and darkness fell in that sudden, irretrievable way it did in winter.

Tomorrow, he would be back at work. He thought of the boy lost in the woods, the grieving father. All the way home, he heard rumblings on the radio about it. Culpability, legality, possible arrests if, God forbid, the child was dead. Something about it felt wrong. Something about it scared him.

Jack's faith had taught him that no single person could be responsible for the well-being of all humankind. There must be secular law, he believed, because people would always transgress moral law. And though in man's law, perfect resolution was unattainable, you could still get close, Jack believed, if your response to life was piety and reverence to God and humankind. He remembered the old blind man in the records office, the Bible in his hand. He thought again of the father and wondered just how the law would play its role in this mess.

That night, he sat in the kitchen for a long time without turning on the light. Later, when it had grown completely dark, he went to his office and sat down on the leather recliner. He turned the lamp on beside him and opened his Torah, turning to Job. "God is wise in heart and mighty in strength," he read. "Who has hardened himself against Him and prospered?"

Though night always spoke loudest to his grief, he tried his best to count himself a lucky man. Graced with God's blessing. A fair and decent man. He tried to find the murmur of his faith, its comfort, its release. But he could not. He told himself that from this day on, he would disavow his son. In his mind, Marty could no longer exist. He thought again of Marty, standing in the hallway, so thin, so dirty, holding on to his mother's jewelry box, of the girl clutching the pillowcase in front of her, and of the thought he'd had that she would hit him over the head with it, knock him out, perhaps even kill him with his prized collection of coins. He closed the Torah and shut his eyes. There had to be fairness to himself. It was not up to him to forgive. This was for God alone.

GLICK

———◆———

It had stopped snowing. He and the dog were still tangled together. But warm. The dog had kept him warm, and this fact amazed him. How had he managed to stay so dry? He felt neither hungry nor thirsty. But when he rose, he realized his face and nose were frigid. He shivered and grew afraid of his circumstances. He looked at his watch: 2:00 A.M. He would not go back to sleep. People died that way in the snow.

He waited. The dog waited, too, awake and watchful. When first light appeared, a husky gray blush, Glick stood up and scrambled out of the ravine, using the tips of his boots to make footholds in the wall of the ice-encrusted gulch. Everything around him had been dusted with the snow, and the crystalline quality of it brought a moment's serenity. Then, all at once, he recognized where he was, knew how to get back. How odd that he had felt so lost.

Glick hoisted the dog out of the ravine—it was not so deep that he was unable to manage it—and within seconds the dog's nose was to the ground, his tail sharp and pointed. The dog made his way up a hill and there, near a grouping of sugar pines, he began to dig and paw at the snow. Behind the dog, up the narrow crags and peaks, the tip of Angels Crest burst through the clouds.

When Glick caught up to the dog, enough snow had been dug away to reveal the tiny face of Ethan's son. Glick knelt down and looked on with wonder. This child. This place. This downy snow, like the fields of heaven.

He dug out the rest of the boy's body. And just as Ethan had said, Nate was wearing pajamas, white, with moons on them. The booties were ripped, no doubt from walking or running. Glick could see that the skin on the soles of his feet had worn nearly away. The boy's eyes were open and he lay peacefully on his side, knees drawn up in a fetal position. His mouth was open slightly, his thumb stuck inside, and Glick leaned over, though he knew there would be no breath. It was then that he saw how Nate's tears had formed two perfect frozen dew drops on his cheeks, and overcome, he gathered the boy in his arms, held him, and wept.

ETHAN

---◆---

The snow had stopped. Everywhere around him a wonder of white and silver light. The silence of the forest was interrupted only by the rush of wind through the trees. It was cold in the truck. His fire had burned down during the night. He opened his thermos, but his coffee was cold. No one would arrive for a while. Maybe if he started searching now, before the people came, he'd find a clue, a track, something he'd missed yesterday in all the bedlam and fear.

He looked out and saw Glick's truck sitting there. Now he'd be looking for Glick, too. It seemed strange that Glick, who was the best tracker in town, and his dog with its sixth sense were missing, too. Vanished, like his son. For the first time, he saw the woods as menacing. Alive and hungry.

He stepped out of his truck. The storm had passed, and he quickly zipped up his jacket and put on his gloves because it was so cold. He held out some hope that a miracle would happen, that his son would be found alive.

He lit a cigarette just as Glick came crashing through the woods and into the clearing. He was out of breath, and when he saw Ethan, he stopped short. They locked eyes for a moment and Ethan saw in Glick's expression every moment of their friendship, and all that had led them here to this clearing on this day, this somber epilogue. Though his son was not with Glick, Ethan saw in his eyes the moment Nate had been found. He knew that Nate was dead.

He felt the blood in his veins constrict, a brute and primal anguish. He fell first to his knees; then he doubled over and lay prostrate on the snowy earth, breathing in its metal scent, feeling everything he ever was or might have been drift away from him and float off into the forest. How, he wondered, could he have gambled so foolishly when the stakes were so high? How would he live with the fact that he alone had allowed his boy to suffer and die in the snowy woods all because of his desire to track a few buck in the silence of the morning?

ROCKSAN

◆

Rosie was still asleep when Rocksan put her boots on, slid into her jacket, and went downstairs to check on the hives. Jane had been up early and had returned to the site to help find Nate. Rocksan did not hold out much hope for him surviving last night's storm, which had been bitter and plentiful.

The storm had blown out, and now a pale blue sky was showing itself beyond the last muscular clouds. She passed the old storage barn and noted the temperature on the thermometer. Twenty-one degrees. Her breath was thick on the air. She'd forgotten her gloves and already the tips of her fingers were stinging from the cold.

When she got to the hives, she saw the drones on the landing board. All of them dead. She had heard other beekeepers call it the massacre of the drones. Every year it was the same thing: male bees systematically killed by the worker bees in vicious attacks that left them dead or dying, their legs broken or ripped from their bodies, their wings torn off. Did it hurt? Did they feel it on some base, cellular level?

She had actually watched it the first year she'd built the hives. It had sickened her. But also, she was fascinated by it. She'd seen the worker bees dragging their victims into corners of the hive and holding them captive while the rest of the horde tore them from limb to limb. It had made her think of the horror of genocide, the lynch mobs, the Nazis, the weird quiet slaughters in the jungles of South America.

When most of them had died, the worker bees had lugged and pushed the dead drones outside. Those who still gasped for breath were left to die an unceremonious death on the landing board. There were always a few drones that wouldn't give up, despite their mutilated bodies. They would try desperately to get back inside the hive. The draw of home, the loss of it perhaps, was too much for them to fathom, so that even knowing they faced certain death by returning, they wished to return nonetheless.

It was a gruesome sight. Rocksan failed to understand why the drones didn't sense the massacre coming and flee for their lives. Why, when they saw the fate of the others, did the remaining bees stick around? She had seen their other instincts for survival kick in. Why not now? Was denial an instinct? Was the hope that it would all work out in the end a genetic trait, the way it seemed to be in humans?

The predictability of their optimism and the confidence they had that it would all turn out okay seemed to her to be the defining characteristic of humankind. Bees, like humans, she thought, seemed to believe that even their senseless mistakes and stupid choices would not, in the end, lead them into the maws of death or disaster.

She watched for a few minutes as the workers hustled their fallen dead over the edge. Then she turned around and went back to the warmth of the house.

JANE

◆

Jane took the pickup and went back to the search site. She knew the instant she drove up that something was different. Something had happened. She saw Glick standing off to the side, a tight circle of rangers surrounding him. When a news camera van drove up and several reporters made their way over to Glick, he was rushed into the back of the sheriff's car and whisked away.

Ethan was nowhere to be seen. Jane got out of the truck and walked over to a group of boys standing near a beat-up Camaro. Every one of them was smoking.

"What happened?" she asked.

One of the boys turned to her and she saw the grim, excited expression on his face: the wide-eyed look people got when horrible things happened, things beyond their control.

"They found the kid. He's dead."

Jane felt as if she'd been hit. She leaned momentarily against the Camaro and then walked off toward the woods. The morning was crisp and cold and sharp. The sun lit up the snow so that it sparkled brightly, blinding her. She thought then of her own son. Of the way she had left him behind the armor of all that booze and the wrongheaded belief that it would set them both free.

A few moments later, she heard the sound of low voices and saw Ethan coming toward her through the woods, carrying his boy in his arms. Nate was wrapped in a white sheet. Behind him, two paramedics carried an empty stretcher and the sheriff walked glumly with them, rounding out the grim procession.

When Ethan came clear of the trees, he looked directly at Jane. Their eyes met, but she knew he wasn't seeing her. He wasn't seeing anything. She saw Nate's feet poking out of the sheet, the bottom of his pajamas worn away, the soles of his feet raw and caked with dried blood. She thought of how she loved him, as if he were her own son. How she would sometimes pretend she had never left George behind, that this little boy, Nate, was hers. She remembered how Nate's love for her sometimes made everything she had done seem okay.

"Ethan," she said.

He looked at her and his eyes came into focus.

"No," he said. "Don't say a word."

She looked at the ground to avoid the stony dead look in his eyes.

"I'm sorry," Jane said.

"Not a word," he said.

Then he was gone. Jane watched as the reporters with their cameras and tape recorders made a beeline toward him. The sheriff, aware of the crowd, seemed suddenly relieved he had something to do and cleared the crowd aside. One of the paramedics gruffly pushed a cameraman away.

"Back off," he shouted. "Get the fuck back."

Ethan picked up the pace. He half walked, half jogged with his dead son in his arms into the waiting ambulance. Once he was inside, the ambulance backed out and, without the siren blaring, it moved from the clearing and disappeared down the dirt road.

Jane went back to the pickup and got inside. It was so cold; she could see a starburst pattern of frost forming at the corners of the windshield. She started the engine, turned on the heat, backed out through the milling crowd, and it all came back to her, the niggling, certain knowledge, when she was just a teenager, that she was gay. The way she got married to hide it. How she would sneak out in search of that arching need for sexual love and then how that all stopped when she got pregnant and had her son. She thought of the way she had left George at barely five months old. She felt like she would be sick because she knew at its most basic, at its most crude, she had somehow believed it more important to her soul that she satisfy her sexual desires rather than her maternal ones.

She had to stop the truck for a minute to catch her breath. She tasted the bile at the back of her throat. She thought of Ethan, of the way he'd carried his boy out of the woods half running, wild. He had seemed surprised that this could actually be happening to him, that this was the turn his life had taken.

She realized she had been lucky, compared to him. But she saw, too, that luck was a capricious thing. It was like anything else. It could change without warning. She thought suddenly of the legend of Angels Crest. How those babies had lived through the infamous storm of 1889 but how most everyone else had died. She had to open the door of the truck so she could be sick.

ANGIE

The early rush was over. Nate was still missing. Angie could not think the word *dead*. But it kept coming at her, blindly, as if she was turning corners on a narrow road and it was there, jumping out at her at every turn.

She had never seen so many reporters. It was like a wildfire, this thing with Ethan. Consuming more and more interest, mesmerizing more people, casting a wider spell. She was concerned about Glick. Last night, she had dreamed about him. A vague, cloudy dream. Erotic and worrisome. She could only remember certain things: his face and his body; a car rushing down a road, then slowing; their arms wrapped around each other, a fumbling, frantic embrace, as if hiding it from someone else.

Now she washed the tables with a hot soapy rag, filled the coffee urns with grounds, wiped down the counter, and prayed silently for Glick's safety, for Nate's safe return, though she knew it was bad and he was probably dead.

All at once, people began to gather around the small TV screen by the cash register on the counter. Angie looked, too, and she recognized the clearing where Ethan had last seen his son. There was a reporter, dressed up in fancy winter clothes, the kind rich folks wore at swanky ski resorts. Her hat was white and had some kind of animal fur around the brim. She was wearing useless but beautiful suede gloves. How vulgar her lipstick looked amid the trees and the deep tragedy that was Ethan's life.

Angie turned up the volume. The reporter was saying that Glick had surfaced early that morning with news that he'd found the body of the young boy. Angie put her hands over her mouth to stifle the involuntary cry. The camera showed Glick being driven off by the sheriff, and the reporter was saying that this had been taped earlier that morning.

Angie felt an enormous, though guilty, sense of relief that he was alive. Her thoughts should have been first and foremost about the little boy. She remembered again the shadowy dream, with the car rushing down the road, of the entanglement of their arms around each other.

Just then, the reporter became animated. The body was being carried by the father out of the woods. The cameraman raced toward the location of all the excitement, but all you could see were the trees and the snow bouncing erratically on the screen. Then suddenly, the cameraman stopped and the shot came into focus. There was a brief image of Jane, standing off to the side of the pond, and then, at last, of Ethan, carrying his dead son in his arms.

Angie turned away from the screen. It was too awful, too exposed. Her hatred for television, this intrusion into other people's lives, flared her temper. How dare they? she thought. This moment would define him forever. She knew that Ethan's hell had just begun.

The door of the diner opened and Rocksan walked in, with Rosie trailing behind. When Rosie saw Angie, she broke out into a run and, rounding the counter, jumped into Angie's outstretched arms. Angie dug her nose deep into her granddaughter's hair and breathed in and out until her nerves were calmed and she felt that all would be all right. That it had to be all right.

CINDY

———◆———

Cindy woke. The brown apartment was bathed in yellow light. She was still in her clothes, one boot still on her foot. Nothing was clear. Sleep had taken her life and run with it. Nothing. No memories even. It was just her, fully dressed, lying here in this room.

The phone rang. The machine picked up, but she didn't hear anything. She realized she must have turned the volume down. Then it all came rushing back. Nate. It was the first formed word in her head.

Nate.

She tried to sit up, but a wave of nausea sideswiped her. The reprieve of sleep never lasted long enough. She reached down on the floor and found the bottle. She took a sip and the heat of the liquor calmed her nerves. She was then able to stand up, and she picked the bottle up from the floor and made her way to the phone. The apartment was so cold, she could see her breath on the air.

She took another sip—the heat of it going down friendly and familiar. She looked at the answering machine. Eleven messages. Her heart began to beat wildly and she knew, of course, that they had found him. Nate.

She hadn't an ounce of courage left. His disappearance had taken it all out of her, and now the phone insisted on ringing and people insisted on leaving messages, and there were eleven messages she could not listen to.

She sat on the bar stool by the counter and waited. The phone rang again. Her nerves were shot. She drank more. Then Trevor walked in. He saw her there and sat down beside her. He did not say a word. He reached over and put his arm around her and she let her head fall to his shoulder. She began to cry.

"He's dead," Trevor said. "Glick found him a mile or two from the road."

Cindy felt herself nodding. She couldn't stop nodding her head up and down. She felt as if she were slowly coming unhinged, that the screws and rubber bands holding her together were finally loosening. That she would burst wide open and fly apart.

"They've taken him to the mortuary next town over. They want you there. There's paperwork, things to sign. Decisions."

"Okay," she said. She could not think of her son. If he tried to enter her mind, she pushed him out. There was no son. He did not exist. If he did not exist, there was nothing to feel at all. She could stay in this cool white space forever. She could be fine there.

"You should get cleaned up."

She nodded again. Trevor looked at the shit-colored carpet. Cindy saw the mud tracks, too.

"What the hell happened here last night?"

"I don't know," she said. And she didn't. She could not remember what she had done the night before, where she had gone. Her gloves and hat and jacket were splayed out on the floor like bodies.

"Cindy," Trevor said. "Cindy."

He was crying.

She stood up. On the counter was the paper plate with the glued macaroni pieces on its edges. She remembered that moment in the hospital, after Nate was born, how he draped his body over her in the shape of an L, sleeping with his head on her breast, his breathing rhythmic and soft against her skin. The strong, sure sign of his air, his sacred breath.

She made it as far as the bedroom and then she sank to the ground. She wished that it had been she who'd been found dead in the snow. She wished she were dead and not her son. She opened her mouth to cry, to say something, but nothing came out. Then she whispered his name. "Nate," she said. "My baby."

JUDGE JACK ROSENTHAL

───────◆───────

Jack awoke. *Marty.* It was his first thought on waking. His heart sank. He drifted toward a memory. So long ago. Marty had just turned thirteen. Jack had found him smoking marijuana in the garage. He'd said, "What the hell is this? What are you doing that you could disrespect your mother and me this way?"

Marty had stood there blinking, ashamed but defiant. He'd put the joint out with his new sneakers. Jack had thought, I paid for those shoes. On the floor was some kind of drawing, something Marty had been working on. Marty, his most precious son. His last-born son, a boy with the fragile temperament of an artist.

"Dad . . . I . . ."

Marty had begun to cry. "What in hell is this?" Jack had said, because now he saw that the drawing depicted a child running from a barrage of rocks, that the children throwing them were laughing cruelly. There were red blotches. Blood? Jack had picked it up.

"What is this obscenity? And these drugs. Didn't we raise you to be different than that, to be more original than that? What is this violence?"

It had ended badly. An argument, the words no longer stored in Jack's memory, but the sense of them locked there forever. The way he had taken the drawing and crumpled it up and thrown it away, to his son's disbelief. And then that day, the very next day, in fact, when driving by, he'd seen his son running from a group of boys—the Richardson twins and the McCudahy boys, plus a few others, ones he didn't recognize. How he had watched his son fleeing.

He remembered how he had stopped the car and cursed the boys, brandishing his arms in anger, telling them to leave his son alone. The music of their hatred rang in the air: "Gas the kikes." And once inside the car, Marty had hit the dashboard, screaming through tears, "Fuck it, Dad. Why did you do that? Why didn't you let me handle it myself?"

After that, Jack had grown afraid of his son, leaving him to devise his own means of protection, leaving him to drift further and further away, ignoring the obvious signs that he was getting into something too deep. He knew he had been wrong to destroy the drawing. But he felt he had been right to come to his son's rescue.

The memory haunted him now. All these years later and he was still confused about his choices, still aware that those two days had been a kind of turning point for him and his son and that he had not handled them wisely, that he had set a course, the wrong one, for his and Marty's entire future.

He thought now that he had intervened at all the wrong times in all the wrong places with all the wrong expressions of outrage and protection. Why had it been so much easier with his other sons? Was it because he had thought them so much less brilliant, so much less fragile? Had it been simply that loving the one more than the others was a sin and, like all sin, had blinded him to better judgment?

Outside, a gray fog glimmered through the half-drawn blind. Like every morning, he cataloged his losses. His wife was dead. She was never coming back. With that came the memories of the swastika on the lawn, the way he'd insisted it remain. His two older sons were grown, with families of their own. And then there was Marty, standing in the hallway with Adele's jewelry box, the fear he'd had that he'd be killed. It seemed all related, all part of the same thing.

He shuffled out of bed and downstairs to the family room. He turned on the TV and learned instantly that the boy he'd searched for yesterday had been found dead in the woods. There was footage of the father carrying his boy wrapped up in a sheet, a brief image of Jane, with whom he had searched. His heart filled with anger and regret and all those sorrowful things he tried to keep at bay every day, and he felt completely lost. God, it seemed, had abandoned him. He found no rescue when he said His name.

All he could think about was the treachery in his decisions. How he had made Adele's suffering worse because he needed to teach a few punks a lesson they would never learn anyhow. How, the night before, he had not demanded his son leave his belongings and go, or else face the consequences. He hated how he would not call the police, he a man of the law, who had always believed that God informed the jurisprudence of men so that they would act in line with His commandments. He hated that with Marty he *had* always intervened at the wrong times and not done so when he should have.

He felt like pounding his fists against the table where he sat, alone in this house that had once been filled with the joy and light of his family. Then he turned all of his anger on the father who ran into the woods to chase a few buck instead of tending to the best interests of his own son. How could a man be so stupid? So willful? So selfish? How could a man put his own needs and desires before the needs and desires of his son?

Jack turned off the television, disgusted. He wanted to throw something through the window. He looked outside at the barren advent of winter. No matter how hard he tried to ignore it, he felt an unfamiliar distance between himself and God.

GLICK

He tried to keep himself still and unfeeling. It was nothing like the LAPD, but still, being in the sheriff's car, driving home to drop the exhausted dog off, then on to the station for that long, slow, dim-witted questioning, he couldn't help but fear it. The last time he had done nothing wrong, either.

But after a few hours, they let him go. He told them what had happened. He'd somehow found himself lost. Slept through part of the night. At dawn, his dog had found the boy. He'd decided to leave Nate there. He'd worried that maybe the authorities would want to investigate. Yes, he said, he had picked the boy up. But this was before reason could take over.

The sheriff took him back to the clearing and he started up his truck. By now, the place was empty except for Ethan's truck. The ground was littered with cups and other garbage, and before he left, Glick picked up the trash and threw it in the bed of his truck. His thermos was outside on the ground, standing upright by the driver's seat. He wondered how it had gotten there. Had he left it that way?

He picked up his thermos and threw it on the seat. Then he drove home to his house on Cage Road, remembered how he had bought the place, in part, because he treasured the irony of the road's name. The dog was tired and hungry. The cats greeted him at the steps, meowing. He fed the animals and took a hot shower. There was beer in the fridge and he drank one down. He ate a bologna sandwich, and as the sky turned black and the long darkness of the night began to fill in the gaps of the earth, he fell asleep.

An hour later, he bolted upright. A dream perhaps, or a sound that was now gone. Whatever woke him, his heart beat mercilessly and he remembered the way he had found the boy and held him and wept.

Awake now, he stared at the cats, who stared back at him from the dresser. The dog was at the foot of his bed, snoring. And Glick remembered.

It was almost sixteen years to the day. He'd been staying at his mother's house because she needed some help. The yard needed work, the house needed a coat of paint, and there was some problem with the plumbing that Glick thought he might be able to fix for her. He'd made a good living fixing up rich people's homes in Malibu and Beverly Hills, so he had the practice, and besides, his girlfriend had left him for someone else and he was alone. He thought it'd be a good place to lick his wounds.

He was outside getting ready to paint when the police drove up. He thought maybe something had happened to his mother and, more distantly, he thought about his girlfriend.

But the cops rushed him and read him his rights and took him off in the car. In handcuffs, he was taken to a room, where they sat him down and started to grill him. He couldn't quite get his head around the notion that they were accusing him of raping someone. An elderly lady in Beverly Hills, the mother of one of his clients. Just the thought of it disgusted him—what kind of animal would do that?—but he seemed unable to convey this to the police. He began to think he sounded guilty. He had no alibi. His girlfriend had left him, so he'd been asleep alone in his room.

They showed him a pair of yellow shorts at the scene and he agreed they belonged to him, but there was an explanation. Did they want to hear? They'd listened skeptically while he told them that he'd taken them off and changed into jeans when he knew he'd be cleaning out a tangle of bushes with stinging nettles and possibly poison oak. He must have left them behind, he said.

They wanted to know how he could explain an eyewitness—the victim herself—who'd picked him out of the lineup. It was then that he decided he'd be better off not saying anything more, and he called someone he knew in Malibu who knew a lawyer.

But you couldn't argue with a witness. He'd spent his savings and then some to try to save his ass, but it didn't matter. The eyewitness—she was old and intelligent and steady as a rock—was unbeatable. Glick lost. He went to prison. He was a sex offender now and he paid for it in every way imaginable, because sex offenders were vermin. He thanked God it wasn't a pedophile charge. He kept to himself as much as he could, reading and watching the minute acts of nature in the yard: the swallows building nests on the razor wire, the snakeskins shed in the spring, the spiders building webs and laying eggs. One year, he watched a caterpillar turn to butterfly, and when the pupa had been left behind, he'd snatched it up and kept it hidden in a piece of tissue until a warden had found it and flushed it down the toilet.

Now Glick hoisted himself out of bed. The dog moved, lifted its head, then went back down. The cats stood up, stretched, and jumped down from the dresser, curling their bodies around his legs, looking for food. The air was so dry he could see how their fur sparked when they walked. He went to the kitchen and looked at the clock over the stove. Almost ten.

Glick remembered it again, finding Nate, the frozen tears, his thumb thrust into his mouth and the icy lifelessness of his body. For so long he had kept so much at bay that now, in this dark place, alone with only the death of the boy and his memories to keep him company, he felt something dark and hard shift within himself. He recognized the anger and the general state of his unhappiness. And he knew that he could stay this way forever. But he also knew, as he had that day ten years before, when he'd poured his drink down the drain and moved to the mountains, that he could die this way. He saw the advancing onset of old age and the company it would keep with his anger and loneliness. The prospect made him afraid.

He whistled for the dog and put on his jacket. He opened the door and he and the dog were slammed in the face by the crisp bitterness of the cold. It took his breath away, and he thrust his hands into his pockets. He got into the truck, leashed the dog down, and drove off toward town.

Main Street was deserted. Angie's was closed. Cars were parked outside of Trevor's Echo. Ethan's hardware store was black. He continued on until he arrived at Angie's house, the simple white clapboard, with its old craftsmanship, the carefully carved latticework on the porch, the ornamental balustrades, and the wide front windows. It was a beautiful house to Glick, simple, small, but sturdy.

A single light burned inside. He saw a shadow cross a wall and then a hand rise up and draw the shades closed. He unleashed the dog and the two of them walked up to her front door.

Glick stood for a moment before knocking. The dog sat obediently by his side. Glick felt the mysteriousness of his longings as they surfaced to the fore. That they now appeared so clearly before him did not surprise him nearly so much as the clear way he accepted them. His loneliness, he realized, had finally spilled over. He was afraid to die this way.

He knocked lightly on the door. Inside, a candle flickered; then a light went on. The porch light followed. Angie opened the door wearing a bathrobe with tiny red flowers on it. In the yellow light of the porch lamp, he noticed a stain on the robe and he saw her humanity there, the welcome of her imperfection. He wanted to reach out, for some reason, and touch it.

"Glick," she said. She did not seem surprised to see him. She looked at the dog. She opened the door wider. "Come in."

"What about the dog?" Glick said. "I don't know what I was thinking bringing him."

"He can stay on the back porch," Angie said. "It's enclosed. Warm enough."

Glick and his dog went into the house. Angie called the dog.

"C'mere, Dog. C'mon."

The dog went toward her, tail wagging. She opened the door to the back porch. The dog went out with regret and obedience.

"Give me your coat," she said.

He took his coat off and handed it to Angie, who put it on a hook by the back door. He wondered about Rosie, then realized she must be asleep. Angie walked back into the house and Glick followed her to the kitchen. She put a pot of water on the stove.

"I'll make some tea," she said.

He nodded. He felt like he might cry. He could not speak. Everything about her seemed kind and forgiving and filled with knowledge and wanting and generosity. He knew that she would have heard how he had been the one to find the body. He was thankful that she didn't ask him any questions.

"Sit down," she said.

But Glick could not sit down. He could not seem to rid himself of the image of the dog digging the snow away from Nate's frozen body or the frozen tears on the boy's cheeks. He remembered all the injustices of his own life, every last detail, as if he were falling to his death and these were his final thoughts. He could not hold on anymore and he let out a sob, and Angie came to him and put her arms around him.

"Okay," she whispered. "It's okay."

Her arms were strong and sure. He had not expected that. She smelled of soap and some kind of powder, a little bitter, like eucalyptus. He cried and let her hold him, and when he had finished, he faced her and put his lips on her lips and they kissed. Again she felt so sure and strong and powerful next to him. He kissed her on the neck and lifted her hands to his face and kissed the palms of her hands and then he went back to her lips. She pushed him aside, but gently, and whispered, "Rosie's sleeping. If you want to stay, you have to be quiet."

His entire body met the invitation and he drew her deeper into the house, kissing her. Finally, she took his hand and, in the dark, walked him to her bedroom and they went inside and lay on the bed. The moon came into the room, cutting the darkness in half by its light. Glick pulled back.

"He'd been crying," he said.

"Who?"

"Nate. There were tears frozen on his cheeks. His thumb was in his mouth when he died."

"Oh, Glick. Oh."

She began to cry, too, and she drew him closer and held him in her arms. Glick wanted to thank her. He wanted to tell her everything—all his thoughts and all the memories that haunted him and all the things that people had done to hurt him. But he said nothing, and when they made love, he kept thinking that there was going to be plenty of time to tell her everything.

ETHAN

Ethan saw his boy lying there in the snow. He was so peaceful-looking. Almost like a doll. For a moment, Ethan thought that maybe he was just sleeping. The wish for it was so strong that he believed it long enough to feel the broad, bright flame of relief. But of course his son was dead.

With the paramedics and the sheriff standing a safe, deferential distance away, Ethan knelt down beside his son.

"Nate," he whispered. "Nate. I am so sorry."

He began to cry again and he lifted his boy in his arms. How heavy death had made him. He brought Nate to his face and kissed his frozen cheek. His skin was blue and his limbs were already set by death and the cold, so that he was stiff and unyielding. Ethan thought of all the life that had once been in his son. He realized that a decision he'd made in a split second had stolen his son's future.

A paramedic approached him and gently tapped him on the shoulder.

"Should we carry him out?" he asked, pointing to his partner, who had propped the stretcher against a tree and was staring miserably at his feet.

"No," Ethan said. "I'll carry him myself."

He turned with his son in his arms and walked toward the path in the snow that Glick had been the first to make. The others followed him, and as they walked, no one spoke. All you could hear was the wind and the sound of the men grunting against the cold and the strain of walking in the dry snow.

When they emerged from the woods nearly thirty minutes later, it was as if the grief had taken over and now he was no longer Ethan. A different man had stepped into his shoes and would see him through this. The old Ethan was gone.

The first person he saw was Jane. He realized that the stricken expression on her face would be the one he would encounter from then on. That all the faces he would see would look like hers. He would now be on this side of pity and compassion. And he realized he would have no words to greet such expressions. As he passed Jane, he told her not to say anything. But it came out wrong. It came out sounding like an admonishment, when what he meant was that the old Ethan was gone and this new man could not account for the actions of the old. That he could not speak to anything that went before him.

He was rushed quickly into the ambulance. Nate was placed on a gurney, and when the paramedic joined Ethan in the back, he covered Nate with a sheet. Ethan took the sheet off, and as the ambulance drove away through the trees, Ethan stroked his boy's cheek.

By then the sun had burst onto the forest and the sky was clear and blue. The world was a brilliant and shining place, and as they drove out of town and down the valley toward the next town, Ethan thought that he might never be able to enjoy such beauty again.

He kept imagining it turning out differently. He was stopped by the finality of it all. Shocked. His life had been so quiet, so uneventful. That he'd chosen to marry an alcoholic was not such a big deal. People married alcoholics all the time. That he'd been divorced was fairly run-of-the-mill, too. The custody battle had been hell. But hadn't he won? Hadn't that win been a decisive vote in favor of his reliability, his fitness as a parent?

Maybe that's what went wrong. When he won custody of Nate, he felt he could finally relax. For the first time in his life, it seemed that he had everything he could want. So what that there was no woman? With Nate, he had achieved a quiet mixture of solitude and companionship. He had relaxed. He had let his guard down. He had made a foolish mistake—one that anyone might make—and he was paying for it now. It was hard not to think that he'd been singled out by fate. People did stuff like this all the time and got away with it. How could he, Ethan Denton, be the architect of this disaster?

It took almost an hour to get to the next town, where the mortuary was, because a road closure forced them to detour through the back roads of the farming communities. They passed acres of orange and avocado groves, walnut trees and stately sycamores, losing their leaves for the winter. Finally, they rejoined the highway and almost immediately exited for the town, traveling slowly on the main road.

The town was not much bigger than his own mountain town, and yet there were things there they never saw at home: McDonald's, a Target store, a Ford dealership. Within the town proper, there was a large main street with liquor stores and a movie theater. The county and state buildings were there, too: a DMV, the hospital where Nate was born, a traffic court. Ethan hadn't been there for months, and even though it wasn't the city, it was still too big, too commercial, too loud for him.

When they arrived at the mortuary, there were reporters everywhere, and Ethan asked the driver if there was a back entrance.

"No man, this is it," the driver said. He had been the one to tap him on the shoulder in the woods.

"I can't go out there. It's like a fucking feeding frenzy."

"Okay. Hold on a sec."

The man got on the radio and talked to a dispatcher. He wanted to drive the ambulance to the hospital instead and have Nate's body moved later, under another cover, maybe a plain car. He was able to get clearance, and in moments they were backing up and driving away, leaving the journalists to stand there with their mouths open, outfoxed and betrayed.

When they got to the hospital, the driver said, "We'll back the rig up to the emergency entrance. Hold on a minute."

Inside the ambulance, Nate lay on a gurney. The glum and silent paramedic who sat beside the gurney looked at Ethan. Ethan nodded and the paramedic quietly covered the boy's face. The act was prayerful and bitter. Ethan felt as though a curtain had been drawn across his life. He knew he would not be able to look at his boy again, and he quickly said good-bye as the gurney was removed from the ambulance and wheeled inside the hospital. Ethan was taken to a room and told to wait for further instructions.

Everything after that seemed remote and unimportant. It became the business of death. His son seemed to have vanished from the radar and the administration of his death seemed to take over. So there were papers to sign and questions to answer. Where and when would the funeral take place? The medical examiner arrived and there were some muted discussions out of Ethan's earshot among policemen and doctors. Plans were laid to move the body to the town mortuary to have Nate cremated.

It was a long blur of events that had little meaning for Ethan and that culminated hours later when Cindy arrived with Trevor, looking pale and small. When she saw Ethan, he braced himself for her drunken vitriol, but instead, she shook her head and cried and rushed into his arms.

They held on to each other and Ethan remembered when he had once loved her and the hope and promise his life had held. He remembered when they'd found out she was pregnant, how scared they'd been, the thought of it like climbing a mountain, filled with fear and exhilaration. He recalled the moment his son was born, its miracle and its mystery. He remembered the first time he had held Nate in his arms and how he believed then that Nate would always guide him from darkness, like the North Star.

"God, Ethan," she said. "What were you thinking?"

He shook his head. "I don't know. I thought he'd stay asleep. I thought I'd get back sooner. I got in my head. I just lost track of everything."

"How could you lose track of everything? It was your son in the car. A three-year-old boy."

"Don't start on me, Cindy. I've always been the one cleaning up the messes."

"Screw you, Ethan," she hissed. "I might be a drunk, but I sure as shit never made a mess this big."

"Maybe if you had kept your pants zipped . . ."

"Maybe if you had *loved* me."

"Stop it," Ethan said. "Goddamn."

He shook his head to get rid of the vitriol. To stop this train wreck from creating more damage.

"Be in this with me. Be in this mess with me, Cindy. I can't go it alone."

Tears were streaming down his face, though it didn't feel at all as if he was crying. He saw her face soften. He saw that though she hated him, she understood him. She knew the depth of it, this loss.

"You took all I had away from me."

"I'm sorry," he said.

"And now you want me here to stand beside you."

He nodded.

"I don't know if I can do that, Ethan."

Trevor walked up and put his hand out for Ethan. They hadn't been friends, not since Cindy left Trevor and chose Ethan back in high school. But Ethan didn't care about all that anymore. How stupid to hold a grudge, to think ill of someone over such small and stupid things. How petty it all seemed in light of this.

He held his hand out for Trevor and they shook hands, and Trevor put his other hand on Ethan's shoulder and for some reason—Ethan could never explain it—he said thank you.

It was dark by the time all the arrangements had been made. A funeral day after next. Ethan had told them to cremate his boy so that his ashes could be spread in the woods. There would be some sort of gathering there where they'd found him. It hardly seemed to matter. Still, Ethan thought that he should pay attention to these details, fearing that later, when it was all over, he would regret not participating.

After it grew dark, the ambulance driver showed up at the mortuary. He was wearing jeans now and a white T-shirt. He wore a heavy jacket and a baseball cap on his head. It took Ethan a moment to recognize him without his paramedic's clothes.

"Listen," he said. "I know your truck is back there where we found your kid. So I was thinking, you know, I'd take you back there if you wanted the ride."

Ethan looked around him. He didn't want to go back with Cindy and Trevor.

"It's no trouble," the man said. "We could stop if you wanted and have a drink. Or not. I have a son about your son's age. I . . ."

"Sure," Ethan said. "I'd appreciate the ride."

The man held out his hand. "Derek," he said.

"Ethan."

They went outside and Ethan got into the man's car, an old Pontiac with a child's safety seat in the back and toys everywhere. As Derek started the car, a black Mercedes pulled into the lot and Ethan had a moment's recognition. He remembered the car, the man who'd arrived to help with the search. Ethan saw someone inside, an older man, duck his head as if hiding. It struck him as weird that it would be the same man. He was afraid, gripped, you might say. Was he being followed?

"You live up there at Angels Crest?"

"Yeah."

"Pretty spot."

"It seems too pretty all of a sudden," Ethan said.

"You wanna stop for a drink? There's a bar just before you leave town."

"No. I think it'd be best if I just got back. But I wouldn't mind buying a bottle and drinking some on the road."

"Well," Derek said. "I guess there're exceptions to the law."

They stopped at a liquor store. Ethan reached into his wallet and gave the man ten dollars. Derek waived it away, but Ethan insisted, and to his relief, Derek took the money.

When he got back to the car, Derek handed Ethan a bottle of Jack Daniel's and Ethan opened it and took a long sip. It went down hard, but he felt his raw nerves instantly deaden. He saw what Cindy might have seen in liquor and felt empathy for her. He handed the bottle to Derek, who looked in his rearview mirror and both side mirrors before taking a sip.

"Got a couple of DUIs behind me," Derek said. "Now with the wife and kid, you know, I gotta be real careful."

Ethan nodded. Everything felt like a lecture. "Must be hard driving an ambulance."

"Well, it's not like the city, where everything is so bloody. You know, not much happens here. Lots of old folks falling down."

Ethan remembered his father. He had seen the old man clutch his side and fall to the ground. He had seen him sit up, gasp for air, die. He remembered thinking at the time that it was merciful how quickly it had taken him.

Unlike his mother, who had lingered in her illness for years. He thought of Nate in his pj's in the forest. He took another sip from the bottle.

"I guess I'll get drunk tonight and face it all tomorrow," Ethan said.

"I'm sorry about your loss, man. Kids. They don't come with guarantees."

"It was my fault," Ethan said. "I can't blame my son. He was doing the one thing he needed to do, which was to find his dad. He went looking for me. I gotta live with that for the rest of my life."

The prospect of it made Ethan think of killing himself. He thought of the old .30-30 Savage in his truck. It was a fleeting thought. It made an impression on him.

"I felt bad for you out there. But I understand why you carried your boy out."

Ethan took a sip from the bottle. He couldn't talk about it anymore. He noticed that it was starting to cloud up again.

"Winter's early this year," he said.

Derek looked straight ahead. "I hope it leaves early, too," he said. "It's already so damn cold."

◆ ◆ ◆

When Derek dropped him off in the clearing, the moon shimmered through the trees. A patch of clouds made way for the stars. The light made Ethan think of Fourth of July sparklers. It was so tender, so delicate. He shook Derek's hand and Derek pulled away after handing Ethan the rest of the whiskey.

"Can't get a ticket," he said.

It seemed so pedestrian—that they spoke of the weather, the seasons, the mundane and trivial things in life. How odd that the world would just go on.

Ethan got into his truck and started it. It didn't turn over right away and he rubbed his hands together to stay warm before he tried starting it again. This time, the truck rumbled to life, and Ethan sat for a few minutes running the engine, waiting for the heat to warm the cab up. He could make out the remains of his campfire from the night before, when there was still hope that Nate would be found alive.

He wondered how Glick had gotten back here and picked up his truck. He wondered how Cindy was doing. He thought of Nate, but a kind of numbness had taken over. Before driving away, he took a long sip of the whiskey.

As he headed back into town, passing Angie's, he saw that the place was packed. There were cars and people he didn't recognize, and it occurred to him that the media might be staked out at his house. He did a quick U-turn at the intersection and headed back toward Glick's house. It was after ten, but he figured Glick would still be awake. He remembered back to the days when he and Glick would stay up all night, sleep a few hours, and then wake up before dawn to go hunting. They could stay out all day without getting tired, though Ethan remembered that Glick would often remind him that he was fifteen years older, a little rougher around the edges.

Ethan drove up the driveway and parked the car. Glick's truck was gone and the house was dark. Ethan grabbed the whiskey and walked up the snowy path to the front door. He knocked, then opened the door.

"Glick," he said. "You home?"

The cats both came running toward the door, meowing. The dog was nowhere.

"Glick?"

He was greeted by silence and the insistent mewing of the cats. They rubbed up against his ankles. Ethan walked in and turned on the lamp by the couch. The house was stale-smelling but spare and clean. It had an abandoned quality to it, as if Glick had left town months ago.

He went to the kitchen. The cats followed him.

"Glick?" he said, even though he knew that Glick wasn't home.

There were some dishes in the sink. The stove was grimy. Ethan opened the fridge. Some cheese, some cold cuts, cat food, a couple of beers, and a jar of pickles. There was mustard and Miracle Whip, a box of crackers, and something in freezer paper—probably venison that Glick had removed from the freezer and had planned to eat.

He took out some cat food and grabbed a couple of bowls from the cupboard. He fed the cats and went to the living room and sat down. The TV was in front of him, but Ethan knew that Glick had never hooked up the cable, so there was nothing to watch but a local station, and even that came in fuzzy. He found his cigarettes in his jacket and lit one up. He hit on the bottle of whiskey. There was not much left.

He lay back on the couch. He remembered how Glick came to town a few months after he and his father had arrived. They had met at the hardware store years before Ethan had taken it over. Glick was buying some hinges.

Ethan knew that Glick had moved into the old house at the end of Cage Road. It had been empty for years, the only house for miles around, and Glick had bought it for a song because the place was so isolated and falling down. Glick had told Ethan he'd read about Angels Crest in a camping magazine. The story about the town's name had stuck with him. How the angels flew over and rested there, protecting those babies. It was nice, Glick said. It harkened back to some other time. When people could hold on to their innocence, in spite of their circumstances.

He remembered that Glick said the article proclaimed Angels Crest a dying town, with a tragic history and no future to speak of. But there was one line that Glick said convinced him to move there. "Angels Crest," the writer wrote, "has enough beauty there to find forgiveness." He had looked Ethan right in the eyes and had said, "That appeals to me."

The two of them, new to the mountains, new to things like hunting deer and shoveling snow and tracking your way out of the woods, had learned it all together. When Glick told Ethan about prison, the wrongful conviction, the anger, Ethan said he'd keep it to himself. But he hadn't, and after he'd told Cindy, she had blabbed it all over town. Glick had shrugged his shoulders. He'd said, "That's okay, man." Ethan remembered thinking that Glick was someone whose past had made him impervious to ordinary betrayals.

Ethan stubbed out the cigarette and finished off the whiskey. He thought he would rest until Glick returned. The house was cold and he found a heavy blanket in the hall closet. He lay back on the couch and put the blanket over himself, drinking in the smell of dust and wool, smells he had come to know living in the mountains. Smells that gave him courage and comfort. The cats finished eating and ran through the living room, feisty with their full stomachs. They went into Glick's room and Ethan never heard from them again.

He closed his eyes. He saw Nate running through the woods, almost as if it had been himself running. He could feel all the pain and misery in it. For the second time that day, he thought of his gun, in the truck. In his entire life, he'd never thought about suicide before. He'd told Cindy once, after she'd passed out bad from drinking and finally come to a day later, that she was a slow suicide. He told her it was the coward's way out.

He thought about the way Cindy's drinking had spiraled into addiction. He had always thought she was the most beautiful creature on earth, with her hazel eyes and her delicate white skin. She was so fragile, so dependent on him. And he liked it. He was drawn to her in a strange way. Her body and her voice and the way she listened to him, the way she touched him, it was like a siren's song. He could not resist her.

Even when her drinking began to get out of control, he still felt ensnared by her. But by the time Nate was born, he was also looking for a way out. The drinking was one thing. Then there was something else. Something he could barely define, except that it was a desire to be alone, to live, strangely enough, like he had with his father. He longed for quiet. For few complications. He craved a sameness, an ordinariness that he did not have with Cindy and the unpredictability that came with her drinking.

He thought of the way he had asked Cindy to stand by him while they were at the mortuary. The desperation he'd felt. It reminded him of something that happened when Nate was about six months old. He had awakened that morning to an empty bed and an uneasy feeling. He had put on his pants and gone to the kitchen, and Cindy was sitting there, staring out the window. It was raining outside. Fall. He remembered the golden leaves falling to the ground. The baby was asleep in her arms, which was unusual, because Nate did not often find comfort in her touch. She was too rough, too impatient, and though it seemed that Nate yearned for his mother, he also rarely seemed to find peace or satisfaction with her.

"He's asleep," she whispered.

Ethan thought then that Cindy looked more beautiful than he'd ever seen her look. Her breasts were engorged with milk, and he could see the outline of them in the opening of her nightgown. He was filled with a sense of hope. But then he saw the bottle of vodka, hidden under some clothes on the chair next to her. He thought that she might have been drinking and breast-feeding. He thought maybe that was why Nate was asleep. Because he was drunk.

"Were you drinking?"

She shook her head. He saw her eyes shift just for a moment to the bottle beneath the clothes on the chair next to her. He saw that she knew he had seen it. The baby stirred and they both jumped a little. The moment seemed fragile and dangerous.

"Did you feed him after you drank, Cindy?"

"No," she said. "Never. I wouldn't do that."

Ethan felt himself fill with rage. He felt himself wanting to tear her apart, to take the baby away from her and throw her out of the house right then. He hated that she lied. He hated that he couldn't trust her. But she was so beautiful, too. She was his hothouse flower, but for the life of him, he couldn't figure out how to rescue her.

"Give me the baby," he said.

"No," she replied.

"Cindy, hand him over."

"You always have to be the good parent, Ethan. You always have to be the one who does it right. You are so perfect, Ethan, that there's no room for me to be good, too."

"Give me the baby, Cindy."

"I'd say you were too good for your own good. Someday, you're gonna fall off your high horse, and then you'll wish you'd taken better care of me."

She wasn't angry. It seemed like she was more sad than anything. She said, "You chose me, Ethan. And now you don't like what you chose anymore, so you're getting rid of me."

She handed him the baby and stood up. She reached for the bottle beneath the clothes without even hiding it. He held Nate and felt relief. He wished he could salvage the good that was left of his wife, love her the way he once had. He also wished she would fuck things up so bad that he'd finally have no choice but to leave.

Ethan looked up at the ceiling of Glick's old house, but soon he had to close his eyes. He was exhausted. Just before he dozed off, he remembered something Glick had told him when they'd had a couple beers one night before the start of deer season. "The guilty ones," Glick had said, "never have any trouble sleeping once they are caught."

ROCKSAN

───────◆───────

When Jane came home with the news of Nate's death, Rocksan felt surprise, outrage. How could something like this be true? Though she had generally kept to herself in town, still, Nate was just a little boy. His death had no meaning, no reason. What greater power than human, she wondered, would profit from the death of a little boy? She realized that only when things seemed unexplainable did her thoughts turn to the gray idea of God. She was glad she had never invested in faith. She didn't need to find excuses to hate the ineffable.

"How's Ethan taking it? Did you talk to him?"

Jane shook her head. "He said there were no more words. Or something like that. He was wild-looking. He walked out of the woods holding his son in his arms."

"Oh God. How awful."

"I threw up."

"Jesus, really?"

Jane nodded. Rocksan was afraid to tread too far into the swamp that contained the past, so she stayed close to Nate and Ethan for now, slogging slowly through it.

"What about Cindy? Anyone know where she is?"

Again Jane shook her head. "Drunk probably," she said. "With Trevor, I'd guess."

Rocksan remembered seeing Cindy one hot afternoon last summer. Cindy had been stealing a bottle of whiskey from the liquor store. Their eyes had met and there was an instant of collusion: No, Rocksan would not say anything. She had walked out without purchasing the soda she had gone there to buy, embarrassed for Cindy, who was still so young. Now, Rocksan felt terrible that she had conspired with her, contributed to her drunkenness, to the illegality of her act. She felt sullied for a moment.

"Poor thing."

"I'm gonna make her a casserole," Jane said.

Jane and Rocksan looked at each other for a long time. The fight from the day before still lingered, and the worries it had brought were still there.

"I thought I'd go finish up with the hives and then come back and help you get things ready for George."

"Okay," Jane said. Rocksan noticed how she dropped her eyes to the ground.

"If your kid calls me a fat dyke, I'll have to kill him and bury him in the yard."

"Rocksan. Jesus."

"I'm just kidding, Beanpole. Lighten up. It's just gonna get worse, so we might as well laugh now."

"That's optimistic."

"Don't get any ideas that that boy is gonna come running up to you with open arms and say, 'Mommy.' First of all, you dumped him and went to San Francisco, where you found some pussy. And second, you live with me, and I am not always a pretty sight. We're lesbians, Jane. He's from Ohio."

"They have lesbians in Ohio. Remember, I slept with a bunch of them."

"Yeah, but he grew up with what's his name. I'm sure he got an earful about how we're fornicating so-and-sos."

Jane nodded. "I know," she said. "I'm not expecting miracles. But remember, *he* called me."

"Desperate measures, Jane. I'm thinking he has nowhere else to go. And besides, do you have any idea what kinda trouble he's in?"

Jane shook her head. It irritated Rocksan no end. Jane dealt with things by ignoring them. She was one of those people who just seemed to hope it would all go away.

"Well, if it's drugs, he's not staying."

Jane nodded.

"So, I'm gonna go take care of the hives," Rocksan said. And to take the edge off, she kissed Jane on the lips. She left by the back door, putting on her hat and gloves. The day had turned radiant. Crisp and sunny, but bitterly cold. Rocksan loved the winter, with its short, solemn days, the quiet promise of spring that came with each new snowfall. She loved bundling up against the cold, the smell of smoke in the air, the night winter sky with its hard lights and brittle stars.

The hives were hushed and still in winter. Many bees would die. Every year, Rocksan would gather a few of the dead bees and send them out to the state laboratory to check for nosema and acarine disease. She would repair the hives damaged by storms. She found peace building new hives, enjoyed the spoils of her solitary labor.

She spent the next couple of hours covering the hives with roofing paper, the last of the winter tasks. At one point, while she rested and looked out at the towering vista of the mountains rising from the trees, she saw a single deer with magnificent antlers grazing calmly on the edge of her property. It hardly seemed possible that a little boy was dead.

◆   ◆   ◆

Jane had made her casseroles and gone to town to deliver them to Cindy and Ethan. While she was gone, Rocksan went to the barn. She found the comforter and a pair of fussy sheets one of her gay friends from her days in the city had given them when they left. She also found the dresser and the rocker, side by side under two old blankets. She uncovered them, and on top of the desk was a box labeled ROCKSAN—PERSONAL.

She had no idea what was in the box. Had probably not opened it for twenty years. She knew it was weird that she still traveled with it, had moved it with her everywhere she'd gone, but for some reason, she never opened it.

She sat down on the rocker and listened to the wind outside blowing through the pines. The smell of the earth was clean. And it was so cold, it almost hurt to breathe. The rustle of little animals, squirrels and mice, kept the silence of the barn company.

She reached over and picked up the box. It was only slightly bigger than a shoe box, taped so securely that when she tried to open it, she could not. She found the toolbox near her workbench and took an old Swiss army knife from it. She tore through the tape with the dull blade of the knife.

Instantly, the aroma of incense wafted out of the box. It was a pleasant smell, ripe and piney-scented. A small plastic box was filled with cone-shaped pieces of incense. She took them out of the box and set them on the desk.

There was a small scrapbook that she remembered from her childhood. When she opened it, several pressed flowers tumbled out and floated to the floor. On one page of the scrapbook, the tiny teeth of her dog had been taped, and beside them a lock of the dog's hair. There was a picture of the dog, Shambala, and then, on the next page, a picture of the dog's grave. She remembered being so traumatized by Shambala's death of old age that she'd sworn off pets forever. And friends, too. And lovers, for a long time. She could not handle the good-byes of things. It wasn't just the dog. It was everything.

There were more pictures, these of her and Angie when they were kids. Rocksan studied the pictures of herself as a baby. In the quiet barn, she said aloud, "I was cute."

Her face was freckled then, her hair red. How had she become so un-freckled and dark? She looked at pictures of her father before he had left them. She had become his spitting image. She wondered if she had his temperament. There was no way of knowing. He had left when she was only six and Angie four. She put the box in her lap for a moment and mulled over the passage of so much time. How had almost forty years just disappeared like that?

There was a picture of the first girl she had ever fallen in love with: Pauline Rheaconty. They were in high school, and Rocksan knew by then that she was gay, had known forever that she was different. She knew she should have been a boy. She used to think that if she had only been born a boy, she would be a more interesting person. What use did she have for her breasts, grown into a D cup by her freshman year in high school? What use was menstruation or even, if she thought about it, her vagina? She had come to admire its power, the pleasure she derived from it, but she knew she would never want or have children. She used to think that her large body—so stout and clumsy compared to her sister's—would be better suited as a boy's body.

Pauline was not gay, and there was an embarrassing scene in the basement of Pauline's house. An unwanted kiss, tears that turned to horror and revulsion. The end of their friendship had loomed in Rocksan's imagination even before she kissed Pauline. The spurned love, the repulsion—she had already known it was coming, even before the kiss was a manageable thought in her head. Her love life and all of its dramas had begun so horribly. But didn't all love?

Rocksan closed the box, but not before removing a picture of her and Angie. They were so young. Their father knelt behind them. He was exceedingly handsome, with his dark Italian hair and his fine muscular body. His eyes were black and romantic. He had an arm around each of his daughters, but he seemed angry and uncomfortable. Rocksan was smiling in the picture, beaming with pleasure. Angie looked straight ahead, expressionless. Rocksan couldn't remember where the picture had been taken, but she did remember her mother holding the camera to her eyes and saying, "Rob, can't you pretend to love us?"

Rocksan wondered what had become of him in the years before his death.

❧   ❧   ❧

The day left quickly. The sky grew dark, the world still. Rocksan poured herself a rare glass of scotch. Jane had wine. A small peace lay over the house. The two of them sat before the fire, waiting. At one point, Jane stood up to turn on the porch light. George should have arrived hours ago.

"Maybe it's his nature to be tardy," Jane said. "His father was late all the time."

"He'll be here."

"Earlier today, when I went to Ethan's house to give him the food, it was locked up. Totally empty. There were some news people snooping around. I left before they could get to me."

"Did you see Cindy?"

Jane nodded. "Yes. I gave her both casseroles. She was practically coma-
tose. She thanked me. She said it was funny who showed up and who didn't.
She said she never would have figured me to come by."

"Well, it makes sense. We are the freaks."

"You are always so sure that everyone hates us because we're lesbians."

"Instead of for our personalities, for instance?"

Jane laughed. She poured another glass of wine. Rocksan liked the angle
of Jane's chin, the sharp cheekbones, the lack of fuss she made over her looks
and yet how lovely she was. She appeared apprehensive and yet serene, too.

"He'll be here," Rocksan said. But she was also nervous. She had left San
Francisco to get away from just this sort of thing, this high drama. She hated
drama now as much as she had once thrived on it.

Jane took a sip of her drink. "I was thinking about Cindy, actually. There
was this thing on the counter in the kitchen. A paper plate with macaroni
glued to the sides. She picked it up and showed it to me. She held it like it
was priceless. Nate had made it. She kept saying, 'I promised him I'd hang
it up.'"

Just then, they heard the sound of a car. It grew louder as it neared the
house, then shut off. Jane reached across the table and grabbed Rocksan's
hand. Her touch felt electric. She looked, to Rocksan, as beautiful as she always had. More so. Her face filled with joy and fear. Rocksan felt her heart
beating. She thought she could feel Jane's, too, pumping through her arm,
into her hand.

The two of them stood up.

"Well, don't just stand there," Rocksan said.

Jane walked slowly to the door. Rocksan followed. She heard voices. She
and Jane exchanged glances.

"Who's he talking to?" she said.

Rocksan shrugged. "Open the door."

Jane opened the door. Rocksan felt herself holding her breath. She
peered over Jane's shoulder. Standing on the porch was a tall, longhaired boy,
the spitting image of Jane, clutching the hand of a very beautiful, very frail,
very pregnant young girl.

JANE

They waited for George while the moon rose. Once again, in the silences that passed between them, Jane saw the image of Ethan making his passage out of the forest, the dead boy in his arms, and it reminded her of all that she feared.

She remembered the dread she'd had that everyone she knew back in Ohio would sniff her out as a lesbian. She was voted prettiest in her graduating class. She'd been a cheerleader. She'd done all the things she'd had to do to hide it.

She'd known her husband all her life. He was good stock. A football star in high school. A beer drinker. A lover of discipline, Jesus, and good reputations. He was the perfect beard. She'd married him. But late at night, when he was sleeping, she'd quietly masturbate to the thought of a woman's touch on her.

Her husband had been such a harsh man, so bitter. He'd even caught her once having an orgasm alone and said, "Don't you know that's a sin?" He'd been turned on, though. He'd fucked her right there, on the spot. She was not surprised, even now, that she had married him. She had always been looking for a way out. Better-adjusted women, women with confidence and courage, would not look toward an asshole to rescue them. But Jane understood, even while it was happening, that she'd chosen Pete because she knew it couldn't last, that he, with his manly-man self, would eventually force the lesbian out of her.

She thought of all those times she'd sneaked out, giving him some excuse or other, and headed for Cincinnati to the girl bars. It became almost like an addiction. She would have a drink, and there'd always be some other lonely, despondent housewife type looking, too. She'd have sex, guiltily, with so much pent-up pleasure that her orgasms would almost make her pass out. She remembered how the first time had been hard, but then every time after that it had been easy.

But then Pete had caught on. He must have smelled the sex on her. He must have seen it on her face, all the anticipation, all that guilt. He must have known on some level, even though he was a fairly stupid man, that she was not what she pretended to be.

When he'd caught her and given her that ultimatum, he'd also gotten her good and pregnant. He had a plan. He warned her if he ever caught her again, he'd expose her. He dragged her to church and made her pray. He would pray fervently beside her. He would whisper in her ear in church, "You got the sexual lust in you." Or he'd say, "You got to ask God to remove that lust." And it always seemed to her that on some level it agitated him sexually. It turned him on.

Jane had to quit thinking about it. It made her stomach hurt. She looked at the clock. It was getting so late. She worried George was lost or, worse, had changed his mind and wasn't coming.

Rocksan looked at her. "He'll be here," she said.

- - -

Earlier that day, Jane had wound her way down the foothills and driven through the town. She was stunned by the onslaught of the media. It made her think of stuffing too many clowns in a phone booth. This town, with its gravel roads, run-down main street, and its deeply private citizens, could not sustain the blitz. She didn't recognize anyone on the streets. Many of the businesses weren't even open, including Ethan's hardware store. But Angie's was packed. As she drove by, she saw people waiting in line for a table, something Jane had never seen before.

Still, she wouldn't be stopped on her errand. She had learned how to treat the grieving when she herself had grieved. After her father had died, and then, a few months later, her mother, she was inundated with flowers. There were flowers everywhere. They were beautiful, but they didn't help.

What she had needed was someone to take care of her. To feed her. Since then, she never showed up at the homes of those in mourning without a casserole. And she always took people a casserole and a bottle of wine when there was something to celebrate, like the birth of a child.

She continued through town and turned left onto the road that would take her to Ethan's. It began as a state-maintained paved road, but as it wound deeper into the woods, the road turned to gravel, and even the county had no funds or the mind to care for it. In the middle of winter, you could not get back there unless you had four-wheel drive. Ethan often skied to the main road and hitched into town, leaving his skis against a tree. He once told her that in all the years he'd been doing that, no one had ever stolen his skis. She remembered just last week he had told her that he wanted to get that road paved, now that he had Nate, in case something happened and he needed to get out of there fast.

The road was rough. The plow had gone as far as the pavement, then stopped. She drove carefully, not yet convinced she needed to shift into four-wheel. She noticed that there were a few cars parked on the side of the road, as if abandoned. City people unable to muddle through. She shifted into four-wheel.

When she arrived at Ethan's, she saw the phalanx of media, and her instinct was to turn around and go back the way she had come. They all eyed her as she drove up. She thought about a pack of wild dogs she had seen once in the city, surrounding a feeble cat.

She parked her car and walked up to the house. A few reporters asked her who she was, but she ignored them. As she walked up to the porch, she was overcome with the memory of Nate, how she often babysat him when his dad worked late or on the occasion of a rare date.

"Ethan?" she called out. She tried the door handle. Someone behind her said, "It's locked, lady." She turned around and faced a portly man in jeans and a lightweight parka. He was smoking a cigarette.

"Did you try it yourself?" she asked.

"Yup."

"Bastard," she said under her breath. Then once again she called out for Ethan, but she knew he wasn't there. She debated leaving the casserole, then figured the people staked out to wait for him would get to it first. Until she and Rocksan had moved to the mountains, she had not realized how glaring the bad manners of urbanites were. She'd once included herself in that category, but she hoped now that she had changed.

As she walked back toward her car, a pretty, young woman with a pen tucked behind her ear walked up to her.

"Are you his girlfriend?" she asked.

"Don't think so," she said. It would have been funny under different circumstances. But the media frightened her. It made her think of her own secrets. And it brought into clearer focus the privacy she had come to depend on in Angels Crest. That the town's insularity and its peace could be so shattered made her see that, in truth, there were no such things as boundaries and limits. She felt vulnerable and exposed as she made her way to the main road. For the first time, she felt real fear for Ethan.

Fifteen minutes later, she was at Cindy's. There was just one news van— Jane noticed it was a national network—parked in the lot of the apartment complex. A car idled on the quiet street; the man and a woman sitting inside were drinking from Styrofoam cups. They watched her. She walked hurriedly, avoiding eye contact with them.

When she got to the complex, Jane walked the two flights of stairs to Cindy's apartment. She had always hated this complex with its brown paint, its cheap stucco walls, its insipid name—Skyview Manors. It sounded so old folks home. She rapped lightly on the door. Trevor answered.

"Hello, Jane," he said.

"You look like you're about to hit someone," she said.

"I was. I thought it was another fucking reporter."

Jane nodded and Trevor opened the door wider for her. She stepped past him and into the messy apartment. Cindy was lying on the couch, her left arm draped over her eyes and her right hand wrapped around an empty glass resting on her stomach. There was an open bottle of whiskey on the coffee table and the ashtray was filled with cigarette butts. The furnace blew hot air into the already close room. When Cindy saw it was Jane, she sat up.

"Jane?"

"I brought you a couple of casseroles," Jane said. She decided to leave out the part about not leaving one for Ethan. She decided it would be best not to say his name at all.

Cindy gestured to a worn-out recliner. "Have a seat."

Jane sat. The room, with its misfit furniture and disarray, was hallowed with mourning.

"Those reporters are something else," Jane said. She felt stupid still clutching the two casseroles in their plastic containers. As if reading her thoughts, Trevor came by and took them. She heard him put them in the fridge. He called out, "You wanna beer or something?"

"Sure," Jane said.

"Thanks for coming," Cindy said. She leaned over and grabbed a cigarette, then filled her glass. She'd probably been a very pretty woman once, but she seemed so old, so worn-out, even at twenty-five. The drink, the bad marriage, and now this. It took its toll on her face. "I never would have guessed you'd come by. But then, there's a few people I woulda bet my life on stopping in and they haven't," she said.

"It's weird that way," Trevor said from the kitchen. "I always say death tells you who your true friends are."

Cindy smiled weakly. Jane remembered the time Rocksan had seen Cindy stealing a bottle of whiskey. She remembered how bad Rocksan had felt. It wasn't so much a morality thing, Rocksan had said. She had felt guilty because her silence had seemed a tacit consent. Jane watched as Cindy poured herself a drink and smoked her cigarette. Her hands shook and she held them out and looked at them.

"Jesus. Look at that. I don't think they'll ever stop shaking."

Trevor walked into the room. "Maybe you oughta slow up on the whiskey," he said.

"Right," Cindy said.

Trevor looked at Cindy. Then he left the room. Cindy leaned back and finished her drink. Then abruptly, she came to her feet. For a moment, Jane wasn't sure if Cindy would be able to remain standing, but she steadied herself and walked to the kitchen. She picked something up and brought it over to show Jane.

"Nate made this for me. He made it for me and I promised him I would hang it up," Cindy said.

It was a paper plate with macaroni pieces glued down and blue crayon drawings on the edges. Blobs of dried glue seeped out from beneath the macaroni pieces. Jane didn't know what to say.

"I promised him I would hang it up, but I didn't do it," she said. "I oughta do it now."

Jane looked at Cindy. Her eyes were nearly swollen shut. Her face was pink and blotchy. She leaned forward and said, "I lost custody of my boy because of my drinking."

Jane nodded.

"Now, I know that you babysat my boy. And I know I told Ethan he shouldn't let you do it. But there's something neither of you two knew."

Jane looked up. She swallowed and said, "What was that?" It was so hard to get the words out.

"I knew he was doing it behind my back, see. And I didn't stop it. I don't care anymore about your sexual proclivities, or whatever that word is. Just that this one day, Nate came home and told me you'd been watching over him. And he told me you let him stay on the swings longer than me or his daddy ever did. He talked about you and his face would light up. I didn't care anymore about who you were shacking up with."

"I—"

Cindy held up her hand. "I know you all think I'm a dirty drunken so-and-so. I know the way Ethan talked trash about me."

"Ethan never—"

"But I saw the way my boy lit up when he talked about you. I wanted him to be happy. You understand."

Jane saw how drunk Cindy was. She didn't think Cindy would remember any of this. Cindy picked up the paper plate with the macaroni glued down on it. She was holding a burning cigarette in her hand.

"I told him I'd hang this up first thing," she said. "I never seem to get around to doing what matters."

Just then, there was a knock at the door. Trevor walked over and opened it. He was smoking a cigarette. He let in three women Jane knew were from the Calvary Church. She did not much associate with anyone from the Calvary Christian Church, but she recognized the three ladies because every year they marched door-to-door collecting for their annual fund drive. They never knocked on Jane and Rocksan's door. Each year, Rocksan was sure to donate a hundred dollars, and every year they cashed the check. Rocksan loved the annual hilarity of it.

Jane turned toward Cindy. "I am so sorry," she said. Her emotions got stuck in her throat.

Cindy looked at her briefly. Her eyes welled up with tears. She clutched Jane in her arms and said, "I won't forget your kindness."

- - -

When they finally heard the car drive up, Jane quickly looked at Rocksan and saw for the first time that Rocksan was nervous, too. Her heart began to beat mercilessly. She wanted to disappear. She was afraid George would find out who she *really* was. Not the lesbian—he knew that—but the secret self. The woman driven away from her son by her fear and her lust and her need for all the things that she thought would better serve her.

She went to the door and opened it. She felt Rocksan standing over her shoulder. She felt herself holding in her breath.

"Jane?" her son said. He had long brown hair, brown eyes, and a sharp chin. Jane felt for an instant as if she were looking at herself. It was unbelievable. The girl took off her glasses.

"Wow, George. You look just like her."

"This is Melody," George said.

"Hello," Melody said. She clutched George's hand, held out the other.

It took Rocksan to knock them all out of their stupor.

"Come inside out of the cold. You must be so tired. And hungry. Well, my God, you certainly are pregnant."

Jane smacked Rocksan on the shoulder.

"Ow," Rocksan said. "What was that for?"

Jane ignored her. She leaned against the wall for support. Why hadn't she learned by now that nothing ever happened the way you thought it would?

ANGIE

———◆———

Waiting tables had almost killed her today. There were so many people, so many strangers—media mostly—that even her regulars didn't come by. When she'd finally closed up, she saw that the bar was jumping, too. She'd heard that about reporters, the way they drank. She wondered where everyone was staying. There wasn't even a motel in this town.

Now she was at home, sitting in the dark. Rosie was asleep. She was thinking how she'd use the extra money she was making to hold a wake, or whatever you called it, after the funeral. She knew Ethan and Cindy didn't have any money. It was the least she could do.

She was cross and hungry, but she couldn't eat. She poured herself a glass of wine and went into her bedroom. She opened the bottom drawer of her dresser and pulled out the photo album she'd kept stashed in the back. She looked through it, at the pictures of her daughter. She said her daughter's name over and over again in her head.

The last time Angie saw her daughter was the day Rachel brought Rosie over. She'd been gone long enough to get married, have the baby, get divorced. A matter of a year. A little less. She'd walked in like it was nothing, left a twenty-dollar bill and a bag of diapers on the counter. And that hateful note: "Dear Mom, maybe you'll do better with her than you did with me."

There had been three letters from Rachel in the intervening years, two postmarked Portland, Oregon, a third Laramie, Wyoming. She'd remarried, said she had a son. Her husband drove a truck. The load, her daughter said, was chickens. Were they dead chickens? Angie wondered. Frozen and packaged? Or live birds? Egg birds?

Angie turned the TV on. The news was blaring out of the tube and once again, as if there were no other news on earth, the coverage was of Nate's death. There was file footage from earlier in the day taken here, in her frumpy town. Glick was being helped inside the sheriff's car. He looked grim and afraid. Angie felt her heart expand, then contract. There were pictures of the milling crowd at the clearing, a shot of Ethan carrying his son out of the woods, someone interviewing the sheriff later in the day. Angie kept the volume low. She didn't want to wake Rosie.

She shut the TV off and went to the kitchen to pour herself another glass of wine. She was too hungry and too tired to eat, and sometimes wine helped her find her appetite. She called her sister.

"We're waiting for Jane's son," Rocksan said.

Angie felt a moment's jealousy. How she wished it was her daughter they were waiting for.

"Lucky her," Angie said.

"Lucky my ass. This is the tempest in the teapot, mark my words, Ang."

"Maybe not."

"Things are kinda depressing, eh? Can you believe that little kid is dead?"

"It makes me miss my daughter, Rocks. I want her home. It's nights like this, I feel so sorry. So guilty. I didn't do the best I could."

Rocksan didn't say anything for a long time. Angie felt miserable in the silence.

"Her dad died, Angie. You can't help that."

"I guess," Angie said. She did not say anything more. She did not invoke the second marriage, how short-lived and violent it had been. Neither did Rocksan. And in that omission, it was clear to Angie how much she had failed. How self-seeking she had been. Maybe her daughter had slipped when her dad had died. But Angie had pushed her the rest of the way down when she'd chosen her desperate need not to be alone over her daughter's suffering. Why hadn't she seen then, the way she saw so clearly now, that in marrying again, she had left Rachel to fend for herself in the wake of her father's death? It was no wonder she'd turned to drinking, to drugs. It was no wonder she'd sought refuge elsewhere.

After she hung up, she went to the living room and kicked off her shoes. She leaned back on the couch and drank her wine in the darkness, keeping at bay her imagination about Nate's last hours alive. When her thoughts drifted to the idea of Rosie in a similar predicament, Angie stood up. She would not allow herself to think it. What use were idle thoughts?

She was fatigued, bone-weary, and she understood on some level that she was depressed. How many years had she spent alone in this house with her troubled memories, without her daughter's clemency, without a man's love? She closed her eyes and felt herself dozing off, only to wake up moments later to the sound of someone knocking. She got up, closed the shades, then checked on Rosie before going to the door.

When she saw that it was Glick, she felt everything about her settle, everything slow down. She felt all her sorrow depart.

"Glick," she said. She worried that she did not seem surprised. But she wasn't surprised. She realized she'd been waiting for this. Waiting for a long time. Now here it was. The thought occurred to her that there was homecoming in his arrival. She opened the door wider and let him in.

She hadn't noticed the dog until Glick said something. She looked from him to his dog and for a moment felt stymied. She realized that of course Glick would bring the dog. He went everywhere with that animal. She understood that the dog was a friend to Glick. She could not keep it out in the night, so she offered the back porch, and Glick seemed to find that reasonable.

When she made him tea, she saw then that he was close to tears and she knew that tonight was different, that from now on everything would be different between them. It was a feeling she had hidden in the remote places of her heart. She had waited alone and patiently but had known—without ever admitting it to herself—that tonight would come, that Glick would come.

She told him to sit down, but he couldn't, and when he sobbed, she went to him and put her arms around him and they began to kiss with such tenderness that, to Angie, it felt as light and life-giving as breath. They somehow made it to her room without waking Rosie, and when he told her about the tears that had frozen in Nate's eyes, she, too, began to cry. It was as if all of her fears and sorrows could tumble out in the space they had between them and yet they could not be touched or hurt by them. She opened her robe and placed his hands on her breasts. She felt the tears warm her cheeks, his touch on her body. She wanted to say, I love you.

JUDGE JACK ROSENTHAL

He had no idea what possessed him to drive over to the mortuary. He knew the boy had been found and would be taken there. He also knew that nothing good would follow this boy's death. He had been a judge for too long not to see the wheels turning in the legal community. Ethan Denton was in trouble.

The night had been so bitter. The stars were fiercely bright against the sky. Jack dreaded the winter and he thought that when he retired, he'd move someplace warm. His mind drifted to Florida, where he and Adele had often flown to pick up cruise ships for their vacations. He thought of the desert. There was a house they'd rented once in Palm Springs. He loved the hot dry air of the desert, the way the light shimmered on the brown hills. He loved the smell of metal in the air, the bloody red blooms of the ocotillo. He decided he would call a real estate agent, maybe find a modest place in the desert with a little land and few neighbors.

He'd arrived at the mortuary just as the father was pulling away. He tried to hide from the father, and the act of ducking seemed so furtive and childish. What was the harm in paying his respects? But when he got to the door of the mortuary, the mortician said there would be no visitors.

"Please," Jack said. "I only want to say a quick prayer."

"It's the family's wishes."

Jack had not expected that he would be turned away. He thought about mentioning that he was a judge. But to use his credentials for personal gain was abhorrent to him. He remembered being pulled over for speeding once. He had taken the ticket, and as they had driven away, Adele had said, "That was stupid, Jack. Why didn't you just tell him who you are?" Maybe Adele had been right. She'd always told him he was too stubborn for his own good. But he could not help the way he loved the laws, especially the small ones that could ensnare even him. Stubborn? Perhaps.

"Please," he said to the mortician.

But the man would not be swayed. He shook his head, avoiding eye contact. "It's against the family's wishes," he said.

When Jack got home a couple of hours later—he'd stopped for a steak and a beer in town—he was greeted once again by the empty house. Its creaking and groaning and shifting was all he heard as he paced the floorboards, remembering the past.

He thought of Marty and wondered where he was, what he was doing. He wondered if Marty had sold the jewelry and his coins. How much money he'd made off of them. He had an image of Marty walking through the seedy underbelly of Hollywood, in the alleys and weedy vacant lots that smelled like urine and semen. He shuddered to think that Marty might be there right now, looking for a place to spend the night. How could a son of his possibly be a drug addict or homeless? Hadn't he provided everything for Marty? His other sons were fine. They had families; they seemed happy. They were successful. What had happened to Marty that he should have turned out like this? Then he remembered the picture he had thrown away, the rescue that had turned bitter, the cries for help he had failed to answer.

He wanted to pray but could not find the words or feel the inclination. He remembered something the rabbi at temple had said once. That one who cries out to God over what is past utters a prayer in vain. It seemed to Jack that all his prayers lately were in vain. He tried to find that spot of solace within him, the place where he kept his faith. But it was empty.

When the phone rang, he thought maybe it was Marty. A small flame of hope. But it was an old friend of his, the retired DA of the city.

"Steven," Jack said. He heard the forced joviality in his voice. He sounded so phony to himself, so desperate.

"How ya holdin' up, Jack?"

"Just fine. Fine. How are you? Is Candy in good health?"

"She's fine. She's in San Francisco visiting the grandkids. She spends all her time there now. I used to feel sorry for myself when our kids were born. Couldn't get Candy to pay a lick of attention to me. But this grandmother thing is even worse."

Jack heard himself chuckling. Steven laughed on the other end.

"What's up?" Jack said.

"Well, I thought I'd give you a heads-up. You know that boy out there in Angels Crest. The lost boy?"

Jack's heart began to race. He thought he could guess what was coming.

"Sure," he said. He did not want anyone to know that he had helped with the search, that he had tried to see the boy at the mortuary. He did not want anyone to know what lay beneath it—his son's betrayal and the shameful way he'd tried to skulk out of his life, all bringing him inadvertently to Angels Crest in the first place.

"Looks like Tom Kraft is gonna prosecute it."

Jack took the phone to the living room and sat down on the couch. He felt as if someone had draped him with a heavy blanket. For a moment, he could not breathe.

"Damn," Jack said. "What kind of charges is he going to bring?"

"Negligent homicide," Steven said.

"Christ," Jack said. "What a bastard."

"I heard that he was going to seek a jail sentence. Word has it that you're gonna get the case, Jack."

Jack rubbed his forehead. He felt his gut constrict and tighten. "This is a bad case, Steven. A really bad case."

There was silence on the other end. Then Steven said, "I knew you'd think so."

"Negligent homicide is a misdemeanor," Jack said. "Maybe he'll plead guilty, save himself from a trial."

"At least there's that hope."

"Jesus," Jack said. "What a terrible waste of the law."

"For some, maybe. Have you been listening to talk radio?"

Jack laughed. "Hell no, Steven. Why would I waste my time?"

"You might want to turn it on. One guy called in, said the death penalty was too light a sentence for the father."

Jack was stunned. "They say it was an accident."

"Well, in this day and age, Jack. You know how it is. You can't be human anymore."

Jack sat back on the couch with the phone in his hand. He felt the thrum and sway of his heart, the blood coursing through his veins. Then without warning, he remembered a moment from long ago. It came upon him suddenly and he closed his eyes. He could remember all of it, the way it smelled outdoors, the sounds, the light. Marty had been swinging from the branches of the sycamore tree in the soft down of early spring. Jack had built the swing for his first son. Had seen his second son use it. Now it was Marty's turn. He recalled the way the sun lit up his boy's hair, the sound of Marty's laughter, the sense that at that moment all was right with the world.

"It's been a long time since I've felt good about anything, Steven," Jack said.

"I hear ya, Jack. I know just how you feel."

"This is a bad case, I'm telling you."

"Yes. But my hopes fall on you to adjudicate it with your benevolent touch."

Jack smiled. Steven loved the flourish in words, the music in language. "That's kind of you to say."

"Your reputation is a comfort. You'll rule wisely," Steven said.

After he hung up, Jack went to the window and looked out at the street. The trees were bare. Long naked arms, with knobby joints. Arthritic. Winter revealed the bones beneath the supple flesh of spring. How could he forget this fact every year?

GLICK

---◆---

When Glick opened his eyes, he couldn't place himself. He thought for a moment he was still back there lost in the snow. He pictured Nate lying beside the tree, the dog digging the snow away from the boy's body. Then he worried for a moment about his dog, because before he actually remembered where he was, he sensed the dog's absence. But it took less than a second for Glick to realize the dog was on the porch and he was here, in this bed, beside Angie, her skin against his. He had not been tender with a woman in so long. He remembered last night, the way they'd touched. He wondered if it had ever been that way before.

It was still dark and the room, with its unfamiliar shapes and shadows, brought him comfort. It smelled of something sweet, like lotion or powder, and there was a reassuring disarray of clothes draped over furniture, paperbacks lying half opened, a glass of water half full on the nightstand.

Angie made a sound and rolled over. She sat halfway up, as if surprised to find Glick there, then sank back into the covers. In the darkness, she leaned into him and kissed him tenderly. Quietly, they made love again, and when they finished, Angie got out of bed and went to the bathroom. Glick heard her shuffling, the sound of the faucet, then the toilet. It grew quiet again. When she opened the door to return to the room, there was a moment before she turned out the light, and Glick saw her illuminated, her long hair draped over her shoulders and the luminous imperfections of her body. He wanted nothing more than to put his hands on her, to warm himself against her, to love her. He was swept so deeply into this view of her, backlit just so, that he was once again aroused. But when she came to bed, he merely held her in his arms, and she said, "You have to go soon. Rosie wakes at seven."

He nodded.

"Come by the diner, though. For some breakfast."

"I will," he said.

They lay like that in the darkness until the first hint of light, when Glick dressed and gave Angie a small kiss on the cheek.

"The dog," she said.

"I wouldn't forget."

"Of course not. It's just that I did."

"Sorry I brought him."

"You can bring him anytime."

He left the room and went to the back porch, where the dog was curled up in a corner. When the dog heard Glick's approach, he stood up and groaned happily. Glick told him to hush, and the dog, seeming to sense the blessedness of the morning, calmed down and walked quietly by Glick's side as he left the house.

❧   ❧   ❧

He saw Ethan's truck in the driveway and was instantly thrown into the still waters of the depression that, he now knew, had been with him for twenty years. He understood that his life would now have to accommodate both sorrow and happiness, that he would have to learn again that there could be joy, as well.

It was a moment of recognition that he would not soon forget. He realized that he should not strive for happiness, that he should never have sought after happiness. That what he needed, what he wanted, was far more complex. He saw now that what a man did that would make him a man had something to do with putting himself above the chase for his own pleasures and the quest for good fortune. Justice seemed a better pursuit, yet when he thought this, he was unsure what he meant.

He entered the house. It was so cold. He immediately turned up the thermostat. The shades were drawn and two bowls were on the floor, filled with cat food that had dried overnight. The stink of it mingled with the musty, closed smell of the house. The dog growled and Ethan, who was lying beneath a blanket on the couch, sat up abruptly. When the dog saw who it was, he wagged his tail and went to Ethan.

"Oh man. I'm sorry," Ethan said. He made as if to stand up, but Glick said, "Stay put, Ethan. It's all right."

Ethan lay back down. He was still wearing the clothes he'd had on when they searched for Nate. His hair was disheveled. There was an empty bottle of whiskey on the table by the couch.

"What time is it?"

"A bit after seven," Glick said. He thought of Angie and of Rosie, just waking up. He wondered what they did in the morning, how Angie got herself ready for work, what she fixed Rosie to eat. He wondered if Angie drank coffee in the morning, or tea. If she listened to the news or watched a morning show on television. He wanted to be there. He wanted to know what she did at every part of the day. He wanted to hear her talk to Rosie, to hear Rosie say something back.

"I couldn't go back to my place," Ethan said. "The newspeople are everywhere. They're parasites, man. They were camped outside my house."

"You can stay here as long as you need, Ethan."

He still had not made eye contact with Glick. He was older by half a life now. In one day, everything about him had changed.

"The funeral is tomorrow," he said, as if picking up a conversation he'd been having with himself.

Glick went to the kitchen and put on some coffee. He turned on the radio, which was tuned to the only station he got out here. Talk radio. Two men were laughing, slicing the morning in parts with their loud voices. One of them said, "We'll be back with your calls." Then they cut to a commercial for a muffler shop.

"Do you want some coffee?"

"No," Ethan said. "I'm feeling real shaky."

"How 'bout some water."

"Yeah," he said. "I'll come get it."

Glick waited by the coffeepot for it to brew. He heard Ethan get up and go into the bathroom. One of the cats bolted through the living room, into the kitchen, and down into the basement, as if spooked by some haunt that Glick could not see.

Glick looked outside his window at the snow-blanketed meadow and beyond that to the forest, which crowded the horizon with its white-topped trees. A light snow was falling. Everything was clean and hushed. There was no hindrance in his mind, no barrier to how far he could see. The dog ran into view, then stopped, sniffed the air, and took off running into the dark woods.

Ethan appeared in the kitchen. Though he stood close to six feet tall, he seemed diminished by his misery. He sat at the kitchen table and held his head in his hands. Just then, the talk show came back on. One of the hosts took a call. The caller said, "There is no penalty great enough for what that man did to his boy. I say fry him. I don't care if he wants to call it an accident. He left that boy in the car. That boy was murdered."

Glick quickly shut the radio off. But, of course, it was too late. Ethan's face had gone white. He sank to the table. Glick went over and sat beside him. He reached out to touch him but found he could not. There was nothing in him, after last night, that could convince him to cross to that place again.

"I'm sorry," he said. "I had no idea it was—that people were talking about it on the radio. I didn't think."

Ethan remained silent.

"You know how people get puritanical," Glick said. "You know that. Hell, back in the day, we mighta been the ones to call. In our ignorance. But we know different now."

"It's okay, Glick. There's nothing you can say. I deserve the harshest punishment."

"It was an *accident*, Ethan. You need to remember that."

"I would change places with Nate if I could. I would rather be dead than sitting here in this kitchen. I am willing to be punished for what I did. I am going to jail. I know they're sending me to jail."

"Goddamn it, Ethan. You gotta stop this now. We don't know anything."

Ethan looked up, and Glick realized it was the first time that entire morning that their eyes had met, and Glick felt sorry for that, sorry that he could do nothing to comfort his old friend. For a moment, it occurred to him that perhaps the only person who might have been able to comfort Ethan would have been Angie.

In a matter of seconds, he relived the entire evening—before his arrival, and then the way Angie'd greeted him on the porch, the stain on her bathrobe, the way she'd kissed him and whispered, "If you want to stay, you have to be quiet." He became flush with the memory. It seemed to be the apology he'd waited for. How strange that it had come in this way, in this woman, in this place, far removed from all the people who had wronged him, from all the people he'd expected to atone for the harm they'd caused him.

"I know more today," Ethan said, "than I have ever known in my lifetime."

Glick nodded. There was really nothing else to say.

◆ ◆ ◆

He was forty years old. That is what he kept telling himself as he drove to Angie's Diner. You are forty years old, so act like it. But he couldn't. He felt like he had back in high school. The way he had whenever he'd fallen in love. His palms were sweaty. His heart beat hard and fast, and his stomach felt queasy. He doubted he had ever blushed in his life and he told himself that he wasn't about to start now. Angie seemed to him to be as unlocked, vast, and open as the forest, to stretch out before him with the same infinite possibility, the same promise.

When he arrived, a mass of reporters with microphones descended on him. He pushed them away. "No comment," he said. He made his way inside, the reporters behind him clamoring, and the sheriff, who was drinking a cup of coffee at the counter, stood up.

"You folks need to respect a man's privacy," the sheriff said.

Something about him—a strange shy authority—made them back down. Glick nodded at the sheriff, who picked up the newspaper beside him and began to read as if nothing had happened.

"You came," Angie said when she filled his coffee cup. "I'm glad."

He looked at his menu. He could not meet her eyes.

"Rosie didn't hear a thing," Angie said.

"That's good," Glick said.

"Coffee?"

He nodded. She turned the cup in front of him upright and poured the coffee into it. In doing so, she leaned close enough to him that he could smell the light powdery scent of her. He wanted to be alone with her.

"Can you believe this circus?" she asked.

He looked around the coffee shop. There were many strangers among the few regulars. At his usual booth, a young woman and an older man sat with their laptop computers. Each of them was typing. They did not speak to each other. Occasionally, one of the reporters would look his way. Glick felt nervous and exposed.

"Ethan's at my house," Glick said. He found himself whispering.

"Oh, that's good," Angie said.

For the first time, he met her eyes. She smiled with warmth. He smiled back and then looked quickly at his menu. He could not make out any of the words, not really.

"I have never seen you blush, Rusty Glick," she said.

"I have never had the occasion to," he told her.

"You flatter me."

"I'm relieved you see it that way."

She walked off and went to the kitchen. In moments, she rounded the counter with three plates and hurried off to deliver them. She returned, wiping her hands on her apron, and pulled her order pad from her back pocket. How many times he had seen her do just that, and yet today it seemed so different.

"You want the potatoes or the grits today?" Angie asked.

"You got hash browns?"

Angie shook her head. "No. Country potatoes or grits."

She looked at him and they both laughed.

"How long we been having this same conversation?" Glick said.

"Forever, it seems."

"Well then, you know the answer."

"Potatoes. And some extra bacon."

"That would do it."

"You're hungry today, huh?" she said.

They both smiled—their private moment—and it seemed so wrong in this atmosphere of grief and voyeurism. He leaned up and she bent over. He whispered in her ear, "You smell so good."

"Well, I guess it's my turn to blush," she said. She turned around before he could see her face, and they didn't talk again until he left.

"Will you be coming by tonight?" she asked as he left his money on the counter.

"If you'll have me."

She inclined her head. Her face was so serene, so filled with warmth. Why had it taken them this long?

"After dark, then," she said. "Rosie goes to bed at eight."

He wanted to kiss her, but he knew it would not be right. So he nodded his head, grabbed a toothpick, and walked out just as Rocksan and Jane were arriving. There were reporters everywhere. He saw how they waited for him. Glick saw a young man and a pregnant girl behind Rocksan and Jane. He said hello to Rocksan and Jane, and Jane stopped him and said, "This is my son, George, and his . . ."

George thrust out his hand. A rise in color started at his neck and crept up to his cheeks.

"My girlfriend, Melody."

"She's pregnant," Jane said.

Glick shook George's hand, which was cold and dry. The isolation of the town, its harsh start at winter and the unfurling tragedy, was reflected back in George's somewhat stunned gaze.

"Glad to meet you," Glick said. "Welcome to Angels Crest."

He glanced quickly at Jane and Rocksan. They both seemed nervous, tense. Glick shook his head of the thought he always had when he saw them—why could he not meet them without imagining them in bed together?—and said, "It's crowded in there."

Everyone looked inside Angie's, relieved, it seemed, to have a place to train their eyes. Glick was not immune to their discomfort, the nature of it obvious, like a banner.

Jane said, "Any word from Ethan?"

Glick thought about it. He decided not to tell anyone else that Ethan was hiding out at his house. "Nothing," he said. "But I know the funeral is tomorrow."

"It's such an awful thing," Rocksan said.

They said good-bye and then Glick made his way toward his truck. He had to fight the reporters. He kept saying, "I got no comment." When he drove off and got a good distance away, he stopped the truck near the cemetery and got out. The headstones were dusted with snow. The trees were bare. Some of the graves were as old as the town. Glick looked up and the snow fell harder, obscuring his view of the sky, keeping his mind in one place, in the center of his life.

ETHAN

When he heard the dog growl, Ethan felt his entire body rise to gooseflesh. It was a new kind of fear: a fear inspired by guilt and mourning. He saw Glick's dog, then remembered where he was. His hangover rounded out his disconnection from all the things that had once been familiar to him.

He was embarrassed to be hiding out. It felt so much like skulking around, so much like what a guilty man would do. But Glick seemed to understand. Glick, with his prison years behind him and all the wrong that had been done to him, was a man who never seemed to judge others. Ethan knew that all the things that had come between them—Cindy and now this—could never bring them back to that place they used to be. He had never had a friend like Glick before.

He tried to appear calm, but he knew that the past two days had written themselves all over his face, etched themselves into his body so that even the way he moved seemed to him to calculate his despair and hopelessness. All of this became heightened, seemed to culminate when the talk radio show came on and the caller said Ethan was a murderer. It was a stunning moment, so perfect in its torment that Ethan felt he had no recourse but to agree with the caller.

It seemed like a long time before Glick left, and not until then did Ethan realize he had not even asked him where he'd been the night before. The ordinary and everydayness of the world no longer interested him. He did not care.

He brushed his teeth using his finger and some toothpaste from Glick's medicine cabinet. He slapped some water under his arms and borrowed a clean shirt from Glick's closet. It smelled of must and wool, like everything in Glick's house. The cats stared out at him from their perch on the dresser.

Outside, it had begun to snow. The air felt warmer than it had the day before, and he wore his jacket without zipping it up. He thought again about the man who'd called in to the radio show to say that Ethan should die for his negligence. He felt the bile rise at the back of his throat. It was not that he didn't wish it himself. He had been thinking that to die did not seem like such a bad thing. It was that others wished it for him. They could not know that living with what he had done was a far greater penalty. He spit on the fresh snow and then went to his truck and started it.

When he was sure the truck would not cut off, he went around the back of Glick's house and found the ax and a pile of wood. He picked up the ax, which pierced the felled tree trunk Glick used as a chopping block, and split a large piece of firewood into three and then again. He slammed the ax back into the tree trunk and made his way to Glick's shed. Inside, he heard the mice scurry for cover as he switched on the overhead light. Beneath the glare of the unadorned bulb, he found a hammer and several three-inch nails. He pocketed the nails and carried the hammer with him to his truck, along with the wood he had just cut.

He drove out of the driveway slowly, looking for people who might have caught on to his whereabouts. But when he got to the main road, the highway was deserted. He turned left, away from town, and headed into the mountains.

The snow was falling harder, and as he climbed the winding roads to the woods, the visibility dropped to a mere few feet. He drove slowly and barely missed hitting two deer that jutted out in front of him and dashed into the woods. The world was so beautiful. He wished for the life he'd once had. A day like this used to bring him calm and happiness. He would work at the hardware store, close early, and spend the day with his son. He'd make dinner or take Nate to Jane's while he worked late on the inventory or the taxes, or had a rare date, dinner and a movie in the next town over. But more often, they'd be alone together, walking through the woods, or at night, he and Nate would lie in bed and make up stories until Nate's eyes grew heavy. There had been a rhythm to his life, a music that sang to Ethan. Every part of his day had been set and occupied by meaning. He had not minded its predictability; it was what he wanted. He'd believed it had all finally fallen into place.

But now it hurt him to see the wonder and beauty of the world around him. He knew he had no way to fit into it anymore. There would be no room for simple pleasures again. How did one ever start over? He thought of Glick, whose life had been ruined by being wrongly accused. How much easier that would be, how much he longed for something that simple, to have at least the fact of being right on your side.

He played over and over again in his head the day he'd left his son behind. And each time, he imagined himself returning to the truck and finding his son still asleep, or even returning and finding his son nearby, wandering close to the truck, not somewhere deep in the woods. Sometimes, he played it back so he hadn't left the truck at all. But it only brought into greater relief his carelessness, his blind bad luck.

Sometimes his mind wandered to Nate in the woods, searching for him, but Ethan could not go far with the thought. When he imagined how his son had suffered, he would cry out every time. How much easier it would have been had God seen fit to take Ethan and not his son. To die did not seem as unfathomable as it once had.

He wound his way slowly up the mountain. There were no other cars on the road, and he knew he had this bad weather to thank for his solitude. He worried that going back up to the place where Glick had found his son would ensnare him in the glare of the waiting media. But no one dared, least of all city people, drive up in this weather. When he finally made it to the clearing where the search party had met, he was relieved to see the place deserted. Soon, he knew, he would not be able to drive up here. The winter would take over and leave the forest to the world of the animals and the towering trees, the memory of his boy dying there.

He got out of his truck and thrust his hands into the pocket of his jeans, feeling the three quarters he had taken from Glick's truck. How long ago that seemed. Several inches of fresh snow had already fallen this morning. The trails and tracks left behind by the searchers were obliterated by the new snow. Ethan zipped up his jacket—it was so much colder in the higher elevations—and he put on a pair of gloves he found in the glove compartment. His gun was behind the seat, and he looked at it for a long time before grabbing the wood, the hammer, and the nails.

He cleared a patch of snow aside and took a piece of plywood from the back of his truck. He put the plywood on the ground and placed the two pieces of wood on top of it in the shape of a cross. Then he hammered the two pieces together. The nails were too long, so he turned the cross over and hammered them flat against the wood.

He threw the plywood in the trunk and held on to the hammer. In his other hand, he carried the cross into the woods. It was snowing so hard that he had trouble finding his way. But he knew this place well and trusted his intuition to lead him back to the spot where Glick had found Nate. On the way, he remembered how he and Glick used to walk these woods every fall in search of deer, how they would spend hours with each other and never say a word.

Nate had begun to understand the significance of silence, too. He'd seemed to have taken his cues from Ethan. He'd seemed to know, like Ethan, that there was a reverential way of walking in the woods. It was half respect, half awe. To talk seemed to sully the silences that streamed through the spaces in the trees. To talk seemed like wasted breath. Nate had already learned this. The irony was not lost on Ethan that he was marking his son's final resting place with a cross.

It took Ethan a half hour to find the spot. Once there, he could not mistake the pine tree where Nate had lain down to die. He made his way to the tree, got on his knees, and held his head down. But no prayers came. They could not. He was a man who had never known God. The closest he had ever come to faith was in the love he had for his son. That was as holy as he had ever felt. He put the cross in the ground and hammered it down, below the white snow, into the frozen dirt.

ROCKSAN

⬧

When Rocksan saw Glick outside of Angie's, she thought for a minute that there was something different about him. She almost asked him if he'd had a haircut. Were his clothes newly purchased? Though she would never have used the word *jaunty* to describe him, he seemed jaunty. At least he seemed less stoic, less brooding. Something alive in his face.

After he left, Rocksan turned to Jane. "Did he seem jaunty to you?"

"Glick? Jaunty?"

"You know. Sprightly?"

"Rocksan, did you spike your coffee this morning?"

Rocksan laughed. "I thought at first he might have gotten his hair cut."

But Jane was no longer listening. Rocksan saw that she was consumed by worry and anxiety. Her face was drawn and taut and she kept jumping at the slightest sounds. The night before had done a number on her. On all of them really.

It took Rocksan to get George and the girl inside. They were all nervous. George's eye kept twitching. He kept staring at Jane, then at Rocksan. His face was exactly like Jane's, except that, unlike hers, it was closed and hard. It was the face of a challenge. A face that said, Prove me wrong. The only one of them who appeared unruffled was the girl, Melody.

The night before, they'd sat down and Jane had offered them some wine. Melody said no, but George said yes. They said it at the same time. Everyone laughed. It was a horrible moment, though, because it didn't seem to break the ice. Finally, George sat up straight. He cleared his throat.

"I'll have some wine," he said.

Jane poured a glass for him and one for herself. Rocksan saw that she drank hers down in two huge gulps. She had never seen Jane do that before. She was mildly impressed, and then amused when George did the same.

They talked for a half hour, maybe more, about the long drive, the strange sights the two of them had seen—three cowboys on horses corralling a herd of cows across the highway in Wyoming, Goblin Valley in Utah, a lone flame red flower jutting out of a snowbank in Arizona. George drank more wine. So did Jane. Rocksan could see both of them slowing down, lubing up, but not in any relaxed way. More like they were hardening themselves for a brawl. And in moments, it fell on them, as if out of the blue.

"Dad kicked us out," George said. "He said I was a whore like my mother."

"Ouch," Rocksan said. That boy didn't wait long to launch an insult. It would have been admirable had it been heaved at anyone else. Rocksan felt her testosterone flare.

"He's sorry," Melody said. "Right, George?"

"I didn't mean anything by it," George said. He looked directly at Jane. "It's just that my entire life my dad said me and you were two peas in a pod. Course, I'm not gay."

Melody cleared her throat. "George is not telling this well at all," she said.

"Boy, you got that right," Rocksan said. She was glad she was getting pissed off. It made it easier to be on Jane's side. Then she realized there were so many sides she could choose from. There was her side, of course. Her father's side. Well, never her father's side. But her girlfriend's side, at least the good Jane side, the Jane side that didn't leave a baby boy behind. There was George's side. He was the one who'd been left behind. Just like her, as a matter of fact, so she could relate to that. And, though she had not heard it yet, she figured Melody most likely had a side, too.

"Here's the story," Melody said. She spoke very softly, very sweetly. Rocksan thought her voice was like water rushing over rocks in a stream. There was something about her that Rocksan liked. It was instantaneous. From the gut. "George and I were Christians."

"Oh God," Rocksan said.

"Please, Rocks. Don't make it harder," Jane said, barely above a whisper.

Her face was beet red. It seemed the effort of talking at all might actually kill her.

"We were all going to the same church. I can't say we were in it, not the way other people were. And you know how you're sort of not supposed to have sex before you get married. . . ."

"It's a stupid crock of shit," George said. "I just went to that stupid church because for my entire life I wanted that bastard to like me."

Melody sighed. She rubbed her belly. "George is feeling hostile because he keeps forgetting that I'm the one who's pregnant, not him, right, George?" She smiled sweetly at George, but you could tell she wanted to clobber him.

"I didn't want to come here," George said. "This was your idea."

"What?" Jane said.

"I suggested to George, after his father kicked him out, that we leave. I suggested perhaps we go to California, though in all honesty, I was thinking more, I don't know, beachy weather. . . ."

"Well, if you don't like it . . ." Jane said. Her face was so red, Rocksan thought maybe she was having a heart attack.

"No," Melody said. She seemed suddenly close to tears. "No. This is all going so horribly. Listen. It was my idea. I thought George should try to forgive you, Jane. It was the only way I would marry him."

George put his head in his hands.

"I don't follow," Jane said. Her lips were pressed tight. Her body was so tense, a vein Rocksan had never seen before bulged in her forehead. This was drama. This was exactly the sort of thing Rocksan had come all the way up here to avoid.

"Okay, look," Melody said. "The truth is, I love your son." She was talking to Jane. It was as if only Jane and Melody existed in the room. Briefly, Rocksan and George glanced at each other. George turned away first.

"But he's very, very bitter, Jane. And I can't marry him till he at least goes to the source and tries to fix it. I don't want to live with someone with that much anger. Plus, we might as well just put it out on the table. He's got a problem with you guys being, you know . . ."

"Thanks, Melody," George said. "That oughta make things easier for both of us."

Rocksan put her hands up in the air, seeing some hope among them for the first time all night. She liked it when homophobes admitted they were homophobes. She saw that as a good thing. She said, "No, this is good. It's good. I used to have this mission of converting homophobes. It was my thing. Converting them or getting rid of them."

"You say that like you're the Mafia," George said.

Jane smiled. She looked at George. "Rocksan scared so many people back in the day, George. She could scare you, too, but she's on her best behavior."

"This is all going very, very badly," Melody said. "And this baby, she's up in my throat. I swear, she's got her leg wrapped around my esophagus."

Rocksan looked over at George. He had his head in his hands again. It *was* going badly, but better than she had expected.

❖   ❖   ❖

Angie's was crowded. Rocksan hardly recognized anyone. She hoped that it would snow harder and get colder and that everyone would go back to the city, or wherever they'd come from. She didn't want anyone to discover her secret. She had chosen Angels Crest because it was a frumpy town that eschewed the vanities of modern culture—drive-through espresso stands, frilly banners on the streetlamps announcing some art show, teahouses with pretentious names like Cheshire Knoll.

Angels Crest, with its dowdy stores and its backdrop of craggy peaks, had been a found paradise for Rocksan. She loved its frigid winters and its silences, which were inhabited only by numbing winds and the sounds of birds. She loved being near her sister. All these people made her nervous. She knew how a place could get overrun.

"Would you look at this?" Rocksan said. "Who are all these assholes?"

Jane shook her head. "It's so sad. The boy is dead and no one seems to have any respect."

A TV was blaring over the counter, and on-screen one of the drunks from Trevor's bar was talking to a reporter about Ethan. He seemed so much larger on television, so much more legitimate somehow, as if the airwaves could shroud even the lowly with a shred of dignity. He was saying that Ethan had always been a loner. He was telling the reporter, a stranger whom no one in town had ever met before, that Ethan and Cindy had had a vicious custody battle. He said, "Ethan seemed like he just wanted to live alone in the woods with his son."

"That's just great. Now the world will think he's some kind of survivalist," Jane said.

George looked at Melody. He said, "This is a bad omen. You're having a baby in a town where a kid just died."

"It's only an omen if you say so. Now take that back," Melody said.

"I take it back," George said.

They were so *weird*. Rocksan looked at Jane to try to get her to see how weird she thought they were, but Jane was busy staring at the floor.

Just then, Angie walked up. She appeared serene, unflappable. How could her sister be so calm?

"Can you get us a seat, Ang?" Jane asked.

"There's a wait."

"Oh, come on," Rocksan said. "Show some balls. Let the media people wait."

"Okay," Angie said. "I'll give you the next table, but you get to quell the riot."

Angie then trained her eyes on George and Melody. Jane actually blushed. "This is my son, George, and his . . . girlfriend, Melody."

"Glad to meet you," Angie said.

"Melody's pregnant," Jane said.

"Jane," Rocksan said. "You don't have to announce it to everyone you introduce her to. It's pretty obvious on its own."

Jane looked like she was about to cry. Then Melody, in a gesture that spoke to Rocksan of Melody's character, put her arm gently around Jane's shoulder and whispered something into her ear. Jane smiled and gazed at Melody with a mixture of gratitude and relief.

It was the first time since George and Melody had arrived that Jane seemed to relax. This was a relief to Rocksan, who felt badly for Jane. Since George and Melody had walked into the house, Jane had grown more and more quiet, more desperate-seeming. Rocksan was relieved when they were quickly seated, despite the glare of the reporters waiting for a table, people who probably knew better than to roust a local. Angie brought them all coffee, except for Melody, who asked for a cup of tea. Rocksan looked at her sister. There was something different about her. Something sewn up, put together, a quality that she hadn't seen in years.

They ordered their breakfasts and sat in their booth, looking at the crowd. One man sat alone with a huge camera on the table, as if the machine were his only friend. He wore a badge with the call letters of a major network on a string around his neck.

"I wonder what happened to Ethan," Jane said. "No one's seen or heard from him."

"He's probably hiding out somewhere. Probably at Glick's," Rocksan said.

"Is this Ethan guy the father?" Melody asked.

"Yes," Rocksan said.

Angie walked up with water and coffee refills. She said, "Those reporters, they've been asking me all kinds of questions. Do I know Ethan? Do I know Glick? When Glick came in the diner, the sheriff had to beat the reporters back."

"That's awful," Melody said. "I feel so sorry for that father. He must hate himself. It was something anyone might do."

It occurred to Rocksan that when Melody spoke, it was always close to a whisper. She was so vaporlike, so ghostly in a way. If Rocksan had awakened in the middle of the night and seen the girl walking through the house in a nightgown, she would have thought she was being haunted.

"Yeah," Jane said. "Ethan's a nice man. Young. Not much older than you guys."

Melody and George exchanged a look. A long silence passed among them. A thousand questions hung in the air. Finally, Rocksan said, "So what happened back in Ohio? Let's hear the story again, only this time can we leave out the insults?"

George sighed. Rocksan could see he felt bad about the way it had gone last night.

"The bottom line is, Dad kicked me out. I was just laid off. And as you can see, Melody is pregnant. Dad couldn't deal with it."

"He did the same thing to me because I was a lesbian," Jane said.

Rocksan quickly looked at George and Melody to see how they would deal with this word spoken aloud. *Lesbian.* But they had no reaction.

Melody smiled bravely. So did Jane. George looked off in the distance. "He was such a jerk, Jane. I mean, you know, all I heard all my life was dyke whore this, dyke whore that."

"That's what he liked to call me, George. What names did he call you?"

George shrugged. Rocksan felt sorry for him then. He seemed to have shrunk. She knew what prejudice did, the poison it was. She knew it was handed down, like certain mannerisms or the way a person spoke or crossed their *t*'s. He had come on strong the night before, but Rocksan could see now, in the way his entire body seemed to shrink in defeat, that he was scared. She saw something glimmer faintly in his eyes. Kindness. Remorse. Hope.

Melody looked at George quickly and George said, "He was brutal, let's just say. But I got used to it. I found a way out of it, mostly. Through school, through my studies. But when he started in on Melody, I knew I couldn't stay much longer."

Rocksan saw Melody reach over and grab his hand. She saw how his hand shook. She saw in the gesture the infinite medicine of love, the balm of someone else's touch. She saw, too, that Melody loved him hard and sure, and the fact that he was so loved by someone made his outbursts seem somehow forgivable.

Rocksan looked at Jane. Her head was bowed toward the table. She could see how Jane was taking it all on, shouldering the burden.

"Look, Jane," George said. There was acquiescence in his voice. "Just 'cause we have Dad calling us names in common doesn't mean I can just forgive you. But I want to. Can that be enough for now?"

"Okay," said Jane. She folded her arms across her chest.

Rocksan was impressed. Jane was holding up after all.

❧ ❧ ❧

Later, after the sun set and Jane and the kids were inside preparing a roast and some mashed potatoes, Rocksan went out to the hives. The night was bitterly cold. A knife wielded at the sky could slice a piece of the darkness out. The storm had passed and the clouds were once again parting to reveal the brilliant light of the winter sky. The stars seemed so close.

The wind howled through the trees. Rocksan turned her collar up against her neck and dug her hands deeper into her pockets. She remembered the most difficult failure she had ever had with the bees. It was shortly after she and Jane had moved to town. She had just set up the hives and was looking for a swarm, in the hopes of expanding what she already had. She called the sheriff and asked him if he would alert her to any swarms in town.

Already, she and Jane were looked upon with suspicion and, by some, with fear. They were lesbians. They were from the city. They kept bees. They were rich. If Angie hadn't been Rocksan's sister, surely they would have been stoned to death for these eccentricities.

About a week later, the sheriff called. He said there was a swarm at the Calvary Church school, in an elm tree near one of the classrooms. The minister was going to call someone to have the bees killed. Did she want them?

She said she did, and the sheriff warned her that she had better not let anyone get hurt. She'd have to get them after school let out, and if any problem arose, *any problem*, she'd be held accountable, financially or otherwise.

She rushed over to the church but was disappointed from the very start. It was a small swarm, probably an after-swarm, and she knew it wasn't enough with which to start a new hive. But she had been a member of the beekeeper's association then, and she'd met up with a pompous old geezer from Vancouver a few months earlier at the annual meeting in Oregon.

He had told her of a technique he'd done several times, with great success, that would safely introduce a new swarm into an existing hive. It involved pouring sugar water on the existing bees as well as the bees to be introduced. She would also have to put a sheet of tissue paper between them, which the bees would then eat through. The theory was that once the bees gnawed through the paper, they would become accustomed to one another.

She thought she'd give it a try, even though something in her gut told her it wouldn't work. Quickly, expertly, she cut the swarm away from the branch and deposited the bees into the swarm box. As she left the church grounds, a minister with a cane walked by and said, "Evening, sister." She realized he was blind and that she had seen him often sitting in the town records office, leaning on his cane, staring at the wall as if he were looking at the pictures that hung there.

By the time she got home, it had started raining and she knew then that it was a bad time to work with the bees. But the man from Vancouver had said his technique worked in any weather. Rocksan had her doubts. She stood before the hives for a long time in the rain. The delicacy lay in the balance between managing the hives and fucking with nature.

In the end, she decided to try it. But nothing went the way it should have. After the first attempt, she returned to the hives a few hours later. There were dead bees everywhere. The new hive she'd gathered from the church had been forced from the other hive. The bees were lying motionless on the ground, soaked from the rain.

She made another attempt, and the second time, the same thing happened. Only now there were more dead and wounded bees. And worse, the bees that had rejected them were in a lather. Rocksan was not wearing any protective clothing. She had been stung twice, something that had rarely ever happened to her. She was devastated by how forlorn the swarm she had found at the church appeared as the bees sought refuge in what remained of their hive together on the muddy ground.

Knowing she would lose them all, she rescued the queen, putting her in a cage, and tried to keep her alive with sugar water. Then she went into the house and called around to see if anyone she knew needed a queen. Her efforts to save the queen grew more and more grim. No one was looking. No one knew anyone who was looking. The prospects were bad, and Rocksan began to feel desperate and foolish and depressed.

She could not help feeling responsible for the deaths of the bees that she had taken down from the tree at the Calvary Church. She remembered the blind minister and miserably, with unusual self-pity, wondered if he would have spoken to her had he seen who she was. She knew that if she let the queen out of her prison, the queen would die. But if she kept her locked up, the queen would also die.

She did not know what to do. What was the most compassionate choice? Should she kill the queen or let her die? By letting her die, would her death be slow and miserable? To what extent did bees feel pain or misery? She hated that having to make this type of decision was the by-product of her interference with nature. She could not keep the queen incarcerated. She could not let her die a long, slow death. She decided to kill the queen herself.

It was one of the most difficult moments she had ever experienced with the bees. Aware of the heartbreaking fate the rejects had met (what deeper pain than to be cast aside, to be rejected?), she knew that in administrating and organizing the lives of bees, she would always be the one who decided and controlled, by mistake or otherwise, whether they lived or died.

After she killed the queen, she went inside the house and sat alone in the darkness. When Jane came home, she tried to explain her despair, but she could not find the words.

JANE

———————◆———————

After breakfast at the diner, the four of them left together in a companionable silence. They drove for a few minutes like that, when George said,
"Why do they call this town Angels Crest?"

"You can't see it for the clouds, but way up there, at an elevation of about
twelve thousand feet, is a mountain, crested into a dramatic peak," Rocksan
said. She was pointing into the distance. You couldn't see anything, because
another storm had blown in and lingered in the higher elevations, covering
the craggy peaks with mist and dark clouds.

"When this town was settled back in the 1800s," Rocksan said, "hardly
anyone made it through the first winter. It was a terrible winter. The worst
on record. You can see pictures of it in the town records office. And there's
an old journal there where you can read how they ran out of food and were
trapped up here. People were dying one by one. All the cattle had died and
there was no way down the pass. But by some miracle, so the story goes, a
handful of babies born that fall made it through the winter. Everyone said
that the angels, on their way somewhere or other, must have rested on the
crest and watched over the children till the winter passed."

"Well, that's pretty hokey," George said.

"Yeah," Rocksan said. "But if you don't worry too much about it, you can
see that it's a nice thing, too."

Jane could hear Melody humming in the backseat. Then she began to
sing, absently rubbing her protruding belly. "Hush, my dear, lie still and
slumber, holy angels guard thy bed, heavenly blessings without number, gently falling on thy head."

No one said a word. Her voice was sweet, off-key, completely unself-conscious. She was staring out the window in the direction of Angels Crest, unaware, it seemed, that anyone else was in the car.

Jane looked out the window, following Melody's gaze to the whiteness of the world and its fragile beauty. She remembered the first thought she'd had when she'd seen George at the door the night before: What would it be like to wear a blindfold and touch his face? She could not believe how big he was. Never, ever, had she imagined him as anything other than twenty-one inches long.

Later, when it all seemed hopeless—it was never going to work, and what had she been thinking anyway?—Jane had carried their two small suitcases upstairs and had shown George the room. She had not expected a pregnant girl, and Jane had a strange ass-backward moment—a dip perhaps into a world she had never known—when she thought the two of them should sleep in separate beds. Then she realized how idiotic that would be. And how stupid, given the limber boundaries of her own life.

"My goodness, George. Look at those sheets," Melody said.

"They seem so . . . *queer*," George said.

Melody giggled. George blushed red. "I'm sorry," he said. "I didn't mean . . ."

"Don't be," Jane said. "They are queer. A friend of ours gave them to us a long time ago. Rocksan dug them out of storage."

Melody rubbed her hand over them. "They're satin," she said.

"You can unpack your things. There's an empty closet there, and that dresser is empty," Jane said. "We can get the rest of your stuff in the morning."

"Oh, there's nothing else," Melody said.

"Two suitcases?" Jane said.

George nodded. "We figured we could buy some things."

"George stole money from his father," Melody said.

"What?"

"Yes," George said. "He kept a wad of cash in the cookie jar all the time. I took it when he told us to leave."

"Made us leave," Melody said.

"My God," she said. "I did the same thing. Was it a cookie jar in the shape of a football?"

George laughed. "Totally," he said. "That's amazing."

For the first time, George really looked at her. Jane had the sense that he was taking her in for the very first time, appraising her with new interest. She saw, for the briefest of moments, recognition, forgiveness.

"It was wrong of him," Melody said. "I won't have a thing to do with it."

George looked at Melody. "Is that so?" he said sarcastically.

She shrugged. "I needed a warmer sweater. What did you expect me to do? Steal it?"

George looked at Jane. "Melody likes to pretend she's righteous," he said. "But she had her hands in the cookie jar, too. She's got enough devil in her to keep it interesting."

Melody slapped George on the shoulder. "Talk to me like I'm in the room. And besides, it's *our* predicament, George. We do what we have to do."

Jane felt suddenly as if she was intruding. They were so odd, so intimate. They seemed to have no fear of the truth—or rather, of unearthing their lies. Like underwear on the line. It didn't matter who saw it. They stole. They admitted it. Done and buried.

"We'll pay him back," Melody said to Jane.

"Like hell," George said. "He's a bastard."

"Well," Jane said. It was suddenly *so* crowded in the room. "I'll leave you to debate your restitution. Good night."

She quickly left the room, and when she got to her room, she saw that Rocksan was already in bed.

"I didn't hear you come in," Jane said.

"And yet here I am," Rocksan said absently. She was reading a book. The title, Jane saw, was *Nectar*.

"George stole money from his father," Jane said.

"Is that so surprising?"

"I guess not," Jane said. "But it's weird."

Rocksan turned the page of her book. She didn't appear to be listening.

"I did the same thing," Jane said. "I took a wad of cash from the very same cookie jar the night I left, just like George did nineteen years later."

Rocksan put the book down on her chest and looked at Jane with a dry expression.

"Like mother, like son," she said.

"That poor bastard," Jane said. "He must hate George so much."

Rocksan put the book on the nightstand and turned off the light. After a few minutes, she said, "It must make him so mad, how much his kid looks like you. You're handsome as a man, Janey."

"Yeah, well, I'm not a man, so don't go getting kinky on me."

"Kinky, schminky."

They were silent for a moment. Then in the darkness, Rocksan brushed Jane's hair back. The tenderness made Jane ache.

◆ ◆ ◆

After the short drive home from breakfast, Melody went upstairs to lie down and Rocksan went to fuss with the bees. Jane knew that Rocksan was always nervous at the start of winter, when it was most dangerous for the bees. Rocksan loved those bees the way people loved their dogs and cats, more so even. George lingered in the kitchen.

"I like your house," he said.

"It's haunted," Jane said.

"Cool," George said. He smiled. It was the first time Jane had seen him smile since he arrived. He looked so handsome. He was such a man. A little on the snotty side, but she felt lenient where that was concerned. These were unusual circumstances. Stressful. A baby was on its way; he was meeting his lesbian mom for the first time. She felt bad for him.

"When is the baby due?" she asked.

"Couple of weeks. But Melody keeps whispering to the baby to hurry up. I catch her doing it all the time. She has powers, Jane. She's freaky-deaky that way. I bet the baby comes sooner."

"There's no hospital in this town. Closest one is twenty miles away."

"We kinda figured. I guess we need to make some arrangement. Call ahead or something."

Jane nodded. "Let's do it first thing when she wakes up. Set up a plan."

"She's tough. I kinda wish she wasn't so tough. Honestly, she's tougher than she looks, and I'm a little wimpier."

"Who woulda thought?" Jane said.

"Is that sarcasm I hear?"

"Yup."

George smiled again. "Look, I'm sorry about the way it started off. The wine. I don't normally . . ."

"Me, too. Me, either," Jane said. She could feel herself turning red. She was aware of her heart racing. All of this was so strange. So almost impossible.

"You have to understand . . ." he said.

"I do . . ."

"He hated you and you left me and . . ."

"I know . . ."

"Sometimes I don't know if I can ever forgive you."

Jane was holding a towel and she put it down and leaned against the counter. It felt as if her entire body were plugged into the wall outlet, charging, buzzing, alive in a way she'd never felt before. Painfully, meaningfully so. "George," she said. "I can't even forgive myself."

"I wish I could ask you why and then stick around to find out. But I don't think I could. Like asking is almost too much, but the reasons are probably worse."

"Maybe," Jane said. "But maybe you could just stick around for a while and save the why for later. Let it unravel itself. It's twenty years behind us. I know I'm asking a lot, but maybe you could find it in your heart to stay for a while and give it a chance."

George shrugged. "We have no place to go. I don't have a job. I wanted to finish college. But Melody got pregnant. I don't know what to do."

"George," she said. "Have the baby here in Angels Crest. And let me take care of you for a while. Till you get back on your feet again." She knew Rocksan would kill her. Why was she always doing this, forgetting to talk to her partner before making huge life decisions? It was a bad habit. She'd have to work on that.

"Part of me wants it so bad. But the other part, the part that got left be-hind by you, it just wants to tell you to fuck off."

"I know," Jane said. She felt herself wanting to cry. But she held on tight, trying to keep a lock on her emotions, making everything inside feel en-tombed. "Let's look at it logically. Where are you gonna go?"

"Melody wants to stay."

"Well, she's the boss. You know that, right? The pregnant woman is al-ways the boss."

George smiled, but it was a sad smile, one that seemed to contain all the unspoken things about Jane, about her pregnancy with him, about her be-ing the boss and leaving him behind. She felt like everything was a land mine, that all of her words had the potential to explode. She also thought if she just had some time with him, he'd learn to forgive her.

"Okay," George said. "But Jane . . . I know it sounds like I'm just some dolt from the Midwest. But I have to say, I don't understand this *gay* thing. I don't *want* my mother to be a lesbian."

"George," she said. "I do appreciate your candor. But it's wrong that most of the world thinks we queer folk have a choice in the matter."

"I guess I'm one of them."

"That's fair. But maybe one day you'll come to see that this is who I am. On the most basic level. It's a biology thing, George. I never, ever would have *chosen* a life that only brought me pain. That would have been insane, don't you think?"

George looked at her with skepticism. He was beet red. It occurred to Jane how much he looked like her, right down to the blush. In the moment that passed between them, fraught with all those unspoken things, she felt the kindest love for him, the most ardent love, a love whose nuance she had left behind and forgotten, until now.

ANGIE

When her sister and Jane arrived, Angie saw how troubled they were. She was constantly amazed by her sister and the courage she had. She thought Rocksan was like a superhero. Serious-minded, filled with so many strange quirks, but powerful, especially when it came to making the right decision, in spite of the way she felt about it.

People didn't see that side of her often. They saw a huge man-woman who could be prickly and opinionated. But Rocksan never went back on her word. She could always see the good and admit to it, in spite of her thick and unruly pride.

When Rocksan sat down at the booth with Jane and Jane's son and his pregnant girlfriend, Angie remembered something from that first year, when Rocksan had just arrived in Angels Crest.

She had just started up with the beekeeping nonsense. Angie remembered how people whispered about Jane and Rocksan. They were lesbians. And they were weird lesbians. They kept bees and had a lot of money, they didn't go to church, and they'd bought that acreage way out at the end of town that no one wanted because there was no water, no septic, and it was overrun by wild berries and poison oak and deer and probably haunted, too, by the old man who'd left that giant dilapidated house in ruins.

One day, Angie remembered, Rocksan had come into the diner. She was wearing those silly rubber boots and a pair of too-large man's painter pants. Her Pendleton shirt had holes in it. Her hair hadn't been brushed, and it seemed like she'd been crying. And Angie remembered being embarrassed by her sister. And afraid for her. People were staring. The lesbian beekeeper was

Angie's sister, and Angie thought the people in town would think less of her by association. She knew how awful that was, but she couldn't help herself.

Rocksan had sat down at the counter and had haltingly told Angie some long, rambling story about having to kill one of her queens. Angie could hardly follow the details. And at first, she couldn't understand why Rocksan was so upset. It was just bees. It wasn't even a dog or cat, but a bunch of stinging, flying insects.

But as she listened, she heard what was beneath the story. The humanity in her sister's endeavors. The goodness Rocksan strived for. She saw then her sister's remarkable and decent self. And she understood then that it didn't matter that it was *just bees*. That what Rocksan grieved was something deeper and more profound. That Rocksan saw her humanity as flawed, her decisions and her desires as reckless. She had decimated a hive, and in the process, she had come to face her own humanness, its folly and arrogance.

Now Angie watched her sister. Her manliness was beautiful, her independence and sense of self miraculous. She was a woman, after all, who cried over bees. She had her brood right there—an emotional and unpredictable girlfriend, a young man, his willowy and angelic-looking girlfriend. There would be a child. That was Rocksan's life. A strange and lovely life whatever way it went.

Angie went back behind the counter, checked the creamers and the sugar bins. She filled coffee cups and water glasses and peered into the kitchen. They were working as fast as they could. They were unused to this kind of rush. She felt both relief and annoyance. She would have money left over this month. But at what expense? Ethan's boy was dead and the voyeurs were out in herds. When would this all die down?

Rosie was in the back, asleep on her little cot. She was clutching her penguin doll and someone, maybe one of the cooks, had covered her with a blanket. Angie thought of her own daughter and wondered briefly where she had gone to, if she would ever be coming home.

◆   ◆   ◆

She worked until she couldn't work anymore. She was weary, but also, thinking of Glick, his touch, the tenderness in his eyes, she was filled with a sense of power and purpose. She took Rosie and headed back to her house. They ate lunch and Angie played with Rosie for a while, building a house out of Legos. When they had finished, it looked nothing like a house, but Rosie seemed proud of it.

"Let's go for a drive," Angie said.

"Can I bring something?"

"Like what?"

Rosie looked around the room. The fish were swimming around in their bowl of water. She pointed at them.

"We can't take the fish," Angie said.

"But I want to."

"How about your penguin? And we'll pick up a Foster's Freeze."

Rosie sulked for a moment, but the promise of ice cream, even in the cold, spurred her on. Angie bundled her in a warm coat and mittens and grabbed her purse. She started the car, turned on the heat, and idled for a while in the driveway. A few cars passed by, strangers probably. Reporters, writers, the curious. Overhead, the sky was free of clouds, sparkling blue, but the air was cold, filled with crystals.

She drove over to the Foster's Freeze first and she and Rosie shared an ice cream, the only customers sitting quietly inside under a crude heater that blew hot air into the room. Then she went by the diner and picked up a few rolls, some muffins, a couple of bagels, and butter. After that, she stopped by the market for eggs, cheese, some coffee, and milk. When she had finished, she got in her car and drove out of town toward Glick's house. She knew Ethan was there and would probably be hungry.

With Rosie humming to herself in the car seat, she drove through town, past her diner, which was empty now except for a few people at the counter and the same couple with the laptops at the booth by the window. As she made her way farther and farther out of town, the air grew increasingly misty. The more trees there were, the darker it was, and she drove slowly, enclosed by the branches of the trees as if by arms.

She had not felt her sadness balanced by joy in years. She realized she had grown wary and scarred by the imbalance, by the sense that since her daughter left, her life had filled with such sorrow that she had not been able to make room for anything else. But that was all changed now. Calmed by the mysterious medicine of being loved.

When she finally got to the end of Cage Road, she saw Ethan's truck in front of the house, but not Glick's. The house—more of a cabin really—was shrouded in the shade of the trees. No sky seemed to penetrate. It struck Angie as a remote and sad place. A way station rather than a permanent home. She thought of Glick living here alone. She pictured him in bed at night, a single lamp burning beside him, a Cabela's sporting goods catalog open on his lap, and his loneliness like another person in the darkened room.

She turned off the engine and saw that Rosie had fallen asleep in the backseat. She opened the back door and gently woke her granddaughter. Rosie began to cry because she didn't know where she was, and Angie picked her up and hummed softly into her ear. Slowly, Rosie began to see that she had been dreaming, that she was safe.

"Where are we, Grammie?"

"Glick's house."

"Is that Nate's poppa?" she asked, pointing to the solitary figure of Ethan standing in the shadows of the curtain at the front window.

"Yes," Angie said.

She let Rosie down and they walked hand in hand to the door. In her free hand, she carried the bags of food. Ethan was there to open the door before Angie could knock.

"Does anyone else know I'm here?" he asked. His face was creased with worry and exhaustion. He drank from a beer can, while nearby a cigarette burned in the ashtray.

Angie had only been inside Glick's house once before and she was not surprised that it was neat and orderly. The furniture was, as she remembered, pleasant enough. The house smelled of must, of being closed in. The relative starkness of the place made her want to be with Glick.

"No," Angie said. "I don't think so. Glick told me in private."

"I must be a burden to him," Ethan said.

"I doubt he thinks so."

"I mean as a secret. Harboring me."

Angie carried the food into the kitchen. She had always liked Ethan, had liked his mild-mannered personality, his sense of fairness. But the divorce and the custody battle had been brutal, had taken its toll. He'd changed, turned more inward, seemed short and impatient more often than before. But the idea of him leaving his son in the truck alone all that time just didn't fit. If Angie knew anything about Ethan, she knew he was a careful and thorough man. Slow to make decisions, not prone, like Cindy, to spontaneity or high emotion. Had the events of the past year eroded some of his caution?

She remembered something that had happened about six months after Ethan and Cindy had divorced. It had been just her and Ethan, late one night at the diner, a few days into hunting season last year. He had been working late doing inventory at the hardware store. And though she was closing up the empty diner, she had poured him some coffee anyway when he'd come in.

The custody battle had been under way a few weeks and it was clear that things had turned ugly. Ethan had seemed depressed, which was unusual. He was the steady type. He never showed you his moods. He said he'd gone hunting on opening day, that he'd ended up tracking the same deer for two days. Day and night, sleeping little, eating less. Then on the second day, he'd finally honed in on the deer as it grazed nearby. It was huge, so beautiful, he said, it made him want to cry. He aimed and quickly, before he could think about it, shot the deer. Exhausted, he'd watched the deer collapse into the brush.

"He got his forelegs under him," Ethan said. He was playing with his coffee cup, looking at the counter. "He was dragging his hindquarters. They were all bloodied up, and when I got up to him, his ears moved. He heard me. He knew it was over. I remember the vapors of steam coming from his nose. It was so damn cold."

Angie had been wiping the counter down. The place was deserted. She wanted to go home. She was so tired. She didn't want to hear about the deer. But he kept talking, as if he needed to.

"The deer didn't turn to look at me, and I was glad for that. It had been a wild couple a days. So I got up next to him and I aimed for the lungs and I shot him. For a minute, he tried to rise; he pawed at the ground. His breath came out from his nose, two lines of steam, and it was getting more and more labored. Just before he died, he shuddered and that was it. He was gone."

Angie could not look at Ethan for a long time. She remembered that finally, when she had the courage to look up at him, she saw that he was crying. And she knew then that the only way a hunter could do what he did was both to love his prey and to desire to kill it in equal measure. She saw that Ethan had too much love and not enough killer. She thought then, though she kept it to herself, that he should never hunt again.

"I brought you this food," Angie said now at Glick's, the memory so fresh that she had a difficult time meeting his gaze.

Ethan bowed his head. "Thanks. I can pay you back."

"It's not necessary. I knew you'd be hungry and going to town would be a burden. The newspeople are crawling around all over the place."

"They've made me sound like some stupid hick, some kinda bad father," Ethan said.

"You don't have to worry about them. They're outsiders. We know you."

"Yeah. Try telling that to Cindy."

Angie studied her hands. She saw that there would be no comforting Ethan. He had gone too far into the well.

"Where's Glick?"

"He went to Calvary Church with Cindy to find a minister. I asked him to help me out that way. The funeral is tomorrow. Cindy knows them over there. She likes the blind one."

Angie liked him, too. He came to the diner every day for a grilled cheese sandwich and a side of slaw for lunch. He lived alone. He smiled often and said little. If you were looking for him, you could almost always find him sitting in the records office alone, his face turned toward the old photos that hung there. No one ever seemed to be looking for him. But everyone knew him; everyone felt his presence.

She looked over at Rosie, who was sitting on the couch, playing quietly with her stuffed penguin. She saw that Rosie sensed the gravity of the situation and seemed to understand that she should not interrupt or cause a fuss. She also knew that Rosie had begun to listen to adult conversation, that it made her still and attentive; that she would not dare do anything to jeopardize the sport of being privy to the lurid world of adults.

"That's another reason I came by," Angie said. "After the service, I'd like to serve everyone something to eat over at the diner. Maybe Trevor can bring some liquor over, some wine or something."

"That's nice of you, Angie, but I can't accept it."

"Why not?" Angie felt a moment's irritation. But Ethan was young. His parents were both dead. He'd had enough of death. She saw his pride stretching out before him like a long, narrow road. He said nothing and sat down beside Rosie on the couch. She held her penguin up to him.

"You can play with him if you want," she said.

Ethan took the penguin and held it in his lap. He looked at the stuffed animal's face without expression.

"Look," Angie said. "You *can* accept it. Don't let your pride get in the way. All you need worry about is keeping up your strength."

He nodded his head. Rosie said, "You can borrow my penguin."

He handed it back to her. "No thanks, kiddo," he said. "But it's a nice offer."

Rosie took the stuffed animal back, and Angie saw that she was relieved that Ethan didn't keep it.

"They're gonna arrest me," he said.

"You don't know that."

"It's been on the radio."

"Nothing will come of it, Ethan."

"They're going to make an example of me. A dumb hick father from the high country kills his own boy."

Angie sat down beside Ethan on the couch. She put her arms around him. "You cannot start thinking about the future, planning what you don't know."

He nodded his head. "I killed my boy, Angie. I'm not afraid to pay for it."

Angie nodded. "Let's just get through today and the funeral tomorrow. Let's just take it one step at a time."

Ethan nodded again.

"Please try to eat," Angie said. She gestured toward the kitchen, where she'd put the groceries, and Ethan looked in that direction, but he seemed unable to focus. He reached over and pulled a cigarette from a pack by the ashtray. There was a bottle of whiskey there, too. Angie got the sense that he was waiting for her to leave so he could take a pull from the bottle and light the cigarette.

She took Rosie's hand and left Glick's house. As they neared the car, Rosie said, "Grammie, you're holding my hand too tight."

◆   ◆   ◆

Later that night, after Rosie had gone to sleep, Glick came to the door. Angie opened it for him, and the dog was there, sitting loyally beside him on the stoop. When Angie opened the door wider to let Glick in, the dog walked straight through the kitchen to the back porch.

"Good boy," Glick said.

Angie went to the fridge and pulled out a bottle of wine. She held it up to see if Glick wanted any and he said he'd rather have a beer if she had it. She said she didn't but that there was some brandy in the pantry. She took his silence to mean he'd take that, and she made a mental note to buy some beer for him.

They took their drinks to the bedroom, walking quietly down the hall. Glick, Angie noticed, was mindful of the fact that Rosie was asleep, her door kept slightly ajar. As he walked past, he peered in for a moment and then continued on to Angie's bedroom, his face open and trusting. It was something Angie had not seen before.

Angie closed the door, and within seconds, the two of them were kissing. She tried hard not to let Glick see how fiercely she'd fallen for his touch, his taste, for the things he said, the way he said them. She tried to keep her breathing simple. Embarrassed by her passion, she made an outward attempt to keep herself from showing it. But her body's response, absent of sentiment and attitude, could not lie. When Glick touched her inside her panties, he looked into her eyes and smiled.

"So it's not just me," he said.

She felt herself blushing—that her body could betray her so—and she turned away.

Later, they lay quietly in bed and said nothing for the longest time. Then Glick turned to her and he said, "Cindy wanted that blind preacher at the funeral service."

"Yeah?"

"He said he'd do it. Walk back into the woods if we helped him."

"He's kind. Quiet, I guess."

"Better than that other one."

Angie nodded. She knew he meant Brother Powell, though she was not a churchgoing woman herself. She knew Brother Powell—he liked his coffee with four sugars and double the cream—and she always shied away from his joviality and forced sincerity.

Angie could hear the wind howling through the trees. She thought it meant another storm was blowing in. For a minute, she flashed on the winter of 1889, when the town was snowed in and all those people—except for the babies—had died. Then Glick touched her gently on the arm. He lifted up and looked into her eyes.

"I want to tell you everything," he said.

She pushed the hair back from his face. His eyes were so clear, so blue, that when she looked into them, she felt as if she were seeing something inexhaustible. She watched his pupils change in increments, widening and closing imperceptibly in size, smaller, then larger, then smaller again.

"It seems like I know it all already. Somehow," she said.

"What I'm saying, I think, is that I want someplace to store all the details. Someplace other than my own head."

For some reason, she could not think what to say next. She felt like she also had too many words, too much to say. She leaned back and took a sip of her wine. "I was at your house today. I gave Ethan some food and told him that we could use the diner after the funeral to feed the guests."

"He told me you were there."

"I felt like I was seeing your house for the first time. I saw you in it, the way of your life, all these years. And I felt something inside me. I wanted to take you away from that."

"I love that house," Glick said.

"Don't get me wrong. It has a beauty to it. But it's much too lonesome."

"You think?" Glick said.

"You can feel the sadness there."

Glick said nothing for the longest time. Angie felt like she might have stepped on his toes. Maybe she had presumed something about him that was wrong, and she feared she might have offended him. But Glick rolled over to face her and he said, "I've only known that emptiness. That's all since they arrested me and threw me in prison all those years ago. I can't tell you, either way, if it's sad inside that house. I am so used to living a certain way, even here, where it's warm, I find myself missing it."

She nodded her head. "It may not seem like it, but I understand. I know what you mean."

"I might sell it someday," he said.

Angie heard the future in his words. She felt the longing and the desire unfurling, and the tight, closed-up way she'd held it all inside her since her daughter left. It felt as if a fist were unclenching inside her. Everything opening up.

CINDY

———◆———

Cindy's apartment was close and smelled thickly of cigarettes. They were watching TV. Some of the drunks from the bar were on-screen, talking to reporters. Trevor stood up then and looked at Cindy.

"I need to put a stop to this."

She nodded. But in a way, she didn't care. It was all bad and it just kept getting worse. Nothing seemed able to get under her skin. Maybe the liquor had finally kicked in. People were going to talk about her and Ethan and Nate and there would be speculation and finger-pointing. That was the way it was. This was her life now.

"You going to the church to find that preacher?" Trevor asked.

She nodded. She smoked. She drank. She remembered the time Ethan had called her a slow suicide.

"Do you want me to take you? I could drop you off there and come back and get you. Or send someone for you."

"No," she said. "I want to take a bath. And you're gonna have your hands full with all them losers talking to the media."

She didn't want to tell him she was meeting Glick. She knew that even though her son was dead, he would be jealous and he would want to talk about it. That's just how he was. But she also forgave him. He loved her. And he was the only one here now. He had loved her all her life. She saw the dignity in him, the unwavering devotion. She felt grateful for that at least.

"Wait a minute now, Cindy. Those *losers* are your friends."

"You think? Then how come they aren't here, comforting me? Why are they opening their big drunk mouths to that pack of wolves?"

"You gotta be fair," Trevor said.

"Do I?"

Trevor put his coat on. He walked over to her and kissed her on the cheek.

"I'll be back later. Don't answer the door."

She nodded. When he had gone, she stood up, and after the dizziness passed, she made her way to the bathroom and turned on the tub faucet. She made the water as hot as she could stand it and then sank down into the steam as though she were being lifted on a cloud and taken away. She closed her eyes and hummed a song that she used to hum to Nate. She was so drunk that she nearly slipped and fell getting out of the tub. The hot water had made her woozy, the liquor traveling through her faster that way.

She dressed warmly and got her parka and a hat from the hall closet. When she stepped outside, she was stunned for a minute by how cold it was. She realized her apartment was overheated and she thought the cold air would help loosen the logy, druggy feeling in her head. She walked down the stairs to the carport and watched as two reporters emerged from a parked car. When they caught up to her, one of them—a man in his thirties, inappropriately dressed for the cold—said, "Mind if I ask you a few questions?"

"Yeah, I mind," she said.

"Did you see your son when they brought him out of the woods?"

"Why don't you all go back to your caves?" she said.

"Did you know they plan to arrest your husband?" This from the lady reporter with the high-healed black boots and fur-lined parka.

"Lady," Cindy said. "My son just died. You wanna show me a little respect here?"

"When is the funeral service?" the man asked.

By then, Cindy had made it to her car. She got inside and pulled away. She saw that she had clipped the man, that he'd had to step back out of the way because she was so close to running him down. Her hands shaking, her heart thumping inside her chest, she reached over and pulled a pack of cigarettes out of the glove compartment. She noticed the shiny tip of her flask. She lit her cigarette and, with one hand on the steering wheel, she checked the flask, but it was empty.

When she got to the Calvary Church, Glick was already there. He was waiting inside his truck and the windows were fogged up. She got out of the car and ran up to his window and rapped on the glass.

"I feel like I might be going crazy," she said. She was shaking so, she could hardly keep standing. She felt like her knees would buckle beneath her.

"It's okay," Glick said.

They walked into the church together. Outside the church, on the blacktop, kids in blue-and-white uniforms were bundled up in coats, playing kickball.

"Nate was going here. He'd just started preschool," she said.

"I know," Glick said. He put his hand on the small of her back and guided her through the church. There were no images of Jesus anywhere, only a gaudy gold cross over the pulpit, where Brother Powell gave his sermons. In a way, it looked more like a high school gym than a church. They walked to the back, where there was a series of doors down a long hallway.

"I ought to start going back to church," Cindy said. She always said that whenever she was inside of one. Then, when she left, she always forgot about it.

They walked down the hallway and Cindy said, "I want that blind guy. Brother Johns, I think his name is. The old guy."

Glick nodded. "Maybe we should go over to the records office."

Just as she was about to agree, Brother Powell walked up. He took Cindy's hand and looked into her eyes for a very long time. She was uncomfortable. She saw the phoniness in the way he held her hand, gazed into her eyes. When his eyes filled with tears, she wanted to smack him across the face. She felt vulgar and spiteful. Nate's death had turned her into a monster.

"I know it sure doesn't feel like it now, but the Lord walks beside you," he said.

Fuck the Lord, she thought. I don't need the Lord walking beside me. I want my son back. But she bowed her head anyway and then wondered why she was so obsequious with the preacher even though she knew he was so full of the Lord that his head might bust. She wondered whether Brother Powell could smell the liquor on her breath. He seemed so sly, so knowing. She remembered how he was always lurking around whenever she had brought Nate to school. How she always avoided him. She remembered how he had told her that God didn't love a sinner. For a moment, she thought he could look into her soul and find all the sin there.

"We wanted to speak to Brother Johns," Glick said.

"Well, I'm sure I can help you with whatever you need," Brother Powell said. His voice was so sugary, so *kind*, but Cindy heard the edge of annoyance there, too. She understood that he knew why they were there and what they wanted. She knew he would do whatever he could to circumvent their wishes, that he wanted to officiate. There was a celebrity, however crass, to her son's death. She understood that he wanted in on it.

"No," Glick said. "We wanted to speak to Brother Johns."

"Well, he isn't here now," said Brother Powell, letting the irritation slip into his words. But then his voice changed and he spoke softly, convincingly kind. He said, "Please. Come in to my office. I want to help."

Cindy was about to follow him, but Glick said, "No thanks. We want to speak to Brother Johns."

Then he took Cindy and turned her around and walked her out of the office. They walked the length of this church that looked more like a high school gym except for its garish gold cross, and when they stepped outside, Cindy felt as though she'd been holding her breath underwater for a long time, that now she could breathe. She felt relieved that her obligation to be kind to Brother Powell, on account of her son, was over. Without Nate enrolled in preschool anymore, she realized she would no longer have to kiss Brother Powell's ass or walk the other way whenever she saw him.

"C'mon," Glick said.

He guided her into his truck, drove to town, and parked at the records office. Cindy followed him inside. It was stuffy and overwarm. She unzipped her jacket as Glick walked over to where all those photos of the town's first residents were hanging on the wall, and there on one of the benches was the old blind preacher. He was leaning on his cane, as if listening to something. The expression on his face was sublime. Cindy wondered if he heard angels singing.

"Brother," Glick said. He cleared his throat. Cindy felt it, too, something holy in the man's presence. She wanted a drink. She realized that whenever she thought too much about God, she wanted to drink. Her hands shook and she craved the life she'd had before, seeing that now it was a much better life than she had once thought.

"Brother Johns?" Glick said.

"Yes," he said. He turned in Glick's direction. "Who's there?"

"It's Rusty Glick. And Nate's mom, Cindy."

The old man nodded his head. He did not speak any platitudes. He offered no condolences.

"What can I do for you?" he asked.

"Brother Johns," Cindy said. "We were wondering if you could say a few words at Nate's funeral tomorrow. It's in the woods. Where they found him. It's a long walk."

The preacher said nothing for a long time. He appeared to be looking at the pictures on the wall. But you could see that he was blind, that his pupils were glassy and opaque. They were a mild shade of blue. Cindy looked at the pictures and she saw the people dressed in their nineteenth-century clothing, the piles of snow everywhere, the photograph of the babies who had survived the storm of 1889, and then the one where years later they had all posed as adults. She saw the black-and-white photograph of Angels Crest. She choked back a sob.

"Do you believe the story about the angels saving those kids back in the day?" Cindy heard herself asking him.

The old man smiled. "I like to believe it. It helps me feel calm, thinking there're angels protecting us."

Cindy sat down on the bench beside the old man and felt things closing up and getting darker. She wondered why the angels didn't save her son. As if sensing it somehow, Brother Johns reached over and found her hand. It was warm and she felt comforted by his touch.

"I can be there at the funeral if you want. I'm not the flashy sort, if that's what you're looking for," he said. "And I'm an old man. I'll have to depend on your help to get me there."

Glick said, "Of course. I'll take care of it."

The preacher still appeared to be listening for something. Or to something that neither Cindy nor Glick could hear.

"I don't know why God does what He does," the preacher said. "That is the riddle of my belief. To love God in spite of earthly pain and suffering."

"It's hard for me," Cindy said, "to believe there're any angels flying around."

"I understand," the preacher said. "Let nothing upset you now. Let nothing frighten you."

"I am so afraid," Cindy said. She felt the words coming out, the sharp edge to them, the way they pained her to speak them.

"Everything is changing. God alone is changeless," the preacher said.

"I wish I believed, Brother," Cindy said.

He nodded his head. He was still holding her hand. She felt how dry and warm it was. She wished she could stay there with him and just stare at the pictures. Say nothing for the rest of her life. Just live in a room filled with other people's histories.

"Thank you," Glick said. "We oughta go."

Cindy stood up. The world seemed to grow narrow and distant. She turned to Glick, standing up and turning her back on the preacher. There was too much not spoken. Too much she couldn't understand.

"Drop me off at the bar," she said to Glick as they walked out of the records office. "And tell Ethan I did what he wanted me to do."

JUDGE JACK ROSENTHAL

———————◆———————

He woke up, startled that he'd napped. It was dark and he looked at the clock. Six-thirty P.M. He sat up and gazed at the outlines of things—the couch where he lay, the curtains, shut against the chilly night, and, farther away, the dining room table with the two candlesticks in the center. He felt cold and reached for the throw at the end of the couch. He put it over himself and lay there quietly, listening to the clock tick and nothing else.

He had an image of his own body, as if he were looking at himself from above. He saw how thin he had become, the places his skin sagged. He remembered a time when he was strong and his joints didn't ache. He had a sense of his bones, their seeming fragility. He thought that if he fell hard enough, he would snap in two.

After a while, he got up and went to the kitchen to fix something to eat. He was surprised at how he had apparently caved in to ennui and listlessness. He knew that this was a sign of depression.

He went to the cupboard and pulled a can of soup out. He found the can opener in a drawer and opened the soup, pouring it and some water into a pan. He turned the heat on low, then retrieved some bread from the pantry and made toast, eating it before the soup had warmed. When the soup was done, he poured it into a mug and sipped it quietly in the darkened kitchen.

He looked outside and saw nothing but the blackness of early winter. How bare and empty it seemed. He thought again about moving to the desert. He wondered if the warm sun would make him happier. He remembered seeing the desert in bloom once. At first, he'd been disappointed because somehow he'd expected more. But the desert's beauty, he had learned, was in the minutiae of its details. Once, on a long walk in Joshua Tree, he'd found a small seashell on the desert floor. He'd picked it up and put it in his pocket.

Now he stood up and went to his bedroom. Beside his bed was a glass container filled with buttons and pennies and a few small slips of paper, fortunes from fortune cookies and phone numbers of people he no longer remembered. Pressed against the glass, facing outward, was a wallet-size picture of Marty, shot just after high school, before the drugs had taken over.

Jack opened the container and dug around until he found the desert seashell. He remembered that in the years since he'd found the shell, he would occasionally sift through the container looking for it and how, whenever he'd find it, he'd feel a deep sense of happiness, of relief. He never understood the pleasure it gave him, but now holding the seashell, which had survived millions of years, from a time when all the deserts were once underwater, brought him a sense of calm. He saw in it the permanence of life, the forgiveness of a God who allowed life to perpetuate, even after you died and were gone.

Now he held the seashell and thought of his boys, not as they were now but the way they were when they were small. He remembered before they were born, how he had wanted children because he thought they would ward off his fears of death. He believed that because they would live on after he died, somehow his own death would seem less frightening.

But after they had been born, he remembered fearing death even more. What if he died and left them without a father? Worse, what if one of them died? It made him afraid, and he would pray fervently, *Please, God, don't let us die.* He remembered thinking, after his first son was born, that parenthood was the hardest job in the world, not just because it was physically taxing but also because it made your vulnerabilities so much more pronounced.

He thought of Ethan Denton out there in Angels Crest somewhere, trying to understand how this had happened. Trying to understand that his son was dead. He knew there would be an arrest any day now. He put his head in his hands and thought of his own son. He kept thinking, At least Marty isn't dead. And yet, he could find no place inside himself to forgive his son.

He knew that to be human meant to walk on a narrow bridge; that the spiritually mature person could do so without fear. But the truth was that the world was full of woes. How did you reconcile suffering with a just God? It seemed suddenly insurmountable. A chasm opening up before him, stretching wider and wider in the darkness.

GLICK

———◆———

That morning, before the funeral, Glick woke up, and there was Rosie standing beside him, staring into his eyes.

"Grammie," she said, still staring at Glick, "why is he in bed with you?"

Angie sat upright, pulling the covers over her naked body.

"Shit," she said.

"You swore," Rosie said.

"Rosie, go out into the kitchen and wait for me."

"Did he get lost?" she asked.

Glick was speechless. He continued to stare back at Rosie. He looked briefly over at Angie as she struggled into her nightgown, which had fallen to the floor the night before. Her face was nervous and filled with worry. He wanted to disappear. It must be so hard to be a child, he thought. To be this child.

"No, honey," Angie said. "He's not lost." She seemed to know that Rosie would not go to the kitchen. Glick in her grandma's bed was far too dramatic to leave behind. So Angie tried another tack. She reached across the bed, her arms open, beckoning her granddaughter. "Come over here," she said. Her voice had turned calm and her face had smoothed out. Glick was amazed. What stunning powers of patience and transformation. He was bewitched by her. But then he remembered he was naked beneath these covers. What would Rosie have made of his nakedness had she seen it?

Rosie went over to Angie's side of the bed. Angie brushed Rosie's hair back from her forehead and whispered something into her ear. Rosie appeared suddenly extremely serious, as if Angie had just given her a very important job. She nodded and walked out of the room, stiff-legged, dragging her stuffed penguin.

"Goddamn," Glick said.

"It's okay."

"Feels bad."

Angie nodded. "She was bound to find out."

"It's too soon."

Angie cast her eyes down toward the blankets.

"I didn't mean because I have some reservations about you and me. I meant because it's too soon for her," Glick said. "And I'm naked underneath these blankets."

Angie smiled. He saw that she was relieved. "Look," she said. "I've made it a practice not to buckle just because it feels bad."

"So, what will you tell her?"

Angie got out of bed and put her robe on. "I don't know. I'll certainly have to tell her we're going to a funeral today. I can't decide what's gonna be the hardest, that or us."

"Maybe I should leave," Glick said.

"Maybe," she said, looking at him sharply, "you ought to stay and have some coffee. Skulking out she knows. Her mother did the same damn thing."

Glick nodded. It was the first time in all the years he had known Angie that she'd mentioned her daughter. He knew to do what she asked.

"Angie," he said.

She looked over at him, and instantly he saw all the tenderness he could want in her eyes. There was freedom in the mercy there, liberty in the calm. He felt all of his anxiety drift away.

"I got to tell you . . ."

She kissed him on the lips. "Save it for later," she whispered. "Save it till tonight."

He nodded. "I'll be right out, then," he said.

He lay in bed for a while longer. It was going to be hard to face that little girl. He thought of Nate, running through the woods so fast and hard that he wore the bottoms of his footie pajamas away. He remembered, suddenly, the gun he'd use to kill deer every year. He thought of his cats, sitting quietly on the dresser, watching the solitary movements of his last ten years. He saw an intricate and puzzling web of all the things in his life, the conundrum of loving a dog and shooting a deer, yearning for love and turning it away at every opportunity, of yielding and keeping at bay. How could a man live a life of such conflict and not go mad? How had he done it all these years? How, he wondered, did you go about making a new life, a life both straight and pliant as a reed?

He stood up and walked to the window. The warmth inside the house had made the windows fog at the corners. Outside, the morning was just beginning to shed its light. He saw in the angle of the sun, the shape of the wind, the high white clouds that it was going to snow. The world was quiet and leaning into itself. He felt something stir in his heart. He knew that he'd been asking why for far too long.

In the kitchen, Rosie and Angie were talking quietly, huddled together, a little team of females. They both raised their heads when Glick walked in. Rosie was stern and unforgiving, but Angie smiled warmly.

"Rosie says she doesn't like you," Angie said.

Rosie folded her arms defiantly.

"Well then," Glick said. "Maybe she'll like the dog."

Rosie looked at Angie with suspicion, as if Angie had been holding out on her and was really a member of the enemy's team. But clearly Angie had forgotten about the dog, who no doubt was waiting patiently, like an old Buddha, by the back door.

"He's on the porch," Angie said.

Rosie looked at Glick. "Go on, then," Glick said. "He won't bite you."

Slowly, Rosie stood up, dragging her penguin by the neck toward the back porch. She looked back once to make it clear that she had no patience for a ruse. Angie laughed quietly.

"Did she really say she didn't like me?"

Angie nodded.

"Jesus. How do you make a kid like you?"

"You show up for them," she said softly. "Every minute of every day, even when you want to stay in bed with the blankets over your head."

Glick nodded. He understood what he was being told. He saw the clear, sharp way that Angie looked at him. He knew that if pressed, she would make a choice and that the girl would win. He realized he was being asked to make a choice himself. They heard Rosie squealing with delight.

"That dog licked my face," Rosie shouted gleefully.

"Oh God," Angie said. "Please tell me he doesn't shed."

"No can do," Glick said. "But I got a way with a vacuum."

Later, they ate breakfast. The dog was granted the privilege of sitting at Glick's side. Rosie tried to feed him some toast, but Glick told her gently that a dog could get used to being spoiled and it was best to keep him a little bit hungry. She nodded gravely, and when it was time to go, Angie buttoned the collar around Glick's coat and said, "She likes that you talk to her like she's an adult."

"Isn't she?"

"Sometimes it seems like it, doesn't it?"

They stood together for a moment before Angie opened the door. The sun shone harshly into the entryway, filling it with yellow winter light.

"Wow," Angie said. "What a glorious day."

"It's gonna snow," Glick said.

"I doubt that."

He nodded. He knew he was right. He was always right when it came to the weather. He didn't bother to prove it to anyone anymore. "Should I pick you up for the funeral?" Glick asked.

"Everyone will know then."

"They're gonna have to know sometime."

"But it's Nate's funeral."

"All right. Let's leave it go for now."

"Besides," Angie said, "I gotta get things ready at the diner. I'll just meet you up there."

Glick kissed her. He felt like he would never have enough of her. He knew that, like the dog, he would probably always go a little hungry around her. That it would be better that way.

He got in his truck, and after he warmed the engine, he took off for his home on Cage Road. The roads were nearly deserted, but he had begun to recognize the cars that belonged to the reporters. They were newer than most everyone's in town. They were big, shiny SUVs that cost more than most people's yearly wages.

When he passed Angie's, he looked inside and saw the melancholy of its empty booths and tables. Angie was late opening up. He wondered if she'd ever been late before. Then he realized she was probably not going to open it, as a sign of respect for those in mourning. He saw the sheriff walk up and try the doors. From the vantage of his rearview mirror, he watched the sheriff peer inside the diner.

When he got home, Ethan was on the couch, as if he had never moved from that place. He seemed so huge, so lumbering in the room, as if his grief had built him up and made him larger than he really was. At the same time, something within him seemed smaller, depleted. Siphoned out by the experience of having to feel this bad every second of every day.

"Did you sleep much?" Glick asked.

Ethan shook his head. "Who you shackin' up with?" he said.

"I'm staying over at Angie's."

Ethan raised his eyebrows but said nothing. After a long silence, he said, "I heard on the radio they plan to arrest me today."

It was Glick's turn to say nothing. He went to the kitchen. The cats came up and rubbed themselves against his legs, purring and meowing.

"Cats fed?"

"No," Ethan said.

Glick fed them and then went to the bathroom to shower and shave. He put on a pair of clean jeans and a fresh shirt. Already, the clouds were lining up in the sky. It was the opening day of deer season. He remembered his premonition, that he might never hunt deer again. He wondered if Ethan knew what day it was. As if reading his mind, Ethan said, "You know, back in the day, we'da been out there for hours, maybe already bagged a deer each."

"Seems like such a long time ago," Glick said.

"Yeah," Ethan said.

His voice was wistful. It caught in his throat. Glick sat down beside Ethan on the couch. From the window, he saw the dog digging in the snow.

He realized there was no single answer to any one thing. That life never of-fered up single answers.

"I'm sorry for everything. I know it's probably the last thing on your mind right now, but I want you to know I'm sorry for what I did with Cindy," Glick said.

At first, Ethan looked at him with a blank, slightly confused stare. Then he nodded.

"It's water under the bridge," Ethan said. "Cindy drank too much. She raised her hand to our boy too much. I had to find a way out. I guess it was as good a one as any."

"I'm still sorry. Somehow I just believed I wasn't accountable to anyone after they locked me up for something I never did."

"I can see how you might feel that way."

"I know it seems small compared to what's happening now. But I wanted you to know."

Ethan put his hand on Glick's shoulder. "It's all right, buddy."

Glick stood up. He was uncomfortable about all this. It seemed wrong suddenly. Though he hadn't been searching for consolation, somehow Ethan had seemed to think that was what he was after. He wanted to tell Ethan that he didn't need forgiveness. He had just wanted to set things right. Why, he wondered, was life so uncomfortable?

"You should get showered up, Ethan. We need to get an early start. I gotta pick up that old blind preacher."

"Why'd she want that guy?"

"I don't really know," Glick said. "But next to the other one . . ."

"Lesser of two . . ."

"He's got something . . ."

"I don't believe in that shit. It's mostly for her. And the kid. You know."

Glick nodded. "There's a clean towel somewhere. Let me find it for you."

He was glad to have something to do. He knew how much Ethan hated anything to do with church, with God. With Jesus especially. He wasn't sure why, except that Ethan had always been opposed to organized things, to creeds and doctrines. He was a forest guy, where the rules were unspoken but obvious. Which made it seem all the more impossible that he'd left his son in the truck alone. He would have known better.

While Ethan showered, Glick went outside to the meadow behind his house. The morning was still and he could feel the storm in his bones. The white pine and Douglas fir around his property were capped with snow, the higher branches laboring under the added weight.

In his travels through the mountains, he had seen white pine that grew over fifty feet. He remembered one spring he'd backpacked alone into the wilds, hiking alongside a creek that was so fresh, he drank from it without boiling the water or filtering it. One afternoon, while ambling along a swift-moving stream, he ran into a black bear. They were not ten feet apart. The bear stood up on its hind legs, and it was so startled it seemed unable to find him, to focus on him. Then, the bear turned abruptly and ran into the woods and disappeared. Glick's heart had filled with a strange hum, the twin emotions of fear and exhilaration. He had felt a sense of purpose and hope, and for a moment he had been unable to walk on. His throat had tightened and tears had sprung to his eyes, though he felt foolish for the rush of emotion and its power.

Now he felt the weight of Ethan's grief and the impact of Nate's death not just on himself but on the entire town. He saw how solitary his life had been, how unaccountable he'd made himself to the world around him, to the people he'd walked beside every day. He remembered the bear he'd stumbled across in the woods and that moment of exhilaration he'd felt. He recognized it now as connection. Though he hadn't understood it then, he knew now that finding kinship with the bear had been his first sense of belonging to something larger than the prison of his loneliness and his bitterness.

As Glick looked out at his land, the dog ran from the woods gleefully and slowed down as he neared him, wagging his tail, his tongue lolling out. Glick recognized joy in the dog's eyes. Everything was new and different. Not the dog's joy—that, he had noticed since he'd rescued the mutt. What was new was the acknowledgment that for so long he had failed to look for the same thing in another human being.

When Ethan had finished his shower, Glick told him to dress warmly and wear a good pair of boots. Ethan looked at Glick and said, "You always did think you were the only one around here who could predict the weather."

Glick smiled. "You were always wrong, seems to me."

Ethan put on his coat and a hat and gloves. Glick watched as he picked up his cigarettes and the lighter and slid them into his pocket. He pulled out some quarters and looked at them before putting them back in his pocket. At the truck, he said good-bye to the dog with a sad kind of earnestness as he climbed inside.

"They're gonna arrest me at the funeral."

"They aren't gonna arrest you at all, Ethan. You didn't break the law. You made a mistake."

"I heard it on the radio. The DA in the city's gone and filed charges. Criminal negligence. I never heard of that."

"Let's just see what happens."

"I deserve it. You don't go leaving your kid in the damn truck on a cold morning. It's just plain stupid thinking. What the hell was I thinking?"

Glick could find nothing to say, because all that came to his head would only make the wound more salty. He thought that Ethan was young and had too much to think about: the hardware store, the divorce, the custody battle, a young son. He thought that Ethan sometimes forgot he was a father, no matter how good a dad he was. But he also thought that Ethan was guileless. Glick thought that Ethan didn't need any more punishment than the punishment inside his own head, the having to live with himself for the rest of his life.

They drove through town and the sky grew darker. The roads were busy now and people were going about their business. Glick drove to the Calvary Church, and the blind preacher was standing on the curb, wearing a dark dressy coat and leather gloves. His hat was lined with fur and he wore a collar and dress pants, though, Glick was relieved to see, his shoes were sturdy.

"Will you look at that?" Ethan said.

"He's gonna freeze out there."

"I swear just looking at him has my gut in knots."

Glick knew what Ethan meant. It was the kindness in his formality. The serenity and the way his posture spoke of the grief. It was the way the old man seemed to take it all so seriously, as if he knew the depths of Ethan's pain.

"That's gonna kill me, Glick. I swear," Ethan said. He began to cry, and Glick slowed down while Ethan tried unsuccessfully to pull himself together. "Goddamn," Ethan said. "This is fucking surreal. This just ain't happening."

"Okay. That's okay, now," Glick said. He heard the discomfort in his voice. He felt so awkward, so ridiculous, his big clumsy manners always getting in the way of being comforting and decent. He felt like a caricature of a man. A stupid, bumbling fool. He slowed down and stopped the truck. He got out and walked up to the preacher.

"Morning," the old man said.

"Morning," Glick said. He took the preacher by the elbow and guided him to the truck. He helped him inside, aware of how slight and thin the man was, how frail, how near the end of his life.

ETHAN

All the way to the mountains, he would weep intermittently and the preacher would pat him gently on the knee in a fatherly way, in a way his own father had never done. As they neared the clearing where it all began, on this first day of deer season, Ethan closed his eyes and he saw his life pass before him, the slow innocence of his childhood, his mother's death, the depth of his father's sorrow, meeting Cindy, falling in and out of love with her, the birth of his son. This last, of all things, the most miraculous moment in his life.

He thought of Nate and how he had wanted to teach his boy to hunt. He thought of his love for the forest, the way the hunt and the woods all came together to form something perfect for him. He thought of all the adventures he'd planned for his boy, now stilled. Quieted by Nate's death.

Now, on the morning of his son's funeral, he knew he would never hunt again, that he could never again find solace in the woods. The loss of his son was also the loss of all the things he had loved. No longer would the forest represent this sanctity. Now he could not look at its solitude without thinking of his son's death.

Glick parked the truck at the clearing. No one was there and no one would arrive for a while. It reminded Ethan of that first day after Nate had gone missing, how he had been searching in the woods alone and then all of a sudden people were everywhere. Now the sky filled with ominous clouds and he saw that Glick was right: It would snow soon. He worried for a minute about the people who would show up at the service, how they would fare with the hardship of hiking out to that place where he had hammered the cross into the ground.

"You're never wrong, Glick," he said. "It's going to snow."

Glick nodded. Ethan turned to the preacher. "Do you feel all right? Can you make the hike? It could take an hour there and the same coming back. Shorter maybe on the return."

"Is it uphill to start?" the preacher asked.

Ethan nodded. "This was the old trailhead to Angels Crest. Took a good day's climb from here to get to the top, and that's if you weren't carrying anything."

"Uh-huh," said the preacher. "I once knew these woods like the back of my hand."

"They built a new trailhead. Farther up by a few thousand feet. They built a wide trail. On a good day, it'd probably take only a few hours. Right?" Ethan said, turning to Glick.

Glick nodded. Ethan was comforted by the fact that none of them made a move to leave the truck. That their politeness kept what they were here to do at bay. Glick said, "It isn't as pretty. And it gets too crowded in the summer."

"Uh-huh," said the preacher. "Course, I haven't been up here in years."

"Did you grow up in this town?" Ethan asked.

The old man turned to him, and Ethan saw the strange transparent bluish color of his eyes, how beautiful they were, how muted and empty. "Yes. Of course. I've lived here all my life," he said. "I was born here."

"Oh?" Glick said. "Where?"

"That old house at the end of town. With the meadow."

"On Cage Road?" Glick asked.

"Yes sir," said the man.

"That's my house," Glick said.

"Well, I'll be," said the man. Then he nodded his head a few times. He patted Ethan's knee. He said, "My great-great-grandfather was born that terrible winter in 1889 that killed most everyone. Back then, it wasn't called Cage Road. There wasn't a name at all. And the original house burned down in 1925."

"Was your great-great grandfather . . ." Ethan said. But he could not go on. He did not want to know. He recalled the town's legend, how the angels saved the children from death. In a weird way, he'd always believed it. It was as much a part of town as Angie's and the town records office. As much a part of the place as the mountains themselves. But now he had to stop and think about it. If there were angels up there, why did they not save his boy?

"He was one of the five children to live that year," the old man said, answering Ethan's unasked question. "I go to the records office because I remember a time when I could see his picture up there on the wall. Before the blindness set in."

Glick and Ethan exchanged glances. Ethan wondered if Glick could see how much he hurt. Glick said, "I can't believe you were born in my house."

The old man nodded. "It was always a solitary place. I always felt lonesome way out there. I couldn't wait to leave it. When I moved to town, I finally felt free."

◆ ◆ ◆

Ethan was the last out of the truck. He saw how the snow had come and changed the place, had made it new again and destroyed the evidence left behind of the search. He saw how pristine and stunning it was and he slipped, for a moment, into the past. He saw the glory that had been his life, the wide-open beauty of it, the hardships, the simplicity even when, back then, it had seemed so complicated and difficult. The beauty of the world made him feel, for a brief moment, like a man who had been delivered of all that had ever hurt or wounded him. The land, capped by snow and the splendor of winter, stretched out before him, miraculous and unparalleled in its breadth and beauty. He saw himself floating above it all, his son in his arms, flying farther and farther away while the snowy world below disappeared from sight.

ROCKSAN

Rocksan woke to the glare of the winter sun bursting through the opening in the curtains, a long sliver of light falling across the bed, across their bodies. Jane was awake beside her, and when Rocksan stirred, Jane put her arms around her. Jane weighed just over a hundred pounds, though her emotions made her seem so much more formidable.

"The funeral's today," Jane said, the sleep still in her voice.

Rocksan nodded. She had heard, the way you do in small towns, that the funeral was this morning. Those who wanted to make the mile or so trek into the woods to the spot where Nate had died so they could mourn were welcome. It seemed to Rocksan that only folks in a town like Angels Crest would find a funeral in the snowy woods standard, even customary.

She thought of those kids—well, they weren't really kids—asleep down the hall in the spare room. She thought of Melody, and her giant belly. She thought of Jane's son—his surliness, his anger, but also that sad, fawning need. She understood it well. She wanted to tell him it wasn't worth a lifetime of holding on to. But she still hadn't let go of her own anger, so what was the point? She was lost to the ways of releasing it. She just wasn't the therapy type. Or the yoga type. Or the Zen type. She couldn't imagine sitting cross-legged and moaning to find serenity.

"I guess the kids will stay here while we go to the funeral," Jane said.

"I hope Melody doesn't burst. They'd have no way of getting to the hospital."

Jane nodded. "It's a worry for sure. I'm guessing we oughta come up with some kind of plan."

Rocksan thought of a screaming baby in that back room. Hadn't she left San Francisco to get away from the stress, the complications, the *need* that others always had? Wasn't this counter to all her carefully laid plans? Retirement in peace. The woods, the clean air. No crap from the past. Why couldn't she just get the hell away from it? She'd come up here to this hick town near nowhere and yet life had still managed to follow her.

"So where do you think they'll go after the baby's born?" Rocksan asked. It made her heart race even bringing it up. She was losing her balls as she got older. She was turning into a little old biddy.

Jane quickly got out of bed and started walking to the bathroom. Very casually, too damn casually, Jane said, "I thought maybe they'd stay here."

Then she went into the bathroom and closed the door.

Rocksan shot up out of bed. She could feel her eyes bulging. She followed Jane into the bathroom. Jane was standing at the sink, clutching it. Rocksan felt her anger creeping up all over her body, on the inside. The boiling blood. It was so familiar. She hated it. She detested it. She was so tired of being so mad all the time. She thought of her sister then, the way Angie seemed to pull something from deep down, some mysterious resource that kept her from being mad, that kept her from hating the world. Rocksan looked at her reflection in the mirror, and her father's face, with its anger and arrogance, stared back at her. In that instant, she saw that she had become him. She had somehow siphoned up his spirit from the dead and made it her own.

"It's probably best if you lie to me on this next question," she said to Jane, her voice so carefully measured that it frightened even her.

Jane nodded. Her face had gone pale.

"Did you already invite them to stay, without talking to me first?"

Jane looked at her hands, which were gripping the sink. Rocksan looked, too, and saw that her knuckles had turned white, the tips of her fingers bloodred. Jane never looked back up at Rocksan again. Rocksan turned and walked out of the bathroom. She walked as far as the door to their bedroom. She thought of her father and the way he had just left with no explanation. She wanted to do the same thing. She wanted to leave all the ropes that lashed her to the earth, to this life with her crazy lover and her pissed-off son and his pregnant girlfriend. But she hated her father so much that she did not want to give his goddamned dead spirit the satisfaction of having won, of having completely commandeered her life. So she turned around and she said, "They can stay a month. That's it."

Later, they were downstairs drinking coffee when Jane looked up, startled, and opened her mouth as if to say something. But then she went back to her coffee, saying nothing at all. Rocksan finished her coffee and was about to leave the table, when Jane said, "Last night, George and Melody were on the couch in the dark. I heard Melody say, 'You gotta live as though you're gonna die tomorrow.' "

"In that whispery voice?"

Jane nodded.

"Are we scared of her?"

Jane smiled. "I don't think so."

"She's like a butterfly or something," Rocksan said. "Like something light and translucent floating on the air."

"Wings," Jane said quietly.

Just then, George came bounding down the stairs. It occurred to Rocksan that there was something puppylike about him. He had a wild sort of energy, untamed and reckless-seeming.

"Melody says she feels too tired to do anything," George said. "I think we're getting close. I don't know how anyone could get any bigger than her. She's a stick figure when she's not pregnant."

"Does she have any cramping, anything like that?" Jane asked.

George shook his head. "No. She's just tired. She says she feels beached, like a whale."

"Why in the hell pregnancy has to be so damned torturous is beyond me," said Rocksan. "And still women do it over and over again. It's a mystery to me."

George poured himself some coffee and sat down. His hair hadn't been brushed and it hung around his face. Rocksan never liked long hair on men. But on George, it seemed appropriate. Quaintly out of fashion. It seemed to make him feel daring. He clearly liked handling it. Now he brushed it back and pulled a rubber band from around his wrist and twisted his hair into a ponytail.

"Melody says it's like being taken over by an alien. She says she can feel everything being used up, all the food she eats, the sleep she sleeps. She says it's like it's being siphoned away from her," George said. He seemed rather pleased and worried all at the same time. He seemed to be in love with the mystery of conception and pregnancy, but baffled by it, too. Like all men and some lesbians, Rocksan supposed.

Rocksan stood up. She was still mad about this morning, still mad that one more time Jane had neglected to confer with her on decisions that completely affected her life. She wished she didn't have to walk around with the word *no* on her tongue. She wished she were more like her sister, who just went with the flow.

"I'm going out to the hives," Rocksan said.

Jane nodded. George grabbed his ponytail and stroked it for a minute. He seemed confused by Rocksan. She supposed he'd never really seen a big fat dyke up close before.

She went to the mudroom and put on her jacket and gloves and hat. Outside, the air had a sheen to it, as if the cold had taken shape and cast a veil over the earth. The trees were still, the pine boughs laden with snow. The manzanita's red bark glimmered in the sun.

Rocksan walked over to the hives, her hands deep in the pockets of her parka. When she breathed, the steam from her mouth came out in big puffs. The world was silent and seemed to be waiting, holding back, bracing itself against the winter.

Rocksan had a hard time believing that she had actually managed to finish the chores, to close the hives up for winter. She thought of the long months ahead, when the hives would remain dormant, when nothing would happen, and how she would long for spring, when she could put her hands on the hives again, combine the weak colonies, look for the queen, and uncap the combs. She loved May especially, when the bees seemed to find their stride and began to do again what it seemed they were made for.

Now she stood over the hives, hunkered down in her hat and jacket and thought of the barren winter ahead of them. She loved how quiet things were in winter, the slow panting breaths of the earth like a denning bear in the cave.

Just then, she heard a sound and, turning around, saw Melody waddling her way over, wrapped in Jane's full-length down jacket, too small to close over her enormous belly. Rocksan felt a twinge of relief. She realized that she liked the girl, but she wasn't sure why.

"Hello," she called. She was embarrassed by her robust greeting. She thought it sounded frantic and a bit too hearty. She wished she was just nice, instead of having to try so hard to be that way.

"Hi," Melody said. "My God it's cold."

"George says you're feeling poorly. Should you be up?"

"Pooh on George," Melody said.

Rocksan laughed. Who said *pooh* anyway?

"He says you're tired."

"Number one, he should try carrying around forty extra pounds. And number two, George wants to think that being pregnant means being sick. He has no idea how alive I feel."

"Yeah. I guess there's nothing too new about the clueless male."

Melody didn't smile. Instead, she looked at the hives and said, "So these are the bees?"

"Yes," Rocksan said. She heard the quiet pride in her voice. She made a note to check that next time. But so few people ever asked about the hives. Most everyone thought she was weird for keeping bees. She flashed on the time she'd scared the bejesus out of those high school kids with her story about the lurid mating rituals of bees.

"I don't know much about bees," Melody said. "I was stung enough. I don't know why. Bees were always attracted to me. My mother said I was too sweet to resist."

"Does your mother know where you are now?"

Melody nodded. "Mmm. She does know."

"Is she . . ."

"My mother lives an alternative life."

"Oh?" Rocksan said. "Is she a lesbian?" The words were out of her mouth before she could stop herself. Melody smiled. It was a smile of great amusement.

"No. I wouldn't say so. She loves men. She can't get enough of them. She's hardly finished with one and she's got another waiting for her in the wings. She likes to say she's a serial monogamist. A passionate lover of men."

"Is she in Ohio?"

"Oh, heavens no. She's here in California. Right now, she lives in a geodesic dome in Julian with an apple farmer."

"Do they grow apples?"

"Yes," Melody said. "She and Hugh—that's his name—won some money in the lottery and bought an apple orchard."

"That sounds like a TV show."

Melody laughed. "My mom is the stuff of sitcoms, that's for sure. She wants to see the baby after it's born. But she'll just keep saying that. She won't ever come. In the language of my ex–Christian brethren, she's a whore."

Melody said *whore* as if it had two syllables. "I'm not mad at her. She doesn't know how to do things any differently. Just 'cause they're family don't mean you gotta love them."

She was good with the hick accent. It made Rocksan laugh.

Melody turned toward the hives. "I heard that smoke makes bees crazy," she said.

Rocksan couldn't believe someone was engaging her in a conversation about her bees. She felt momentarily giddy. No one except Jane ever talked about the bees.

"Actually," Rocksan said, tempering her voice, trying to sound nonchalant, "smoke is the great equalizer."

Melody laughed. "Yeah. George and I know all about that."

Rocksan looked at Melody. Was she talking about pot? It seemed so unlikely. But then, why not? Melody, and George, for that matter, were surprising, people who could not easily be nailed down.

"Can you open one of those hives?" Melody asked. She winced for a moment and held on to her stomach. Rocksan wondered what blips and kicks went on in the mysterious universe of the pregnant womb.

"No. It would be a bad idea," she said. "Bees get especially upset if the hives are opened when it's cold out. They'd likely charge and sting the crap out of us."

"Oh. Well, I suppose that wouldn't be very good."

"If they did it, though, you could light something, a mossy piece of wood. The smoke would drive them to the safety of their hive."

Melody appeared suddenly thoughtful. She looked up at the sky, where high storm clouds were beginning to form.

"There's this book I was reading on the coffee table in there. You folks from California are really funny, the things you read."

"What was it? The book?"

"Zen and the Four Elements."

"That's Jane's," Rocksan said. "I'm not the Zen type."

"I didn't even know there were four elements," Melody said. "You would think there were hundreds of them. But this book was saying that fire is one of the four elements. So I was thinking, since fire's been around since cavemen, it must speak to the bees of something ancient. It might make them afraid," she said. Then, almost as an afterthought, she added, "But they could be responding to something else. Something we would never know. Something that has slipped away over millions of years. An ancient call of some kind."

Rocksan felt herself growing still, listening. She was amazed that Melody had said this, that Melody saw the bees as something more than stinging insects. She, too, had wondered why smoke was so profoundly effective in calming the bees. When it came to the bees, everything had a deeper meaning. And now, this pregnant girl, hundreds of miles away from home, who apparently believed people should live their lives as if they were going to die, was responding in the same way, saying the same sorts of things about the bees that Rocksan might say. How odd that two such different people with such different temperaments could think in such similar ways. Rocksan loved the strangeness of the world, the odd little alignments and divergences, the wondrous surprises of affinity.

"We have fallen out of touch with the forces of nature," Rocksan said quietly, almost with shyness. "But I expect the bees have not."

Melody smiled. She winced again and groaned happily. She said, "I think the baby is coming soon."

"Are you okay now? I don't know too much about this baby thing."

Melody waved her hand in the air. "Being pregnant, it occurs to me for the first time that every single one of us has a mother. I never really thought about that before, in that way. We were all fetuses, carried along by our mothers."

Rocksan thought of her mother, how hardworking and selfless she had been. How she had hardly ever smiled. How she hadn't gotten married again. How she'd weathered her husband's departure with a maddening stoicism.

"My mom is really sort of dead to me," Melody said. "I don't know about this thing you and Jane got going. Being lesbians. I'm not troubled by it. People have their own business. I just wanted to come here 'cause I really wanted to be around someone's mom. It's hard being pregnant, doing it on your own."

For some reason, Rocksan was touched. She wasn't sure why. Melody was strange that way. It made Rocksan think that sometimes you just met people whom you could love right off the bat. Just like that. You'd forgive them anything because something present and alive inside of them spoke to something lost inside of you.

"I'm not really the maternal type. Believe it or not, though, Jane is."

"I told George he has to forgive her or he'll turn into a wrinkly old bastard with a puckered mouth."

Rocksan nodded her head. She saw Melody wince and clutch her belly again.

"This baby is dropping every day. I think her damn head is poking out."

"Gads," Rocksan said. "That sounds so horrible."

Melody laughed. "Boy, you sure *aren't* the maternal type, are you?"

❧ ❧ ❧

Jane was quiet on the way to the funeral. She seemed as if a great weight had been lifted from her shoulders. Or more had been added. It was so hard to tell. Rocksan had evidently missed something.

"You wanna talk about it?" Rocksan asked.

"He really hates me. I think me being a lesbian grosses him out."

"Everyone gets used to everything over time, Jane."

"Yeah. But he also hates me because I left him behind."

Rocksan put her hand on Jane's knee. "It's twenty years of bullshit, Jane. You can't expect it to fix itself overnight."

Jane nodded. She looked miserable. The clouds were growing thicker. She thought of the funeral, the task of hiking into the woods, of the somber hours that lay ahead of them. She thought how city folk would never turn out for a funeral where you had to work your muscles and your grief at the same time.

"I'm sorry about before," Jane said.

"That's okay," Rocksan said. "I'll just make George pay for it. There's lots of work around the house he could do."

"You are such a bitch, Rocksan."

"Thanks. Just this morning, I felt like I was losing my *cojones*."

"You'll be dead and your *cojones* will still be screaming at somebody. The undertaker. Giving orders."

Rocksan smiled. She sort of liked the image. She drove on for a while. A silence filled the car, but it seemed pleasant, in spite of their reason for driving. She thought of Melody. How Melody had spoken of the bees with such interest, as if she could see why Rocksan cared so much about them. She thought of Melody giving birth and then of a baby screaming. She'd never thought babies were cute. They all looked like wrinkly faces carved out of apples. But still, she had a brief, weird fantasy. She was standing by the hives, talking to the baby, conjuring up the beauty of the bees for her. She saw herself and the child cleaning the feeders together, changing the queen, mourning the massacre of the drones.

"Melody will need some time to rest after that baby is born," Rocksan said. She stared straight ahead. She saw Jane look up at her. She would not meet Jane's eyes.

"Are you saying they can stay longer?"

"I'm not saying anything, Jane, except that every one of us had a mother once."

Rocksan looked over at Jane. Jane appeared confused. "Huh?"

"It's just something I was thinking about is all," Rocksan said.

A moment passed. Then Rocksan said, as gently as she could, "Next time, you gotta talk these things over with me. We can't keep going on like this. We gotta learn to talk to each other."

Jane nodded.

"Just talk to me. I'll try to be like Gandhi or someone and not bite your head off before the words come out."

Jane seemed speechless. Rocksan realized it was the most conciliatory she'd been in a long time. Maybe ever. She and Jane fumbled for each other's hands. There was something earnest in it. Something shy and new. Rocksan's heart filled with both celebration and sorrow.

They drove the rest of the way in silence. Then they reached the clearing where Ethan had last seen his son alive. There were cars parked everywhere and people standing about. At the trailhead, she saw the old blind preacher talking to Cindy and Ethan. She saw Glick standing off to the side, as if he were waiting for something, and for some reason she thought of her sister. She stepped out of the car and knelt down to tie her boots up tighter. It was going to be a long walk.

JANE

——————◆——————

After Rocksan left to fool with her bees, Jane had found herself alone with George. She was very nervous. She remembered all that liquor she'd had to drink twenty years ago in order to leave her son. She had a vague idea that a stiff drink would be good about now. But then she saw herself in his face, the structure of his bones, the brown of his eyes, the hurt there.

"What's up with her and those bees? Is that some kind of gay thing?"

"George, you can't be serious?"

"I'm not. I'm being a bastard."

"That's cheap."

George nodded. "I'm my father's son."

"You sound like a bad movie of the week."

"Maybe so. But it's the truth. It's who I am."

"So you believe that people are a certain way? They can't change?"

He shrugged. They were silent for a long time. Jane saw that he was nervous, uncertain. At one point, he started to say something, then changed his mind. Finally, he broke the silence.

"When Melody goes into labor, you guys know what to do, right? Like where to take her. Shouldn't we go into that town with the hospital and do something in advance of the birth?"

Jane nodded. "I think we should. Let's talk to Melody about it."

An awkward silence passed between them. Something fluid, moving. A flashing thought, darkness. There was a memory of something she could not grasp, something dark and painful. Faces in a room. Snow. A sudden burst of light. She thought of Nate, dying in the woods. She thought of her son, alive, sitting here across from her. How unexpected life was. How mysterious.

"George," she said. "We need to work some things out between us . . ."

"I know," he said. It was as if he had just experienced something sensory, too. Some moment had passed between them. "Really, I *want* to forgive you. But you know how that goes. Then what's left? All I've known since forever is how to hate you."

Jane bowed her head to the table. She thought about what Rocksan had said earlier. That people got used to anything. She knew that she lacked patience. She always forgot that nothing stayed the same. She tried to tell herself this now. To tell herself that in time, this would be resolved one way or the other and this terrible feeling would be replaced someday by something else.

"You have to try, George."

"It feels so desperate," he said. "So forced."

"But everything new feels that way."

He shrugged. His face had gone red. So had hers. They shared these traits. They shared their eye color, their bone structure, the texture of their hair. They both blushed. They both cried easily.

"I was always afraid I would be gay," he said. "Like I would inherit it from you."

"See. So you do believe it's not a choice."

He shook his head adamantly. "Can't you see where I had to believe it was? That it is?"

She nodded. "It's doesn't make me a freak," Jane said.

"Not in your book."

"Don't be cruel, George," she said.

He leaned forward and put his hand out, then drew it back. She saw regret on his face. He was her son. *Her son.*

"I'm sorry," he said miserably. "I don't mean to hurt you. I'm so sorry," he said.

She nodded. "I understand."

"Do you?"

A shadow crossed the room. She looked outside. The clouds were really stacking up. This was so hard, so painful. She just wanted him to forgive her. Why wouldn't he do what she wanted?

"The funeral is in a couple hours," Jane said. "I should get ready."

George looked outside, too. He said, "I feel so sorry for that dad. But the whole thing was his fault. What a stupid move, man. People just make stupid moves, all the time."

Jane stood up. She knew he was really talking about her. She looked at him, the way he bent over the table, as if the air had been let out of him. She saw that he was crying silently, and she wanted so much to put her arms around him. She understood then, in that moment, with the clouds darkening the room, just a few hours before the funeral for Nate, that the key to her release had never been in winning his forgiveness.

"You make me want to be a better person," she said.

He nodded. He was overcome. He brought his hands to his face. He covered his eyes, and she saw how strong and beautiful his hands were, how much they were shaped like her own hands.

❖ ❖ ❖

As Jane and Rocksan pulled up to the clearing, Jane saw all the cars and she felt a sense of belonging and sorrow. She realized that this was her life, this place with these people who would turn out despite the threat of snow, for the arduous funeral of one of their own.

She thought of her son—*her son*—back home with Melody, of the two of them planning their lives, beginning. She understood that this was no time to make mistakes, that now was a beginning for her, too. She saw the tapestry of her life spread out before her, all the fits and starts. She knew that she could not destroy this chance. How did you stay on course? By what power could you learn to make the right choices, to do the right thing?

After Rocksan parked the car, four rangers in separate trucks drove up. They stopped at the edge of the clearing, but kept their trucks idling. One of them got out of his truck and walked over to each of the other three, spoke briefly, gestured with his hands and pointed to the edge of the clearing, then returned to his truck. After that, they all lined their trucks up, forming a kind of barricade around the clearing. Almost in tandem, like a dance, Jane thought, they stepped out of their trucks and stood there, like sentinels, leaning against their vehicles, each with an official park ranger hat on his head and their matching government-issued winter parkas snug against their bodies. She saw the formality in it. The respect. She understood what a fickle thing luck could be.

ANGIE

How malleable children seemed. How willing to accommodate. But Angie knew it wasn't true. At any given moment, they would seem to absorb a new situation, take it in stride, accept it. Then three weeks later, they were throwing things at you, acting out in a way that made it clear how badly you had betrayed them.

Angie had seen it with her own daughter. When Angie had brought that truck driver home and married him, Rachel had gone along with the program. But once Rachel understood that the man—drunken, overweight, mean—wasn't going away, she shut down. She was never the same, even after Angie kicked him out. Rachel had had enough of betrayal. She was a closed book by then.

Now, after she kissed Glick good-bye and watched him drive away, she turned back to Rosie and began to fret. Rosie had seemed okay in the end. She'd played with the dog. She'd responded to Glick's gentle recriminations about feeding the animal at the table. She'd even managed a laugh. But Angie knew better. She knew it could all head south at the slightest provocation.

Angie watched her granddaughter playing with some toys on the floor. She went over to her. She said, "I am never leaving you, Rosie."

Rosie nodded her head.

"Do you understand what I'm saying?"

Rosie looked up at Angie and nodded her head again. She was solemn, even a bit afraid. Angie took a deep breath. She thought of Ethan for a moment, the way he had left his son in the truck. She saw that except for the details, she had done the same thing with her own daughter. Her daughter hadn't died. But she was lost to Angie forever.

Rosie grabbed a piece of Angie's hair and curled it around her fingers for a moment. Then she said, "Why isn't my mom here? Or my daddy? Are they coming back?"

Angie sat on the floor. "I don't think so, baby." Sometimes, Angie thought, you had to tell the truth in a rush, like pulling a bandage off the tender skin. The smart always came, sharp but short.

"Why?"

"Even though your mommy loved you very much . . ." Angie had to stop for a moment. She thought about how even before Rosie had been born, this moment existed in her future, that she'd had a hand in creating it.

"Even though she loved you, she was not able to care for you."

"Did she die, like Nate?"

"No," Angie said. "She just didn't have the—"

"Doesn't she love me?"

"Yes. She does love you. She does. That's why you're here with me, as funny as that sounds. If she had kept you, sweetie, she would not have been able to take care of you the way I can."

Rosie nodded. She seemed to understand. But Angie knew that to think Rosie understood any of this would be her downfall. It had been her downfall before. She had to remain vigilant. She had to remain consistent. She had to remember that Rosie *did not* understand, no matter how adult she seemed. It was a ruse children learned. They learned to be sophisticated, to trick adults into thinking they understood the ways of the world. And adults, Angie had learned, were so desperate for the way out that they failed to see this smart, this subtle ploy that children played on them.

"Where's my daddy? Nate has a daddy."

"Your mommy and your daddy got a divorce, honey. They don't live together anymore. I don't know where your dad is. I don't know where your mom is. I wish I did. I wish I could bring them home for you."

Rosie nodded. Angie could see how she was fighting back the tears. Her lips quivered and her chin rippled.

"Rosie," Angie said. "You are number one in my life. No one will ever re-
place you."

Rosie looked up at Angie. She was crying. She said, "I don't know what
my mom looks like. How come there aren't any pictures of my mom? Or my
dad?"

Angie stood up. She held out her hand for Rosie. Rosie took it and stood
up, too. Together, they walked into Angie's room. Reaching into the bottom
drawer of her dresser, Angie pulled out the photo album she had stuffed
there after Rachel had left. Now she realized how wrong she had been to
keep it hidden. She opened up the photo album and showed it to Rosie.

"Now, I don't have any pictures of your daddy. His name was Robert
Preston. But this here is your mom when she was thirteen. See how you
have her very same eyes?"

Rosie stared at the picture with a kind of wonder and disbelief. She nodded her head.

"And this one here is the last one I took of her. She was just nineteen."

It was a picture of Rachel standing outside the house with a cigarette in
her hand and a swagger in her pose. She was smiling, and the bones in her
cheeks were so pronounced that her smile—half mocking—looked fragile.
It could have been something else even, not the smile at all that made her
seem so fragile. You could see the anger and the hurt in her eyes. You could
see the defiance.

"Did my mom smoke?"

Angie nodded. "Yes."

Rosie looked at Angie as if she were appalled. "That could kill you,"
Rosie said.

Angie put her arms around Rosie, who still clung to the photo album. "I
love you, Rosebud."

Rosie did not seem to be at all interested in what Angie was saying. She
was trying to look at the photo album. But Angie knew better. She knew
that Rosie was listening to those words, clinging to them as if her life depended on it. She knew that Rosie's seeming indifference only meant that
she had already learned the stupid ways of adults.

"You can keep these pictures," Angie said. "If you want, we can hang some of them up in your room."

Rosie nodded solemnly. She took charge of the photo album. She held on to it tightly.

Later, Angie bundled Rosie up and took her to the diner. Hilda was waiting outside in the cold.

"What the hell?" Hilda said.

"Sorry I'm late."

"You treat me like chopped liver."

"Sorry."

"I can't walk out there in those woods. That's a good thing for you, so I can stay here and get the food ready. But damn, you left me standing out here in the cold for"—she looked at her watch—"fifteen damned minutes."

"You swore," Rosie said.

"Damn straight I did," Hilda said.

Rosie's eyes widened.

"She's all bluster, honey. Don't mind her," Angie said.

"What about the kid? You aren't making her walk back in those woods?"

Rosie was standing beside Angie, clutching the photo album and her penguin.

"Of course not. I was hoping you could keep her with you," Angie said sheepishly. She felt bad. But what could she do?

"No, Grammie."

Hilda bent down. She looked at Rosie, who had always been slightly cowed by Hilda's girth and her booming deep voice. "You gonna help me?" Hilda asked.

Rosie shook her head. "No, you scare me," she said.

Angie and Hilda looked at each other. Hilda raised her eyebrows. "She's spoiled. She's surly, just like you," she said.

"I'm surly?" Angie said.

Hilda nodded as Angie opened the door. "It's a hidden trait of yours. You only show it to the help."

Angie found herself smiling. Hilda was so *weird*.

They went inside and Angie spent an hour setting up. She put plates and silverware out on the counter. She filled the coffeepots and told Hilda not to start brewing the coffee until people began arriving. She put tea bags out and cups and glassware. She put the napkins in a basket. She started preparing sandwiches. A few people came by, tried the doors, but when they found them locked, they moved on, or knocked on the windows to be let in. Each time, Hilda shouted. "We're closed. Can't you read the damn sign?" Then she'd look at Angie or at Rosie, who was engrossed in the photo album, and she would say, "Where's the damned respect?"

Angie said good-bye to Rosie and Hilda and headed for the mountain. She saw that some of the reporters were heading that way, too, and she felt bad. She hoped they were too feeble from living a city life and wouldn't—or couldn't—make the trek back into the woods. She could not imagine it, and she wondered if there were any means to keep them out of the funeral service. She knew that the old blind preacher would be conducting the service, and she worried about that, too. Could he make it out there? And what would he say? She thought about him for a minute, how he was always around, always present, but how you never knew anything about him. She wondered if he was too eccentric to say the right things. Then she worried, because she knew there could hardly be a right thing to say. The circumstances were so unforgiving.

Behind her and in front of her, a line of cars snaked their way up the mountain. She recognized only a couple of them and was relieved when she finally arrived and saw that the rangers and the sheriff had made a barricade. They were stopping the cars and letting only people from the town into the clearing. She saw the frustration in the reporters' faces. She heard one of them say, "Officer, this is public land. We have the right to use it."

When she parked her car, she spotted Glick immediately. He waved and headed toward her. She looked around and saw the old preacher talking to Cindy and Ethan. She saw her sister and Jane. Rocksan was kneeling down and tying the laces on her boots. Angie slowly stepped out of her car.

"You made it," Glick said after walking up to her car.

"Yes," Angie said. She felt like she might cry. She was overwhelmed. She felt the full weight of Nate's death. She thought briefly of her daughter, but more so of her absence. She thought of Rosie. The image of Rosie clutching the photo album. She felt herself taking in a breath, and suddenly Glick was there, holding her up.

"Steady, there," he said.

"I don't know what just came over me."

"It's okay," Glick said.

"I feel so dizzy."

"They're arresting Ethan after the service."

"What the hell for?"

"Sheriff told him the charge is criminal negligence."

"What the hell is that?"

Glick shrugged. He had Angie by the elbow. If people noticed their intimacy, they didn't seem to make much of it. For a moment, Angie thought their union might just slip into the fabric of the town's life, that no one would care that much. Not now. Not when something else mattered so much more. She thought how odd it was that you could go about your life and forget how profound and also how trifling it was, until something like this happened.

"We're pretty much ready to hike in. Brother Johns says he's ready to go," Glick said.

"I'm afraid, Glick."

"It might be we all are," Glick said.

Angie walked with Glick, and everything seemed to be happening in slow motion. She had a moment's understanding of her own mortality, of life's wistful end. She saw how small she was in the grand scheme of it all, how insignificant really. She felt as though she were not a single individual, but part of a vast and enigmatic sea of living things. She had an image of a school of fish and then a flock of birds, of their ever-changing but constant motion forward, sideways, and back. You could not take one step, she thought, without holding the rest of humanity's hand. She reached for Glick's hand, tears streaming down her face. Glick leaned over. He said, "I love you."

She nodded, crying more now.

She looked up at all the people in her town, at the media cordoned off to the side, kept out. She saw Rocksan and Jane talking quietly to each other, Rocksan gripping Jane's hand with might. She saw Cindy and Ethan and Trevor huddled together like one single person. She saw the preacher standing alone, leaning against his cane as if listening for something. She imagined Nate lying in the woods, dying. She saw him take his last breath. She comforted herself by imagining his soul, like a piece of tissue paper, rising up out of his body and floating gently away on the breeze. Floating away and disappearing, until it was only a memory in her mind's eye.

CINDY

———————◆———————

Cindy was riding in the back of a gold station wagon. Her father was driving. Her mother was sitting beside him, stroking the back of his head. She saw the glimmer of the silvery nail polish on her mother's fingernails, the long fingers, the rounded bones of her knuckles. Her mother turned around and smiled. In slow motion, her mother said, "I love you."

Cindy opened her eyes and, groggy from the dream, remembered that it was the day of Nate's funeral. Trevor slept deeply beside her. He was on his stomach, and Cindy could see the tattoo of the naked lady he'd come back with after a drunken high school weekend in the city. She thought about waking him, then changed her mind. Quietly, she got out of bed and put on her clothes.

She went into the living room and was glad to find a nearly full bottle of whiskey on the coffee table. She took a swig, grabbed her purse and her keys. She put the bottle in her purse. She wrote Trevor a note, saying she would see him later at the funeral. She took her heavy parka off the peg by the door and wrapped herself in gloves and a hat. She opened the door and braced herself for the cold. Outside, she saw the same reporters in the car, parked across the street, as if on a stakeout. The engine of their car was running and the exhaust made a plume of smoke in the cold air. She walked up to them, feeling ballsy from the swig of whiskey, and knocked on their window. The man rolled the window down. He looked at her expectantly.

"If I see you at my son's funeral, I'll kill you," she said.

The man smiled. He looked like a punk. A smart-ass. He did not appear to be moved by the threat. She wished she had a gun so she could show him how serious she was. She wished she could pull a gun out of her purse and place the barrel against his skull. She knew she could have done it. Her son's death had turned her into something else. It seemed like there were no more stakes anymore. Nothing to stop her. With first light of day and the whiskey warming her throat, she felt raw and capable of anything. The cold rounded out her sense of vengeance.

"You aren't killing anyone, Mrs. Denton," the man said.

"Try me," she said.

She walked away and got into her car, wondering if they could smell the liquor on her breath. She drove out of the carport. The couple in the car followed her. She drove slowly through town. When she passed Angie's, she saw Angie and Hilda talking by the door. Angie's granddaughter was holding a large book and a stuffed animal. As Cindy passed, the three of them walked into the diner.

Cindy drove on. She wanted to go out to Glick's house to see if he and Ethan had left yet, but she had enough sense not to lead the predators to their prey. She turned on the radio and, as she knew it would, the news soon turned to Nate's death. It was then that she heard that her husband—ex-husband—was going to be arrested that morning. She immediately took the bottle of whiskey out of her purse and had a long sip, and the liquor going down calmed and detained her thoughts. With Nate gone, she felt like there was nothing holding her to the earth. She pictured Ethan and she wanted to be with him. She wanted to stand by him, as he had asked her to do. It seemed the natural course to take, as simple as breathing. She would stand beside him not out of desire or love, but for her son. She had the idea, however drunken and muddled it was, that Nate would wish it that way, that Nate was guiding her. She knew it might just be the liquor talking. But she thought it wasn't.

She slowly made her way up the mountain. She was nearly alone on the road, except for the reporters behind her, and she wondered if anyone was going to show up for the funeral. She knew that it would be a hardship for people to walk back into the woods in the snow to the place where Nate had died. She worried that maybe no one would come.

The reporters who had been following her lagged farther and farther behind. The roads, which Cindy knew well and navigated with ease, were icy and curvy. A stranger would be afraid of the roads. She sped up and drove even faster, and when she arrived, she pulled up beside Glick. She got out of the truck and Ethan walked over to her and put his arms around her. She felt the familiar warmth of his embrace, the smell of him. It sent her back. Her head was spinning. She felt, for a moment, like she might faint. The reporters took a picture. She saw the flash go off in the woods, like a stain in the air.

"Cindy," Ethan said. His voice was muffled by her jacket. "God, Cindy. I . . ."

"It's okay," she said. She saw their lives, the way they had snaked in and out of joy and rage, and she could not close the door on it. She thought of how she would never see her son again. She saw Ethan as her last link to Nate. She was broken and deserted. When they disengaged, he said, "You got anything to medicate?"

She pulled the bottle from her purse and gave it to him. She watched him take a deep sip. He screwed the cap back on, wiped his mouth with the back of his hand, and gave it back to her just as the preacher approached them.

"You must abandon yourself to God," the preacher said. "You must admit your faults to Him."

Cindy stood there beside Ethan, aloof and alone, miles away from God. She felt her disenfranchisement from the world, from the people who were arriving there to be with her and mourn with her. She felt that her alcoholism—for that's what it was—and the mark of her son's death upon her made her separate from everyone else on earth except for Ethan.

"I can't have faith," she said to the preacher.

He took her hand in his and held it, and she could smell the scent of his old age, even through his coat.

"You must have faith. Only God will relieve you from this."

"Please," she said. "Don't talk about that now."

The words came out in a hushed, harsh whisper. It was as if she were losing her voice. Ethan held her other hand. He leaned over and said, "Stay close."

Then the reporters tried to get at them just as the sheriff and the rangers arrived, and there was a flurry of people. The breathlessness of their need was suffocating. How weird it seemed that these strangers had desires, when it was Cindy whose mouth felt open, whose needs were gaping. Cindy watched with a kind of disbelief as the sheriff ushered the media out beyond the barrier that he and the rangers had created with their cars. Then the sheriff walked up to them and, with his eyes cast downward, said, "Ethan, I got to tell you some bad news."

Cindy watched Ethan's expression. It did not change at all. He seemed prepared for the news. Cindy was glad that she had heard on the radio that Ethan was going to be arrested; otherwise, she might have made a spectacle of it. She might have gone hysterical.

"I know, Sheriff. It's okay."

"We're gonna do it easy, though, okay? No handcuffs. No big to-do."

"What's the charge?"

"Seems like it's gonna be a misdemeanor. Criminal negligence."

Ethan nodded. Cindy had never heard of criminal negligence. She turned to the sheriff and said, "But there isn't anything criminal. It was a mistake."

The sheriff could not meet her eyes. "Charges were filed by the DA down valley. I can't speak to them. There's a lawyer there waiting to take your case. A public defender."

Cindy heard the words *public defender*. She thought of her welfare check sitting on the counter. She felt low and criminal, even though she had not been the one to leave Nate in the truck. She felt like she was exactly what they were saying about them on the news: hicks, drunks, rednecks.

The sheriff was talking, Ethan was nodding, and Cindy was thinking how she was a hick, a redneck, a drunk. She saw how Ethan never broke. He remained stoic and silent. Like he'd always been. She thought of the nature of their long relationship, how it was just like her to choose someone who could never give her what she most wanted. What she most needed.

"Ethan," she said. "Ethan. Let's go do this funeral and get it over with."

The endlessness of her days stretched out before her. She wished she could just die. But she knew that she could never take her own life with a gun or a blade. She thought that maybe, someday, she would be driving and she would just glide off the edge of the road, float down until she crashed. She wouldn't even know what hit her. It would be a blessing. And maybe by then, no one would know who she was. No one would care. That would be the best way to go—if no one cared who you were. A slow suicide.

Ethan turned to her. He said, "It's time. Let's go."

JUDGE JACK ROSENTHAL

He did not tell anyone that he had helped search for the boy. Nor did he tell anyone that he had gone to the mortuary and skulked around, hiding when the father drove by, begging to be let inside. He did not understand these things himself, and now the case had landed on his docket, as he knew it would.

As he sat in chambers, reading over the brief, he saw that Tom Kraft, the prosecutor, wanted to make Ethan pay hard. Jack read it over three times. That morning, on his way in, he'd heard Kraft on the radio. He was distressed that Kraft was going to try the case in the media. He hadn't wanted to listen to Kraft's interview, but prurient interest won out. It was clear, Kraft had said to the reporter, that Ethan Denton had committed a heinous crime and needed to be punished for it.

Jack knew Kraft well. He was a young man with big dreams. He was also wiry, cross, and sharp. When you met Tom Kraft, you were struck first by his intelligence, then by his irritability, which came across in the small, neat way he dressed and the fastidiousness of his manner. He was a man who was wound tight and seemed to bear his intelligence with a great deal of anguish. He was someone who thought too much. At the same time, his obvious political aspirations made him unable to live a strictly intellectual life. Kraft had to play to people, to woo his conservative constituents. Everyone knew he was planning a run for the state legislature. Among a certain set, Kraft was wildly popular. Among others, he was reviled. Jack tried to remain impartial, but of course he could not. When he read the complaint, filed with an almost beautiful scrupulousness, its words echoing Kraft's neat, controlled voice, he felt the hairs on the back of his neck rise.

He used to see Kraft jogging in the park near their house when he and Adele would walk in the evenings. Kraft would smile tightly, nod his head, and say, "Afternoon, Judge." Jack had always been irritated by Kraft's pointed deference. He saw in it a subtle anti-Semitism. He couldn't say anything out loud, because Kraft would never expose himself in an obvious way. But Jack saw it in his eyes. The "Jesus killer" look. Kraft never made anything seem personal. But you always knew it was.

Jack had heard that Kraft was going to bring the Family Services file between Ethan and his wife to bear in court. He was going to drag every detail out of it and somehow string together enough stories to prove that Ethan had a legacy of prior bad behavior. He had said on the radio that he was determined to prove that Ethan was a man whose entire history of reckless acts had led to the final one: the death of his son. He used the word *criminal* over and over again, and each time he did, Jack felt something brittle and sad stir within him.

For Jack, the case was something other than that. He saw in it the embodiment of sin and repentance. *Teshuvah.* Returning to one's true nature, returning to God. It was the sin in it, the rebellion against God and the subsequent debasement of Ethan's truest self, that most attracted and interested Jack. Jack did not see the case as one that required the emotional toil of legal wrangling, the posturing and vengeance he had come to expect when crimes involving children were tried. He saw it as an opportunity for atonement. For Ethan to right himself before God and the people who loved him. Otherwise, he believed, Ethan would not commence to live his life again.

But from the looks of it, this case would be tried in the court of public opinion. Today's moral climate frightened Jack. And though he hated to admit it, Kraft scared him, too. He saw Kraft's willingness to drag Ethan and his family through the mud as a corrupt but very real expression of his power. That he could get away with it signaled a larger dishonesty and a breakdown, Jack thought, in common decency.

Jack knew Kraft and men like Kraft, who were swayed by the rhetoric of family values. Jack was no fool. He had turned the radio on. He had heard the public outcry. The thunder. For every parent who could identify and empathize with Ethan, there were five who could not, who vociferously ordered his execution. This was going to be a bad case. Jack hoped only that Ethan would plead guilty or no contest to avoid a trial. But in that case, the sentencing would be up to Jack. And Jack understood there was no right decision. That any decision he made would be too personal, too painful.

Jack rose stiffly from his plush leather chair. His chambers were beautiful, smelling richly of leather and wood. He put his robe on over his street clothes and looked outside at the prickly winter morning and the bare trees lining the courthouse steps.

On the wall beside the window were his diplomas and the many honors and awards he'd won over the years. There were pictures, too, of his family, of him and the various dignitaries he'd met, of his vacations to remote and exotic places. There was one picture of his family taken almost thirty years ago. He took it off the wall and stared at the faces of his sons and his wife. He looked intently at his own face, at how young he had been, how rugged and hale. He had once been so strong and so active. How slowly age had taken away his vitality. So slowly, in fact, that he had failed to see it until everyone was gone.

He thought of Marty. He knew that it was wrong to have a favorite son, but he had never been able to shake it. His thoughts turned to the Torah and he remembered the story of Abraham and Isaac. God Himself had acknowledged that Isaac was Abraham's favorite son. He had told Abraham to take Isaac and tender him as a burnt offering. Jack had always been struck by the fact that Abraham hadn't, in the end, killed his son. It seemed to him that Abraham had been bluffing all along, that he'd never had any intention of giving his son up for God. But wouldn't God have known that? Didn't God know everything?

Still, Jack had read the story over and over again, and he believed in his heart of hearts not only that Abraham had never fully committed to killing his son but that God would never have forced his hand. God had to be bluffing, because who could love a God of such cruelty, a God who would make a man kill his favorite son?

Jack stood up and walked to the bathroom. He turned on the hot water and splashed it on his face. He thought about Ethan, of that split second when he decided to chase the buck and leave his son asleep in the car. He thought of his own son, lost somewhere on the streets of Hollywood. He remembered how he had sat at his kitchen table and wondered how a man could do that to his own son. Now he was not so sure how he felt, exactly, only that he believed at the most basic level that Ethan did not need to be punished for his error. He did not need to go to jail. Society was not in danger because of the acts of Ethan Denton. At the same time, Jack honestly believed that there had to be some *reparation*. That only in repentance could Ethan shield himself from ruin.

Jack stood up and looked at himself in the mirror. He was shocked by the old man who stared back at him. He remembered how Marty had stood on the landing of the stairs with the stolen items, the way he had been unable to say anything, how that moment had called for Jack to step forward in forgiveness and understanding.

The thought suddenly crossed his mind that he was not without sin of his own. He realized that in loving Marty the most, he had cheated his son out of parental love and given him instead his vain and desperate worship. All of his choices, he now saw, had been made from that frantic love and the fear that drove it.

He peered at his reflection. He wondered what Marty saw there. He wondered what God could see. How could he stand in judgment of another man, he thought, if he did not look to see that his own house was in order?

GLICK

---◆---

Slowly, the procession of mourners walked into the woods. Glick was in front of Angie, and all the while he was aware of her presence, of the heaviness of her sorrow behind him. He wished he could hold her hand. He kept remembering how he had found Nate in the woods. The preacher leaned heavily on his arm while, across from him, Ethan took the old man's other arm and walked in tandem. Behind them, Cindy walked alone, her head bowed, her hands clasped in front of her as if in prayer.

Around him, the earth was a silent vista of snow and trees and winter birds. Saplings from last spring poked through the snowbanks. The wind, which had quieted now that the clouds had completely moved in, rustled from time to time through the tops of the pines. The quiet shuffling of the mourners behind him seemed holy, and Glick felt, even in the midst of such pain, his connectedness to the world, to the people he had lived among for the past ten years. He kept his eyes trained in front of him, narrowing his mind, taking on the burden of the preacher's weight. On the other side of the preacher, Ethan steadied the man's pace as well, stumbling once in a while from the burden.

As they neared the site where Glick had discovered Nate, he remembered how he had found himself lost in the woods, stuck in a ravine with his dog and his misery. He remembered the fear he'd had of death and the way he'd waited almost breathlessly for first light. How odd it was that once the sun had risen, he had known exactly where he was. He had not been lost at all, and yet *he had been lost*. Glick wondered how these things fit together, what he was meant to glean from them.

He remembered picking the boy up and holding him in his arms, and he knew now—though he hadn't then—that the moment he'd made connection with the boy, his life had changed. Now he thought about the boy's final repose—the tears frozen on his cheeks, the worn feet of his sleeper, the sad and anguished way he'd curled up in a fetal position to die.

Glick felt the sorrow rise to the back of his throat and he steadied himself as a helpless sob made its way out of him. Ethan turned to look at him, and Glick saw that he, too, was crying. Between them, the old preacher walked on steadfastly, with a kind of unwavering loyalty to the somber procession, his eyes fixed forward blindly, seeing nothing.

ETHAN

All the while, as they walked, Ethan remembered Nate when he was alive. He remembered the way Nate would come into his room in the morning and sleep the last few hours before sunrise on the pallet on the floor. The way he smelled of sleep and of fresh bread's sweetness. He remembered the way Nate would run through the woods, laughing with delight, how inquisitive he'd been, how gentle with the glorious world that surrounded him. Nate alive filled Ethan's heart with joy, and that's what he held on to as he steadied the preacher and walked into the darkening woods.

But as the threat of snow deepened and the woods began to grow more ominously shadowed, he could not think of Nate alive anymore. His image of Nate's final hours, his final breath, the last moments of his life turned him stony. It was *so* hard to walk. When he thought of his son, lying on his side, his thumb in his mouth, weeping and calling out his name—he could hear Nate crying for him—he wished that the earth would open up and swallow him whole. At one point, as they neared Nate's final resting spot, Ethan turned toward Glick and saw that he was crying. Tears streamed down his own face, and he felt the preacher hold his arm tighter and he wished, for the thousandth time, that whatever cruel God had seen fit to take his son had taken him instead.

When they made the final bend in the path to the place where Nate had died, with the long line of mourners behind him, Ethan saw the crude cross he had pounded into the earth. He saw the fresh snow that had fallen on it. He felt his knees buckle, and in spite of himself, he began to slide slowly to the ground. He thought it so ironic that the elderly preacher was trying in vain to hold him up and not, as it should have been, the other way around.

Suddenly, Glick was there, and with the preacher's help, and Cindy's help behind him, Ethan felt himself being hoisted to his feet. He found the strength in his legs again and he vowed that for the rest of his life he would simply black out all his thoughts. He would begin to do it now, and within seconds he found his thoughts narrowing down, closing up. Very soon, all he could do was merely see the quiet, snowy earth around him, the snow-shrouded cross before him, and the darkening sky above him as a flurry of white and delicate snowflakes began to cascade earthward.

ROCKSAN

For some reason—Rocksan was not sure why—when Ethan fell to the ground, she saw the image of her father a few weeks before he'd left. He had been mending a broken gutter on the roof. She remembered watching him the moment the ladder had given way beneath him and he'd fallen to the ground, his arms and legs flailing in the air. She could recollect the fear she'd felt seeing him lose his balance and crash to the ground. She remembered the thought she'd always had, till then, of his invincibility, and she realized there in the snowy woods as Ethan collapsed that her father's abandonment of her and her mother and sister was inextricably wound up with the way he'd fallen helplessly off the ladder.

Now, as the first snowflakes began to pierce the sky, she watched Glick, the old preacher, and Cindy wrest Ethan to his feet. She thought that later, years from then, she would view it as the single most pitiable moment of the entire day. She saw then that Ethan was lost, that he was a man who, like her father, would be of no more use to the people who loved him. She could see the broad stretch of his life, the grief that would accompany him everywhere he went for as long as he lived.

Then, with no warning whatsoever, she felt tears flood her eyes and she realized she was crying for the first time in decades. She suddenly turned to Jane and grabbed her and sobbed into her coat, and Jane, surprised and taken aback at first, did nothing. Then she felt Jane's arms come up, those slender, delicate arms that she had held and loved and known for twenty years, and wrap themselves tightly around her. She could find no words because her voice was tied up with the task of weeping. She felt her grief leave her and spill out into the quiet air. She felt the woods take it and lift it high up into the air, and the more she sobbed, the more sorrow she released to the woods, until Jane was whispering into her ear, "I love you. It's okay. We'll be okay . . ."

She bowed her head then and said a prayer, which was something she had not done since her father left. She silently whispered to the woods, *Please, please watch over him,* and she did not know whom she meant, if she meant her dead father, or Ethan, or Nate, or if she really meant all the lost souls surprised by the world's capricious cruelty, surprised to discover that they had once held joy in the palms of their hands without even knowing it.

JANE

———◆———

Jane walked beside Rocksan near the middle of the procession. She felt warmed by those around her, as if in a safe harbor of moored ships rocking gently to and fro. She could not believe how many had turned out for the funeral. She was gladdened that the media had been cordoned off so that the people of Angels Crest could mourn in peace. Jane felt the power of their numbers, the luminosity of their collective grief, shining radiantly, pulsing as if alive.

The sorrow she felt brought back the memories of those first few months after she'd left her son behind. The pain of it came back in a visceral rush and she had a memory so complete that for a while, instead of mourning Nate's death, she was back there, mourning the death of her old life, the loss of her son. She realized that because she left her son, she had never fully celebrated the birth of her new life. Could not.

Then when Ethan stumbled, she felt a powerful kinship and sorrow for him. She worried that he might find no way to swim back to shore, that Nate's death had left him permanently marooned. He would be alone for the rest of his life, no matter how many people surrounded him. Then, just as she was lost in this thought, Rocksan, without warning, began to sob.

She had never known Rocksan to cry. She had never seen her shed a tear in the twenty years they had known each other, and it struck her as the single most frightening thing she had seen in her life. But then she felt relieved. She saw in Rocksan's tears an inexplicable sense of the permanence of their love.

Jane put her arms around Rocksan's girth and held her tight, slowing the procession behind her. She was grateful for the way everyone behind her waited until Rocksan had spent her grief. When they stumbled on, Jane understood that this was one of the most important things to happen since the birth of her son, and she would not forget it.

When they all finally made it to the site of Nate's death, where a crude cross had been hammered into the ground, the snow began to fall, and Jane wondered at the community of all of them, at the solidarity that Nate's death had brought among the disparate souls of Angels Crest.

The preacher began to speak, his voice barely audible above the brooding song of the woods. "Merciful God, be Thou now unto us a strong tower of defense...." Jane looked at her neighbors and her friends. She held her lover's hand, and she thought of the grace in her son's homecoming. She closed her eyes and bowed her head because her gratitude overflowed but her sorrow was deep. And all the while, the blind preacher spoke. "O wind of God, come, bend us, break us, till humbly we confess our need; then in your tenderness remake us...."

ANGIE

When the snow began to fall just as they'd all assembled at the spot where Nate had died, Angie remembered how once, when her daughter was only two or three, they had hiked into the woods for a picnic. It was a spring day and the morning had been clear and cold, cloudless. A brilliant day full of promise. Angie's husband was still alive. Life seemed good and right.

They had gone into the woods (so close to this very place, in fact) only a half mile or so when a freak storm from the north roared to sudden life. Without warning, Angie and Rachel were freezing and wet and the darkness preyed on Angie's fears. She remembered thinking then that she must not ever show her daughter this fear, that she must take her daughter from that predicament—that's what it had become—and get her warm. That she must be brave because life was so precious and could so abruptly be taken away. She remembered clutching her daughter's hand, leaving behind the picnic basket, and running out of the woods to the clearing and the car, sitting inside, her heart pounding with relief.

Now, as the preacher began his mourning prayers, Angie knew, like Ethan, that she had made mistakes that had cost her dearly. Nate's death, to her, seemed a warning that you must live your life as if it will all be gone in an instant. She saw Glick standing beside Ethan, his body strong and powerful, and she saw Cindy, like a wilting flower, on the other side. She watched the preacher with a kind of awe, because she had never really paid any attention to him except to feed him on his daily sojourns to the diner and to pass by him once in a while as he sat alone in the town records office.

She heard his voice, its quiet, reverential sway. She heard his words, the melody in his prayers. "Hear our hearts' sorrows, and heal us; cleanse our transgressions and mend our wounds. Set us on our feet; harden us against ourselves, we who crave for ease and rest and peace, so that we may overcome this grief."

Angie heard in his words not just condolence for Ethan and the loss of Nate but also comfort for herself and the difficulties of her life. She saw her life now as it was. This gift, this burden. She wished that Ethan, that she, that all of them, could learn their lessons without such anguish.

She shut her eyes and tried to remove the thought of Nate's terror, of her own daughter and the preciousness of her daughter's childhood. She saw that to be a parent you had to have nerve and strength, but, more than that, you had to have the courage to forgive yourself. She realized that, as a mother who had failed, she'd spent her life since then hurrying from darkness. Now she began to understand that suffering was not meaningless, even though its meaning might be hidden for a long time. She saw that everyone's life was filled with upsets and woes; that suffering was wasted on the one who could not see that in community and connection lay redemption.

She kept her eyes closed, pushing aside her sorrow long enough to express her thanks for Rosie, whom she now saw as sent to her so that she could discover all the good hidden away inside herself, so that she could look at her reflection and say, I forgive you.

CINDY

It was the strangest thing, how she could feel so sober, so clearheaded. It was as if Nate's death had finally come home and found a place within her. She felt his death in every nerve, in every breath and every movement. In all her gestures, she felt it, without relief, taking over, so that even the liquor no longer had consequences.

She walked behind Ethan, confused by all the feelings she had for him: love, anger, pity, hatred. She wondered how she would walk on, how she would face the rest of the day, the rest of her life. Somewhere behind her, she knew, Trevor was walking, and she felt pain about that, too, that she could not find the solace in him that he was willing to offer, that she could not give him what he wanted: her grief, her sorrow, her need for rescue.

As they neared the site of the funeral, Cindy saw Ethan stumble and fall, and everything inside her fell with him. It was as if she were really the one crumbling to the ground. When she stooped down to help him up, their eyes met and she saw in them his need to be forgiven, his need to be loved. She felt as though she were looking at her own image. It was so painfully strong that she had a picture of the two of them lying there with their arms wrapped around each other in the snow like one single person, waiting for death to take them.

When they finally assembled around the cross in the snow—who had put it there and when?—she looked at the feeble preacher and saw for the first time how strong and invincible he was, as if his faith and not his bones were holding him up. When she looked at him, it appeared to her as if light were pouring out of him, long beacons of golden light.

She had never seen faith like that before in anyone, and she felt sorry that she had not tried harder to find God or religion or whatever it was that people found. She saw how it was an act of faith simply to have any at all and she knew that now it was probably too late for her to find rescue in God. She had no place to start from, no trust. She had no belief to hold her over until God, as people said He always did, redeemed her.

The preacher began to speak. His voice seemed to shake, but he also conveyed a strange kind of power and force. She noted how finely, how politely he had dressed, how cold he must have been. His determination and his quiet solicitude shamed her. She knew she would never be like that, could not be like that, that her life was one of weakness, driven by fear.

He seemed to be praying out loud, saying things that had no relevancy to her son's death, to the pain within her and that strange undrunken clarity she felt that brought on the force of her grief. She looked around her at the other mourners, how hard they wept or how fiercely they stared straight ahead, their eyes unwavering but their hearts open and fragile.

Then without any warning, the preacher, who sensed where Cindy stood, turned to her and said, "I cannot explain why some people die and others do not, why cruelty has to be a part of death, why God can't see fit to remove cruelty from the death of a child. Even though I am a preacher, I cannot supply the answers you are looking for. I am sorry for that.

"I can only say that my faith in God must encompass all things in God's world, that I must accept His gifts as well as the pain with equal amounts of faith or I will die myself. I see your suffering. I want to remove it from your heart, but I cannot. Except to tell you that if you open your heart, you will find solace; if you surrender, you will find a way to forgive and to be forgiven. Do not curse God. Do not curse Ethan. Do not curse yourself. You must find your way down this road, but know that you are not alone, for in your darkest hour, God will seek you out, and if your heart is open, you will find salvation."

Cindy closed her eyes and imagined her son running through the grass, running with the light on his hair, his joyful laughter. She saw him running into her arms; she saw herself picking him up and swinging him in the air. She saw the laughter on his face, the joy. She saw him running off again, running farther and farther away, the grass stretching out before him endlessly and his back to her, getting smaller and smaller and finally disappearing altogether beneath the bright blue sky.

JUDGE JACK ROSENTHAL

———————◆———————

The judge left his chambers in search of coffee. His secretary offered to bring some in for him.

"No thanks, June," he said. "Take a break yourself, if you want."

He went outside to a coffee stand and stood in line behind several men and women in dark business suits. The air was sharp and crisp, wintry. He gathered his coat around him tightly and watched as a flock of small blackbirds swooped in tandem, as if they were one animal in the sky. The delicacy and grace of their flight moved Jack for a moment and he watched them alight on the telephone wires above him and be still.

He knew that Ethan Denton would be coming in this afternoon for his arraignment. Jack had seen his name on the docket and he knew well the attorney who would represent him, a sharp young public defender who had moved here a year ago from San Francisco. Jack had heard that Celina Cervantes left San Francisco because her husband had found a job here as a pediatrician. He knew that the courtrooms were full of attorneys like Cervantes, those whose lives held so much hope and promise. They were young and good-looking and successful, with big homes in the new development by the golf course. They had nice cars, beautiful children, and the money for private schools and tropical vacations.

He worried that Cervantes was a little too comfortable and did not fight hard enough for her clients. But it was not something he could quite put his finger on, because he had never seen concrete evidence of it. It was something subtler, something under the surface. The privilege of a certain set made for entitlement, young people, it seemed, who had less drive, less persistence and rigor. Less at stake than he'd had when he was starting out.

The standards, Jack thought, were lowering not just in the legal profession but in the world at large, too. Human conduct seemed subtly worse in general. Jack made himself think of the kindness of individuals. He knew it was dangerous to generalize. As he sat on the bench and sipped his coffee in the cold, he condemned his thoughts, because he knew on some level that he was jealous and afraid. He felt suddenly old and useless. How did you make something new of your life when you were nearing its end?

After he finished his coffee, he made his way back to the courthouse. He was to be in court in fifteen minutes. He hurried past the throngs of people and made his way inside the overheated building.

His chambers were on the second floor. As he went into the stairwell, he heard the door open behind him and he turned around to see Tom Kraft, dressed in his usual impeccable suit, his hair perfectly combed, his face pink and shiny from the cold.

"Morning, Judge," Kraft said.

"Hello, Tom."

"Cold out there."

"It sure is," Jack said.

They began to walk up the stairs. Kraft was filled with energy. It seemed to spark off of him. He was wound up tight, but he kept a smile on his face. There was an overwrought, slightly frantic pleasantness about him that made him seem inscrutable. It occurred to Jack that it must take a lot of work to be Tom Kraft, to be so wound up and yet maintain such a pleasant front.

"Guess we'll be meeting later today in court," Jack said.

Tom looked rather appalled. It usually was not good form to talk about an arraignment. But something about Tom inspired Jack to forget formality. He knew it was driven by his dislike for the man. He was egging him on. He knew it and yet he couldn't stop himself. And besides, it was a shitty thing to do, having Ethan arrested on the day of his son's funeral. He despised Kraft for just these kinds of shenanigans.

"Yes, sir," Kraft said pleasantly. But you could see the tension, the energy behind it.

"Let's try to keep the circus out of it. All right with you, Tom?"

Tom smiled at Jack. It seemed like his smile would break off his face and shatter onto the floor in a handful of tiny pieces. "Ah, Judge. You know how I love the limelight. Now c'mon. Don't let's take the fun out of it."

Jack smiled. He held the door open for Tom. Tom said, "After you, Judge."

Jack was embarrassed by the way his breathing came out winded. The walk upstairs and the high emotion of meeting Tom in the close, overheated stairway caused his heart to beat unnecessarily fast. When they parted at the door to Jack's chambers, Tom said, "See you in court, Judge."

Jack went inside his office. He turned the heat down. He felt himself sweating. He went to the armoire and opened it up. He turned on the television set inside. It was already turned to the local news station.

On the TV screen, a reporter—that same woman with the fur-lined hat and leather gloves he'd kept seeing—was talking into a microphone. The snow was falling hard. As Jack tuned in to what she was saying, the camera zoomed in on the sheriff's car pulling out of the very same place Jack had gone to help search for the boy. Briefly, before turning back to the departing car, the camera focused on the crowd at the clearing, and remarkably, he saw Jane, the woman he'd searched with, stepping into a car with a large, manly woman.

The reporter was saying, "As you can see, the sheriff of this small mountain town is driving Ethan Denton away. Denton was arrested just moments before, after emerging from the woods with the town's preacher and several other mourners, in connection with the death of his three-year-old son. His arraignment is scheduled for this afternoon."

Just then, the camera returned to the reporter and a tall, handsome man walked by with the waitress from the diner. The reporter turned to the man and said, "Excuse me, sir, I'd like to ask you a few questions."

The man turned directly to the camera. "No comment," he said.

"Are you a friend of Ethan's?"

The man looked at the reporter. "Lady," he said. "You need to get your damn camera out of my face."

He heard the waitress—Angie was her name—beside him say, "Let's go, Glick."

The reporter turned toward the camera. "And there you have it, folks. This community is very protective of its own. Not many are talking about the terrible—"

The judge turned the television off. He thought about Tom Kraft, of the way he smiled like he wanted to explode. Then he looked at the wall and saw the picture of his family. He focused in on Marty. He wondered how different he was, really, from someone like Ethan Denton.

GLICK

———————◆———————

The walk back to the turnout where the mourners had parked seemed so much faster than the walk into the forest. They were all cold, wet from the snow, and relieved that it was over. You could see it in the way they hurriedly entered their cars and drove off with little to say and a sense of purpose. The promise of hot coffee and a warm plate of food drove Glick to turn his own thoughts outward, away from this sad place, this snowy forest.

If not for Angie, though, he might have decked the reporters who came at them like a swarm of gnats. He heard her voice beside him, calming him, moving him forward. When he got to his truck, she said, "Come with me, Glick. We'll get your truck later."

"But the preacher," he said.

"Oh, right. I guess you'll need to give him a ride."

Glick nodded. It killed him that he couldn't drive back to town with Angie. He wanted to be near her, to smell her scent, to be comforted by her serenity and her calm. He wanted to hold her hand, to connect himself to something that held the promise of life, of comfort and reprieve.

He watched her drive away as he slowly helped the preacher into the truck. The old man had some difficulty maneuvering himself comfortably into the seat, and Glick made sure that his overcoat was tucked inside the cab before he shut the door. He longed for a sip of a hot whiskey, something to tear at the ice in his blood. He thought he would not find comfort until he could be in Angie's arms.

But once he turned out of the clearing and onto the main road, he was suddenly aware of his breath. He felt as though a huge weight had been lifted from his shoulders, as if he could now begin to breathe regularly again.

"It feels like I've been holding my breath," Glick said.

"I know what you mean," the preacher said. "I have never got used to speaking at a graveside. I was glad when Brother Powell took over the church."

Glick looked out the window. The trees whirled passed, a sea of green lit by the luminous snow. The snow fell softly to earth.

"You were a pro out there," Glick said. He decided he liked the old guy.

"I can't say that I have ever felt comfortable pretending to know how to make people feel better," he said. "Brother Powell, though, he has a talent for that."

Glick sighed loudly and the preacher turned toward him. Glick looked right into his eyes. They were wet and opaque. There was nothing to latch onto. What was it like to be blind? He wanted to know what you *saw* if you could not see.

"When did you lose your sight, Brother?" Glick said.

The old man shook his head. "I lost my vision when I was just a kid living out there on Cage Road. They say I got cat-scratch fever. I dunno. Some say my mother had syphilis and I got the blindness through her womb."

"How old were you?"

"Oh, about five or six when I lost sight altogether."

"Do you remember?" Glick said. "Do you remember what it was like to see?"

The old man shook his head. He removed his hands from his coat and set them on his lap, as if in quiet prayer. He seemed to have sunk into a dream state. His face was slack and calm, his eyes open. He was so still, Glick thought for a moment he might have dozed off to sleep. Glick thought of the preacher sitting in the records office day in and day out, as if he could actually see the pictures on the wall. He remembered what the preacher had said about being the great-great-grandson of one of the town's first children. He wondered what it meant for the preacher to see how his fate had been so clearly mapped out for him.

As if the preacher were reading his mind, he turned to Glick and said, "I feel marked. Like as though God marked my spirit for His own. My being here at all as God's will. You understand?"

Glick said nothing. Then the old man seemed to snap out of his strange reverie. He said, "You live out there on Cage Road. That's hallowed ground, my friend. Sacred in its bitterness and loneliness. You ought best find yourself something else."

"What do you mean?"

"It's a lonely place out there. As a boy, living out there, I always felt I was living on the very edge of the earth. My great-great-grandfather, one of them babies that made it that first winter here, he built the first house. Then it burned down and he died inside. And his son built the new one, where you live now, and he died, too, out there in the woods. And it seemed from then on, every generation, something tragic had to happen out there. My mama, she died out there, too, in that very house, going mad and blind herself. So you see, it's a place for the sorrowful."

Glick thought of his house, of the silent woods that surrounded it. He realized that he had lived there alone for ten long years, that most of his days and nights were spent in solitude. He recalled how he would sometimes go days without speaking to another soul except the animals—his dog and the two cats. He remembered the way the moon filtered in his bedroom on clear nights, of the rage he'd contained within the walls of that house. He remembered the thought he'd had after he'd found Nate in the woods. That he would die alone in that house if he didn't do something about it.

"It is a sorrowful place," Glick said. "You know, it got to be so I felt wedded to that sorrow."

"You best get yourself out of that house," the preacher said. "Leave it for the forest to consume."

When they reached Angie's, Glick parked the car and then helped the preacher out. He said, "You're coming in for some lunch, right?"

But the preacher just shook his head. He thanked Glick and made his way to the records office. Glick watched him walk inside and disappear from sight.

When he opened the door to Angie's, the first thought that came into his head was that he was home. The rich smell of bread and frying bacon and hot coffee seemed to penetrate all the way through his clothes and into his pores. He wanted nothing more than to sink into his favorite booth and order up a plate of eggs and hash browns and bacon.

Angie spotted him and came over.

"C'mon," she said. "Folks are getting good and drunk."

"That sounds like it might be just the thing."

Angie nodded. "You might as well know that I have never been drunk in my life."

"I'm not surprised."

"I don't intend to start now."

"That's okay with me."

"And since I'm getting the record clear and the slate clean, I know all about you and Cindy, even from the other night, 'cause I saw her follow you home, but you don't owe me any explanations, and that's all I ever want to say about it."

Glick felt himself turn hot. Surprised, he looked at Angie, who was flushed, too. He nodded, shamed, and they walked together to a table where Jane and Rocksan were sitting with Jane's son and his pregnant girlfriend. Other people were filtering in and heading for the liquor and the food. The room was filled with relief and sadness.

"I'll get you all some food," Angie said.

Glick took hold of her hand. "Why don't you sit down here and I'll get the food."

Angie smiled. "You know how long I been waiting tables?"

Glick leaned over and whispered in her ear, "From now on, all the tables are gonna turn and everything will be different."

He kissed her ear very softly and went to fill her plate.

Later, as night fell, Glick went home, fed the cats, and retrieved the dog. He then drove over to Angie's house and deposited the dog on the back porch. Angie made some dinner, a plain meal of soup and mashed potatoes, some leftover ham from the diner, and then put a very cranky Rosie to bed. As Rosie and Angie walked down the hall, Glick heard Rosie ask Angie accusingly, "Is *he* sleeping over again?" He did not hear Angie's response, just the warm murmur of her voice.

Glick stood up and carried the dinner dishes to the sink. He began rinsing them and putting them in the dishwasher. Above the sink was a small picture of Angie and Rosie standing formally in front of some kind of amusement park ride. Their smiles seemed forced and formal, and yet there was something unbearably sweet about the two of them standing there side by side.

As Angie walked back into the room, he saw her reflection in the window over the sink. She moved slowly, and before she realized he was looking, her expression was closed and tight. But then she smiled at him in the window and walked up and put her arms around his waist. She rested her head against his back. Outside, the night was black. Glick turned off the water and the two of them stood like that for a very long time. At last, Angie pulled away and sat down in one of the dining room chairs.

"All day long, I kept thinking about Nate lost in the forest, looking for his dad. I am so glad the day is over."

Glick sat down beside her but remained silent.

"When my daughter was little," she said, "before my first husband died, she would stay so close to my side. Anywhere we went, she would never wander off. If she lost sight of either of us, she would get hysterical. But you know, as she grew older, after her dad died and I got remarried, she couldn't wait to get away from me. I was always losing her places and then she would suddenly turn up. Just like that, out of the blue, like she had to make up for all that fear of losing me before." Angie was looking off in the distance. "I think about her every day. I pray every day that she will come home. Turn up one more time, out of the blue."

Glick looked at his hands, so oafish, so clumsy, resting there in his lap.

"I have waited so long to talk about her," Angie said. "I hope you don't mind."

Glick shook his head. "I don't mind," he said.

She stood up then and Glick saw that it was time to shut off the lights and go to bed. He followed her to the room. She went into the bathroom and Glick sat uncomfortably on the edge of the bed. He was unsure what to do. Should he remove his clothes and get into bed? Everything seemed suddenly so painfully awkward, so difficult. He tried to appease himself with the thought that one day, if he was lucky, getting into bed with Angie would be as natural and sweet as dozing off to sleep beneath a warm sun.

Angie came out of the bathroom wearing a robe. She took the robe off and beneath it was her nightgown, a white cotton one with tiny pink flowers on it. He was again dazzled by her brilliance, the serene beauty of her face, the way her hair hung down her back, the lack of flash and glitter in her cotton nightgown. How sexy it seemed in its plainness. She seemed to have undergone some kind of transformation in the bathroom, as though her entire spirit had been lifted by something. She smiled at him and he was able to muster a smile back.

"Poor you," she said, getting into bed. "Don't worry. Soon it won't be so awkward."

He laughed. "I feel like I'm in high school."

"Me, too," she said.

"I suppose I should wash up."

He went to the bathroom, relieved by the ordinary task of washing. As he brushed his teeth and washed his hands and face, it occurred to him that he had longed for ordinariness in the company of a woman since the day of his arrest. He realized he had not had it until now, that living on Cage Road had been a form of prison, too. He remembered what the preacher had said to him on the long drive back to town: that the property was "sacred in its bitterness." He had not known its history, had never bothered to find out. Now it seemed the preacher was right, that he should leave there as soon as possible.

When he returned to the bedroom, Angie was lying still beneath the covers, her eyes closed. She had turned off the overhead light, and the faint yellow glow of the lamp beside the bed lit her up, so that she appeared to him to be the color of burnished gold. He blinked a few times, but still the image of her that way remained, and he took that golden glow as a real thing, like the lamp itself, or the bed she lay upon. He began to undress. She opened her eyes and then sat up slightly to pull down the covers for him. When Glick got into bed, he stared up at the ceiling for a long time. Then he turned to her and said, "I think it's time to sell the house on Cage Road."

She rolled over. She put her hands on him and they made love, softly, quietly, far into the night.

ETHAN

He was prepared for the arrest. In a way, it was almost a relief. The sheriff didn't bother to handcuff him. It was all done very politely. The sheriff handled Ethan with deference, told him kindly that they'd better head to the city now.

Cindy offered to follow them into the city so he could get back to town after it was all over. She said she had nothing else to do. Ethan didn't want to tell her he might not be coming home. He was too relieved and grateful for the offer. He was afraid to go alone. She slipped him her flask before he got into the backseat of the sheriff's car, and he took a sip and handed it back to her.

As they drove out of the forest and hit the highway heading toward the city, Ethan felt a palpable relief not to be back in the snowy woods. He realized that he would never love the backcountry again, and for this, too, he mourned.

"Sheriff," Ethan said, "do you know what criminal negligence is?"

"Naw. It's a legal tangle. Something I figure some lawyer made up along the way when nothing else fit."

"Thanks for holding the media back," Ethan said.

The sheriff looked at Ethan in the rearview mirror and nodded. Ethan saw the toothpick hanging out of the sheriff's mouth. He saw the pity in his eyes. He wanted to be out of the range of such empathy. He looked down at his hands, examined them, turning them over and back again. How fragile his body seemed, how vulnerable.

As they neared the city, the snow had turned to rain and then finally petered out altogether. The clouds hung heavily in the sky. They neared the jail and courthouse, a gloomy complex of modern buildings, and Ethan saw that there were reporters everywhere. People were carrying signs exhorting the use of the death penalty, quoting apocalyptic Scripture from the Bible, or showing their support for Ethan.

"Jesus Christ," the sheriff said.

"Shit," Ethan said. "They're gonna crucify me."

He turned around, but they had lost Cindy miles back, even before they'd left the county. Ethan felt afraid.

"All right," the sheriff said. "We're gonna have to walk up to the jail together here. Now don't do anything foolish, understand? Keep your fists in your pockets and your mouth shut tight."

"Goddamn," Ethan said. "When am I gonna wake up?"

❖ ❖ ❖

Ethan was booked at the county jail. His picture was taken, along with his fingerprints, and they put him in a cell with two other inmates—a drunk who was passed out and curled up on the floor, and a young-looking guy with a black eye and the word NAZI tattooed on his hand—one letter on the back of each of his fingers, above the knuckle.

Ethan looked at the Nazi and sat down on a bench that was permanently set into the wall. The walls were made of hard plaster. There was no window, and the faint smell of urine and body sweat hung in the air. The Nazi glared at him and Ethan felt weak and small. He considered the possibility of getting beaten. But the thought of it didn't cause him any fear.

He was told that a public defender would be by shortly and then an arraignment would follow. He did not know what an arraignment was exactly, except for some vague television version of it. He pictured a clean, open courtroom, well-dressed lawyers standing around politely. His idea of it came from the movies and the crime books he read from time to time. In reality, it was all so different. Shoddier, meaner.

"You that man killed his son?" the Nazi asked.

Ethan looked at him but didn't answer. He felt such hatred well up inside him that he was at a loss as to what to do, how to react, how to even speak without conveying the hatred. He wondered why he felt the need to be polite to a punk kid with a black eye and a foul tattoo on his hand.

"They said you were coming," the kid said. He seemed to beam and drip with revulsion for Ethan, and the irony of it was not lost on Ethan. What a little prick, he thought. He had an image of his son running through the woods, running away into the forest. He heard his boy laughing joyfully, running into the woods.

"Some people say you oughta fry for it. But me, I beg to differ."

Ethan stared at the ground. Against the wall, the drunk made a noise and then was silent.

"'Course," said the kid, "everyone knows, even dumb shits, that you shouldn't take your eyes off a kid."

At that, Ethan stood up and grabbed him by the collar and thrust him against the wall. The kid registered surprise and then fear. Ethan felt his rage bubble forth. He spat when he spoke.

"You shut the fuck up or I swear I'll kill you."

The two of them remained locked there for a moment longer, Ethan holding the kid by the collar against the wall, the kid shocked and surprised by the brutishness and unexpectedness of the act. It occurred to Ethan how silly it was that they should be standing there like that. Then he thought that he was acting just like a criminal. You put a man in a cage, he thought, and he becomes what he will.

Just then, Ethan heard people walking up, their loud voices echoing down the hallway. He let the punk go.

"You keep your fucking mouth shut," he hissed, "or I'll kill you."

The Nazi was stunned. He tried to wrest his dignity back. He spat on the ground and turned away.

A cop and a young woman appeared at the jail cell. The cop began to unlock the cell door. He said, "This is Celina Cervantes. She's your attorney."

"Hello, Mr. Denton," the woman said. She was startlingly beautiful, with long black hair and olive skin. She was dressed in an elegant and expensive-looking suit. The skirt, Ethan noticed, went past her knees. Her leather high heels were immaculate. Everything about her sparkled and inspired confidence. She was both sexy and maternal, a combination that stirred Ethan with a complex set of feelings. He had the surreal image of himself placing his head in her lap and weeping while she stroked his hair and murmured words of comfort. He wanted to be led away from this jail cell, this predicament, and into the arms of a woman like her, someone who could be so strong-looking, so beautiful, so motherlike, a woman who would give him comfort and expect nothing in return.

"How are you holding up?" the attorney asked.

The cop reached for his handcuffs, but the attorney glared at him.

"That won't be necessary, Officer," she said. "Really. He's not a hardened criminal."

The cop appeared momentarily flustered in the attorney's presence. He put the handcuffs away and looked at Ethan.

"It's up to my discretion, buddy. Don't fuck things up."

Ethan nodded. He realized he had entered a world where he had no rights and that in that region he could be treated any way anyone deemed appropriate. He thought of Glick spending all those years in prison for a crime he had never committed. He felt a new sense of respect for Glick, a new kinship. He realized how little time it took to be demoralized, to have your dignity taken away from you. For the first time, he thought of the possibility that he might actually serve time. He didn't think he'd have the resources to come up with a new way to be a man in a place where the regular rules no longer applied.

He remembered a few years back, before Glick slept with his wife, how they had wrapped up a good day of hunting with a bottle of whiskey. They had sat at Glick's house, getting slowly drunk out by the woodshed. Glick had told him what had happened in prison, how he'd been raped and left for dead. Said it was the first he'd ever told anyone. He remembered seeing Glick a few days later, the embarrassment of it between them. Glick never mentioned it again, and Ethan was left to wonder how a man survived a thing like that.

As he walked down the hallway with the attorney, Ethan realized that the only function this all seemed to be serving was to take him away from any thoughts he had for Nate. Instead of the constant image of his son running through the woods looking for him, Ethan now saw that he was being

forced to divide the loyalty of his grief between Nate's last hours on earth
and his own fate. Above all, this bothered him the most. He had come to
rely on the strange comfort of his grief, of the way it had taken him over
completely, of the way he felt it was the only service he could offer his dead
son. This new diversion, where he was forced to find concern for himself,
was the final insult. Why should he matter at all?

He and Ms. Cervantes—how beautiful and starlit she seemed—sat in a
small interrogation room. Ms. Cervantes looked at him with a pleasant
smile. He could make out what he thought was a mixture of pity and polite
solicitude. He saw in her eyes, as he saw in the eyes of everyone he came into
contact with, the narrow relief she felt that this tragedy was not her own.
How brilliant it must feel, at the end of a day, to walk away from his loss,
from the untidy mess of his life.

"Here's where we're at," she said. Ethan heard the way she countrified her
accent, her language. He knew that no educated city-slicker attorney would
phrase a sentence the way she just had. He had read enough books and seen
enough TV to know that educated people did not talk the way a man of his
class did. "You're being charged with criminal negligence."

"Excuse me," Ethan said, "but what the hell is that? I have never heard of
that before."

She smiled patiently. She was all patience and understanding. It began to
make Ethan nervous and uncomfortable. He wanted to tell her to stop trying to comfort him, to talk instead with her big attorney words, to treat him
like he was smart and knew something.

"Plain and simple, negligence is a person's failure to act reasonably, the
way most people might act in a similar situation. When they refer to criminal negligence, they imply that there's a degree of recklessness added to it."

"But I didn't think it out. It was an accident."

"Make no mistake about it, Ethan, you are not being tried for murder
here. There is no dispute over whether or not there was any intent."

"So what do they want? What are they trying to do?"

"Okay. Here's the lay of the land. Listen carefully. You have to understand that the DA—his name is Tom Kraft—is trying to build a career.
This is the best case to come to him in a long time. You have seen the me-

dia out there. You know that what happened to your son"—here, Ethan saw that she bowed her head slightly and gently folded her hands as if in prayer—"has touched a nerve with a lot of people. So, you see, it's a good case for Kraft. He plans on really milking it. Now if you plead guilty, you avoid a trial. If you plead not guilty, there will be a trial. I want to advise you now that if you go to trial, Ethan, Kraft will drag you and your ex-wife and every detail of your divorce and the child-custody battle, all of it, through the mud. He will have every intention of establishing a pattern of behavior that will prove you are reckless. He will go after you."

"It was a *fucking mistake*," Ethan said. His head was pounding. He thought of Cindy out there somewhere with her whiskey.

Ms. Cervantes nodded her head. She licked her lips and pressed on. "Having said all that, I think a jury trial can work to your advantage. I think we can mitigate some of the damage that Kraft will be able to call up by appealing to the jury's sense of . . . *empathy*. Everyone who is a parent knows on some level that right now you are suffering the worst form of punishment. And, also, that it could have easily been them. You may get off with a verdict of not guilty. But I warn you, it will be brutal. It will go on for a long time. And public sentiment right now seems to be evenly divided. I won't lie to you, Ethan. This case *will* be tried in the media."

Ethan looked at Ms. Cervantes. He wondered about her life. He thought of her as someone who would never be caught in this situation. He saw her as blessed. Blessed with beauty and brains and money. He felt resentment and admiration for her all at once.

"What would you do?" he asked.

"I'd go to trial. Judge Rosenthal is a fair man. I'm a good attorney. We can beat Kraft."

Something in her last words caught his attention. He suddenly felt as though he were a pawn in a game that was much larger than he could ever have imagined or understood. Ms. Cervantes talked fair. She seemed fair. But what was this really about? Did she dislike Kraft? Was she ambitious, too?"

"Is my wife, my ex-wife . . . is she out there? Can I talk to her for a minute? Privately?"

Ms. Cervantes pressed her lips together. She put both hands on the table and pushed herself up. "Of course," she said. To Ethan, it sounded curt. "I'll go get her."

Ethan sat alone in the room. There were no windows. It was painted an institutional green, the color of pureed peas. He thought then of his son, lying down to die, his thumb thrust in his mouth, the tears in his eyes. He clung to his grief, to its pulsing glow.

Cindy arrived and sat down. She looked at Ethan. Her eyes were swollen nearly shut. Her cheeks were blotchy and pink. She seemed to be trembling slightly.

"Jesus Christ," she said. "Look what we've done."

Ethan nodded. "I did it."

"But if I hadn't—"

"It was me. My fault. You got nothin' to feel badly about, you understand."

She nodded. Ethan saw her bite her lip, hold back tears. For the first time, he saw her as courageous. As better than he'd thought her to be.

"The lady attorney says I should go to trial. She says she can beat the DA. She says we can appeal to the sympathy of the jury."

"What do you think?"

"I'm no criminal. I made a mistake. I don't know." He felt frantic. His heart raced. Everything was happening so fast. How could a person be expected to make a decision, any decision, after his boy just died?

"So then maybe, you know, you should go to trial."

"Only thing is," Ethan said. "Only thing is, they'll drag us through the mud, Cin. They'll try the case in the media. It will be a big thing. Like O.J. Every day, we'd have to walk through a crowd of reporters. They'll dissect everything in our lives. The drinking. You know, how we fought over him."

Cindy nodded. She appeared grim and afraid. She seemed to be shrinking before Ethan's eyes. He saw how he had ruined her.

"Whatever you gotta do, Ethan, you gotta do. I got to tell you it's hard for me right now being here. But he was our son."

She seemed to be getting smaller and smaller before Ethan's eyes. He saw the damage he had already done. He saw how his arrogance and selfishness had destroyed his marriage and killed his boy. He saw what it might do still. He reached across the table.

"Listen," he whispered. "I guess I've done enough damage. I guess I've ruined everything. So now, thinkin' it through and all, I see how I can't do it. I can't drag you through it. I'll plead, baby. Okay. I'll plead."

Cindy nodded her head vigorously, all the while growing smaller and smaller before his very eyes.

- - -

Ethan had to sit in jail for another couple of hours. The Nazi was gone. So was the drunk. At last, a jailer came for him. His attorney and Cindy met him in the hallway.

"Ready?" Ms. Cervantes asked.

Ethan nodded. Together, they left the jail and made their way through the crowd of reporters and onlookers to the courthouse. When they got inside, they were met by more media. Cameras were everywhere. Ms. Cervantes said over and over again, "No comment." Ethan and Cindy held hands. Ethan's heart raced. He tried to remember his son, but he couldn't picture Nate. He couldn't find Nate anywhere. He worried that the media and the circus around him would take him away from the flame of his grief. He wanted to feel that pain. It was the only thing he had left.

When they arrived in court, though, it was suddenly quiet. It was hot and close, humid. The room smelled the way it had when he was back in school on rainy days. There was an institutional smell of papers and paint and concrete floors. The judge was behind the bench. There were several men in dark suits conferring together at one end of the courtroom.

Cindy took a seat. The room was empty. Ethan said, "Where is everyone?"

"The judge ordered the courtroom closed," Ms. Cervantes whispered. She guided him by his elbow up to a table on the right-hand side of the courtroom. Ethan was too afraid to look at the prosecutor. There were three men standing there. He wasn't sure who Tom Kraft was.

From there, it went so quickly that by the time it ended, only moments later, Ethan felt like he'd missed it. The judge barely looked up from the bench. But something about him struck Ethan as familiar. He felt as though he had seen the man somewhere before. The judge said, "How do you plead?"

Ms. Cervantes told him to stand up. She told him what to say.

"Guilty, Your Honor."

The judge's face remained impassive. He looked at the prosecutor. Ethan followed his eyes. He saw the man he guessed was Tom Kraft rise up heavily from his seat. He could see the man's narrow lips, the way they were set around his mouth so tightly and squarely.

"We request he be held in lieu of one million dollars, Your Honor."

"That's ridiculous," Ms. Cervantes said. "He has no record. He clearly is not a risk to society, Your Honor. He's not a flight risk."

The judge still had not looked at Ethan.

"I'm waiving bail, Mr. Kraft. He's released on his own recognizance. I'll rule one week from today on his plea."

The judge hit his gavel. Ethan thought he could hear Cindy quietly weeping behind him. He turned around to leave. The judge called out to him.

"Mr. Denton," he said.

For the first time, they made eye contact, and in that moment Ethan knew where he'd seen the judge before. He recognized him as the stranger who had pulled up in the Mercedes at the search site, the same man, he now realized, who had been ducking for cover when they'd passed each other at the mortuary. He was startled. Something made him afraid. He did not know the habits of judges and lawyers. He did not know what anyone in this strange place was after, what levels of corruption and deceit existed in the courtrooms of America, what nuance of kindness and care was true and real. But he felt intuitively that he should say nothing about it. That he should remain still and quiet, unsuspecting.

"Yes?" Ethan said. He heard the tentativeness in his voice, the fear.

"I'm sorry for your loss," the judge said.

They remained locked in each other's gaze for another few seconds, and in that short amount of time, Ethan knew to keep his instincts intact, to trust them like an animal. He murmured a thank-you and turned away. He couldn't even be a hundred percent sure he was free to go, but it seemed that way. He saw Tom Kraft grimace at the other end of the courtroom. He knew, at least, that for Tom Kraft the party was over.

"You're free to go," Ms. Cervantes said. She was smiling pleasantly, genuinely. "Be back here next week. The judge will sentence you then. Call me to double-check the time. And we'll need to go over some of the details of the sentencing hearing. You'll want to prepare some kind of statement."

She handed Ethan her business card. It was hard to believe that it was over.

ROCKSAN

———◆———

She had decided, before the funeral was even over, before the preacher had even neared the end of his sermon for the dead boy, that she was going to get good and drunk. Rocksan also made another decision. It was less articulated than the first, less simple. But she saw, in the funeral and in the shocking and strange turn of events in her own life, that there was only one choice involving the administration of her brief occupancy on this earth. Tomorrow you could be dead, she remembered thinking as she and Jane walked out of the woods. She had made the decision to celebrate her good fortune, her good life and its fine bounty. Nate's death, though immensely sad, had made her comprehend how lucky she was.

On their way to Angie's, they stopped to check on George and Melody, who both wanted to go to the diner. They said they had talked about it. Though they didn't know Ethan or Nate, they said they felt driven to pay their respects.

When they arrived, Rocksan saw that the crowd at Angie's had found a collective drunken relief among themselves. She joined in, until finally Jane insisted they get home. She was afraid Melody was going to have the baby right there on the floor of Angie's, in the midst of a funeral meal.

They drove home in silence for a long time. Then Melody said, "If it's a girl, I think we ought to name her Jane."

Immediately, Jane laughed. "Oh my God. You can't be serious?"

"Are you serious?" George asked.

"Well, I just think it's such a lovely name."

"Forget it," George said. "No offense, Jane. But . . ."

"None taken. Honestly, Melody, it's sweet, but I'd be horrified."

Rocksan saw Melody shrug her shoulders in the backseat and look out the window. She never seemed to be too troubled by anything. Rocksan had never met anyone who was so even-keeled, so dependable in mood and spirit.

When they finally got home, it was late afternoon and everyone was tired. After talking quietly to George and Melody in the living room, Jane went upstairs to lie down. George and Melody were left sitting on the couch, and in moments, both of them were asleep, George sitting up, Melody lying down, her feet spread across George's lap.

Rocksan was too logy and whiskey-riddled to rest comfortably. But she was also tired and, in the end, sad. The loss of Nate, though she'd hardly known the boy, had sunk into the deep places of her heart.

She went outside to the hives, which sat silently in the brooding quiet, like tiny homes in an empty town. Rocksan thought about Angels Crest and she remembered when she'd first arrived in town, when she'd first heard the story of the settlers dying that terrible winter, how quaint it had seemed. She recalled her arrogance, thinking she was some hot-shit San Franciscan with her bad lesbian self. Everything in Angels Crest had been so picturesque, so slightly beneath her. She could hardly recall that person. Now she saw that in reality, this world was, in many ways, much less provincial than her life had been in San Francisco.

For the first time, she really thought about the Angels Crest myth. How terrible it must have been that all those people had died. And yet, how strange that those babies had managed to stay alive. What caprice, what providence had mapped out their destiny with such surprise and grace? She could see why others would believe in angels. She also could see why she could not. It was hard to cast your lot with the angels when all your life people had ostracized and ridiculed you.

She turned her attention to the hives. They looked so somber, sitting there all sealed for the winter. Though she'd requeened late, Rocksan had faith that the bees would survive the winter. But she had seen a hive destroyed by winterkill. It was only a few years ago, when the weather had turned too cold and the bees slowly starved to death because they'd refused to break the cluster they'd made around the queen to keep her warm. The queen eventually died, too. Rocksan had tried to find comfort in the inevitability of it—they were either going to freeze or starve to death.

But when she'd found dead bees with their heads poked into empty comb cells, as if searching for one last drip of honey before dying, it had turned her heart. Hundreds of dead bees had lain on the bottom board, and the few that remained alive had been loopy and disoriented, huddled together to stay warm. But they'd died, too, and without a queen, the hive was decimated. There was no hope for rebirth.

Rocksan remembered that winter and how much the devastated hive had broken her heart. Now she equated it with the first winter in Angels Crest, when all but a few of the settlers had died. Again she wondered what fate had intervened to spare the lives of those few children. She saw the broad province of human life, drifting through the ages, of those who died young and those who lived long. She saw her own life as a gift—how strange that she had never thought that way about it before. She was shocked to feel tears spring once again to her eyes.

She could not account for this sudden sentimentality, this sudden ease for crying. Had it been the death of the little boy? Had it been the arrival of Melody and George, the prospect of a new life entering theirs? What could possibly have come uncorked, unscrewed, set free within her? She looked off into the distance at the snow-cloaked mountains and the graying dusk. She felt a clear understanding of life's ebb and flow. She believed, perhaps for the first time, that she fit somewhere in humanity's web, and something—a broad, shimmering tide of forgiveness—seemed to release itself within her, so that all around her the world seemed to glow with a bold, humming life.

JANE

◆

After the funeral, Jane felt hollowed out. She and Rocksan walked somberly toward their car, holding hands. She realized it was one of the few times they had ever displayed any public affection in Angels Crest, and she noted, too, that no one seemed to care. It was as if the death of Nate, the arrest of his father, and the unanimous contempt they all held for the media had made them equal in one another's eyes.

They had stopped at the house to pick up George and Melody, and when they arrived with the other mourners at the diner, Jane worried that Rocksan would get drunk and embarrass her. She was always worried when Rocksan drank, because she would get even more rowdy, more obnoxious. Back in the day, when they lived in San Francisco, Rocksan would hold court, delivering her irreverent drunken diatribes against the establishment. But that was fitting in a place where flamboyance earned you stripes. Here, in this town they now called home, on the saddest day anyone of them could remember, flamboyance would mean immediate ostracism.

But it turned out that Rocksan kept her drunk confined to their table. Melody seemed preoccupied by her pregnancy, and George rolled his eyes the second time that Rocksan spilled her drink. But there was no scene. It occurred to Jane that perhaps Rocksan had finally been tamed. Still, she was relieved when they left. She could not understand the growing boisterousness, the startling sounds of laughter as the mourners drank more and more whiskey and beer. She felt an ache within her that only a good night's sleep and some time would heal. She could not remove the image from her mind of Nate running frantically through the forest in search of his dad. Children knew only a few things, and one was that their parents would always be there to rescue them, no matter that it wasn't always true. She hoped that when he laid down to die, he believed his dad would be coming for him soon.

When they got back home, the house was cold. Jane turned on the furnace and Melody and George grabbed a blanket and went to lie on the couch.

"The thought of climbing those stairs," Melody said. "I wish this baby would stay dropped. She drops, then crawls back up into my throat."

George looked at Melody with concern. He said, "You still have a couple weeks till your due date."

"Screw the due date. This baby is not gonna stay in me for two more weeks, you can be sure of that. I am, from this moment on, willing her to get the hell out. I can't stand another second of it. I keep peeing on my damn self."

Jane remembered being pregnant with George. She remembered those last few weeks. She had bought into the lie that pregnancy was beautiful and peaceful and miraculous. No one had told her about the hemorrhoids, the vomiting, the constant leakage of God knew what kind of fluids on her underwear day in and day out. She thought she was supposed to be happy during pregnancy. But she had blown up like a whale. She had lost her balance. The last month of her pregnancy, she was always falling over.

"Oh, Melody," Jane said. "I do remember that."

George looked at Jane and she wanted to tell him everything. What it had been like the moment he arrived. How beautiful he had seemed to her, in spite of his colicky entry into the world.

"You, George, were a gorgeous baby. I had a C-section because you just didn't feel like dropping. . . ."

"Oh God, please don't tell me that," Melody said.

"And so you came out so perfect, with none of that conehead stuff," Jane said. "They let me hold you for a moment before they took you away, and I remember thinking that it was all worth it."

George was smiling slightly. He said, "Dad never told me anything about it. You know, he hired this lady, Mrs. Mullick, to come in every day and take care of me. She was there for almost ten years."

Jane looked at the floor. "I am so sorry. . . ."

"I don't see how we can get past this if you keep apologizing, Jane," George said wearily.

"Be nice, George," Melody said.

"I don't have to be nice. Jesus Christ," George said.

Melody smiled weakly at Jane. "He thinks he's pregnant, too," she said. Then she turned to George and said, "I'm the only one here who gets to be a bitch."

"I'm sorry," George said. "It's just with that dead boy and all these re-grets . . . I just want it to be easier. I want our baby to come into something easy."

Jane nodded. "George, life is so hard. I don't mean to start acting like a mother now and be giving you advice. But I have to say that life is hard and you are young and the baby *is* coming into a good place. You and Melody will be wonderful parents."

George nodded. "I just feel like that dead boy is a bad omen."

"Only if you say so," Jane said, aware she was mimicking Melody.

"He gets glum sometimes," Melody said. "But I never do. That's why we get along so well."

George leaned back on the couch and Melody stretched out on the couch and put her feet on his lap. Jane put the blanket over her. Her big belly loomed over her tiny frame.

"I'm so tired," George said.

Melody rolled her eyes. "I'm the pregnant one, George," she said. "You keep forgetting that."

Jane looked at her son. His eyes were closed. He was leaning back into the couch. His face was so adult-looking, the bones as if carved out of stone, so fine and sharp and clear. She felt her heart beating with pride and she worried that for the rest of her life she'd never get to show it to anyone.

"George," she said. He opened one eye, then the other. "You were such a beautiful baby," she said.

Jane went upstairs to lie down. She felt a bad headache coming on. She felt bleak and wretched and filled with grief. She wished Nate had been found alive, and for a moment she pretended it was so. She saw the joy on his father's face. The relief. She felt a deep welling of anger rise within her. Why did a little boy have to die? It seemed so wrong. It *was* so wrong.

She stood by the window and watched Rocksan make her way to the hives. Rocksan looked them over, walking quietly beside them. Everything about her seemed strangely reverential, at peace. Jane had never seen Rocksan so still, so tranquil-looking. Then, to her surprise, she watched as Rocksan began to cry. She remembered the way Rocksan had bawled like a baby in the woods during the funeral and she thought that it was a miracle. It was something she had never seen in their twenty years together, and now it had happened twice in one day.

Jane watched Rocksan standing solemnly out by the hives. It had taken her all the time they'd been together to coax out even the smallest details about Rocksan's father. It occurred to her that perhaps Rocksan had not been crying—was not crying now—for Nate at all, but for herself and her own terrible losses.

She left the window and went to the bed. She lay down and closed her eyes. She realized that Rocksan had probably saved her from herself all those years. She thought of her son downstairs, of the baby to come. She pretended that many years had gone by and all was forgiven and all the wounds had healed.

ANGIE

That night, after the funeral, long after Glick had fallen asleep, Angie lay awake thinking of her daughter. She had not allowed herself to think of Rachel for any length of time in the past because it brought forth too much pain. The extent of her own culpability in Rachel's disappearance had never left her.

Now she remembered back to the time when Rachel was young and playful and happy. She traced her thoughts to her marriage to the truck driver, how then, and only then, Rachel had turned away, started smoking and drinking. Angie realized now, too late of course, that the two of them would have been fine alone. Why had she felt the need to muck their lives up with an ill-suited marriage?

Glick made a noise in his sleep and rolled over. In the dark, she could make out his form beneath the blankets. She felt a surge of love for him. The years alone had taken their toll on her. The wanting, the desires—both sexual and emotional—had lain far in the recesses of her mind. Now, whenever she looked at Glick, they burst through. She wished that Rachel would come home. She wished for the circle to complete itself.

She knew that the funeral and Nate's death were stirring up her own sense of loss. She told herself that it would pass in time, that grief was never as hungry as it seemed at first. She knew that she was amazingly skilled at shouldering the burdens of her sorrows and that this wound, which had been opened simultaneously by Nate's death and her love for Glick, would close back up and return to the small corners of her heart.

Finally, she felt sleep coming. She gave herself over to it, lying close beside Glick, smelling his scent, taking comfort in his being there. You cannot hold on to what you haven't got, she told herself, and finally, at last, sleep came for her.

In the morning, Angie woke to an empty bed. She felt afraid and upset for a moment, but then she heard voices outside. She looked at the clock and was shocked to see it was past 8:00 A.M. She had decided the day before to keep the diner shut up for the day and now she rose stiffly and somewhat guiltily from her bed and went to the window.

A wan sun shone down on the wet earth. Outside, Glick and Rosie were dressed for the cold. Steam poured forth from their mouths as they shouted and played with the dog, who looked like he might simply drop dead from the bliss of all that attention. Rosie was throwing a ball to the dog and the dog did not seem to mind that it went neither in the right direction nor very far. She heard Glick say something to Rosie and Rosie answer back. Glick bent over, laughing, and then he picked up the ball and threw it for the dog. Rosie shouted gleefully when the dog jumped high in the air and caught the ball in his mouth.

Angie went back to the bed and sat in the silent room, hearing the faint sounds of their voices outside and the ticking of the clock in the hallway. She saw the curious atlas of her life, the roads connecting the destinations, the way no route ever seemed fixed, no avenue untenable. It seemed to her that her life was playing out exactly as it was meant to be, that nothing, *nothing*, ever happened without a reason. She saw that she'd had to lose so much so that she could be here, in this moment, a different woman, a lucky woman, listening to the laughter of the people she loved most in the world drift gently on the cold winter air.

When she finally pulled herself together, she put on some clothes and went to the kitchen to scare up breakfast. She made some eggs and some fried potatoes. She sliced up a few bananas and put them in the blender with a cup of yogurt and a little orange juice. She dug some bacon out of the freezer and fried it up, and finally, just as everything was cooking at its peak, Glick and Rosie came inside. She heard Rosie slam the door and race down the hallway toward her room as Glick made his way to the kitchen.

He leaned over and gently, awkwardly kissed her on the cheek. His lips were cold. He made her feel so rare, so precious. His deference to her, the way he handled her with tentative but oddly sure hands and glances, made her feel beautiful, as priceless as history, as valuable as the future.

"You okay?" he asked.

She nodded. "You?"

"Good," Glick said.

Angie noticed that his nose was running. He was red from the cold. He rubbed his hands together and blew on them.

"So cold," he said. "Jesus."

"It's always like that when the storm has passed."

"You feel like the world will break apart, it's so cold," he said.

She poured Glick some coffee, then went back to her cooking. Rosie came into the room with the photo album and sat down beside Glick. She began turning the pages of the photo album and humming to herself. Angie could tell that Rosie wanted Glick to ask her about it. Finally, when he didn't and she could no longer stand it, she said, "This is my mommy."

She turned the photo album toward Glick and he looked carefully at the page of pictures.

"She's pretty," Glick said, and Angie was glad that he sounded sincere.

Rosie turned the page for him. "This is her. And this is her, and this is her. And this is Grammie."

Rosie was pointing at all the pictures. She was turning the pages for Glick. Glick remained quiet, tracking the pictures not like an adult trying to please a kid but like someone who was interested. Angie saw how he was filling in the gaps left behind by her daughter's absence, and she felt that familiar pang for her daughter, who in so many ways completed her story. Finally, Rosie turned to the last page; then she closed the book and slid off the chair with it in her hand and left the room.

"Your daughter is pretty," Glick said. "Like her mama."

Angie smiled. "She really is pretty. She got the best of me and her dad. A blend of us. Amazing how she didn't really favor either of us, but both of us at once."

"What was your husband like?"

"You mean her dad?"

Glick nodded.

"He was a nice man. Very plain in so many ways. Uncomplicated. He was gentle and kind and, well, honestly, a little dull. But I liked him that way. I find I like things a little dull."

Glick smiled and then took a sip of his coffee. Angie admired his beauty, the way his eyes—so boldly blue—sank deep into their sockets, the fine angles of the bones in his face. She felt herself desiring him, and she turned the bacon and buttered some toast and flipped the potatoes, aware of the strange erotic swell that was taking over. The smell of the food, its greasy spatter and richness, the wan sun, the palest of Glick's scent still on her skin—all this befuddled and bewitched her. She felt herself turning red, and when she looked at Glick, she saw that he, too, was at once filling with desire, that he had been watching it fill her. Their eyes met and they smiled at each other with a sly kind of acknowledgment, as if to say, I want you, too.

Glick said, "I can hardly look at you."

She said, "Honestly, Glick. I feel ridiculous."

He laughed. She did, too. When Rosie came running into the room, she stopped for the briefest of moments, as if her radar had been stung by the power of what went on between Angie and Glick. Then she sat down with her photo album and said, "Can we go on the snowshoes today?"

Angie looked at Glick. He nodded. She said, "Sure."

Then Rosie turned to Glick. "I want you to bring that dog," she said, sassy and adultlike.

CINDY

When it was all over and the judge had let Ethan go, Cindy was as hollow as she could ever remember feeling. As they drove in the darkness back to Angels Crest, she saw the enormity of the last few days as if it all lay below her. She turned to Ethan and said, "I feel like I'm outside myself, looking at my life like I'm not in it anymore."

Ethan didn't say anything in response, and his reticence and silence were a welcome thing, something she had learned to appreciate when they were married because the chatter in her own head was so loud, so boisterous. She went over those last few terrible moments in the jail, when Ethan made the decision not to go to trial. She saw it as the one thing that might someday, years from now, when the bitterness was not so unforgiving, redeem him in her eyes.

She had a vague feeling that now was the time for her to change her life somehow. She didn't know what she meant by this thought, only that something different had to happen. She thought that if she didn't do *something*, then she would never get over the loss of her son, the destruction of her life.

When they finally got back to town, it seemed deserted. Angie's was closed, a few lights glowing mournfully in the back. The bar was open and Cindy saw some people she drank with standing outside, smoking cigarettes in the cold. When they passed the hardware store, Cindy saw Ethan lower his eyes.

When they arrived at the clearing where the mourners had parked and gathered before the hike into the woods, only Ethan's car was there. In the moonlight, it seemed the loneliest thing Cindy had ever seen. She turned and said good-bye to Ethan, and for a moment their eyes locked. She saw in his gaze what they had once been to each other and what they had become.

"Cindy," he said.

"Get some sleep, Ethan."

Soon she was driving alone in the woods, her headlights illuminating the canopy of trees, the cold, snowy banks, and the narrow curves in the road. Her sorrow made everything stand out so clearly. The details of the woods were remarkably apparent, starkly drawn, as if they'd been penciled in with a sharp point. She seemed to see every pine needle, every indentation on the bark of the trees, the point at which a snowbank ended and the atmosphere began.

Then she realized that she wasn't drunk and that though she'd taken an occasional sip from her flask, she hadn't been drunk most of the day. She wondered over that for a minute, over the fact that she wasn't sick from the lack of it, that she hadn't craved the drink, hadn't longed for it, desired it to death. She saw for the first time how encompassing her loss was, how it had taken over even the fierceness of her longing for booze.

She drove slowly and kept the sorrow at bay by not thinking of her son or of Ethan, or of the tragic way their lives had run, focusing instead on the clarity of the woods, the crisp outlines of the landscape against the starlit night. She thought only of the quiet woods, the sleeping animals, the bears making their dens for the winter, the rodents gorging and stuffing themselves for the bitter months ahead, the owls with their beady, cold-lit eyes, searching for prey. She thought of these things over and over again until she left the piney cavern of the forest and started to make her way toward the town, passing the house where Jane and Rocksan lived, then entering Main Street, passing the bank, the library, the records office, the hardware store, and Angie's, until she finally reached Trevor's bar and parked the car.

She got out. The night was cold and sharp and bitter, and when she breathed in, her lungs hurt, reminding her that she hadn't smoked in hours. She dug in her purse for her cigarettes, and when she found them, she lingered outside and looked at the stars. She remembered driving in the back of the station wagon with her mother and father when she was a little girl.

She remembered her mother saying that when you died, you turned into a star. She looked up and picked a star and decided that it was Nate. She said, "Mommy loves you, Nate. Don't forget that."

She was so close to leaving the bar, so close to *not* having a drink that she almost turned around and got back into her car. But then she thought that it was enough just to *think* about not drinking. It was something she hadn't done in—how long, years? So for now, it was enough. And when she made the decision to go inside, she had two simultaneous thoughts. The first was how good it would feel to drink and the second was that it hadn't been her mother—could not have been, since she would have been too young to re-member—who told her that about the stars at all. It had been her drunken grandmother, who'd sat up one night and blurted it out just before she died, telling her that the best thing about dying was you got to be a star in the sky and shine forever.

Inside, the bar was smoky and dimly lit. A cluster of people were stand-ing near the dartboard, boisterously laughing at something. It seemed weird that anyone could laugh. That there was anything worth laughing over. Shouldn't they be grieving? Then she realized that of course they wouldn't be grieving. The loss was hers.

A few people were sitting at the bar. When Trevor saw her, he came out from behind the bar and walked over to her. He helped her off with her coat. He said, "You okay? What happened? Is Ethan back? Is he in jail?"

"Trevor," she said. It was odd, but she was whispering, as if it could still all the noise around her. "Gimme a sec, wouldya?"

"Sorry," he said. He sat her down, then went behind the bar, and poured her a glass of whiskey. "It's just, you know, I was so worried. I kept thinking about you."

The others nodded at her. June Moon, the town's aging flower child, smiled. "Hiya, kid," she said.

"Ethan pleaded guilty," Cindy said.

"What the fuck?" Trevor said.

"He wanted to get it over with."

"Is he in jail?"

"It doesn't work like that, Trevor. Jesus. Could you let me have a drink. I've been down valley all fucking day long. I'm thirsty and tired and I just feel like . . ." She didn't finish the sentence. Couldn't.

"Sorry," he said. "I just . . ."

She downed her drink. "He has to go back in a week and the judge is gonna sentence him. That's all I know, Trevor. Really. That's it."

Trevor nodded. She could see he was trying to keep quiet. She felt her heart beating steadily, like a rocket, but unfaltering and strong. She thought of her son lying down to die in the woods. She thought of her son as a star.

"I gotta go home, Trevor. I gotta go. Can I take some whiskey with me? There's nothing in the house. And I haven't eaten a thing. Can I get a sandwich or something?"

She knew the kitchen behind the bar—such as it was—was closed.

"I can make it myself," Cindy said.

"No, no. I'll make you one. Ham? And cheese?"

She nodded. Trevor said to the folks at the bar, "Be right back."

Everyone nodded. No one was in a hurry. June Moon scooted over to her. She sat down next to Cindy. She said, "Honey, I am so sorry."

Cindy nodded. She realized that no one in here was her friend. They were all a bunch of drunks. They were too consumed by their need to drink to be entirely selfless enough for friendships. She knew this because she was just like them. She saw it all so clearly now. How she had spent her life in this bar with people she'd once thought were her friends but who hadn't even shown up at the funeral or her house. Jane, the lesbian, had brought her not one casserole, but *two*. She thought of the casseroles sitting in the fridge in her shit-colored apartment. She had forgotten there was food at her apartment. All she wanted was some whiskey, something to eat, bed.

She stood up, went behind the bar, and poured herself another drink. It wasn't an unheard-of thing to do, but still, everyone eyed her jealously from their bar stools. She had a terrible thought. She thought maybe they wished that some horrible disaster had befallen them so they could get away with the same thing. She had to get out of there.

"Trev," she shouted toward the kitchen. "I gotta go."

She took a bottle off the shelf and walked out of the bar. It was so cold outside, it felt like a slap in the face. Trevor came up behind her, a sandwich in his hands. It was unwrapped and sloppily made. Cindy noticed the meat hanging out of the sides. It had been like that all night. Everything so clear and defined. All the things in her visual field bigger, brighter, all the details easy to see.

"What the . . ." Steam poured forth from Trevor's mouth and Cindy could make out the crestfallen fury in his eyes.

"I have to go."

"You can't just take the bottle. I mean, you can. But . . ."

"I'm sorry," she said. She started to cry. She just wanted to be sitting in her shit-colored apartment getting slowly, deathly drunk. All of a sudden, that was all she seemed capable of doing. Reluctantly, she held the bottle out to him.

"No, it's okay. You keep it," he said. "I'll close up early. I'll come over."

She shook her head. "You don't have to do that, Trev."

He opened her car door for her. He said, "I'll see ya later." He'd forgotten to give her the sandwich.

When she got home, the apartment was too hot. She hadn't turned off the thermostat before the funeral. She had the vague worry, as she did every month, that she wouldn't be able to pay the heating bill. She sat down on the couch and drank straight from the bottle. She went into the kitchen and jabbed a fork into the casserole and took a couple of bites. It tasted good, so she scooped some out and put it into a bowl and warmed it up in the microwave. When it was hot, she went back to the living room, picking up the paper plate with the macaroni on it that Nate had made for her, and sat down on the couch. She ran her fingers over the macaroni on the plate and she ate the casserole, which was warm and delicious, like something a mother might make for her family. She drank until she felt the familiar obliterating comfort of the liquor, and all the while she ran her hands over the macaroni on the plate. She hoped that Trevor wouldn't come over, but she knew he would. She knew that if she didn't get out of Angels Crest, Trevor would always come over. He would always be there. When she thought about it drunkenly, it didn't seem like a bad thing, but it also seemed like a terrible thing.

She stood up. She thought of her son, her boy, whose face she had stroked and also hit, whose face she loved and cherished, her boy, who lay on top of her their first night in the hospital, with his tiny feet holding him up and his small wrinkly body lying across her breast, her boy as a star. She went outside and stood behind the motel-like railing in front of her apartment and looked up at the sky. The lights at the apartment complex were too bright to see the stars, so she grabbed her coat and her bottle and her cigarettes and went out into the parking lot, as far away from the lights as she could.

Her breath was thick and steamy in the cold air. The night was black and rigid. She drank and smoked and looked up at the stars. She saw the stars and she picked one out again and began to talk to Nate as if he were still alive. She told him she loved him, that she was sorry, that she would always love him no matter what. She said she wished he hadn't died at all, but also that he hadn't died the way he had. She told him that she hoped he hadn't suffered. She felt as if Nate were right there beside her. She no longer thought about him running wildly through the woods. Now she saw him as a star, shining brightly in the sky, forever and ever.

JUDGE JACK ROSENTHAL

───────◆───────

One thing Jack had always prided himself on was his ability to know and understand his emotions. The babbling of his joys and irritabilities. He attributed this knowledge to his lifelong effort to keep himself in line with Torah, with faith. On any given day, any discontent could be met head-on with this trick of his—prayer and solitude. It always allowed him to find the seeds of his dissatisfaction.

But when Ethan Denton arrived in his courtroom, Jack felt a strange wave of vertigo, a sense that the world was coming undone and there was nothing, not even God, to hold on to. He had no memory of such a sense of powerlessness, of falling, of collapse. He was a judge, a father, a learned man, a man of God. He was a man people respected, a person people trusted and turned to. In his later years, young people had even turned to him as surrogate for their own absent or dead fathers. Jack's sense of loss as Ethan trudged into his courtroom was terrifying. And in turn, he was stupefied by his own fear.

Ethan, he now saw, was entirely broken. Utterly humbled by his grief. Jack thought of Job, but he saw that Ethan had no faith to sustain the circumstances of his present life. He was a man with nowhere to go, nowhere to turn for comfort. Jack noticed Ethan's ex-wife, the woman with the pink streak dyed down one side of her hair. He wondered what it must be like for her to be there, sitting behind the father of her dead boy, the man who had been responsible for the death.

He was relieved and not at all surprised when Ethan pled guilty. He saw that a man as broken as that had nothing, really, to fear. He listened quietly to the plea and he saw the pain on Ethan's face. He put himself in Ethan's shoes and he thought of his son Marty. What if Marty had been lost and died in the woods? What if Marty had not even lived long enough to steal his mother's jewelry or to offend him? Jack wondered if the pain surrounding Marty would have been different if it had been mitigated by time. He was ashamed for pondering the thought, for almost wishing his son had died young and innocent instead of living long enough to hurt him.

As Ethan stood before him, almost noble in his misery, Jack saw what a puny and cowardly man he himself had become. For the first time, he wondered if abnegating his responsibility for his son to God had marked the beginning of all his wrongheaded thoughts and now this sense of powerlessness.

At the end of the proceeding, Jack met Ethan's eyes, and he knew then that Ethan recognized him. As he held the man's gaze, he saw his own folly. Sitting here on this bench after having searched for the boy, after showing up and *ducking* at the mortuary, constituted a conflict of interest so deep, so egregious that should anyone discover it, he would end his long and highly regarded career with a stain. He wondered if Ethan would say something, but when they looked at each other, he saw that Ethan would probably keep it all to himself. Ethan was a stoic man. Jack knew intuitively that Ethan was a man who did not speak easily. A man for whom words almost always failed.

After it was over, Jack drove home and poured himself a drink of scotch. He saw that the cold and lack of attention had killed his wife's herbs. He took the small potted plants off the windowsill and carried them outside, where he left them because he could not bring himself to throw them away. He had the vague hope that they were like hibernating animals and would be restored in the spring. He realized he knew nothing of plants, gardening, the things his wife had had a deep and abiding passion for. It made him feel her absence more acutely.

He sat on the couch, loosened his tie, sipped the scotch. God how he hated ties, with their staid, conservative patterns and the way they hung around his neck like a noose. He wondered who the hell had invented ties, with their symbolic masochism. It seemed suddenly bizarre, even clinically sick, the unspoken way men walked around all day with decorative ropes around their necks.

He felt lonely and bitter. He poured himself another drink and went into his bedroom, the one he'd once shared with his wife. He lay down on the bed and stared up at the ceiling. He kept imagining that boy running through the woods. He had images of Marty as a boy, playing under and in the trees outside, laughing. He pictured Marty as an adult, a drug addict, skulking around the house, stealing things to pay for his habit. He saw himself wandering through the woods looking for another man's son when, really, it should have been his own son he was rescuing.

When the phone rang, Jack jumped, spilling some of his drink on his shirt and tie. He took the tie off and, with disgust, tossed it across the room. He sipped his drink. He did not want to talk to anyone. He was angry and bitter and he knew he'd have to pass some kind of sentence on a man who, from all that he had seen, had made a mistake. A *mistake*. Did he have the right to force another man's atonement when, in fact, the only crime committed was one of selfishness and recklessness? And didn't Ethan, who had to look at himself in the mirror every day for the rest of his life, didn't he suffer punishment enough just by remaining alive to live it over and over again?

The phone stopped ringing and the message machine picked up, but there was only silence, the sound of someone breathing, and then the click of someone hanging up. Jack immediately thought of Marty. Ethan's hearing was in a week. How was Jack going to sentence a man who had most likely already sentenced himself to a life of regret and sorrow?

ETHAN

As the week passed before his sentencing, Ethan kept thinking over and over again that someday in the future he would look back at this week and not remember a thing. He had found a way to suspend his life, to keep it hanging in the balance, without much effort. He did not think of the particulars of his grief. It hung over him like a fine dull mist.

He did not answer the door when anyone came calling. He did not pick up the phone. Once, he saw Cindy standing at the end of his property line, forlorn and wistful, but he did not go out to talk to her.

But every day, for that week before his sentencing, he drove to the site of his son's final resting spot. He took toys and flowers and pictures. He filled the spot with anything he could find. One cold clear night, he woke up and saw that the mercury had dipped below ten degrees. He drove up the mountain with one of Nate's coats. He laid the warm jacket over the spot where his boy had died. He felt like he was slowly going insane.

The media had thinned out. Now that the boy was dead, the funeral passed, all they waited for was the sentencing. The town had closed around Ethan; they had built a fortress of solidarity and silence. No one spoke to the reporters anymore, not even the drunks. But he knew they awaited him in the city. He knew they'd be there like the vultures they were, dogging him, taunting him with their ravenous questions, their greedy curiosity.

The day of the sentencing rose bold and clear. The sun was bright and yellow and it was almost impossible to look at the snow without sunglasses. Ethan felt as though he were in a torture chamber of light and beauty, because he could not grasp the beauty nor feel the beneficence of the sun.

Cindy agreed to go along with him in case he'd have to stay. He needed a ride and she offered to drive, which surprised him but also did not surprise him. When she arrived, she smelled of liquor and perfume. He noticed that she wore a skirt, with sensible black shoes and stockings. He had never seen her dressed like that. It goaded him into sorrow because the shoes were plastic and the skirt looked cheap. And he was wearing a tie that he'd borrowed from Glick. It was out of date, wide at the bottom, and smelled of mothballs. They looked like who they were, and he was ashamed of this. He looked over at Cindy and reached out for her hand. He was nearly beside himself with the irony that in spite of all they'd been through, Cindy was the only person he could tolerate.

She pulled out her flask on the way and handed it to him. He took a sip.

"It's cold out there," he said. The weather. How stupid. How mundane. His grief made it too hard to talk about anything other than what did not matter.

"It's always better when it snows," she said.

"Isn't it weird how it snowed only while Nate was missing and only on the day of his funeral? Doesn't it seem strange that it hasn't snowed at all since?"

Cindy nodded. "It's like everything bad came together and made it worse."

"That's what I been thinking this whole week. Maybe if it hadn't snowed . . ."

"We can't go there, Ethan."

He heard the unspoken in the air. The real question, the true accusation, was, Maybe if he hadn't left his son in the car in the first place . . .

"I swear, Cindy, I don't know why I did it."

She took another sip. "It's water under the bridge now, Ethan. You can't crucify yourself. It's done."

He held his hand out and she handed him the whiskey. He took a long sip. He welcomed the way it went down. He wondered if he'd be in jail tonight. Would he go to a federal penitentiary? How long would he spend behind bars? The thought of it didn't frighten him. He owed a debt, not to the world, but to his son. What bothered him most was that society had made this its personal problem. He wished, not for the first time, that there were no laws, no people imposing their ideas for atonement and reparation on him. His suffering was complete. No amount of jail would change that. He did not believe he needed to pay society back. He merely wanted to find some way to forgive himself, to show Nate, wherever he was, that he was sorry.

As they neared the courthouse, his heart began to pound in his chest. He was afraid, he realized. He was scared of the media and the staid formality of the institutions that meted out justice. He was afraid for Cindy. She had lost so much weight. She seemed so fragile, so broken.

"Okay, here goes," Ethan said. He looked at Cindy, and at the same time, the two of them took a deep breath and got out of the car. As they made their way up the courthouse steps, the media descended on them. Flashbulbs went off. Reporters hurled questions at him. Ethan wished the sheriff were with them. Suddenly, Ms. Cervantes appeared and raced down the courthouse steps.

"Why didn't you call me back?" she said. She seemed angry. "I've been calling you all week. Where have you been?" Then she turned to the media and shouted, "No comment" as she hustled Ethan and Cindy up the steps of the courthouse and into the building.

"Did you prepare that statement? If you had called me back, Ethan, we could have gone over the proceedings." Ethan did not understand why she was so upset. This wasn't happening to her. Nothing seemed to make any sense to him now that he was here. He felt as if he had finally lost his mind, because everything seemed suddenly ludicrous and surreal. Was he dreaming? Was he going to wake up? He had a strong sense that he was just about to roll out of bed and find Nate there on the pallet on the floor, where he liked to sleep, wrapped warmly in the sleeping bag.

They walked briskly down the hallway. The place seemed deserted. He felt like they were the last people on earth. They rounded the corner and mounted the stairs, Ms. Cervantes taking two at a time in her expensive black pumps. Ethan noticed how slim and taut her calves were, what a beautiful body she had. He pictured her at the gym, running and running on a treadmill. He pictured men ogling her.

When at last they arrived at Judge Rosenthal's courtroom, there were people everywhere, milling about. He realized that the members of the media had planted themselves right outside the doors of the courtroom, an ambush waiting for him and Cindy. An explosion of questions filled the air. Flashbulbs erupted. Cindy grabbed Ethan's hand and began to cry.

They managed to get inside, where Cindy fell into a chair. Ethan and Ms. Cervantes sat beside her. The judge was already there. He was hearing a case. There were several attorneys talking. One of them said, "Your Honor, she was *out* of town at her mother's *funeral*. She didn't skip. She was at *her mother's funeral*."

Ms. Cervantes turned to Ethan. She leaned up and straightened his tie. He was shocked, but an eerie passivity had overtaken him and he didn't protest. He pictured her doing the same thing for her husband, absently, an act not so much of love as of habit.

"Judge Rosenthal is a fair and decent man," she said. "I have it on good authority that you are getting the minimum sentence. Relax. We'll just get through this one minute at a time."

She looked quickly over at Cindy. She nodded her head and Cindy sat up and wiped her eyes. Ethan saw Cindy clutching her cheap purse with one hand, a tissue crushed in the other. He reached out and grabbed her hand, forcing her to let go of the purse, so that it rested in her lap, unattended and sad-looking. She kept crying softly, quietly. He saw the last five years of her life pouring out of her eyes. He leaned over. "It's okay. It's okay." He must have said it ten times. She just kept nodding and crying.

"Are you prepared to speak? Ethan? Have you prepared yourself to speak to the judge before sentencing?"

"I forgot. . . ." He hadn't forgotten. It wasn't that. He just didn't care. Nothing mattered anymore.

Suddenly, they were standing before the judge. Ethan wondered what he would say. He looked back at Cindy. She was still crying softly. He looked up at the judge and saw that the man looked terrible, as if he'd been up all night. He appeared ragged. His expression was grim.

"Good morning," the judge said.

Ms. Cervantes gave a tight smile. She nodded. At the other table, to their left, the prosecutor stood with his hands clasped behind his back. He was ramrod straight, his face expressionless. Ethan expected to have some kind of feeling for him, some kind of hatred, but when he looked at the man, he felt nothing. His heart beat heavily in his chest. Ms. Cervantes and the prosecutor sat down. Ethan sat with them. A moment passed. The judge looked at a file. Ethan saw that the judge's hands were shaking badly.

"Okay," the judge said. "Mr. Kraft."

The prosecutor stood up. "Thank you, Your Honor." He began to talk, but Ethan heard nothing of what he had to say. He realized that none of this meant anything to him. The prosecutor droned on and on. He kept saying how terrible the case had been for him, the personal anguish it had caused him. Ethan found it unbelievable. Who were these people? How had they managed to enter his life without his wanting them to? He thought briefly of Glick, who had spent all that time in prison for something he hadn't done. He felt the enormous runaway-train power of the law. He saw how once it got going, it couldn't ever be stopped, that there was no getting off.

Then Ms. Cervantes was talking. She was telling the judge that he should be lenient, that no sentence would equal the horrible punishment that Ethan now suffered. Finally, Ms. Cervantes leaned over and whispered to Ethan, "Go ahead." Ethan looked at her. She whispered, "Stand up. Didn't you prepare a statement?"

Ethan stood up. He felt as if he were underwater, that everything was happening in that slow, murky underwater way. Or as if in a dream. He was in one of those dreams where he was trying to run from something but couldn't get his arms and legs to move. He cleared his throat. The judge looked at him, and he had the sense that the judge was looking to him for answers, as if Ethan held the secrets of the universe and wasn't really on trial for killing his son. The judge seemed breathless, on the edge of his seat.

Ethan looked at the floor and began to speak. He said, "You cannot know my agony. You cannot understand my pain. There is nothing you or the law or this court can do that will punish me more than the punishment I already feel. It doesn't really matter to me anymore. If I could trade places with my son, that would be the only mercy."

Ethan felt himself beginning to cry. It occurred to him that there *was* nothing left in this life for him.

"I will serve whatever time you give me, Judge. But you have to know . . . you have to know that nothing can bring my son back. Nothing. The time for rescue is over. It's too late."

He sat down. He didn't really know what he had just said. He didn't know what he meant about the time for rescue being too late. He did not understand anything that was happening here, in this place, removed from the place where his son had died. Now his son's death stood before him in stark relief against these bizarre proceedings, this outlandish formality.

Finally, the judge spoke. But again, Ethan did not hear the words. He noticed only that the judge looked miserable and worried and fearful, as if something much, much more was at stake. As if his entire life depended on this moment, this place, this time, these people.

At the end, they locked eyes for a long moment and the judge, who appeared suddenly ill, turned away before he sentenced Ethan to counseling, community service, and the minimum time in jail—thirty days. He asked Ethan when he would like to begin serving his time. Ethan looked at Ms. Cervantes. She raised her eyebrows, and he whispered in her ear, "Tomorrow."

And then it was over. Ethan had to fill out some papers and arrange for an arrival time with the jailor. As he and Cindy walked outside, the media waited breathlessly, slobbering all over them. A couple of local cops made a sort of barricade around Ethan, but he didn't care anymore, because nothing, he knew, could ever hurt him again, or touch him, or disturb him. The rest of his life would be spent with Nate. Only Nate.

When he and Cindy got in the car, Cindy at the wheel, they pulled out of the parking lot and drove away. Cindy drove for a long time and neither of them spoke. Then the city was behind them and they were at last on the county roads, among the avocado trees and orange groves, the nut trees with their shimmering silver leaves, swaying in the light and wind.

Cindy stopped the car beneath a sign on the side of the road that noted the turnoff to Angels Crest, population 354, and Los Angeles, nearly four hundred miles the other way. Ethan suddenly remembered how they had come home from the hospital with their tiny newborn baby and he had stopped the car at this very sign and pulled over. Cindy had been momentarily irritated because she hurt and wanted to go home, but he'd pulled a piece of paper out of the glove compartment and written the number 5 on it. Then he'd found some electrical tape and gone outside and taped it over the number 4 on the sign, so that it read ANGELS CREST, POPULATION 355.

He turned to Cindy, and he saw that she was thinking the same thing, experiencing that same moment in time. At once, they were both sobbing, holding on to each other and crying. Ethan let the tears flow from his eyes. He did not censor them; he did not edit his grief. It poured forth like a mountain stream in the springtime, pure and white and clear. They held on to each other like that for a long time, and for Ethan, it was like sitting in a place where nothing but memories existed, whisking past them like iridescent veils, completely, frustratingly, out of reach.

At last, Cindy broke the silence. "I sit here at this fork in the road," she said, "and I wanna go the other way."

❧   ❧   ❧

Later, night fell and a brutal cold seemed to lay itself down on the town like some sort of sleeping, heavy animal. No one was about. Angie's was deserted. The media had closed shop and left. Darkness. A brilliant canopy of stars. Ethan and Cindy stopped at the liquor store and Ethan sat in the car, hidden as best as he could, while Cindy picked up some liquor and some food. They had decided she would tell Walter, who owned the liquor store, what had happened, because he was the biggest gossip in town, and that way, everyone would know.

When they got home, Ethan emptied his pockets of money, including the three quarters he had found in Glick's truck the first day of the search. Then he joined Cindy on the couch in the living room, inside the house they had once shared as husband and wife. They drank until they both agreed they felt nothing but the dull ache of their sorrow. Some of Nate's toys were visible here and there, and Cindy retrieved a plastic garbage bag and started throwing toys inside. She went through every room, while Ethan sat in the kitchen and watched her walking back and forth, picking up everything—toys or stray articles of clothing—and throwing them in the bag. When she was done, she sat back down.

"I'll help you do the rest," she said. "Another day."

"You're stronger than I ever gave you credit for," Ethan said.

"Funny how it takes the worst to find out the best in people."

Ethan leaned back on the couch. He said, "Let's go to sleep."

They both stood up and went to the bedroom. Ethan did not turn on any lights. They lay down on the top of the bed in their clothes—Cindy in her cheap skirt and Ethan with the borrowed tie—and wrapped their arms around each other. In a little while, Ethan reached down for the folded extra blanket at the end of the bed and pulled it over them.

"We'll get through this," Ethan said.

"Sure," Cindy said.

In moments, with Cindy's steady, familiar weight beside him, Ethan fell into a dreamless landscape, stilled beneath the pall of grief.

GLICK

---◆---

Glick felt bad that the only tie he had to lend Ethan was out of fashion. Its colors were bold and sickly—blue and a shade of orange that made him feel vaguely nauseated—and it was too fat at the bottom. It was the same tie he had worn during his own brush with the law, back when those colors were the height of fashion and he was young and innocent enough to think that the hands of justice would sort out the mistake and end his nightmare.

The law, he used to think, was fair. An innocent man would never be punished, because the law would never allow for such injustice. Now, his ideas of fair and right were different. And the tie, though he'd kept it, remained way in the back of his closet, a reminder of those days when all had seemed lost.

He suggested that Ethan go to town and buy a new tie, but Ethan said there wasn't any time. When Glick said he'd follow him into the city and be there to support him, Ethan shook his head vehemently.

"No, man," he said. "Cindy said she'd drive me."

Glick thought he understood. It did not surprise him that the two of them—Cindy and Ethan—would face this together. He remembered how they had once loved each other so richly, so resolutely. He also remembered how much they had grown to hate each other. The passion between them, whether love or hate—it didn't matter which—would always be there. He understood that the two of them had found a link to the one thing they could both love: their son.

So he wished Ethan good luck and told him to call when it was over. That night, he and Angie were eating dinner when they learned that Ethan had been sentenced to only thirty days. They were both glad. Angie said that perhaps tomorrow they could go out to Ethan's house, take him some food. Maybe now, she said, he'd like the company.

The next morning while Angie worked at the diner, Glick cleaned the yard and fixed a few broken things—the screen door needed a new hinge, the drawers in the kitchen were all off their tracks, and a shelf had fallen in the kid's room. He ate lunch at the diner and he and Angie kissed in the alley behind the kitchen while her granddaughter slept on her cot, her photo album on the floor beside her, as if dropped in sleep.

Later, he took the dog out into the woods and they walked for miles in the waning light. The day was cold and beautiful, silenced by the way the deep part of winter was coming, waiting for the quiet solitude of the season, waiting for the pause to end, for spring to return.

As he walked, Glick realized his heart was not filled with that sense of waiting anymore. He saw winter for what it was; he didn't think past it. He didn't hope for something better, for the end of something, for the beginning of something. It had been years, but for the first time he felt planted in the here and now.

He walked toward the trailhead for Angels Crest. He remembered finding Nate's body, and he walked past the site where the funeral had been. Near the cross, a pile of toys and clothes had been heaped, and Glick felt his heart tightening for Ethan. He saw fresh footprints in the snow, heading away from the site, toward Angels Crest. He followed them for a while, knowing somehow that they were Ethan's. He thought for a minute that he ought to track his old friend down, make sure he was okay, but he knew that the rest of Ethan's days would be swept up by his grief and that he probably needed the solace of the woods, the quiet of the forest. Then he realized that Ethan was probably already in jail, already serving the first day of his sentence. Glick felt a twinge of guilt that his own life had seemingly sorted itself out. Overnight. He was unused to the thought that from now on he might be happy.

He stopped for a moment and looked up at the tip of Angels Crest jutting up into the cold blue sky. He listened to the wind blowing through the tall pines. Somewhere a jay screeched and then was silent. The dog stopped, too, and listened. All around them, the snow glistened in the waning light of day. The silvery scent of the woods filled him with calm. Glick looked behind him and could see through the trees all the toys piled near the place where he had found Ethan's son. Again, he looked up at the glorious peak and he saw, as if from a long ways away, the broad expanse of his life, the curving path that had led him here, to this place, to this moment in time. He thought of all that he had endured, of all that would yet come to pass. He knelt down and pet the dog and said, "C'mon, Dog, let's go home."

ROCKSAN

The day after the news of Ethan's sentence had swept through town, Rocksan woke to the sounds of Melody and George. George was saying, "Are you sure? Are you sure?" And Melody was crying out, "Oh my God, it bloody hurts."

Rocksan looked over at Jane, who was lying beside her in the bed. At that moment, Jane's eyes flew open and she and Rocksan both jumped from beneath the covers. Like a pair of doddering old aunts, they reached for their respective robes and ran down the hallway to the spare room.

"Guys," Jane said. "You all right?"

Melody opened the door. "It's time," she said. At first, she seemed calm as a breeze. Calm like summer. Warm and easy and tranquil. Then Rocksan noticed that she was sweating and her hands were trembling and she held her belly. "It hurts, Jane," she said. "Why didn't you tell me it would hurt this much?"

George was throwing clothes into a suitcase. He was wearing pajama bottoms and no shirt.

"How far is the fucking hospital? Can we get there in time?"

"Quit your cussing, George. You're making the contractions come faster," Melody said.

"I'll get the car," Rocksan said. Then she turned to Melody. "You're early."

"I never did have a good sense of timing," Melody said. Then she winced and grabbed her belly and cried out. "I think I'll stay right here in this house and have this baby on this floor."

"The hell you will," George said.

Suddenly, Rocksan looked at Jane and Jane looked at her, and without thinking about it, they embraced. It was quick. It was the shortest embrace Rocksan could ever remember, and yet she felt as if something had been mended, some tear, some impossible rip that could never quite be sewn up but might work okay with a couple of staples and a little glue.

"I love you, Beanpole," she whispered, her heart racing because a baby was coming and because of something else, something she could not put into words.

"Me, too," Jane said.

"Get the fucking car," George said.

Melody looked at Jane with an apology in her eyes. "As God is my witness, I have never heard him swear like this before."

Quickly, Jane and Rocksan packed up a few things for the trip to the hospital, which was twenty miles away. It was what they had all planned. They'd even called and talked to a nurse there, telling her they'd be in to look at the place, have a talk before the baby came.

Melody made it downstairs, but she got only as far as the couch, where she lay down in apparent agony. Rocksan could see that the contractions were coming faster and harder. Melody began to cry out, then said, "I don't think I'm gonna make it to the hospital."

"Oh God," George said. "What do we do?"

"Be quiet, George," Jane said. Then she stood straight and bold and said, "Melody, get down here on the floor and hike up that nightie."

Melody lay on the floor and winced, then let out a loud scream, which was met by George's scream. Melody kept screaming and telling them all that it hurt like bloody hell. George grew more and more frantic. Just like a man, Rocksan thought. And some dykes.

"For God's sake, George, calm yourself," Jane said.

Rocksan was amazed. She had never seen Jane so commanding. She was glad, because it sure as shit looked like Melody was going to have her baby right there on the living room floor. Rocksan watched Jane spread Melody's legs apart and look at her privates. Then she looked at Rocksan and said, "This baby is crowning. Call the hospital and ask them what the hell I'm supposed to do."

Rocksan quickly retrieved the phone. By now, George was silent, in awe, it seemed, of this miracle. Or else unable to speak from complete terror. Rocksan told him to get some towels from the hallway closet and, because she had seen it on TV, instructed him to go to the kitchen and boil some water.

She called 911 and they patched her through to the hospital, where a nurse got on the phone and relayed instructions to her, which she, in turn, relayed to Jane. All the while, Jane was calm and collected. She looked like a goddamn warrior.

"You look like a warrior, Jane," Rocksan said. "You look like a goddamn lesbian warrior."

Jane laughed for a moment and then she stopped laughing and said, "Here comes the baby."

The whole time, Melody screamed and grunted. "Damn," she said. "Damn."

"Push," Jane said. "Push. Harder. Harder."

"Goddamn," Melody said. Her face had turned beet red. The veins were bulging in her forehead and neck. Meanwhile, George had brought the towels. Rocksan caught a brief glimpse of the blood and the mess and she thought about how they'd have to clean the whole thing up once it was over. She thought about their house, this place that had been haunted and filthy and decayed when they bought it, and how she and Jane had patched it back together with all the love and patience they could muster. She thought of her bees, their silence in the cold as they waited for winter to end, and all the hope they brought in the spring when they burst from the hives and brought the flowers to life. She thought also of her father, who had left her when she was so young, and she wished he hadn't died, so she could be given the chance to forgive him, just as George now had the chance with Jane.

Then all at once—it was like that sigh just before a snowstorm, when everything becomes intensely quiet, brilliantly so—the baby's head spurted out and Melody began to cry, and there it was, in Jane's warrior arms. A little girl.

"Well, shit," Rocksan said, "would you goddamn look at that!"

JANE

She caught the baby in her arms and it threw up and began to cry. Rocksan, who was on the phone with a nurse, relayed how to cut the umbilical cord, which was easy enough, and Jane looked at her son, but she couldn't see him because everything had become misty and white, as if she were about to faint. But she didn't faint, not at all. Instead, she looked at her granddaughter and realized that for once in her life there were absolutely no words to describe her feelings.

George had calmed down considerably. He had sat, finally, at Melody's head and whispered things in her ear, which, Jane noticed, seemed to have had a calming effect on Melody. Jane felt a welling of pride for the way he pulled it together, for his decency, for his eagerness and youth and his new baby. For the life he would lead as a father.

Jane took one of the towels George had brought and she wiped the baby off, because she was covered in a strange whitish coating. The baby cried and cried, and Jane wrapped her up and covered her head and gave her to Melody and George. Melody put the baby to her breast and the infant took the nipple and began to nurse.

After she handed the baby over, Jane felt her insides tumble, because she saw how she had both given and received a gift all at the same time. She saw how it was all jumbled up, giving and receiving, loving and wanting and needing and having and giving. She saw how all her weaknesses and her lack of courage, and all the things she most despised about herself, had taken flight as the baby fell into her arms. She thought that maybe she would never suffer again, not in the way she had suffered these past twenty years.

She stood up, tears streaming down her cheeks. She looked at Rocksan and laughed. She said, "I have always been the one who cries."

Rocksan laughed, and Jane said she'd be right back. She walked out the back door and surveyed the land and the sky. In the distance, the hives sat quietly, silently, almost desolately. Soon the ambulance would be there to take the baby and Melody and George to the hospital. She thought briefly of Nate and Ethan. But she could not dwell there, and she looked once again at the hives and knew they were filled with bees, humming and alive, and that come spring they would be ridiculously industrious, making love to the wildflowers that crowded all the free space on their land. Looking through the window, she saw Rocksan on the telephone, probably already blabbing the news of the baby to her sister, and she thought of her son, how far they had yet to go. She thought that later she would make a casserole and buy a bottle of wine.

ANGIE

Early that morning, the day after Ethan had been sentenced, he arrived at the diner. He said he was going to report to the courthouse or jail. He said he wasn't sure what he was supposed to do next, where he was supposed to go, but that he was heading for the city to get it over with. He kept looking back at his truck on the street. Once, when Angie looked at it, too, she saw his old gun leaning up against the back window of the truck, his heavy winter parka propped on the barrel.

"It's only thirty days," he said. He asked for a cup of coffee to go. He nodded at Angie and said good-bye. For some reason, she noticed his heavy hiking boots, the gloves poking out of his back pocket.

Later, Glick came by. While Rosie slept, they made out like teenagers in the alley. She felt blushy and hot and embarrassed. When she had to get back to work, Glick told her he was going to take the dog for a walk but that he'd be back before dark.

After he left, Angie went over to the little cot where Rosie was sleeping and she saw the photo album that had replaced the penguin as Rosie's favorite object. It lay open on the floor, and there was a picture of her daughter smiling out at her. Angie picked the album up and studied the picture, memorizing everything about her daughter's face. She looked at Rosie asleep on the cot and for the first time she saw the resemblance between Rosie and Rachel. It was in the eyes and the mouth. She saw Rosie's small hand twitch in sleep, open and close. Her eyelids fluttered. Angie hoped her granddaughter's dreams were easy and slow and filled with blue and white child-ish things.

Just then, the door to the diner opened and the old blind preacher walked in for his lunch. Angie closed the photo album, taking one last look at the picture of Rachel before ordering up the preacher's usual grilled cheese on rye and a side of slaw.

CINDY

———◆———

When she woke up, Ethan was still asleep beside her and the day's first light had not yet broken through the morning. The clock read 5:00 A.M. Cindy felt the hangover, the sorrow, the unbearable numbing pain of her life. She tried to tell herself that in a year's time, maybe two, the pain would lessen. She tried to tell herself that though it might never go away entirely, her grief would one day wither like an old mountain thistle and lose its prickly thorns.

She rose from the bed quietly so she wouldn't wake Ethan and then tiptoed to the living room. The bag of Nate's toys was leaning against the couch. There were a couple of twenties and some other loose bills, along with three quarters, on the kitchen counter. She figured Ethan wouldn't be needing the money right away, since he would be getting three hots and a cot for the next thirty days. So she took it. Just like that. She put it in her pocket.

She didn't bother putting her shoes on. They were cheap and ugly, and she threw them in the trash before she found her keys, grabbed what was left of the whiskey, and slipped quietly out into the icy chill of morning.

She drove through the silent town and made her way home to her shit brown apartment at the Skyview Manors. She parked her car, which was low on gas, and walked in her stocking feet up the cold steps to her apartment.

The place was overly warm. Once again, she had forgotten to turn off the damn heat. It wouldn't matter anymore. She gathered her underpants and her bras from the top drawer in her dresser. She went to the closet and took a stack of clothes hanging there. She grabbed what jeans and sweaters she could find scattered on the floor in her room and carried them all into the kitchen.

She went to the bathroom, gathered some toiletries, and put them in a makeup bag that was under the sink. She walked through the bedroom to the kitchen. On the counter was the plate with the glued-down pieces of macaroni on it. She picked it up and looked at it for a long time. Then she put it back down on the counter and shoved her clothes into a plastic garbage bag. She grabbed her keys and the welfare check that had arrived a few days before, then quietly walked to the door with her heavy winter coat in her hands. She was wearing her stupid cheap skirt, but she didn't feel like changing. She grabbed her shoes and a pair of boots that were by the coat-rack and then stepped outside, closing the door quietly behind her.

She quickly put her boots on and walked to her car. She threw her clothes and her toiletries in the trunk and checked her purse for the whiskey. She pulled it out and took a sip, a long sip, and instantly her nerves calmed and she felt a sense of clarity and determination that only the rush of whiskey ever gave her anymore.

She put the car in reverse and backed out of the parking lot of the Skyview Manors, then drove through town, past the hardware store, past Angie's, the records office, past Cage Road, where Glick lived, past the library and the Calvary Church, where her son had gone to school, had just begun his life.

She stopped for ten dollars of gasoline and then used the quarters she had found at Ethan's to buy some gum. She turned out onto the main high-way and made her way toward the fork in the road, where an ambulance rushed passed her, heading, it seemed, toward town. There at the fork, she pulled over and stopped one more time at the sign where she and Ethan had wept. She looked at it for a minute. ANGELS CREST, it read, POPULATION 354. She remembered Jane and Rocksan and Jane's son and his pregnant girlfriend and she wondered if, when the baby was born, someone would think to change the sign the way she and Ethan had done when they brought Nate home from the hospital. POPULATION 355, it would say again.

Then she figured it didn't matter anyway, because Nate's death and that baby's birth would even the score and it would seem like nothing in Angels Crest would ever change. People died young and unexpectedly, like her son, and others lived for a long time, like the old blind preacher, and they would always be going to Angie's for coffee and the hardware store for nuts and bolts and the bar to ease their pain.

She took another sip from her bottle and then drove off just as the blackness of the early morning gave way to the faintest, the very faintest glow of light.

JUDGE JACK ROSENTHAL

———◆———

He left the courthouse feeling ill and tired. The day had started miserably. Soggy skies but no rain, just wet. Wet air, wet grass, wet streets. Then he'd battled the media and the inanity of the reporters. He detested the way they asked questions, as if they were really hurling stones. By the time he'd sentenced Ethan, he'd felt flush with fever. His stomach roiled. He didn't even have time to ruminate after sentencing Ethan because of the steady stream of crackheads and petty thieves parading through his courtroom. In his chambers at the end of the day, feverish and sick, he changed into his street clothes.

On his way home, in a blur of sickness and sweats, he thought about the sentence he'd given Ethan, the way he had arrived at it. He'd known in the intervening days, after the arraignment, that he'd have to come up with something. While he had some measure of the depth of Ethan's remorse, he'd convinced himself nevertheless that he could calculate a fair sentence in accordance with the law. But in the end, he saw only that he was a slave to the law, that he had let it bully him for half his lifetime. A truly moral man, he told himself, would have let Ethan go. Instead, he'd bestowed the cowardly sentence of thirty days. An appeasement, he knew, to society and to his long-standing belief that there had to be rules and there had to be consequences.

He turned into his driveway and trudged up the walk. Inside, he went first to the kitchen and poured himself a glass of water. The back of his throat was parched and he put his hand, which felt big and ballooned by the fever, against his burning forehead. He was sweating profusely now. He

reached for a towel and stumbled, steadying himself against the counter before wiping his wet skin.

He could not get the look on Ethan's face out of his mind. The way he'd
stared at the ground when he'd spoken, the lack of any expression whatsoever on his face when he'd heard the sentence. The man was so polite, so
stoic. Jack remembered the time, after he'd helped look for the boy, he had
cursed Ethan, had lashed out at him in his thoughts.

Now he knew so clearly, so evidently, that really it was himself and his
stupid arrogance he loathed. He felt wretched. His body was revolting from
some virus or other and his heart felt far from everyone, especially far from
God. He sat down and closed his eyes, remembering the way his children
had clucked their tongues as kids whenever he would get mighty with God.
How obvious to him now that the tenents of his faith rested solely on the
flimsy structure of his ego. Somehow, though his children hadn't had the
language for it, they had known. They had been smarter than he was.

He felt sick to his stomach, and in moments he had to run to the bathroom to throw up. His gut was churning and twisting. The sour burned at
the back of his throat. He lay with his head against the cool porcelain of the
toilet and once again emptied his stomach. He had to clutch his bowels from
the cramps, and in seconds he was forced to unbutton his pants and relieve
himself in a confluence of pain and apprehension.

When he had finished, he stumbled from the bathroom and made his
way upstairs to his bedroom, where he lay down on the bed he'd once shared
with his wife. He thought again of Ethan standing before him. He replayed
every word that Ethan had said, relived every moment. *The time for rescue is
over. It's too late.*

He sat up and, as if in a dream, reached over to his nightstand for the
glass jar that contained the desert seashell and the buttons and the old fortune cookie fortunes. The picture of his son was there and that, it seemed,
was what he was searching for. He looked at it through the glass, rolled the
glass against his forehead, and felt the balm of its cool surface on his fiery
skin. He reached inside the glass—how old and gnarled his hands were, and
those fingers, so thick and dry and aged—and slid the picture out. He
pressed the picture against his chest, mistaking it for a minute for something

that would quiet his pounding heart. What was he thinking? This was his son. This was a picture. He peered at it, and though it took a minute to focus, he saw at last Marty's clear face, his smile, the tranquillity of his youth.

He thought of the boy, Nate, who had been lost in the woods. How he had died up there in vain, with no one to rescue him. Jack sat up, afraid, his heart racing. What end had been served by Nate's death? He could not believe that a just God could be so cruel. He remembered the hours and hours he'd spent praying, and also the pining vulgarity of his prayers, the way he'd turned to God out of need and hunger rather than praise and kindness.

Jack knew now what he had always kept at bay. He was a man whose faith was so thin, so phony, that he would use God to justify the wedge he had driven between himself and his wayward son, the love of his life.

He began to cry and he held on to the picture of his son. He managed to get out of bed and make his way toward the bathroom. He had some idea that if he could just get a cold, wet cloth on his forehead, he would feel better. But he only got as far as the foot of the bed, where he slid to the ground, still clutching the picture of Marty. He closed his eyes and once again saw Nate. But the image vanished and what he was really seeing was Marty roaming the streets of Hollywood, strung out on drugs. Once more, Jack heard Ethan's words. *The time for rescue is over. It's too late.*

Jack opened his eyes and Ethan was standing there in front of him. Jack sat up.

"Ethan?" he said. He reached out, thinking that Ethan could give him a hand up. But Ethan stood still, polite, stoic, saying nothing.

"Please," Jack said. "What else could I have done?"

Still Ethan said nothing. Jack began to weep. He was aware that Ethan would find his tears cowardly and disappointing. "What would you have me do?" he said.

And then at once, Ethan put his hand out and Jack reached for it. As they touched, he felt something change in his heart. Whatever it was seemed to have nothing whatever to do with God or the law. It seemed profoundly more ineffable than his understanding of either. It was a steady drumbeat, a sense of yearning, of striving, of grace. It was also filled with loss and despair. The marriage of hope and impossibility. It made him feel strangely elated and free. That was the word he came up with: *free*. He remembered what he had taught his sons about the Torah: "What is hateful to yourself, do not do to others."

It seemed so simple. The judge looked at Ethan. Then he looked at the picture of Marty again and thought, It is only too late for rescue when you quit breathing altogether.

ETHAN

Ethan woke with a start. The first thing he thought of was Nate. Nate disappearing without a trace in the woods. Vanished. Gone. Now dead. He looked at his hands in the morning light, at his arms, at the wonder of his form and shape. This body, this package. *Me*, he thought.

When he saw that Cindy had gone without waking him, he was relieved. He wanted to take himself to the jail, to face the next thirty days alone starting now. But going alone meant he would have to find a way to have the truck picked up. Or maybe he could store it. Or lend it to someone. He really didn't care what happened to it.

He dragged himself from bed and showered. He went to the kitchen, too hungover for coffee, and noticed that his money was gone, including the three quarters he had taken from Glick's truck the day Glick showed up to help find Nate. He was glad they were gone, that Cindy had them. He wasn't sure of their significance, only that they carried the weight of that day and he could neither spend them himself nor keep them.

He decided to drive to the diner. Maybe by then he would be able to drink a cup of coffee. He was supposed to report to the courthouse by 10:00 A.M. and it was only 6:30. So he had time. He thought maybe he would take a walk in the woods. Visit the grave site one last time, because by the time his thirty days were up, the winter would have fully barreled in and buried the cross he'd hammered into the ground.

He drove through the quiet streets. As he passed his hardware store, a weight fell on his shoulders. He realized he hadn't made arrangements to pay the mortgage or have someone mind the store. Suddenly, it all seemed too complicated. Things had happened too quickly. There were too many details, too much hassle. His son was dead. He did not care about the store, the mortgage. He could not find a way to care about anything. He realized that he really had nothing to live for.

He stopped at Angie's, ordered coffee, and told Angie that he was heading to the city. But instead, he made his way up the winding slope to the turnout where just a short while ago the media, the sheriff, the search and rescue rangers, and the townspeople had all assembled to help him find his son. When he arrived at the turnout, he thought of all that activity. It had been like a machine moving along with its own energy source, gaining momentum and steam as time went by. Now the spot was deserted. A few pieces of garbage and someone's baseball cap were all that remained.

Ethan put on his parka and grabbed his old dual-sighted .30-30 Savage and a box of shells. He set off into the woods. He decided to hike to the top of Angels Crest. It was a glorious day, and though the trail was probably covered in snow, he knew the way with his eyes closed. It would be a hard walk, but Ethan felt strong, sure. For the first time since his son had died, he felt steady on his feet.

The sun was vivid and bright, the snow alive with crystals, and the air cold and fresh. He stopped first at the site where Nate had been found and where they'd had the funeral service. He knelt in the snow and he clasped his hands together and he whispered to his son. He told Nate how sorry he was, how much he loved him, how he would be with him soon enough.

Then he set off into the woods and walked. He thought of nothing and of everything. He thought of Nate playing in the yard, coloring in his coloring books, walking through the woods. He saw Nate over and over again, smiling and beckoning to him. He did not think of Nate's last hours on earth. He did not think of the many and different ways his son might have suffered. If he felt himself going in that direction, he veered away from it and he thought all over again of Nate playing in the yard, or coloring, or walking in the forest.

Ethan walked for hours. He never felt hungry or tired. Once, he leaned down and cupped a handful of snow in his gloved hand and ate it very slowly, savoring the taste. When he saw, at one point, that it was well after four in the afternoon, he was surprised. He felt as if he'd been walking only an hour at most. But here he was, over six hours late for his appointment with the jailor, and he knew they would probably be out looking for him. He also knew, by the shape of the mountain, the way the light refracted off of it, that he was near the tip of the crest.

Funny, but up till now, he had hardly noticed the way the setting sun had changed the shape of the woods. He had always prided himself on the awareness he had for the subtle nuances in the forest, the way certain elevations had a different scent, the way the waning light always made the woods look smaller and less forbidding, and the way his breathing changed, growing shallower and more labored with each foot he gained in altitude. But he was not at all aware of his body and barely aware of his surroundings except to feel them in the essential way he had always felt them, as if they were a part of him.

When he reached the summit, he looked out over the valley. He could see for miles. The air was clear and the sky was so blue that Ethan felt himself welling up with joy. He had never seen anything, he thought, more beautiful. He sat on the ground and propped his gun up in a way that would make it easy for him to pull the trigger. He made sure that he buttressed it against an immovable rock to mitigate the kick, so that there would be no mistake.

He thought of the angels and how they had long ago saved those babies. He also thought of how they had not saved his own boy. He looked out at the forest below him, at its beauty and its radiance. He felt its kindness and the particular way the woods had cradled him and kept him safe for so long. He closed his eyes and imagined Nate running through the woods, running with the tree-dappled light on his hair, his laughter echoing back and forth among the ancient boulders while the music of his voice danced among the trees. He saw Nate running fast, beckoning to him, running farther and farther away, the meadow grass stretching out before him endlessly, his laughter growing fainter and fainter, his body smaller and smaller as he finally disappeared beneath the bright blue sky.

In Memory of

Harvey Schwartz
Robert W. Littlewood